SECONDHAND SKIN

A SOULBOUND UNIVERSE NOVEL

HAILEY TURNER

Cover design by James T. Egan, www.bookflydesign.com
Beta reading by Amanda Viecelli.
Developmental Editing by Mackenzie Walton.
Edited by One Love Editing.
Proofing by Lori Parks: lp.nerdproblems@gmail.com
Proofing by M.A. Hinkle.

WELCOME TO THE WORLDS OF HAILEY TURNER

Urban Fantasy
Soulbound

Science Fiction Romance
Metahuman Files

Steampunk-inspired Epic Fantasy
Infernal War Saga

CHAPTER ONE

The end of May in New York City came with a burgeoning heat that Wade Espinoza never really noticed. Being a fire dragon came with some perks, and not being bothered by heat or really feeling cold was one of them. During the cooler months of the year, he usually forgot his jacket or sweater at home, which resulted in odd looks from fellow New Yorkers and resigned scolding from his pack.

But it was almost summer, and Wade was happy to leave the cold-weather clothes he never cared for shoved in the back of his closet whenever he left for school, work, or to handle their pack business. The one good thing about jackets, though, was their pockets, which could carry snacks. The pockets of his jeans were never deep enough, even for the short walk home after a night working a shift at Tempest, his pack's bar.

Tempest was the epicenter of the New York City god pack's outreach for pack needs. It was neutral territory, open to anyone who wandered inside, and Wade had been helping to supervise the staff there since he turned twenty-one two years ago. He was, admittedly, a terrible bartender, but he could pour a beer, a glass of wine, or a shot of whiskey with the best of them. As far as bouncers went, when the need arose, no one was better than him.

Wade's one-bedroom condo was located in the East Village, the same neighborhood he'd lived in since joining the New York City god pack five years ago. The condo overlooking Avenue A was cozy and messy and where Wade stored his various hoards until someone from his pack inevitably showed up and told him to clean the place. The building was also where his favorite food cart made a special stop once a week. Wade looked forward to the food cart's arrival every Tuesday morning for a tasty, greasy breakfast of the best kind after a work shift.

He could already smell the bacon, egg, and cheese sandwich before he turned the corner, along with the unwelcome pungent scent of sulfur and the sound of heckling from people who weren't local to the neighborhood. He wrinkled his nose as he caught sight of three men standing in front of the food cart parked halfway down the street, light shining through its open window. It was almost 6:30 a.m.—he'd closed the bar at 4:00 a.m. and stayed late to handle some pack business—and he was now late for his breakfast pickup.

Clearly, some assholes were trying to steal it.

"Give us the money and we'll let you keep parking here every week," one of the men on the sidewalk said.

Or not.

"Are you seriously trying to do some racketeering? In my neighborhood? In front of my building? With my favorite food cart?" Wade asked loudly as he lengthened his stride.

The small group turned to look at him, the cocky expressions on their faces not impressing Wade. The scent of sulfur got stronger, the particular odor of *demon* making Wade scowl. Gross. If they ruined his breakfast sandwiches, he was going to be so pissed.

"Keep walking," said one of the men—an ifrit, if Wade had the scent right, and he usually did.

"Uh, no. You're in my territory. *You* walk."

One of the ifrits swaggered closer, flashing sharp teeth and giving off a threatening aura that might have worked on a mundane human but which Wade only found laughable. He'd faced down plenty of demons and gods in his twenty-three years, and Wade hadn't found anything dead or alive these days that he couldn't eat, ifrits included.

He flashed his own teeth, the skin on his face getting that particular itch that happened when he shifted mass just enough to push dragon scales through it. The ifrit froze midstep, one foot hovering over the sidewalk as all the color washed out of his tanned face.

"Walk, or I get a side of demon with my BEC," Wade said. The group of ifrits as a whole spun on their heels and sprinted away with a burst of supernatural speed without another word. Wade snorted, clearing smoke from his nose. "And don't come back!"

Wade was still scowling in the direction the ifrits had run off to when he stepped up to the food cart's open window. Paolo leaned through the opening, turning his head in the same direction, but the ifrits were already gone.

"Thanks, kid," Paolo grunted. He was a tall, burly cook in his late thirties. His entire family ran a food cart business in New York City, and Wade had hit up every single one of them in his time living there, but he liked Paolo's BECs best.

"Have they been by before?"

"First time for mine."

Wade turned to look at him, frowning as he dug out his wallet. He'd lived around Patrick Collins for years and knew how to read between the lines of what people said and meant, thanks to the mage and former special agent of the Supernatural Operations Agency. "But not for the rest of your family?"

Paolo grimaced as he shoved away from the window to rummage at the counter to his left. "Some of the cousins said they got hit up by a gang the other week. They closed the carts early rather than pay."

"Were they in pack territory?"

Paolo snorted out a laugh as he came back with a bulging plastic bag. "You know we only park in pack territory. Werecreatures make great customers."

Because werecreatures, like magic users and Wade and others who were part of the preternatural or supernatural communities, needed more food than mundane humans for energy. He was thankful for the fact that, tithes to the god pack aside, Marek Taylor was a billionaire who never minded Wade's grocery bill. "Yeah, but which one?"

"The carts were in Downtown Manhattan and Midtown."

Wade knew every single werecreature pack in those neighborhoods and made a mental note to send an email to those particular pack alphas. "I'll let the packs know to keep an eye out for the ifrits."

"Is that what they were?"

"They were assholes."

"*Dumb* assholes."

"That's the only kind."

Paolo laughed and handed Wade his bag of precious BECs. "Your breakfast. On the house today."

Wade made a face, then quickly pulled out a hundred-dollar bill and shoved it in the tip jar bolted to the food cart's counter. "Thanks."

Paolo didn't even try to stop him. "See you next week?"

"I'll be out of town."

"Then let me know when you're back, and I'll stop by."

"Thanks," Wade called over his shoulder as he walked toward his apartment building. He dug into the bag and pulled out a steaming hot BEC, unwrapping it to take a large bite. He had eleven more in the bag and ate through three of them before he even made it to the front door of his apartment on the third floor. Putting his key into the lock, he shouldered the door open while shoving the last bite of his latest BEC into his mouth to free up his hands.

Wade snagged another sandwich, carrying the bag with him into his bedroom, which was a mess by Patrick's standards but perfectly comfy by his. The custom-tailored suit Sage Taylor, his god pack's dire, had paid for was currently at her mansion on Fifth Avenue, but Wade needed to change his clothes anyway. Lillian Taylor, Sage and Marek's daughter and Wade's favorite niece ever, had hit the toddler stage of being particular about the scents that came around her. She threw a temper tantrum when any of the core of the god pack smelled like someone else.

So Wade ate the rest of his BECs around a quick shower and getting dressed in new clothes, tossing his old ones in the direction of the overflowing laundry basket in the corner. At some point, he'd have to actually do his laundry, but he figured he had enough jeans and T-shirts in his dresser and closet to get him through another couple of weeks. He ate his last BEC while running out of the building to catch his rideshare, phone chiming with an incoming text from Patrick.

Where are you?

On my way. Wade slid into the back seat of the car and snapped a selfie, sending it to Patrick.

Judging by the crumbs on your face, you ate already, didn't you? Sage made waffles.

Don't eat my waffles! A few seconds later, Wade received a selfie of Patrick holding an entire Belgian waffle on a fork and staring at the camera. *That's just mean.*

I'm feeding it to Lillian.

Wade groaned, knowing he couldn't deny his niece anything to eat. *Fine. But only her. Be there soon.*

Heading Uptown on a Tuesday morning wasn't as bad as going in the other direction, but it still took some time to get through rush-hour traffic. Wade passed the time scrolling through one of his favorite social media accounts, checking out any new restaurants in Manhattan that he needed to add to his list of places to try. Some of the viral food dishes looked absolutely ridiculous, which meant, of course, he wanted to eat them.

Eventually, the rideshare dropped him off in front of an Art Deco mansion overlooking Fifth Avenue and Central Park, the entire block god pack territory by virtue of Sage's name being on the deed of trust to the building. Wade had a key to it, just like he had a key to Patrick and Jono's building in Tribeca. Marek had dropped a ridiculous amount of money to buy an entire four-story condo building with a rooftop patio and garden, had it renovated into a single connected home, and then gave it to Patrick and Jono three years ago.

Despite Patrick and Jono being the alphas of the New York City god pack, neither of them, nor Sage nor Wade, called the ancestral territory in the Upper Manhattan neighborhood of Hamilton Heights home. They left those blocks of buildings to the rest of the god pack that had built up around them after the Battle of Samhain at the end of the world.

Linh Nguyen, Camilo Rivera, and Sahil Agarwal had been the first god pack members Jono had accepted into their ranks a few years ago, and they pretty much oversaw the housing situation in Hamilton Heights. The underground challenge ring was an aspect of the territory there that both Jono and Patrick detested and which the Crescent Coven had done multiple cleansing rituals to eradicate the rancid vibes there that always creeped Wade out.

Usually, a god pack clustered together in their territory and didn't have their alphas and dire living somewhere else. Usually, a god pack wasn't headed up by a mage and a werewolf who once channeled an animal-god patron. Fenrir had faded away after some time had passed, unlike the Norns, who Wade knew still claimed Marek as their seer. Marek hadn't lost a shade of color since the Battle of Samhain, but Wade knew the world was washed out for him, with some colors fully gone. He wasn't blind and driven mad by the Norns—yet—and hopefully wouldn't hit that unwanted but inevitable milestone for a few more decades. He had a daughter to raise, after all.

A daughter who shrieked gleefully the second Wade stepped through the front door of the grand apartment Sage and Marek called home in the massive mansion.

"Uncle Wade!" Lillian screamed, throwing her arms up and

sending pieces of Belgian waffle flying into the air. She wiggled out of her booster seat with the nimble fearlessness that only came with being born a werecreature, but she still wasn't quick enough to outmaneuver her mother.

"Oh, let's not take a header to the floor," Sage said, scooping Lillian up and settling the little girl on her hip.

Lillian smacked a sticky hand against Sage's cheek before pointing at Wade. "Uncle!"

"Hey, hey, how's my favorite girl?" Wade asked as he hurried through the living area over to the crowded dining table. The curtains were pulled back from the wall of windows, showing off the sunny view of Central Park.

Sage handed Lillian over with a tired smile. "Not done with breakfast. She wants a piece of fruit in every single square of the waffle and each square cut into a piece by itself. Have fun."

Wade kissed Lillian on her forehead, smiling when she giggled. "Of course she does."

Lillian's hair was a medium brown, grown out long, with soft, loose curls she got from Marek. Her brown eyes and the natural-born ability to shift into a weretiger she got from Sage. Her stubborn nature, they liked to joke, she got from Patrick through osmosis. Wade had made it his duty to teach her about the tastiness of snacks, and every time she hit a food milestone, he was there to share it with her.

Syrup and whipped cream–covered Belgian waffles dotted with fruit was definitely a meal they'd shared before. Wade sat in the last empty seat at the table, settling Lillian on his lap. Jono reached across the table with Lillian's plastic plate and cartoon-themed utensils, which Wade snagged and dropped in front of them.

"You're late," Patrick said from Jono's left.

Wade snorted, picking up a blueberry and putting it into a waffle square. "Had some pack business after we closed down the bar, and then some ifrits tried to mess with my favorite food cart outside my place."

Patrick frowned at him, the redhead reaching for the syrup to pass that over. "What were ifrits doing on your block?"

"Trying to start a shakedown business. I don't think they knew it was my block."

"Are they dead?"

"I'd be even later if they were because I'd probably be calling from the PCB."

Patrick made a contemplative sound before drinking his coffee. "Casale wouldn't let you get processed for something like that."

"He's no longer bureau chief of the Preternatural Crimes Bureau."

"No, he's just the police commissioner now."

Their god pack had open communication with the New York Police Department through Casale these days. After the Battle of Samhain, the last act of the outgoing Mayor Doyle Ferbenn—the human identity for the Dagda—had been to appoint Casale to lead the NYPD, not just the PCB. Out of everyone who could've taken over that role after the Battle of Samhain, Casale was top of the list, and no one on either side of the political divide had complained about it, even several years on.

Wade finished fixing Lillian's waffle and handed back her fork. "One square at a time."

Lillian stabbed her fork into a square topped with a strawberry and whipped cream and shoved it into her mouth, smiling around it. Wade snorted and took the plate Sage had made for him that she passed over. "We're expected in Central Park in thirty minutes, so eat fast."

Emma Zhang laughed from the other side of the table. "Like you need to tell Wade that."

Wade tossed a blueberry at her, which she leaned back in her chair to catch in her mouth. Beside her, Leon Hernandez did Wade a solid by passing over the coffee carafe so he could pour himself a mug of what was Kona by the smell of it.

Emma and Leon lived on one of the lower levels in the mansion, co-alphas of their Tempest pack. They'd owned the bar that held their pack's namesake before gifting it to Jono to help him establish a business for his residency in the States. Wade still thought Jono and Patrick should just get married. The paperwork seemed a lot simpler that way.

"Who's babysitting my girl?" Wade asked.

"We are," Leon said.

"Linh is proxy while we're all gone for a week, but we're not advertising our absence," Jono said as he stole some bacon off of Patrick's plate.

"It better only be a week. I need to be in DC for that trial, and Priya wants me to consult on a new case, but the evidence she wants me to review is restricted to SOA headquarters," Patrick said.

"You're the one who told Gerard we'd accept his wedding invitation, no matter when or where it was."

"I couldn't tell him *no*. I just thought he'd hold it somewhere in Ireland, not past the veil."

Wade liked former Captain Gerard Breckenridge. The half-fae immortal-born Cú Chulainn had been a huge help at the end of the world, but Wade also liked the way he could piss Patrick off. He found it hilarious. The rest of the Hellraisers, Patrick's old Mage Corps team, hadn't been half-bad either.

What Wade didn't much like was going past the veil. Every single time they'd done so, it had been because of a fight. He just hoped Gerard's upcoming wedding to Órlaith wasn't going to devolve into a feud of some sort. Wade had been assured they'd all get to eat the food without it impeding their ability to get home, and he was looking forward to dessert.

"Chew faster," Sage said, looking at her watch.

Everyone dug in, shoveling food into their mouths and finishing their breakfast quickly. Wade cleaned his plate before Lillian finished hers, but he stayed at the table when everyone else left to gather their things. Their wedding clothes would be carried over in garment bags, but Wade let Sage handle all of that while he kept Lillian distracted from the fact they would be leaving.

Going past the veil always messed around with time. Spending a day in Underhill would have them losing a week or more in the mundane world. It would be the longest time spent away from Lillian for Sage and Marek, as one of them typically tried to stay behind with her, even with the pack on hand. Gerard had allowed a plus-one for Sage and Wade, and Marek had decided to come along.

Wade didn't have a plus-anything at the moment, and he was fine with that. He still had one more year of college before he'd earn his BA in Humanities, and Wade had no desire to get sidetracked any more than he already had during and after the Battle of Samhain. Being in college was always a nice excuse for whenever General Noah Reed inevitably called him up every six months or so to see if he wanted to join the military and be trained by an actual dragon. Wade kept hanging up on Patrick's old superior officer, wondering when the other dragon would figure out the answer was, and would always, be *no*.

He'd done his time fighting, both with his pack and when he'd been forced to as a young teenager in order to survive the wrath of a god. Wade's therapist had given him the green light years ago to say no to whatever he didn't want to do, and he was going to stick to that. Reed could keep listening to the silence of an ended call.

"I have your clothes," Jono said when he wandered back into the dining room, two garment bags draped over one arm and a Louis Vuitton duffel bag held in the other.

Wade glanced down at Lillian's almost empty plate. She still had her fork clenched in one little hand, but she'd been poking at his phone for the last couple of minutes, watching a cartoon. "I think she's done."

"Playtime?" Lillian asked, looking away from the screen and giving him a sticky-looking smile.

"I think it's bath time for you."

Wade picked her up and held her aloft over his head easily, spinning once and no more than that because he didn't want to upset her stomach. She shrieked gleefully at him, and he carried her upstairs. Emma met him at the bathroom with a smile. Lillian didn't mind going into her aunt's arms too much, but it still took a few minutes before she was distracted by bath toys and bubbles and Wade could make his escape.

Everyone who was leaving had already exited the apartment, with Patrick holding open the door that led to the foyer and the elevator. "Ready?"

Wade nodded and lengthened his stride. "Are we walking into the park?"

"The hawthorn path isn't accessible by car, so yes, we're walking."

Wade stepped past Patrick into the foyer, then ducked into the elevator that Jono was holding open. He nearly tripped over the small carry-on Sage was bringing along but caught himself in time. As the doors closed, Wade's sharp hearing picked up Lillian's angry cry as she realized her pack was leaving.

Sage let out a soft little sigh, to which Marek said, "It's only a day or so, sweetheart."

"But it's a week for her," Sage replied.

"She's in good hands."

Emma and Leon might not be god pack, but they were still *pack*, and Wade knew Lillian would be safe. "We'll need to bring her back something. Gotta bribe our way back into her good graces."

Patrick scowled over his shoulder. "Do *not* bring back any snacks for her to try."

"Hey, the fae promised the food would be safe!"

"No," everyone in the elevator said in unison.

Wade rolled his eyes. "Fine."

He'd still try to sneak something back for her, even if it wasn't food.

CHAPTER TWO

The palace in the Seelie Court, where the Spring Queen ruled, was gold and shiny and full of things that Wade *itched* to take home with him.

Sage leaned across Jono in the row of flower-covered wooden chairs they sat in and tugged at Wade's arm, forcing him to look away from the intricate jeweled headpiece a *duine sídhe* wore one row up and two seats down. She raised an eyebrow at him. "You are *not* allowed to pickpocket anything."

Wade lifted both his hands, empty of shiny things, even if Sage didn't know his pockets weren't. "I wasn't!"

"You were thinking about it, and the answer is no."

Wade wisely said nothing to that, tapping his foot against the mossy ground. The wedding wasn't being held in the throne room he'd only seen once before but in a grand living hall whose walls were massive tree trunks, the roof made of high, leafy branches, and a waterfall of flowering vines at the spot up front, where Gerard waited for his bride. He was flanked by Patrick, Keith Pearson, two other former soldiers, and a handful of fae, all of whom were the equivalent of his groomsmen. There'd been a word for it that Wade had heard in the fae's chosen language and which his brain had roughly, if easily, translated into English, but he couldn't remember what it was now.

Everyone past the veil referred to Gerard as Cú Chulainn, but he answered to both names. Their arrival in Underhill that morning had occurred amid a massive celebration leading up to the wedding ceremony, and Gerard had made sure to be the one to greet them when they'd first set foot through the veil. He hadn't changed since the last time Wade had seen him four years ago—still tall, his light brown hair grown out from the military cut he'd once sported, slightly pointed ears peeking through the mass. His silver eyes had been full of laughter when he'd welcomed them, but now those same eyes were staring down the aisle as everyone started to rise.

Jono discreetly elbowed Wade in the side, and he hastily got to his feet, tugging his dark green suit jacket with its gold trim straight. The suit was an elaborate design created by a fae tailor in Manhattan, but he still felt a little underdressed compared to some of the other Tuatha Dé Danann surrounding them. He craned his head around, peering at the other end of the hall, where a line of banners swayed in the soft breeze, music rising into the air among the beautiful, crystalline voices of fae singers.

The music didn't follow familiar beats, some of the sound registering at high notes Wade knew mundane humans wouldn't be able to hear. He dialed down his hearing a bit as a literal parade of fae—winged, hooved, and not—danced their way down the center aisle, tossing flower petals, bits of moss, and sparks of magic into the air where pixies cavorted around. Wade batted away one of the bitey little things when they got too close, to which Jono shot him an aggrieved look.

What? Wade mouthed at him.

Jono didn't respond, and they went back to watching the spectacle that preceded Órlaith's grand arrival. As the Summer Lady to the Spring Court and the granddaughter to the current ruler, Órlaith was walked down the aisle by the goddess Brigid, the pair a sight to behold amidst the extravagant celebration.

Órlaith's long orange-red hair fell down her back in loose curls and a few braids, with flowers woven through it. The elaborate golden crown she wore sparkled with colorful gems, the brilliant diamond in its center something Wade really, *really* wanted for his hoard. But he never stole from friends and so pined from afar, half wondering if he could find a good substitute in the palace after the ceremony, something no one would miss.

Maybe.

The music tapered off, those in the procession standing aside amidst the crowd as Órlaith made it to the front. There was no giving her away, only Brigid having her stand before their people and beside Gerard as she took her spot in front of everyone to give a blessing as only a goddess could.

"May the memories you make and share never be forgotten," Brigid said in her opening speech, power in her words and voice that Wade could sense. It wasn't a spell, merely how the Tuatha Dé Danann prayed, he guessed.

The ceremony itself was an involved thing that took a few hours, tradition twining Gerard and Órlaith together in their own sort of legend. Gerard only had eyes for his bride throughout the entire ceremony, and Órlaith never looked away once. It was sickeningly sweet, and Wade was happy for them, but he was even happier when it was over and they were married, and the entire party left the living hall for the palace gardens and the endless mounds of food waiting for the guests there.

"Wade—" Jono said.

"Be right back," Wade said before swiftly cutting through the crowd with one goal in mind.

He'd leave the mingling to the rest of the pack. Wade was far more interested in the epic food options on display for the guests to eat. The long tables in the many gardens set aside for the food were piled high with roasted game, grilled vegetables, salads of all sorts, an entire table filled with bread from savory to sweet, another table dedicated to potato dishes of all kinds, and a completely separate garden reserved for all the many desserts on offer.

Wade took a moment to stand there in pure bliss before getting in line and grabbing a thin wooden plate off the stack at one end of the feast table. Apparently, the fae were all about getting your own food on your own time and partying it up in the gardens with all the guests who'd been invited. None of the typical sit down at a fancy table and be restricted by courses trend that always left Wade hungry.

The celebration was supposed to last for a week, but Wade and the pack were definitely not staying that long. So he was going to make the most of the food while he had the chance. That meant making a mini mountain on his plate from just the first table alone. Pleased with his efforts, Wade grabbed a fork and made his way back to the others, shoveling food into his mouth as he went.

Sage was the first one to spot him, a resigned expression crossing her face. "Why am I not surprised?"

"They said it was safe to eat," Wade protested around a mouthful of food.

"Chew with your mouth shut," Patrick said, gently knocking a fist against his shoulder.

Wade eyed Patrick's suit, noticing the shiny jewels sewn into the lapels and cuffs of his jacket and the edge of his vest. The dark green fabric almost matched his eyes, while the gold broach he wore looked more like a medal than an adornment for a wedding. The other three Hellions nearby seemed to have the same sort of jewels on them, while the fae who had stood with Gerard did not.

Patrick caught the direction of his gaze and tapped at the intricate gold brooch. "It's a gift from Gerard to us mundane human groomsmen. No, you can't have it."

Wade stabbed at a piece of meat on his plate that tasted like chicken and bacon roasted together and took a bite. "It's shiny."

Patrick reached out and snagged one of the long slices of bread smeared with something that maybe tasted like onion on it. He shoved it in his mouth before Wade could properly protest. "Oh, that's good."

"This is my plate," Wade grumbled. "Go get your own."

"I think that's a great idea."

Patrick grabbed Jono by the hand and dragged him off toward the nearest garden dishing out food. Keith did a double take from where he stood some yards away before hurrying over. "Where'd Razzle Dazzle go?"

"To get some food before Wade eats it all," Sage said, heading in the same direction.

Wade was left behind, but he didn't mind so much, content to plow his way through his first plate and watch everyone around him enjoy the wedding celebration. Everyone was discussing the nuptials and Órlaith's gown and Gerard's formal return and a bunch of other details that had no bearing on him or his pack. Honestly, it sounded boring.

He finished his first plate and wandered into a different garden that was saturated in a floral scent from all the flowers blooming around the next food table he was going to try. Most of the dishes on this one seemed to be full of pots with stews and soups and baskets of thick bread in all kinds of shapes and flavors. Wade spent a good hour sampling every single pot on the table, one small bowl at a time.

He took a break after that, wandering off to watch some of the performers and drink some of the mead on offer at various refreshment stations. It was sweet and thick on his tongue, and he wondered if they'd let him take a bottle or two back home with him. It wasn't as good as Thor's in Chicago, but he'd take what he could get.

By the time he decided he wanted something sweet, the dessert table in a different garden filled with topiary was pretty packed, but there was a spot of space around a dark-haired fae that would give him a perfect opportunity to grab some cake. Wade snagged a plate, sidestepped around some chatting fae who clearly could've caught up somewhere else, and planted himself firmly in front of a platter that held one last slice of something that smelled like it was baked with honey and hazelnut.

Wade slid the last slice onto his plate with his fork and was contemplating something else to go with it when the dark-haired fae made a displeased sound from his left. "That slice was mine."

Wade glanced at the fae, eyes narrowing as he took in the dark purple clothing, silver adornments in the sunset-orange hair, and pale yellow eyes staring at him like he was a bug. He sniffed delicately, getting a whiff of the fae's scent, and wrinkled his nose. "Oh, you're from the Unseelie Court."

The fae looked absolutely affronted at that. "I am *not*."

"Sure." Wade reached for the nearest serving spoon and dumped a scoop of what might have been a parfait onto his plate. "I didn't think Gerard had invited any of you."

The fae stepped close enough to be a threat, but Wade knew better than to give ground. He merely raised an eyebrow and reached for a different serving spoon, never breaking eye contact, and scooped another dessert on his plate.

A muscle in the fae's too-beautiful face twitched. "Mortals aren't welcome here."

"I have a fancy invitation that says I am."

He didn't bother telling the fae they were wrong about him being mortal. *Technically*, dragons weren't immortal, but their long lives made it seem that way to mundane humans who lived only a fraction of the time they did. It was something he was working through with his therapist, the knowledge that he'd outlive his pack and their future generations. But the fae didn't need to know that.

"I believe the mortal came as Lord Cú Chulainn's *personal* guest, Lord Diarmait," someone said with a surprising hint of a Boston accent to their voice.

Another fae slid around a group of people waiting for their turn at the dessert table but not willing to get in the middle of the argument. Wade couldn't help but take a second and maybe a third look at the newcomer. He smelled a lot like the sea, all salt and ocean when Wade took a breath, but also something else he couldn't really place. He just knew he'd bottle it if he could.

Oh no, he's hot.

Wade just managed not to blurt out that thought, unable to look away from the stupidly handsome fae who came to stand near him. He was dressed as elegantly as everyone else in an outfit of brown and deep blue. He wore a rich-looking fur cape that Wade really wanted to touch and half thought would make a great throw blanket in his apartment.

The fae would also look really good in his apartment.

He had a face that could probably let him walk a New York Fashion Week runway, with enough freckles that Wade wished he could count them. Wade knew it was impolite to stare, but he found he couldn't look away, lungs drowning in an ocean scent he didn't much mind despite being able to breathe fire.

"Riordan." Wade glanced at the first fae, watching his lips curl over teeth that looked a little too sharp to ever be found in a human's mouth. "You would speak up for mortals."

"Nothing wrong with most of them," Riordan replied coolly. Wade silently mouthed the name, liking how it felt on his tongue.

"One hopes he will not stay long."

"Only long enough to eat all your cake," Wade retorted, wrenching his attention away from Riordan.

Lord Diarmait—and wasn't that a stupidly pompous kind of name—who claimed he wasn't part of the Unseelie Court didn't make a scene when he left the line, but the sheer dismissal of Wade's presence was patently rude. If he cared at all, he maybe would feel embarrassed by the fae's actions, but he didn't.

Wade was pretty pleased with himself for snagging the fae's gold bracelet when he'd turned to leave though. He twirled it around his index finger while staring at the newcomer.

Riordan made a strangled sort of sound. "That's not yours."

"It is now," Wade said cheerfully as he pocketed the bracelet. It'd make a great gift for Lillian. "I didn't need the help, but thanks anyway for getting him away from the table. He was blocking the panna cotta."

Riordan glanced at the dish in question. "That isn't panna cotta."

"Oh? Then what is it?" Riordan said something in his language that Wade's brain squeezed out as "Yeah, no, that's panna cotta."

He'd never questioned how he could just understand people who hailed from the supernatural and preternatural communities. Mundane human languages he'd have to learn the old-fashioned way, but if it was spoken by people who originated from beyond the veil or outside human norms, he generally had no issue understanding them.

Sometimes it paid to be a dragon.

Riordan laughed. He had a really nice laugh that Wade kind of wanted to hear over and over again. "I suppose it's pretty similar. I won't stand in your way of it."

He stepped aside, and Wade had the ridiculous urge to reach out and yank him close again. He couldn't ever recall feeling this way outside his pack, and even then, this felt different. "Thanks. What are you having?"

"Not the panna cotta." His tone was teasing, as was the look in his warm brown eyes, making something weird and warm flutter in Wade's chest. "I'll let you go first."

Wade filled up his plate with some more dessert and picked up a goblet of a syrupy-looking drink. He waited for Riordan to fill up his plate before the two of them wandered away from the dessert table.

"Did you come here by yourself?" Wade asked, totally not trying to dig for information. Really.

"Just me," Riordan said. "My clan is back home. What about you?"

"I came with my pack. They're around here somewhere."

Riordan glanced at him. "Do you need to get back to them?"

"Probably," Wade said reluctantly. "You could eat with us if you want?"

His hopes were dashed when Riordan shook his head. "While I came alone, there are some people I need to speak with still."

Wade tried not to let his disappointment show. "Oh. Sucks that you have to work during a party."

"Hopefully, it's worth it." Riordan hesitated a moment before saying, "The celebration will last a while. If you're still around over the next few days, maybe we'll see each other again."

"Maybe." Wade forced a smile. "Nice meeting you anyway."

Wade left to go find his pack before he did anything stupid, like blurt out he thought Riordan was cute or offer the fae his number. He found his pack sitting at a table underneath a tree, some of Patrick's old team huddling with them. Those few were mundane humans, and Wade figured they felt safer with his pack than by themselves, even with Gerard's promise that no harm would come to any of them.

"Did you clean out the dessert table?" Patrick asked as Wade approached.

"No." Wade reached between Patrick and Keith and dropped his plate between theirs. "I'm sitting here."

"Pushy," Keith muttered around his fork, but everyone on the bench scooted one way or the other to make some room.

Wade sat down, pressed elbow to elbow between Patrick and Keith, and then dug into his plate of delicious sweets. He half listened to the conversation around him, content to eat his way through the options he'd picked. Everything was really tasty, and he silently bemoaned the fact he wouldn't be able to find any of it back home. He was scraping his fork over the now-empty plate sometime later when Patrick perked up, causing Wade to look around.

Gerard and Órlaith extracted themselves from a knot of guests nearby and made their way to the table, smiles on their faces and looking incandescently happy. Patrick stood, needing to lean against Wade to free himself from the bench, leaving behind his half-eaten plate. Wade watched Patrick approach Gerard before sliding Patrick's plate closer.

"That's not yours, mate," Jono replied idly.

Wade sighed and slid the plate back to Patrick's spot. "Fine."

"I don't know how you're still hungry, considering the amount of food you've eaten," Keith said.

Wade shrugged. Being hungry was a background sensation that he dealt with by snacking. He was still a growing fledgling and would be for the next few centuries, according to Reed. Shifting mass took effort and energy, and Wade preferred his human form rather than his dragon form on a daily basis. His pack kept him fed—it had been one of the first things they'd done for him after he escaped the last fight ring Tezcatlipoca had thrown him into. Wade still remembered how Jono had emptied an entire vending machine at the PCB for him while he waited in that interrogation room, scared out of his mind and refusing to show it.

Wade hadn't believed he was safe at that time and didn't believe it for weeks, even after Tezcatlipoca had been dealt with back then. Eventually, he'd learned that Patrick and Jono had meant it when they'd said they would keep him safe, and Wade would be forever grateful for the kindness they'd shown him over the years. He could look on his fucked-up past before finding his pack with clearer eyes these days. His therapist called it progress. Wade called it growing up. It helped to do it with a family rather than in chains.

"Enjoying the food?" Órlaith asked from behind him.

Wade hastily moved his fork away from Patrick's plate. "It's really good."

Órlaith reached out to ruffle his hair, and Wade allowed it. He'd liked her ever since their first meeting when they'd rescued her on the Skellig Islands, and she'd been angry rather than scared of her predicament, taking the rescue in stride. "Eat as much as you want. There's plenty to go around."

"Are you sure about that?" Jono drawled. "He could eat you out of house and home. He's done it to us before."

"Hey," Wade protested. "You gave me a credit card for a reason!"

"Yes," Marek said wryly. "I'm thankful I can cover the monthly bill."

Wade picked up something that was a cross between a grape and kumquat and lobbed it at Marek's face. The seer moved to catch it with his mouth, hazel eyes crinkling as he chewed. Wade took the teasing in stride, well used to everyone complaining about how much he ate, even as they shoved food onto his plate and bought him snacks.

"I wish you could stay through to the end of the celebration, but I understand why you all must go," Órlaith said.

"Before you leave later, we wanted to give you a token of our appreciation for coming," Gerard said.

Wade perked up at that. "Gifts? Where's mine?"

He leaned away to get out of swatting distance from Jono and ended up almost making Keith fall off the bench. The other man squawked, but Wade grabbed him by the arm and hauled him upright again.

Órlaith laughed as she gestured gracefully at several fae who walked toward the table holding ornate wooden chests. "Yes, we have gifts."

Wade wasn't sure if it was normal for fae to hand out gifts at a wedding rather than accept them, but he wasn't going to complain. He itched to find his but politely waited until it had been handed to him. The carved box was small, fitting in the palm of his hand. When he flicked it open, he found a gold ring with a fire opal set in the band. An artisan had carved a delicate design into the opalescent sphere, the runes not anything Wade could read, but he could sense the magic in it all the same. Whatever spell had been laid upon the ring, it wouldn't affect him.

He still took it out of the box and promptly put it on his right middle finger.

"There's a protection spell in the fire opal. It will lend aid to whoever you tell it to, giving them whatever they need in that moment," Gerard said.

"Oh," Wade said, pleased with that, thinking about all the ways it would've come in handy in the fights leading up to the end of the world. If it would help keep his pack safe, then it was both shiny *and* useful. Which meant he was never taking it off. "*Awesome. Will people know it's an artifact?*"

"Some very strong magic users may be able to."

Wade narrowed his eyes thoughtfully before adjusting his aura so the intricate barrier that disguised his soul and kept him appearing human to the world at large expanded just enough to incorporate the ring and its magic in his shielding. It felt like shifting mass in a way, the edges of himself smoothing out with the adjustment.

Gerard blinked at him, raising an eyebrow. "Huh. I guess that's one way to hide it."

"It's mine now. I don't want people to try to take it."

Wade peered at the gifts the others got, noticing that jewelry seemed to be a theme, something that no one complained about. Sage got a new pendant, Marek a ring, Jono a bracelet that Gerard promised would adjust when he shifted so he wouldn't lose it, and Patrick received a necklace with a flat medallion stamped with what Wade had a sneaking suspicion was Gerard's family crest or its equivalent. Which probably meant something, though he didn't know what, even if Patrick seemed to.

"Oh, you *asshole*," Patrick said, eyes wide as he stared at the medallion.

"I don't let my people go," Gerard said plainly, reaching out to scrub his fingers through Patrick's neatly styled hair to mess it up like any older brother would. "You and the other Hellions will always be part of my story, and that means you're family."

"I told you not to make him cry," Keith said with tears in his own eyes.

Wade knew this was probably some kind of goodbye for the old

Mage Corps teammates. Gerard had promised the Cailleach Bheur he'd return home, and that meant leaving the shores of America behind. So Wade left them all to their goodbyes and their hugs in favor of finding some more food.

Eventually, the daylight faded into evening, and someone did a fancy spell that seemingly pulled the stars above down to the land to burn in the air above the garden. Wade wandered through the feast tables, picking at his food, feeling fully satiated for once by the time Sage found him when he was thinking about finding a place to nap.

"We're heading back," she said.

Wade downed the drink in his hand and left the cup in a shrub. "Okay."

As fun and entertaining as the wedding had been, he was looking forward to sleeping in his bed, whether the one at his condo or the rooms he'd long since claimed as his in the other pack apartments.

Sage rounded everyone up with a firmness that always came in handy as dire. They said their goodbyes to Gerard and Órlaith, and a pair of fae attendants were tasked with escorting them to the cross-roads and beyond. They all stuck close when they crossed the veil, the fog of the empty space disconcerting in a way that made Wade want to stretch his wings. The desire to do so faded once they made it back to Central Park, coming out on the hawthorn path in the center of that urban greenery.

It was noon when they finally returned to the mortal world. Wade pulled his cell phone out of his pocket as Patrick conjured up a mageglobe, the tickle of a look-away ward passing over his skin. Wade let it settle around him and ignored it as he waited for his phone to turn on and connect. When it did, he snorted at the date. "It's June. We lost a week."

"That's about what I expected," Patrick said as they traipsed out of the shrubbery and onto the asphalt path that would take them back to Fifth Avenue.

They were all tired and full of food. Keith and the other Hell-raisers said their goodbyes on the sidewalk just beyond the edge of

Central Park, insisting they could catch a taxi or rideshare back to their hotel. The rest of them trekked back to the Art Deco mansion that was home and were greeted by a harried Emma, who promptly deposited an irritable Lillian into Sage's arms.

"Oh good, you're back," Emma said. "The Boston god pack has asked for assistance for a problem their dire refuses to talk about over the phone."

Wade groaned, the sound mingling with the rest of the protesting noise his pack made.

There went his nap.

CHAPTER THREE

"I can't go to Boston," Patrick said, sounding frustrated. "I'm scheduled to be in DC this coming week for a federal trial."

Wade pried the bottle cap off his beer, the metal bending beneath the force of his grip. The Corona fizzed a little up the neck as he tipped it against his lips and swallowed half of it. Patrick was staring at his phone, scowling at whatever his calendar app was showing him. The week lost to Gerard's wedding meant everyone was playing catch-up almost immediately when Wade really would've preferred a nap. Food comas were the worst.

"Marek is scheduled to go to Silicon Valley for a tech conference later this week, and I'm not leaving Lillian while she's sick," Sage said. The poor little girl in question was sitting in her lap, looking miserable with a stuffy nose and big, watery eyes. Sage gently smoothed her hand over Lillian's sweaty hair before bending to kiss the top of her head. Emma had given Lillian a potion before they arrived, but the common cold was stubbornly tenacious, even for werecreatures.

Jono grimaced, sharing a glance with Patrick. "We've all been gone for a week, and I need to stay here to handle any of the problems that cropped up while we were past the veil."

As one, the rest of his pack turned to look at Wade, who paused in leaning back to finish the rest of his beer. He stared at them, then groaned. "Is it my turn?"

Patrick put his cell phone back in his pocket. "It's your turn."

Wade chugged the rest of his beer and set the bottle on the coffee table in the living room. "What's the deal with their dire not wanting to talk over the phone? And why aren't the alphas asking for help?"

"She wouldn't say," Emma replied, a little grim.

"I wanted to defer to Patrick and Jono since it deals with another god pack's territory," Linh said. She had only arrived a few minutes ago, having been notified they'd all returned home and needing to trek down from Hamilton Heights. She'd held down the fort in their absence, but while she could act in Patrick's and Jono's stead as proxy when necessary, some decisions she prudently left to her alphas to decide. Sending aid to another god pack with little to no information on *why* aid was being requested was one of them.

Wade knuckled one of his eyes and sighed. "Can I sleep first?"

Jono ruffled his hair in passing before scooping Lillian up into his arms to rock her a little. "Patrick and I will make some calls when we get home. You can stay over tonight. You won't be leaving today."

Wade grunted his agreement. When everyone split up twenty minutes later, he followed Patrick and Jono downstairs to their car in the garage, climbing into the back of the four-door dark gray Mercedes-Benz that was Jono's favored vehicle in the city these days. Patrick still had a soft spot for the Mustang he'd driven for years, but when Jono had finally bought a car, he'd gone for a bit of luxury. Wade could appreciate the leather seats, which he sprawled across and dozed on during the drive to Tribeca.

He only opened his eyes when they'd parked in the garage and Patrick had opened the passenger door to tug on his ankle. "Come on, get up. You'll feel better napping on a bed."

Wade groaned but slid out of the car, hiding a yawn behind his hand. Patrick had already ditched his suit jacket, the clothing draped over one arm. Wade took that as permission, and by the time they made it to the elevator, he'd shed his own jacket. He drew in a deep breath, the scent of Underhill fading beneath the permanent scent of *pack* that saturated the building.

Patrick always had a lingering bitterness to his scent from a soul wound that never bothered Wade, while Jono's had lost the hint of ozone that had been present when Fenrir was his patron. They were what Wade considered home though, a calming presence that had always stilled the churning in his gut and panic in his mind once he'd finally realized they meant it when they promised they wouldn't let anyone hurt him.

He hadn't believed them when they first rescued him from a god's clutches some years ago, too used to punishment and pain to trust a kind hand back then. Wade tried not to think too much about the dark years that came after he was taken from his mother, when he'd worn a god's collar and been enslaved. He'd worked through a lot of his anger, fear, shame, and self-hatred with the aid of his therapist, something Patrick had advocated and paid for once they took Wade into their pack when he was eighteen.

But learning to understand that none of what he'd experienced—the fights to the death, the forced thievery, the unwanted touches—was his fault had taken time. All of what Wade had survived had left its mark on him, but the reminders weren't as brutally stark when he was surrounded by his pack and the people he loved who loved him back. Healing wasn't linear, and that was okay because he was better today than he'd been at fourteen, and Wade would be forever thankful for that.

"Go shower," Jono said, giving Wade a gentle nudge toward the stairs once they were inside the condo. "You can nap after. I'll make dinner tonight."

Wade nodded and took the stairs to the second floor of the three-story condo, where his bedroom was located. Both Sage and himself had rooms in the condo, the core of their god pack always represented in some way wherever Jono and Patrick lived. Their god pack had grown, sure, but Wade knew the four of them would always be a step outside everyone else due to what they'd all gone through and survived.

He pitched himself into the bathroom attached to his bedroom and stripped out of his clothes to wash off any last lingering traces of Underhill. Then he pulled on a pair of boxers and flopped on his bed, rolling around until he'd dragged the blankets around him like a burrito and promptly passed out.

Wade woke up sometime later to the late-afternoon sunlight streaming through the cracks in the blinds and someone poking him in the stomach through the layers of blankets. He grunted, opening one eye and working his chin over the edge of the blanket to glare blearily at Patrick.

"Jono made lasagna," Patrick said.

"Did he make me one?" Wade asked through a cracking yawn.

Patrick snorted. "Yes."

"Awesome."

Jono was a great cook, a skill Patrick did not share. Wade liked eating food but was too impatient to really want to cook. He *could* cook—better than Patrick—he just preferred ordering his meals delivered straight to him.

"Be downstairs in five minutes, or I'm eating out of your pan," Patrick said.

Wade squawked a wordless protest, but Patrick had already escaped by the time Wade rolled himself out of bed. He hastily pulled on a pair of sweatpants and a clean enough T-shirt before making his way downstairs. He could smell the lasagna before he reached the kitchen, two pans of the delicious, delicious pasta sitting on the island.

Jono was pulling a tray of garlic bread out from the oven and didn't even turn around when he said, "Go sit down. We're eating at the table like civilized people."

Wade withdrew his finger from the top of the lasagna pan that was his and sighed. "Fine."

Patrick was already at the table, a huge Caesar salad sitting toward one end and bottles of beer at everyone's place setting. Wade took his usual seat and rested his elbows on the table, watching Patrick scroll through his phone. He made a thoughtful sound that had Wade perking up and wanting to steal his phone to check his texts.

"What's that noise for?" Wade asked.

"Spencer is thinking of retiring," Patrick said.

Wade wrinkled his nose. "Does the SOA know he'd retire so he could spend the rest of his life with Takoma?"

He liked Spencer Bailey but much preferred Spencer's psychopomp. Fatima was adorable and mischievous, and Wade had liked her since he first met her in London. Takoma, on the other hand, was someone Wade didn't particularly care for, but then again, he didn't like vampires, whether they were in love with a friend or not.

Patrick shot him a pointed look. "No, and we're not going to tell them that."

"Do I look like I spend time around SOA special agents anymore?" Wade reached for the salad bowl and served himself a heap of it. "Anything new from Boston?"

Patrick set aside his phone and took the salad bowl from Wade when he passed it over. "Sage got us information on their dire. Her name is Ella Dean."

"And the alphas?"

"Married couple. Different from the alpha who was in charge before the Battle of Samhain. The Salem god pack said they haven't had as many issues with the Boston god pack since Harper and Casey Jenkins took over." Patrick finished serving himself and Jono and set the bowl back on the table.

"So why is their dire reaching out to us and not the god pack alphas?"

"Ella wouldn't say when I spoke with her. She just insisted that it couldn't be over the phone, that it had to be in person."

Wade frowned. "You sure it's not a trap of some sort?"

"I don't rule anything out, which means neither are you."

"Well, yeah. That goes without saying."

Jono came out of the kitchen with two lasagna pans in hand. He placed one on the trivet in the center of the table and the other on the trivet in front of Wade. Wade promptly picked up his fork and knife and dug in before Jono returned with the garlic bread.

"There's been nothing in the news about anything weird going on in Boston while we were gone," Jono said as he handed one-half of an entire baguette to Wade.

"That doesn't mean anything," Wade said around a mouthful of pasta.

"Chew with your mouth closed," Patrick said.

Wade made a face and chewed fast, the heat of the lasagna right out of the oven not bothering him at all. He broke his portion of the baguette in half and rested both pieces over his dish to soak up some of the sauce and cheese. "So I'm heading over there blind? That's never fun."

Patrick and Jono shared a look before Jono spoke. "You want another pack member to go with you?"

Wade shook his head. "No, it's fine. I can handle it."

All the rest of their god pack members had their own duties within New York City to handle. In a city still recovering from the veil being ripped open through it a few years ago, every member of their god pack was needed to help keep the peace between the packs under their protection and the rest of the supernatural community. Of those who could be spared, Wade had the unique advantage of being impervious to magic, demons, and other supernatural kind of problems. Usually, eating them fixed whatever was wrong.

He'd need to remember to pack some extra mouthwash.

"We know you can handle it, but the second you think things will go tits up, you ring us," Jono said, pointing his fork at Wade.

Wade nodded and preened under the praise, still not above wanting to make them proud. Then he dug into his lasagna, determined to demolish it.

Jono and Patrick switched to talking about things that weren't pack related at the table, a rule Sage had initiated in her home and which they'd carried over here. Pack business engulfed their lives so much that trying to carve out time for themselves took effort some days. Listening to them talk about mundane errands and where they should go for their next date night was a nice reminder that they'd all survived to be able to enjoy moments like this.

Their relationship made Wade sometimes think about wanting something similar one day, but it was a need he always passed on. He didn't care about the details of everyone's love life, mostly because he was really only familiar with the opposite from when he was a young teenager. Yeah, he found people aesthetically pleasing, but his therapist always said he didn't have to act on it if he wasn't ready, and that was okay.

So he looked, and sometimes he thought about kissing someone, but it never became more than a fleeting thought. His pack never teased him about his lack of a partner and didn't let anyone else do so either. Though considering his background, Wade would most likely have to find someone with a lifespan close to his own, and there were very limited beings out there that could check that box. For now, he was content to be with his pack, spoil his niece rotten, and add to his current hoard.

"Is there dessert?" Wade asked as he put the last bite of his lasagna in his mouth. He'd finished the entire dish, along with the bread and his salad, but there was always room for dessert.

Jono rolled his eyes, but his smile was fond. Wade wasn't surprised when he got up and pulled an entire Junior's cheesecake out of the fridge. He cut a large slice for himself, a smaller one for Patrick, and then gave Wade the rest of the cheesecake. Wade happily ate his way through one of his favorite desserts. By the time he finished, Jono and Patrick had abandoned the table for the couch, and Wade took it upon himself to clean up the kitchen.

When the dishwasher was running, the last scraps of food eaten, and the counters wiped down, Wade claimed the part of the sectional that Patrick and Jono weren't sprawled across, pulling out his phone and bringing up a game to play while the other two binged a show that he remembered being popular a few years ago.

"I can tell you how it ends," Wade said absently.

Patrick kicked him in the shoulder. "You do that, and I will empty out your snack cabinet."

Wade sniffed haughtily at that threat. "You would never."

"Both of you shut your gobs and let me watch in peace," Jono said.

They settled down for a comfortable night in, the companionship of pack something that Wade knew he would always want in his life, no matter how long he lived.

CHAPTER FOUR

The private jet finally rolled to a stop in the private hangar at Boston Logan International Airport. Wade was on his feet before the flight attendant was cleared to open the door, retrieving his backpack from the storage unit in the back. His luggage was on the tarmac when he finally clattered down the jet stairs, waving a cheerful goodbye to the pilot and flight attendant on Marek's payroll.

A four-door gray Audi waited for him on the tarmac, the driver's-side door open and key fob handed over by the delivery person. Wade took it with a nod of thanks before chucking his luggage in the trunk and getting behind the steering wheel. He dropped his backpack on the front passenger seat, rifling through it for a can of Coke that he put in the cup holder.

Getting out of the airport was an exercise in patience that had Wade sighing heavily and drumming his fingers on the steering wheel in time to whatever song randomly popped up on his playlist. It was a better use of his hands rather than flipping off everyone who tried to cut him off. Wade often thought New York City drivers were the worst, but clearly, they had nothing on Massachusetts drivers.

His GPS was supposed to take him directly to the Ritz-Carlton, where Sage had made his reservation, but Wade detoured to the first Dunkin' Donuts that showed up on the map. He took the last exit before the Sumner Tunnel and drove only a handful of minutes before he saw the Dunkin' on the right-hand side. Wade parked, left everything but his wallet, cell phone, and the key fob in the car, and hustled inside.

Only a couple of people were in line, getting late-morning coffees, and when he finally made it to the register, Wade used his fingers to tick off his order. "I want a large coffee Coolatta, extra whip, a dozen donuts, two dozen donut holes, and all of your hash browns."

The employee blinked at him over the register, finger hovering over the screen to enter in his order. "Uh, *all* of the hash browns?"

Wade checked the time on his cell phone, calculated how long it would take him to get the food and then get to the hotel to check in before having to meet Ella at noon, and then sighed. "Okay, however many hash browns you can fry in the next ten minutes."

He knew from previous experience that if he asked for the bags of unfrozen hash browns to fry himself, they'd say no. Corporate entities were so stingy.

The employee gave him a long, disbelieving look before rapidly tapping in his order and telling him the cost. "What donut flavors?" the employee asked as Wade paid with his credit card.

"Surprise me. I like them all."

The donuts came first, and he sat with his boxes and bags of doughy goodness, cramming one after the other into his mouth while he waited for his hash browns. He'd eaten his way through nine donuts by the time his hash browns were handed over in a plastic bag. Wade mumbled his thanks around the donut holes he was chewing and left with his haul of food. He organized everything within easy reach on the front passenger seat, happy now that he had something to snack on.

Driving into Boston proper reminded Wade why he hated driving in cities and much preferred the subway or someone else behind the steering wheel. By the time he pulled into the valet strip in front of the Ritz-Carlton's entrance on Avery Street, he'd yelled at a dozen drivers and honked out a symphony. Sighing, Wade put the car in park and gathered up his backpack and the now-empty donut box. It was barely a thirty-second walk from Boston Common, and he could smell a lot of grass when he got out of the car. It made his nose twitch.

"Checking in?" the valet asked when Wade tossed him the keys after unlocking the trunk.

"Yup. I'll be back out for the car in about twenty minutes."

"Of course. We'll bring it around when you need it."

Wade hauled his luggage out of the trunk and wheeled it toward the hotel entrance, the doorman having already opened the door for him. He waved off a staff member who offered to take his luggage and only got halfway through the lobby before an older man whose hair was trending silver at his temples peeled away from where he was loitering near the front desk and came over to greet him.

"Mr. Espinoza, I'm Harry Adams, general manager of the hotel. I wanted to extend a warm welcome to you and let you know that if you should need anything, we're here to provide it," the man said smoothly as he gamely took the empty donut box before offering his hand in greeting.

Wade, having spent years around the kind of wealth most people could never even fathom, followed through with the handshake and an easy smile. He figured he had to be in the system, with Sage providing his information, for them to know him on sight. "Thanks. I'll be wandering around Boston for the most part and don't know when I'll be leaving. I hope that won't be a problem."

"Not at all," Harry demurred. "The presidential suite is yours for as long as you need it."

"Great. Mind showing me to it?"

Wade wasn't one to stand on ceremony, and the clock was ticking for him to get to his meeting with Ella. Harry and his assistant showed him to a private elevator, handing over a discreet black key card that Wade shoved into his wallet.

"That key card accesses the elevator and your suite. If you lose it, please let us know, and we'll promptly issue you a new one," Harry said on the elevator ride up.

Wade nodded, only half listening as Harry droned on about what the hotel offered. All he really cared about was if they'd have a decent selection of snacks.

The elevator slowed to a stop seconds later, and the doors opened on a small foyer. Harry crossed it and used his own card to open the door to the presidential suite before handing it to the woman who'd accompanied them. "Stephanie will be your dedicated concierge while you are here. Anything you need, she will ensure it is provided. All her information and what we can provide will be in the contact book on the desk."

The space was huge, easily bigger than the average New York City apartment. Windows overlooked the city and Boston Common, a fireplace was integrated into one of the walls of the living room, and Wade could see the spacious bedroom down the hall. The penthouse had a sparkling kitchen and a dining room with a table that could easily fit the core of his pack. The space smelled like cleaning chemicals and nothing else. He wondered if that was standard practice for whenever Sage traveled.

"Thanks," Wade said. "I need to head out for a meeting."

Harry and Stephanie were quick to say their goodbyes, leaving Wade to get settled. He wheeled his luggage into the bedroom and chucked it in the closet before dumping his backpack on the bed. He had his keys, wallet, and phone in his pockets, sunglasses perched on his head, and fifteen minutes to get to Faneuil Hall for his meeting with Ella.

Wade had a feeling he was going to be late.

Hurrying out of the suite, Wade took the elevator back down to the lobby. He had to wait a couple of minutes for the valet to bring his car around and then drove where his GPS told him to. The beginning of June felt like the start of the summer tourist season now that Memorial Day weekend was behind them. Lots of people were out on the sidewalks on the late Wednesday morning, all of them dressed for the sunny day. Despite the pedestrian crowd, the parking garage on State Street wasn't completely full.

Wade parked, locked the car behind him, and jogged for the exit, clattering down the stairs rather than using the rickety-looking elevator. He bounded onto the sidewalk and hurried toward where everyone else in the vicinity was heading: Faneuil Hall.

It smelled like chocolate outside, which was just unfair. The cobblestone square he ended up in was dominated by the redbrick and white-trimmed building of Faneuil Hall. People drifted in and out of its door for the visitor center, but Wade wasn't interested in history or a tour. He had his sights set on the statue of Samuel Adams near the center of the square. That was the spot where Ella had told him to meet her. Sage had done a deep-dive search on her, so Wade knew what the dire looked like.

Ella leaned against the base of the statue, eyes glued to her cell phone. She wore white jean shorts, a pink crop top, pink sandals, and rose-tinted sunglasses. Her blond hair was styled in waves and fell loose nearly to her elbows. The designer purse slung over one shoulder was all white leather except for the gold chain. She looked young for the pack rank she held, but Wade knew better than to dismiss her outright. One didn't become dire of a god pack without being able to handle themselves and the threats directed toward their alphas with lethal intent.

"Ella?" Wade called out.

Her head snapped up, revealing perfectly applied makeup that wasn't melting off from the heat. When she spoke, Wade was surprised to hear a thick Southern accent fall from her lips, as if she'd walked right off a plane from Atlanta, Georgia. "Who's asking?"

Wade came to a stop a little ways from her, lifting his hand in a casual wave. "I'm Wade. Sorry I'm late. I had to check in to my hotel first. Sage said you were contacting her on a secondary phone, and I didn't want to call it."

He didn't state what god pack he was from, not out there in the open. Ella's eyebrows arched over the rims of her sunglasses. "I was expecting one of your alphas."

"They're busy, and so is my dire. You get me instead."

Ella pursed her lips. "Well, I suppose you have rank enough to help us."

"Trust me, I can handle whatever problem you got." Wade glanced around at the groups of people scattered across the square. "Did you want to talk out here, or do you have somewhere else in mind?"

Ella put her phone away in her purse. "Not out here. It's too open. I only wanted to meet here because it's not anywhere they'd expect me to be. I hate the tourist areas of this city."

"Then where do you want to go?"

"We're getting an early lunch."

"Great. I'm hungry."

"You smell like you already had donuts."

"Eh, those were a snack. I could do with a solid meal. Lead on."

She led him barely half a block away to a restaurant that served up a menu full of fancy bar food. The interior was all dark paneled wood and a long wall of windows overlooking the street and the square they'd left behind. The place was casual enough, and since Ella didn't take off her sunglasses, they had no hassle from the hostess about being seated.

Ella requested a table as far in the back as they could get and away from the windows. Since it wasn't the weekend, the hostess was able to accommodate them, and they had at least two empty tables between them and the next group of diners. It probably wouldn't last, but it was fine for now. Wade took the menu he was handed and gave it his undivided attention.

Neither he nor Ella spoke, not until the waitress came by to take their orders. Ella got a Crab Louie salad and a hamburger, while

Wade's order of a burger, two lobster rolls, a bowl of clam chowder, and two sides of fries could've fed at least three people. The waitress eyed them warily after taking their order but was polite enough when she brought back their drinks. Ella's fruity cocktail was rimmed in sugar, while Wade stuck with a beer.

"So," he said in a low voice. "There aren't any other werecreatures within hearing distance, and there's no active magic in here. You ready to tell me what's going on?"

Ella narrowed her eyes. "How can you be sure? You don't smell like a magic user."

Wade knew he probably didn't smell like anything to her except a mundane human. He'd learned to hide his soul and what he was years ago, able to pass as human when he wasn't. "Look, you asked for our help, and I'm helping. You gotta trust me if you want us to work together. You weren't forthcoming on the phone to my pack, but I'm here now, so what's going on?"

After a few moments of silence, Ella forced her shoulders out of the hunch they'd settled in and leaned forward, dropping her voice so low it was barely a whisper. Wade still picked up her words as clearly as if she'd screamed them. "Our alphas were taken hostage two weeks ago by a local mobster during a meeting over territory borders. We weren't willing to move our boundaries, and Niall took offense to our rejection. So he took our alphas and bound the rest of us who'd come along for the meeting from talking about what happened or from asking for help from those within the city who call it home. He said we had a month to accept his terms, or he'd kill our alphas."

Wade leaned back in his chair and crossed his arms over his chest. "But you were able to reach out to us?"

"Yes." Ella managed a fleeting, strained little smile, there and gone in a second. "The terms didn't say anything about asking the enemy for help, and I know my pack wasn't on good terms with yours before my alphas took over. You technically counted as the enemy for this."

Wade's eyes never left her face, seeing his own visage reflected back at him on the lenses of her sunglasses. "That sounds a lot like the fae."

Ella shrugged, fiddling with her fork before reaching for her drink to sip it. She didn't confirm or deny his statement, which made him wonder if the binding wouldn't let her talk about what this Niall was. "Niall didn't smell like fae. The people with him were mundane humans and a sorcerer. Nothing out of the ordinary."

"Except for how he got the drop on you and your alphas and kidnapped them."

Ella set her drink down with a grimace. "Yes."

"I hate to ask, but are you sure they're still alive?"

Her jaw worked for a moment before she finally answered. "No. We haven't seen them. But I'm not willing to say they're dead until I see bodies first."

"You're dire. Why not take over as alpha?" Cold rage wasn't a comfortable scent to breathe in as it poured across the table to him, stinging his nose. Wade hastily held up his hands. "Whoa, okay, I didn't mean to piss you off. I'm just saying, if you took over the Boston god pack even temporarily, that might break the spell he's got on you so you could talk about this problem with your allies. But I'm not a magic user. I don't know if that would work."

"I'm not—" Ella cut herself off, swallowing her anger and schooling her face into an expression of calm neutrality as their waitress returned with her salad and Wade's clam chowder. Neither moved nor spoke until the waitress had walked off. "I'm not taking the position that rightfully belongs to my alphas. Not when they aren't here to defend it. That's *my* job."

Her hissed-out statement actually made Wade relax a little. Loyalty was something he understood, and he didn't think she could be all that bad if she wasn't gunning for the role of alpha of a god pack. But then again, it could all be a ruse.

Ugh, he was thinking like Patrick.

Jono would say that was probably a good thing.

He shoveled a few bites of his soup into his mouth, not bothered by the heat of the chowder. It tasted great. "Who else knows your alphas are missing?"

"None of the packs under our protection, but that won't last for long. There's only so many times I can push off a mediation or a territory fight between packs."

Wade made a face at the mention of fighting. Most god packs allowed for disputes to be handled in a challenge ring, something his pack had put a stop to. While they couldn't stop all the packs under their protection from squabbling and getting into skirmishes, the outright murderous aspects of the challenge ring had been put to rest. Right now, the only thing their underground space in Hamilton Heights was used for was citywide meetings for all alphas.

Wade didn't think the Boston packs worked like that.

"Okay, so we can assume packs are getting suspicious. Any challengers in the god pack who have tried to take over?"

Ella stabbed at a shrimp and popped it into her mouth. "A few."

"Are they dead?"

She bared her teeth at him in a hard smile, incisors sharper than they would be on a mundane humane. "They probably wished they were when I finished with them."

Wade had a feeling Sage might like her. "And anyone else outside the packs? Night Courts? Covens? Hunters?"

Their waitress came back with the rest of their food before Ella could answer. The table wasn't big enough for all the plates, so Wade ended up piling the lobster rolls together on one and started on his hamburger first.

"I don't know," Ella said once their waitress left, sounding frustrated. "I've had our god pack searching for any sign of our alphas, but we can't outright ask people. The binding won't let us, and even if we could ask, it would put us in a bad position."

"Sounds like you're ripe for a takeover, either from a werecreature or something else."

"Not someone?"

Wade picked up a fry and dunked it in the ketchup he'd squirted on his plate. "In my experience, it's not always werecreatures gunning for the top spot."

They'd dealt with hunters and demons and all manner of gods for a period of time before the end of the world. The lure of power drew from all corners of this world and past the veil. The Boston god pack had a power vacuum their missing alphas had left behind, and in a city this big, the fight to fill it or control it was going to be messy when it spilled out of the shadows and into the lives of mundane humans.

"I think I need to know more about this Niall guy," Wade finally decided.

"My research is back home in our territory, but it isn't much." Ella hesitated a moment, catching his eye through her sunglasses. "I'd offer you a place to stay, but you said you had a hotel already, and I don't want to put you at risk."

Because that was a surefire way to bring down the wrath of his pack, and these days, no one wanted to face them.

"Nah, the hotel is fine. I'll swing by to get copies of your research and talk to some other people in your pack. I won't stay long in case Niall or someone else has your territory under watch. We can make plans to meet tomorrow morning. How about we do breakfast?"

Ella nodded, a cautious sort of relief loosening her body. "That could work."

"Great."

They finished their meal in a companionable enough silence. Wade paid for both of them, and they went their separate ways, pretending to be friendlier than they were upon leaving in case anyone was watching.

Yeah, he was definitely thinking like Patrick.

CHAPTER FIVE

 above the waves as below. Sound traveled differently through water; an echoing, droning tone from boat engines, propellers, and the indistinct back-and-forth chatter and echolocation of marine life.

Riordan Maguire of Clan Maguire swam through the waters of Boston Harbor in selkie form, nose closed and eyes open, fully aware of his surroundings and the passing ship traffic above. Visibility below the waves wasn't the best, but his heightened vision helped him to navigate well below the threat of propellers as he bypassed the ships. He had plenty of open water to swim through, all of it familiar, even if the faint, echoing thrum deep in the water was new.

The sonorous vibrations weren't typical of any animal or supernatural creature Riordan was familiar with in the past few hundred years he'd been swimming in the harbor. The sound echoed from past the islands that dotted the harbor and bays, rising and falling in pitch at the very edge of his hearing. All his instincts told him something out of the ordinary was in the ocean, but he hadn't found any evidence of what it could be.

He shoved that thought aside and focused on traversing the

channel that led to Boston proper. It was late afternoon, trending toward evening, which meant people were out and about still, and he needed to be mindful of being sighted. Some fae were skilled in the kind of magic that would keep mundane humans from noticing them at all. Selkies were decent at glamour, but that wouldn't make them invisible. Riordan stuck to the left-hand side of the channel, swimming with significant speed toward the commercial piers that dotted the shore there.

The Drydock Green Space was an area of land that tipped into the water between the cruise terminal and a commercial fish processing pier. The space was open to the public, far from the hustle and bustle of Downtown Boston. While it wasn't the best place to come ashore, it was by far the easiest in the area and a favored launching spot for his clan if they couldn't be at the beach. As the water grew shallower, Riordan somersaulted into a shift, coming up into waist-high murky water in human form with his deep brown and cream-spotted sealskin clutched in his hands.

"*Maidir le ham diabhal,*" a familiar voice called out to him. "I have your clothes. You need to stop leaving them shoved under the nearest rock, boyo."

Riordan made a face at where his older brother stood on the rocky shore, Donal shaking said clothing in his direction. "Where else do you want me to hide them? And don't you dare say the nearest bin."

He tied his sealskin around his waist. Glamour could hide his pointed ears but generally not his clothes or lack thereof. Selkies had no qualms about showing skin in either form, but mundane humans could get ridiculously prudish about it. The last thing he wanted was for someone to call the cops on them.

"You could try your car," Donal said, passing over the clothes and shoes once Riordan made it to him. They were of the same height and shared their mother's brown hair and eyes, but Donal had far more freckles than Riordan and was older by about a century. "Well? How was your patrol?"

Riordan grimaced as he hastily yanked on his clothes before undoing his sealskin, shaking it out into the guise of a leather jacket that was definitely far too hot for the weather today, but it never bothered him. Wrapping himself up in his sealskin, even on land, was like wrapping himself up in a soft, comforting blanket.

"No," Riordan confessed. "My search came up empty, like always."

Donal grimaced and headed toward the flatter greenery of the mainland. "So did everyone else's today. Don't blame yourself for that. Saoirse never would."

They'd been searching for their little sister's sealskin ever since it had been stolen as a way to get their clan under the thumb of an enemy. Saoirse had been frantic after the attack, bruised and shaken. The perpetrators had only taken her sealskin—changed at the time into the form of a fashionable coat—and left her battered in a club two weeks ago. They hadn't demanded she come with them, though she'd confessed she'd felt the hideous pull of power in her soul that urged her to go to the thief who held her sealskin now. She was able to remain with the clan so far, though Riordan knew that wouldn't last for much longer.

Ever since her sealskin was stolen, Riordan had handled several calls regarding his sister's future and his clan's anticipated subservience. If they defied the demands placed on them, Saoirse would be forcibly called to her new mate's side, bound to the person who held her sealskin. If they caved, she'd be allowed to stay with her clan, but her sealskin would be hidden somewhere they could never find, forever keeping them in line.

Neither option was a good one, and Riordan had spent every spare hour he could in search of his sister's skin, to no avail.

"You came back early," Donal said once they made it up to the grass and the pavement. "I was surprised to get your text. You could've come home first rather than go on patrol."

The cement was warm beneath Riordan's bare feet, shoes dangling from his fingers. His feet were still damp from his swim and he had a towel in his trunk he was going to use to clean up with before putting on his sneakers. "The wedding is over and I needed to clear my mind."

Riordan tried not to hunch his shoulders. He had gone to Underhill as a representative of their clan to Cú Chulainn's wedding. Riordan would have preferred staying in Boston and handling the mess they'd been dragged into and sent his brother. But Donal couldn't make clan decisions with other fae, so it had been up to Riordan to go.

"Did anyone take you up on our request for help?" Donal asked.

Riordan shook his head, lips pressed tight together for a few seconds before he spoke. "No. Mostly, they wanted to know why we weren't going home."

"Back to Ireland or Underhill?"

"Does it matter?"

They weren't the only clan of selkies calling the United States of America home, but they'd been in Boston longer than any of the others. They'd come over before the Great Hunger but were followed decades after by the desperate Irish who managed to flee the devastation. Underhill hadn't yet sprouted hawthorn paths into the Americas at the time; those had come later, with belief fed by the Irish.

Riordan's clan and others had made the new land home as best they could, knowing back then that traveling beyond the veil was nearly impossible without returning to Ireland. But it had put them —for a brief moment in time—out of reach of those who knew about their sealskin.

Eventually, the fae found their way to foreign shores, spreading roots into a land that welcomed everyone from all walks of life, whether mundane or magical or something else. Several hundred years later, and they'd watched Boston grow from a colony to a thriving modern city, one they'd sunk their own business ventures in. It made returning to Underhill difficult. Leaving a place where they were comfortably entrenched in the supernatural community to a world past the veil where they'd have no political leverage after being gone for what might have been thousands of years in Under-hill wasn't enticing.

"Water off the pelt, boyo," Donal said. "I hope the rest of the wedding was nice."

"Sure," Riordan said, thinking about the mortal at the dessert table whose name he'd failed to get and had been kicking himself over ever since. The dark-haired young man who'd talked back to Lord Diarmait had immediately caught Riordan's attention in a way no one else ever had. Even now, Riordan couldn't stop thinking about him, but he didn't tell Donal that.

Riordan firmly told himself the fixation would pass.

Donal clapped a hand onto Riordan's shoulder, giving it a squeeze. "Come on. Let's head to the pub. You look like you could do with a pint."

Riordan nodded tightly, knowing he was being uncharacteristically quiet, but he hated coming back empty-handed.

When they reached the cars, he wiped off his feet before putting on his sneakers and getting behind the steering wheel of his Corvette. Donal was already driving away, taillights bright against the June twilight. Riordan started the engine and drove after his brother, weaving his way through traffic in the South Boston neighborhood his clan had called home for centuries.

His immediate blood kin had owned a tract of land near the beach and had kept it, even through the period of historical discrimination against the Irish and the fae. These days, the surrounding streets were filled with homes and apartment buildings, and theirs was no different. Clan Maguire had built a number of homes on the two blocks of land they owned, the squat-looking triple-decker buildings mostly filled with clan members. The corner building that Riordan and his siblings called home also housed a pub on the first floor, a local spot as much as a destination one.

The Maguire Pub on the corner was the original location of the Irish pub and restaurant business empire he and his siblings had created and still presided over. They had locations in many big cities on the East and West Coasts, close to the oceans or other waterways. They were in the process of opening a new location in New York City after a multi-year delay, thanks to the Battle of Samhain, but it had been paused yet again while they dealt with this current threat to their livelihood.

Riordan drove down the easement that cut the block in half, parking in their home's garage in the rear of the building. Donal pulled in behind him, his headlights switching off. The triple-decker home was half a block down from the pub, which made it easy to lock everything up behind them and make their way between buildings to the street out front.

They walked in an easy silence toward the pub, the door propped open to let in a breeze. Entering, they passed through a silence ward that kept the raucous sound of the pub inside the walls. The noise hit Riordan's ears like an explosion: music, laughter, and the sounds of televisions showing whatever game was on. The Red Sox were playing an away game, and quite a few patrons were dressed in their team's colors.

A server twisted around a group of boisterous twenty-something guys, moving with a grace that hinted at her years spent dancing back in Ireland before coming here for school. Sophie was a sweet girl, took no nonsense from anyone who came through the door, and always had a cheerful attitude. So her faint frown was concerning.

"Saoirse's in the back, looking a bit glum," Sophie said, her Dublin accent not the only one Riordan could hear within the walls of the pub.

"We'll check on her," Riordan promised. Sophie nodded and left with her tray of empties, easily weaving through the crowd. Donal shoved at Riordan's shoulder, and he got moving.

The pub took up the first floor of the building, lit with amber lights scattered throughout on the ceiling and wall. The wooden tables weren't bolted down, which meant they were easy to pitch together for large parties, of which there weren't any tonight. Mostly, it was small groups drinking beer and eating pub food. Riordan's stomach growled as the smell of fish and chips hit his nose when he passed a table.

"Didn't eat while you were out?" Donal asked.

"I wasn't focused on food."

"I'll put in an order for us."

Donal peeled off, heading for the kitchen. Riordan continued to the table in the corner where their sister sat, methodically tapping the fingers of both hands against a half-empty pint glass. When Saoirse spotted him, she gave him a tight little smile. "What's the *craic?*"

"Sorry, *a dheirfiúr.* I didn't find it." Saoirse ducked her head, fingers stilling on the pint glass. Her auburn hair was scraped back in a tight ponytail, making it easy for him to see how she squeezed her eyes shut, clearly trying not to cry. Riordan kicked the chair next to hers out from beneath the table and sat in it, slinging his arm around her shoulders and pulling her in close. "Sure look, we'll find it."

Saoirse leaned into him, still clutching her pint glass. "I shouldn't have gone to that club."

"None of that. It's not your fault you were out having fun with your friends. That's not a crime. You didn't lose your skin; it was stolen from you."

"And now they're using it to hurt the clan."

"We'll get it back."

Saoirse raised her head, eyes dry despite the wretched look in them. "We're running out of time."

Riordan didn't argue that fact because it was true. They were days out from the deadline they'd been given, but he'd be damned if they were forced to choose between the clan and his sister's life.

Having their sealskin taken from them by someone they didn't choose was a nightmare every selkie carried in their bones. To have themselves bound—mind, body, and soul—to someone who would only keep them as a prisoner simply because that person held their sealskin was something every clan guarded against. They were taught young, the rules ingrained deep, to never let go of their sealskin.

Saoirse hadn't let it go willingly—she'd had it ripped from her.

"We are not letting you go," Riordan promised in a low voice, heart aching with wanting to make that statement true.

Saoirse curled her fingers around his wrist, giving him a strong squeeze. "You don't have a choice."

Because the magic in her sealskin would be too much to resist after a time, the pull their people were born with demanding she be reunited with it. If she went, Riordan knew they would never get to see her again and that she would never know the ocean again.

"Hey, lass," Donal said quietly when he arrived a few minutes later with two pints of Guinness, one of which he placed in front of Riordan. "How are you doing?"

"I'm all right for now."

Donal didn't appear to believe her, the same way Riordan didn't, but he left it alone. "Our food should be out soon."

"Good, because I'm starving," Riordan said.

"Then you should've eaten some fish."

Riordan made a face and reached for his Guinness. "I'll take it fried."

Donal sat across from them, lounging spread-legged in the chair, one of his feet knocking against Riordan's on accident. "The wedding was a bust when it came to looking for allies."

Saoirse leaned forward to rest her chin on her hand with a resigned air about her. "We can offer the clans in Underhill nothing, and other fae won't even look twice at us for the same reason. We've been too long here, they always say."

"Going back won't help you," Riordan said stubbornly. She'd never be able to stay, not with her sealskin held in the mortal world. It would drive her mad.

Saoirse shrugged, gaze dropping to the tabletop. "I know."

Her quiet resignation cut like a knife to the heart. Riordan shared a quick look with Donal, who shook his head minutely. Riordan opted to bite his tongue and change the subject. "How's the office been?"

Saoirse had always had a head for business, more so than he and Donal in some areas. It's why she was CEO of their restaurant empire while they worked under her as vice presidents and directors, but the pub here was more a second home than the crown jewel of their business. "Good. I think the new executive assistant will work out."

"We trust your judgment."

Her smile this time was small and pleased. Riordan tweaked her ponytail, ignoring the falsely outraged squawk she let out. She shoved at him hard, nearly causing his chair to tip over. What could have devolved into a familiar sibling squabble was stopped by virtue of their food arriving. Riordan's stomach growled loudly, but he refused to be embarrassed when Donal laughed at him.

They dug into their fish and chips, with Donal having ordered Saoirse her favorite shepherd's pie. It was nice having a meal together, the rest of the crowd keeping their distance as they ate. Most of the patrons tonight were kin or clan, with a scattering of mundane humans and a witch who always came to read at the bar and eat an order of curry chips. She never seemed bothered by the noise, and Riordan knew she wasn't using magic to silence the area around her.

He'd finished the last of his meal and most of his Guinness, contemplating a second pint, when the pub went quiet in a way that made all his hair stand on end. Donal went rigid in his seat, nostrils flaring to catch the scent of whoever had walked in. Riordan drew in a deep breath, ignoring the scent of the sea from their people and finding the one that put a faint hint of alarm on Donal's face.

"What's a werewolf doing out here?" Donal hissed.

Riordan's eyes widened as he caught sight of who was making their way toward them. "Not just a werewolf. God pack."

Clan Maguire had no territory issues with the Boston god pack for at least the last fifty years. So there should've been no reason why Casey Jenkins, alpha and co-leader of the Boston god pack, was taking up space in his clan's pub. Casey was in his mid-thirties, fit and well-muscled in a way that came from fighting, not working out.

Riordan had ordered his clan to steer clear of all werecreature territory when there had been challenges going on two years ago. The resulting shake-up in the god pack had seen Casey and his wife, Harper, on top of the whole mess. As far as werecreatures went, the pair could've been worse. They were fairer than their predecessor, less inclined to try to annex territory through any means necessary.

That didn't mean they were kind—much like the fae that followed in his wake.

"Ah, there you are," a voice said, the sound like an oil slick on Riordan's skin, human or otherwise. "So glad we could finally meet in person. You've been ignoring my calls."

Donal stood, turning to face the newcomers so his back wasn't to them. Beside Riordan, Saoirse went absolutely still, but the sound of her heartbeat kicked up to a hummingbird pace. Riordan blindly reached for her hand, gripping it tight as their unwanted guests drew closer.

"Niall," Riordan said evenly. "Our time isn't up yet."

Niall Noígíallach, Boston's most underrated mobster, smiled wide enough to show his back teeth. Wavy blond hair fell to his shoulders around pointed ears, framing a beautiful face dominated by teal-colored eyes. His suit was subtle in its flashiness: designer, exquisitely made, but no hint of a brand name on any of his clothes or accessories. The thick gold and diamond rings on his hands were the obvious markers of wealth to mundane humans. To the supernatural community, it was his status as a Seelie *duine sídhe* that made everyone steer clear.

Selkie clans didn't mingle with the *daoine sídhe* all that often. They might all be fae, but some fae thought they were better than all the rest, and selkies had never had enough clout to matter in the Seelie or Unseelie Courts.

Niall was one of those kinds of fae, the sort to always find a way to get exactly what he wanted, no matter the damage done. His territory was a carved-out corner in Beacon Hill and several floors in a skyscraper in the heart of Downtown Boston and had been for the past three decades, ever since he'd slipped out of a hawthorn path in Back Bay Fens to make all their lives difficult. He wasn't someone the kin would ever trust, and the clans had all kept their territory borders good and tight against Niall's insidious encroachment.

But it hadn't been enough.

"Clear the pub of everyone but clan," Riordan said as he stood, letting go of Saoirse's hand.

He didn't need to raise his voice; every supernatural creature in the bar would have heard him. Those that didn't have enhanced hearing would be notified to leave by staff. It took only a few minutes to send everyone off, their bartender and servers handing back credit cards from open tabs and voiding all the transactions to get everyone out faster. It was a minor loss, considering what had walked through the door.

Riordan watched Niall get comfortable at a different table, making it clear he expected Riordan and the others to come to him as if he were some king lording it over them. Casey stood at his back like a guard dog come to heel, which made Riordan's skin prickle. No god pack alpha would ever be so docile, and Casey was known for being devoted to his wife and changing how things were done in the Boston god pack. That she wasn't there with him was another red flag.

Standing behind them was another fae, one that left Riordan uneasy at her presence. She wore glamour he could sense but couldn't see through, appearing as an old human woman with dyed dark green hair to his eyes. That much power was concerning, and Riordan wasn't the only one who seemed put off by her presence. Donal and Saoirse were just as wary.

The older fae said nothing, and Niall didn't seem subservient to her in any way. But neither did she appear in thrall the same way Casey was. She could be another one of Niall's victims, but Riordan wasn't so sure.

Her eyes looked too hungry to be trustworthy.

When the pub door locked behind the last patron, leaving only those selkies who were part of Clan Maguire inside, Riordan finally spoke. "What do you want?"

Niall raised a finger and wagged it at him as if he were a dog. "Ah ah ah, you aren't in charge here."

Riordan looked at the older fae. "Is she?"

Niall outright laughed. "No."

For some reason, Riordan couldn't tell if that was a lie or not. "This is our territory."

"Not for much longer." Niall's gaze slid sideways to where Saoirse stood. "You're looking particularly lovely tonight, Saoirse."

"Fuck off," Saoirse snapped, arms crossed tightly over her chest.

Niall didn't seem all that put off by her attitude. "Is that any way to speak to your master?"

"She's not going with you," Donal snarled.

"This isn't an argument you can win. You know that." Niall crossed one leg over the other, ankle resting against his knee. "I have her sealskin. You are in no position to argue."

"You haven't called for me," Saoirse said.

"Which is why I am here."

Fear sliced its way through Riordan, a helpless sort of sensation gripping his heart and making him want to scream in rage. Only he couldn't. "You can't have our sister."

Niall's smile was as cold as the Arctic Ocean some of the kin called home. "I already do. I've allowed her to stray from my side to show you I can be benevolent."

Riordan outright scoffed at that. "If you were benevolent, you wouldn't have sent your people to take her sealskin in the first place."

"If your kind weren't meant to be owned, then Danu would have never allowed you to separate yourselves from your sealskin. But you can, and it is on others to see your kind rightfully handled and owned."

"You won't own any of us."

"On the contrary. I will own your entire clan before the month is up, and then I will move on to your kin."

Niall spoke frankly, with the casual cruelness of one who knew they'd get what they wanted no matter the cost—to themselves or others, so long as they won. Riordan clenched his teeth together until his jaw ached, refusing to show his anguish, for that was a weakness none of them could afford. "You only have one of our sealskins."

After the attack on Saoirse, Riordan had forbidden his clan from going out alone and warned others of the threat targeting the kin. Everyone was on edge, and the reason for that unease sat in his pub, smiling around poisoned words.

"Yes, but it's the one that matters at this time." Niall sighed in a put-upon way that was all an act. "My terms aren't unreasonable."

"You want our clan in exchange for my sister's freedom. That won't happen."

"Do you think you'll find her sealskin? I know you've been swimming the waters of Boston Harbor and canvassing the streets, searching for it. Your efforts are meaningless. You will never find it."

The mention of his failure stung, but Riordan refused to rise to the bait. "We'll find it."

Niall waved off his words. "You won't. But I'm willing to make a bargain with you, and I don't ever offer those lightly. I will trade her sealskin for yours, Riordan, clan chief of Clan Maguire."

"No," Donal snapped, taking a threatening step forward.

Casey moved, a blur of preternatural speed that Donal barely dodged. Casey's claws at the end of his fingertips sank into the wooden tabletop instead of soft flesh. The expression on the god pack alpha's face never changed, remaining a blank mask. It further reinforced to Riordan that Casey wasn't there of his own free will, not after Niall's little speech. Casey retracted his claws and stepped back, still saying nothing. Riordan wondered if he could even speak without Niall's permission.

"Then your sister stays with me, and if you wish to see her again, you will hand over your clan. If you don't, you will spend the rest of your lives wondering where she is, how she is doing, if she is alive—"

"Stop," Riordan ground out, not liking how Saoirse suddenly bit back a strangled noise that was too close to a sob for him to ignore.

Niall was no longer smiling, brilliant teal-eyed gaze locked on him. "You have options, something I rarely give. Trade your sealskin for your sister's and hand over your clan. Or keep your freedom and know you will spend the rest of your lives never knowing about hers."

It wasn't a bargain; it was a death sentence either way one looked at it, and Niall knew it. Riordan forced his voice steady when he finally spoke, words coming out a rasp. "I need time to think about it."

"Riordan, no," Saoirse protested.

"This isn't a negotiation, so don't try to change the terms of the bargain," Niall said.

"Right. It's more of a hostile takeover," Donal muttered.

Riordan tipped his head in agreement, never looking away from Niall. "A few more days won't matter, will it?"

The other fae tilted his wrist and pulled back the sleeve of his suit jacket and the button-down beneath it to check the time on his Rolex. Then he looked at the old woman, and Riordan half wondered if he was asking for permission. "You've had two weeks. I'll give you one more."

That Niall didn't demand an answer right then and there proved to Riordan the other fae believed them to be trapped in a corner with no way out. He'd take joy in watching them squirm like fish in a selkie's teeth. The terms of the bargain were harsh, and they could only agree to it in the end—whichever clause ultimately won out.

Niall left with Casey one step behind him and the old woman following in their wake. She'd not spoken during the entire meeting, but the look she tossed over her shoulder on the way out sent a cold shiver down Riordan's spine.

The door shut behind them, leaving a heavy silence in the pub that was only broken by Saoirse. "You should let me go with him."

"No," Riordan said, turning to gather her close for a bone-creaking hug. "I won't let him have you."

"You can't let him have the clan. He won't stop with ours if you do."

Clan Maguire was the largest selkie clan in the northeast, entrenched in Boston and the surrounding area and stretching up and down the coast for centuries. Giving Niall power over them would mean giving up territory they'd held since coming to these shores. It would mean selling out his people. Riordan couldn't do that to the kin who looked to him to keep them safe overall, but neither could he give up his sister to a fae who hid his cruelty behind pretty smiles.

"I'll find a way out of this," Riordan promised.

Which was a daunting task, because a fae's bargain was never meant to be fair, even when offered to their own kind.

CHAPTER SIX

WADE ATE A HEFTY BREAKFAST MADE BY THE PRIVATE CHEF THE HOTEL
offered before leaving to meet with Ella. He made a pit stop at
Dunkin' on the way to the god pack territory out in the Forest Hills
area of the Jamaica Plain neighborhood. Ella had given out the
address at the end of lunch only a little reluctantly. Not because she
didn't trust Wade in her pack's territory but because she didn't know
what the fallout would be if Niall had their home under surveillance.

Wade didn't notice anything out of the ordinary when he parked
in front of the triple-decker home on Walk Hill Street. He peered at
the pale blue siding and white-trimmed windows, noticing there
was enough space on either side between its neighbors that could've
been filled in as apartments back home. The space and the numerous
trees dotting the street was a little mind-boggling coming from a city
as packed in as Manhattan.

He got out of the car, peering down the street in both directions,
taking in the area. He drew in a deep breath, parsing out the scents.
It definitely smelled like werecreatures lived there. He'd bet good
money every single house facing the cemetery in Franklin Park was
owned by the god pack. The park itself was surrounded by a low iron

fence that wouldn't keep any werecreature out. He wondered if they had permission from the city to shift in that greenery.

Locking the car, Wade carried his three boxes of donuts with him up the walkway to the house. He shoved the last bite of a chocolate old-fashioned into his mouth and would've knocked, except the door opened before he could do so. Ella stared at him, gaze flicking from his face to the boxes.

"Is there even any left?" she asked, clearly remembering their lunch.

"Uh, I can get more delivered?" Wade said a little sheepishly. "I didn't want the car to smell like donuts because then it'd make me hungry later. Can I dump them in your trash?"

Ella sighed and stepped back, gesturing at him to enter. "Come inside. The trash bin is out back."

She took the empty boxes from him and passed them off to an older man who appeared behind her, his bright amber eyes the same color as hers. Wade glanced around, not seeing the usual setup of food and drink on the hallway credenza that he was used to back home. "No hospitality?"

Ella arched an eyebrow. "Do I need to ask that of you?"

Wade raised his hands in a fending-off gesture. "Nope. I just have a mage in my pack, and I'm used to us offering it. You might want to make it a standard procedure going forward."

"I'll mention it to my alphas when we get them back."

Wade shoved his sunglasses on top of his head, looking around curiously at the home. He could hear a couple more people in the home that he couldn't see and wondered how many pack members were going to be present for this little meeting.

Ella seemed more at ease today than she had yesterday out in public. Maybe it had something to do with being in her own territory, but she didn't seem so stressed, despite the situation. She led him to the dining room adjacent to an open kitchen. Someone had left a bag of Oreos on the island, and Wade's fingers twitched with the urge to grab it and eat the remaining cookies.

A small stack of folders sat on the dining table next to a laptop. Ella claimed the chair in front of the laptop and waved casually at the folders. "I've had my pack looking into Niall so you can see what we're dealing with. It's not much. He hasn't been on our radar as a threat, to be honest."

"Fae can afford to play the long game. If he's targeting you now, I'd bet he's been planning it for years."

"You're still certain he's fae?"

"I'd bet the no-limit on my credit card he is."

Wade sat in the chair next to Ella. He opened up the folders and laid them out on the table to get a better idea of what he was dealing with. After so many years working alongside Patrick and Sage, he knew a bit about investigative work. It wasn't something he'd ever want to make a career out of, but if it helped his pack, then he was all for it.

"Niall Noai—you know what? I'm not gonna butcher that," Wade said, squinting at the printout of a news story about Niall's real estate empire, which probably only scratched the surface. "He's Irish. Looks like an asshole."

"Because he's Irish?"

"No, because he's pulling sneaky shit." Skimming through the documents provided a superficial background on the man who Wade didn't believe for a second was mundane human. "He doesn't look like a fae in the photographs, which makes me think he's using glamour. I won't know until I see him."

"You don't have any magic."

Wade hummed. "Glamour doesn't work on me."

He could always see right through it to what was hidden underneath. Magic made his skin itch if it was strong enough for him to even notice it. Mostly, he didn't, unless someone was lobbing military-level attack spells his way. Then he just got annoyed.

Ella closed the laptop and watched him flip through what little her pack had managed to find out about Niall around the magical restrictions placed on them. It wasn't anything like the dossiers

Patrick sometimes came home with or the legal brief and evidence Sage worked on. It was lacking solid information, probably because Ella and the rest of her god pack couldn't talk about Niall. Fae and their magic were insidious that way, all twisty when it came to reading between the lines of what was said and what was meant.

"Do you know where he likes to hang out?" Wade asked.

Ella eyed him dubiously. "Sorry, but you don't look like you'd fit into the places Niall likely haunts. He doesn't strike me as the type of guy to go to a local bar and watch the Red Sox or Bruins play. His net worth is probably in the multimillions. He's a burgeoning hotelier, as far as our research shows."

Wade wasn't impressed. Marek was a billionaire, and he was pack through Sage. Wade was well versed in the kind of money that could buy a small country as opposed to a single hotel building. "I wasn't asking if I—"

A loud banging on the front door had Ella's head snapping around, eyes narrowing. Her nostrils flared, and Wade drew in a breath as well. Something like sea salt hit the back of his throat, making him think of the ocean. The house wasn't close enough to the harbor to see the water, much less smell it, which meant whoever was on the porch wasn't mundane human.

Footsteps thundered on the second floor before clattering down the stairs. Ella stood, her chair nearly toppling over. "Stay here."

She darted away with preternatural speed. Wade easily tracked her exit and gave it, oh, thirty seconds before he got up and made his way down the hall to the front door. The argument happening across the threshold probably wasn't one they should've been having so openly, but when tempers were high, people never thought rationally.

Other members of the Boston god pack stood with Ella in the front hall, ready to back her if the argument turned into a fight. Wade couldn't see who was on the front porch, but he could clearly make out the anger in their faintly Boston-accented voice. A jolt of recognition shot through him as Wade realized he knew one of the voices.

"—want to speak with your alphas right now," Riordan snarled.

"They're unavailable," Ella replied with all the icy politeness a Southern belle could give. "You coming here like this could be construed as trespassing."

Riordan let out a sharp laugh. "You think I want your territory? Nah, lass. It doesn't come with oceanfront property. Casey came into *my* clan's territory last night playing attack dog for a bastard, and that means your pack owes us a damn explanation."

Ella drew in a sharp breath before saying, "I will let you inside if you take hospitality. If you decline, this conversation is over."

"We'll keep our word."

Two people stepped into the home, both of them tall and dark-haired, similar enough in looks they had to be related. Wade's attention latched onto Riordan, the same fae who had tried to dissuade him from interacting with the Unseelie fae at the dessert table during Gerard's wedding.

He's still hot.

It was unfair how ridiculously good-looking Riordan was, especially in the leather jacket he wore today. Wade had thought he was over mourning the fact he'd never thought to ask for Riordan's phone number, and yet, here the fae was, waltzing back into Wade's life to tease him. It just sucked that he was arguing with Ella because that put him on the opposite side of Wade.

Then Wade's phone rang, making him jump. He quickly turned his back on everyone in the hallway, digging his phone out of his pocket. Patrick's name came up on the caller ID, and Wade knew better than to not answer.

"Hey," Wade said in a low voice, stretching out the word as he retreated back to the dining room with quick strides. "People can hear you."

"Line and location not secure? Got it," Patrick said.

"Pretty much."

"I'm on the way to the airport. Are you somewhere safe, at least?"

Wade scratched at the back of his head and made a face down at the folders on the table before sliding over to the kitchen island and the bag of Oreos there, left woefully unattended. "Uh, sure."

"That lacked conviction."

Wade unfolded the bag and slid the carton out, pleased to see at least half the Oreos were left. It would be a travesty if they got stale. Really, he'd be doing everyone a favor if he ate them. "I'm at the Boston god pack's home."

"Who's having a row?" Jono asked from the background on Patrick's side of the line, clearly eavesdropping.

Wade heard him perfectly fine, even without Jono being on the phone. "Some fae just showed up."

"What?" Patrick said sharply.

Wade shoved two Oreos into his mouth and chewed, speaking through the mouthful. "Gotta go. Bye."

He ended the call, silenced his phone, and shoved it into his pocket. If he didn't see the next call from Patrick, then he could honestly say he missed it. Picking up the bag of Oreos, Wade headed toward where the raised voices were coming from, which turned out to be the front room that overlooked the street and the park beyond. He leaned against the doorway, eating the Oreos one by one as he watched the drama play out.

The Boston god pack stood on one side of the room facing off against the pair of fae who didn't seem intimidated by werecreatures at all. Wade's attention lingered on Riordan in his leather jacket. The day was set to be a warm one, but he didn't seem bothered by the encroaching heat. The leather jacket fit him like a second skin almost, and Wade wondered what it felt like. His fingers itched to steal it, to add it to his hoard. Maybe it would get Riordan to follow.

Wade paused mid-chew, poking at that thought. Weird to think about wanting someone *and* wanting to act on it. He hadn't felt that urge in, well, what seemed like forever.

"You're sure you saw Casey?" Ella asked, staring at the newcomers.

"He nearly broke a table trying to go after Donal here. Yeah, we saw him."

Ella opened her mouth to talk, and the next second, she doubled over, clawing at her throat. Wade tensed, smelling a subtle hint of magic that abruptly faded once Ella let out a ragged breath. The fae, for their part, seemed a little surprised at her reaction.

"Are you all right?" Donal asked, sounding genuinely worried.

Ella opened her mouth again, thought better of it, and sighed in frustration. Wade dug another Oreo out of the bag. "She can't talk about it. None of them can."

The two remarkably human-looking fae finally seemed to notice he was there. Riordan's eyes widened, nostrils flaring, presumably taking in Wade's scent. Wade knew all the other man would really get was mundane human, false as that scent was. It would've been the same scent he'd have gotten at the wedding. If Wade didn't adjust his aura to the particular shielded level Reed had taught him years ago in Central Park, he'd just come across as a bit *strange*.

A bit dangerous.

He always weirded people out. It was hilarious some days.

"You're here? What *are* you?" Riordan asked, sounding a little bewildered and a lot less angry.

"A problem," Wade said cheerfully. "Don't make me yours. You won't like that."

Riordan's gaze dragged up and down Wade's body, making him blink as he realized he was being checked out? Yeah, he was definitely being checked out by the hot guy.

Riordan tilted his head, a contemplative look coming to his eyes. "I don't mind problems like you."

Wade nearly choked on his Oreo and had to cough out some crumbs. "Let's get back to you having seen Casey with Niall the asshole."

"You know Niall?"

"No, he just looks like an asshole. I'm a pretty good judge of character."

"You saw him in a picture," Ella said.

"He stole your alphas. That's asshole material right there," Wade retorted.

Ella made a face. One of her pack members, a guy twice Wade's age, spoke up with the thickest Boston accent he'd heard since arriving. "If Wade can speak for us, we should let him."

Ella shared an unreadable look with each of the werecreatures in the room with her before letting out an aggrieved huff. "Wade, this is Riordan and Donal Maguire, of Clan Maguire. They hold territory along the harbor shore."

"We've met," Riordan said.

"Did you, boyo?" Donal asked sharply. "When?"

Riordan rounded on the other man, saying something in the fae's version of Irish that had Wade's brain squeezing tight in his skull for a second or two before it started processing the language.

"How do you know him?" Donal was demanding.

Riordan glanced back at Wade. "He was at Cú Chulainn's wedding. He got in an argument with Lord Diarmait at the dessert table."

Donal reared back a little, head swiveling around to stare at Wade. "And the kid is still alive?"

"He was there as one of Cú Chulainn's personal guests with a group of other mortals. Everyone had strict instructions to leave them all alone."

Wade continued to pretend he couldn't understand them. Ella, however, seemed annoyed at their rudeness of excluding everyone else from the conversation. "Wade is part of the New York City god pack. He's agreed to help us with a problem."

At that, both of the fae froze where they stood, their attention zeroing back on Wade like a heat-seeking missile. Donal swallowed. "New York City?"

Wade wiggled his fingers at them. "My pack isn't looking to expand up to Boston. I'm here as a courtesy."

"When Brigid called for aid, the clans up here answered. We heard the fight against the gods was led by your pack," Riordan said slowly.

"I don't remember seeing you on the streets."

"We fought at the Battle of Samhain in the Hudson River."

Wade made a face. "Water fae? No wonder you got stuck fighting against the Norse dead."

"We're selkies."

Wade's gaze lingered on the leather jacket Riordan wore and the stylish brown coat Donal had on. "Sealskin?"

Maybe he could hoard Riordan after all if Riordan was willing.

A wary look came to Riordan's deep brown eyes. "Off limits."

Ooh, a challenge. Wade liked those—when it came to stealing.

He'd never tried to steal someone's affections though.

"Niall kidnapped the alphas of the Boston god pack two weeks ago and gave the rest of the pack an ultimatum to fall in line and hand over their territory, or he'd kill Casey and Harper. What did he do to you?"

Both the selkies seemed startled at his statement, the pair looking to Ella for confirmation, which she couldn't give. She just stared back at them with a grim expression, mouth pulled tight. "Wade isn't from around here, and we couldn't ask for help in Boston. Take what he says as truth."

"The terms they were given sounded like fae words. If you've had a run-in with Niall, maybe you can confirm for me that he *is* fae. Ella thinks he's just a mobster businessman."

"He's fae," Riordan said, crossing his arms over his chest. "Part of the *daoine sídhe*."

"So he's a lord or whatever? Demigod? Did he get kicked out of Underhill like Tiarnán?"

Riordan blinked at him. "How do you know the Lord of Ivy and Gold?"

"He's my dire's boss."

To be fair, Tiarnán was back in Brigid's grudgingly good graces after the Battle of Samhain. Something told Wade that whoever or whatever Niall was, that wouldn't be the case with him.

"How high up are you in the New York City god pack?" Donal asked curiously, eyeing Wade with a frankness that was much more businesslike than his brother's intense stare.

At that, Ella laughed. "High enough you won't want to mess with him. But it sounds like we're on the same side here, and Wade can be of help. So what does Niall want with you?"

Riordan and Donal were quiet for a good long minute before Riordan finally spoke. "Our sister was attacked two weeks ago. Niall's people took her sealskin. He said he'd give it back in exchange for mine and control of our clan, or he keeps it and Saoirse forever, and we'd never see her again."

Wade crumpled the bag of Oreos in his fist, destroying the rest of his cookies. "Oh, fuck that."

He didn't condone what basically amounted to slavery. He'd been there, survived that, and wasn't willing to leave anyone else in that kind of horror if at all possible.

He pushed himself off the doorframe and stepped into the living room, tossing the Oreos bag onto the coffee table. "It sounds like this boils down to a territory fight, only Niall is going about it by taking hostages to get you to comply. I'm going to need to see a map of everyone's territories, and you'll probably want to form some kind of official alliance for this mess."

He knew the Five Boroughs like he knew what was in the hoard in his apartment these days. All he knew about Boston was food places he'd seen on social media that he was hoping to hit up while there.

Riordan eyed Ella with a healthy dose of judgment. "Can you even speak for your alphas while they're in captivity?"

"Honey, it's not your fault you're a little slow on the uptake, but yes. I'm dire for a reason," Ella bit out.

"Whoa, don't go at each other's throats. You're both on a time-line you can't afford to miss," Wade said, cutting Riordan off as the other man opened his mouth to argue.

Riordan scowled at Ella, but his tone was grudging when he spoke to Wade. "I can't speak for the other clans with regard to an alliance."

"I'm not asking you to." Riordan stared at Wade, and Wade stared back, arching an eyebrow for good measure. He could outstare anyone and had when it came to the last snack in his pack's various homes. The only person he ever lost to was Lillian because she deserved to win every time. "The Boston god pack will keep its word. You need to promise to keep yours as well. Neither of you want each other's territory; you just want your people back."

Riordan's eyes were big and brown, and Wade was about five seconds away from getting distracted by counting the freckles scattered across his sharp cheekbones when the other man finally broke their staring contest.

"Clan Maguire will ally with the Boston god pack. We cede no territory," Riordan said.

"On behalf of my alphas, the Boston god pack agrees to the terms of the alliance and also cedes no territory," Ella said. She extended her hand to Riordan, and he accepted her handshake without trying to out-squeeze her.

Wade clapped his hands together, looking at them. "Great. Now that we're all friends here, one of you gets to play tour guide for me."

CHAPTER SEVEN

language.

Riordan squinted at his older brother before shoving his sunglasses onto his nose. "Careful isn't going to get Saoirse's sealskin back."

"I'm not talking about Niall. I'm talking about Wade most likely being part of the core of the New York City god pack. You know what that means."

Riordan let his gaze slide away from Donal to focus on where the young man in question was talking with Ella. He didn't answer immediately, letting his attention linger on the New Yorker in their midst.

Wade was taller than Ella and nearly at eye level with Riordan, leanly muscled, with skin Riordan was certain would tan darker given enough time in the sun. His dark brown hair was shaved short underneath while grown long up top, wavy and messy in a way that made Riordan itch to get his fingers in them and put it to rights. He looked less like he was playing dress-up now than he had during the wedding. Wade couldn't be older than twenty-one, at most, and Riordan had a rule about not tumbling mundane humans into bed.

And there was the problem. Wade looked and smelled and laughed like a mundane human, but looks could be deceiving.

Everyone in the supernatural and preternatural communities knew the core of the New York City god pack as it was now was a legend in their own right. Jonothon de Vere had been the mouthpiece for Fenrir, the first god pack alpha in far too long to carry the favor of an animal-god patron. Patrick Collins had been god-touched in every way that mattered, whether he accepted that or not. One didn't get the entirety of the gods of heaven—Seelie fae included—fighting alongside him without being chosen by them.

Sage Taylor was a dire who could go toe-to-toe with the fae and outbargain them at their own game half the time. All signs pointed to her being one of the Lord of Ivy and Gold's legal protégés, which would make her a force to be reckoned with in a few years' time.

Wade was something else. Something different. None of the rumors that had crawled out of Manhattan after the Battle of Samhain could agree on his role in the pack or during that near-world ending fight. Riordan's clan and their kin had been water-bound for all of that fight. He'd never seen the fighting in the streets and so couldn't say for certain that the wildest rumors about the New York City god pack's fourth-ranked pack member were true.

What he did know for certain was they'd have that god pack knocking on their front door, looking for retribution, if Riordan let anything happen to Wade.

"I'll keep an eye on him. I have zero interest in meeting his alphas," Riordan said. He didn't tell Donal that he had one hundred percent interest in Wade for other reasons that had exploded in his face the second he'd caught sight and scent of the other man.

His statement seemed to satisfy Donal though, who reached out to grip Riordan's shoulders and give him a little shake. "Don't lose your skin. Come back whole."

"Always."

They'd driven to the Boston god pack's territory in Donal's car, and he left with a squeal of tires too loud for the weekday morning. Riordan waited only mostly patiently for Wade to finish up his conversation with Ella. After another minute, Wade jogged to where Riordan stood on the sidewalk.

"Which car is yours?" Riordan asked.

In answer, Wade pointed a key fob at the pristine Audi parked on the street, causing the headlights and taillights to flash as the alarm beeped once. "I'm driving. Your first duty as tour guide is to find us breakfast."

Riordan stared at him. "Are you serious?"

Wade's stomach growled, but he didn't seem embarrassed at all. "I'm not sightseeing on an empty stomach."

"We're not sightseeing at all."

"That's where you're wrong. Get in, seal-boy."

"*Seal-boy*? I'm older than you."

"Yeah, yeah. Everyone in my pack is older than me except my niece. That doesn't make you special."

"And how old are you?"

Wade walked around the car and opened the door. "Twenty-three. Old enough to drink if that's what you were worried about."

Wade got behind the steering wheel and started the engine. Riordan stood there on the sidewalk for a few seconds more, staring in disbelief at the car, before shaking his head and getting into the front passenger seat. The leather seat was contoured in a comfortable way, but he still had to move it back a little farther than Wade's so he could stretch out his legs.

Wade fiddled with the GPS on the car's dash touchscreen, frowning as he poked at the map there. "Ella said Niall is some wannabe hotshot CEO but that he didn't look or smell like fae when he attacked. You said he was fae, so I'll trust your insight there. What's his background? Seelie? Unseelie? Please tell me he's not related to the Sluagh in any way."

The casual way that Wade spoke about the Unseelie fae's undead hunters that made even other fae run and hide had Riordan side-eyeing Wade. "You seem to know a lot about the fae."

"Nope," Wade said far too cheerfully as he finally tapped at one of the addresses listed in his search and pulled into the street. "I just know what I've fought against."

"Niall isn't tied to the Sluagh. Most of us fae think he's prayer-born, or maybe he got lucky and fell into the Cauldron."

Wade's fingers stilled on the touchscreen. "That sounds like a god. I hate dealing with gods."

"You're not too far off."

Wade groaned. "Ugh. I'd ask Gerard for help with the bastard, but he's on his honeymoon with Órlaith right now."

Riordan suppressed a twitch at the casual way Wade spoke about one of his people's most dangerous warriors. He knew Cú Chulainn had gone by several names over time, each one intertwined with the one of legend. That Wade named him like a friend was more proof he had people behind him who wouldn't like it if he got hurt. "How do you know Cú Chulainn?"

"He was Patrick's captain when they were both in the Mage Corps together. Good guy. Has a spear I want but he keeps too close of an eye on it for me to nick it."

The British term was odd. Riordan never heard Americans use it all that much. "You seem close enough if he invited you to his wedding."

"I went for the food, and I like Órlaith. She's nice."

Riordan couldn't really remember if anyone had ever called Brigid's granddaughter *nice*. The Summer Lady was ruthless in defense of her Court and queen, to say nothing of those people she considered friends. "Niall isn't like them."

"You said he's practically a god. That's what prayer-born means, right? Sort of like Santa Muerte. Some kind of folklore believed by enough people to earn a godhead. So, I mean, technically, he's like them."

At that, Riordan did twitch because mundane humans didn't

know much, if anything, about godheads. He himself didn't have one, being a mere immortal like almost every other fae in Underhill. "We don't know for sure. Niall does what's best for Niall and has ever since he held court in Ireland as a mortal."

Wade sighed, sounding aggrieved in the way Saoirse got when he or Donal asked her to do something she didn't feel like doing. "I hate gods. I'm not cut out to deal with them. That's Patrick's specialty."

"Then why didn't he come?"

"Because the government is paying a huge expert witness fee to him for a trial in DC, and we're all about making the government pay through the nose in my pack."

The GPS finally spouted out a direction, and Riordan looked at the dashboard screen as Wade dutifully turned left onto American Legion Highway. "You're going to Mike's Pastry?"

"You can't pretend to be a tourist if you don't do touristy things."

Donal was going to kill him if he ever found out Riordan had stepped foot in that tourist trap. "Look, if you want cannoli, I'll take you to Modern Pastry."

"No, no, we're going to Mike's Pastry."

Riordan frowned at Wade, studying the younger man's profile. He didn't have any freckles, but Riordan was struck by the length of Wade's eyelashes and how he didn't have even a hint of stubble. As attractive as he was, it wasn't enough to stop Riordan's annoyance from rising. "How is acting like a tourist going to stop Niall when we're on a countdown?"

"Ella's research said his business is downtown but that he lives in Beacon Hill. We'll get some food, then do some scouting."

"The North End isn't within walking distance of Niall's office downtown or Beacon Hill."

"I bet you swim for miles in Boston Harbor. Don't tell me you can't do some long-distance walking?"

"I have a car with air-conditioning for a reason."

Wade shrugged, drumming his fingers against the steering wheel for a few seconds. "Heat doesn't bother me. Letting some asshole enslave the supernatural and preternatural communities up here in one of the bigger cities in the Northeast does. Trust me, seal-boy. I have a plan."

The plan in question turned out to be to get cannoli first, and no amount of protesting could get Wade to change his mind.

"Look," Wade said with a loud sigh after they'd parked the car in a lot. "Niall has his business in a pocket of fae territory that everyone ceded to him before I was even born. We're going to trespass, but I'm not trespassing without a snack."

"Don't god packs all make a big deal about not trespassing? As in, don't do it?" Riordan asked dubiously.

Wade smirked, reaching out to pat Riordan on the shoulder too quick for him to pull away, but Wade didn't try to grab his leather jacket. "Only when we don't want to piss people off. Now, come on. I want cannoli."

Riordan watched Wade walk off, gaze lingering on his trim waist and nice, denim-clad ass. "You know, I asked for help, not trouble."

"Lucky for you, I'm both."

Riordan huffed out a quiet laugh despite the situation. Wade seemed sure of himself, despite his age. But if he'd survived the Battle of Samhain, then Riordan supposed he knew how to handle himself in a fight—something they were bound to find if they went hunting after Niall.

He flexed his hands, absently wishing he had claws like Casey for when they came across other fae during their exploration today. Selkies in their seal form came with sharp teeth that could rend flesh from bone and blunt claws that couldn't do damage the way werecreatures were capable of. What magic Riordan had was tied to his sealskin—water magic when in the sea, glamour to hide his fae ancestry when walking amongst mundane humans, shapeshifting, and loyalty. Not much good on dry land, and loyalty was a double-edged sword if it wasn't given willingly.

Riordan easily caught up with Wade, the smell of sugar and yeast thick to the point of cloying in the air the closer they got to the cannoli shop, something mundane humans wouldn't really notice. The line outside of Mike's Pastry was already long, and he dreaded waiting in it. Being surrounded by tourists was never his idea of fun.

Wade didn't care, lining up with phone in hand. Riordan glanced at the screen since Wade clearly wasn't hiding it, raising an eyebrow at the number of unanswered texts he was scrolling through. "Something happen back in New York?"

"Nope. I hung up on Patrick back at Ella's," Wade said.

"And everyone's calling you for that?"

"They're a little overprotective sometimes."

Riordan made a mental note to make sure Wade didn't get a mark on him while in Boston. Donal's warning was sound; he did *not* want to deal with the New York City god pack any more than necessary. Wade was enough.

Wade was fine, in more ways than one.

His skin prickled, being so close to the younger man, an itch Riordan forced himself to ignore. He knew what it meant, but he didn't have the time or the right to pursue it, not when Saoirse was still at risk. Besides, he'd promised himself long ago he'd never give his sealskin to a mundane human, fixation or no fixation.

It didn't matter if it meant he'd be giving up the one person who could be his mate.

Wade ignored him for the most part as the line inched its way to the inside counter with all its many cannoli on display. Only when Wade was called to the counter did he finally look up from his phone. He ignored the marzipan cookies and other pastries, clearly on a mission, and Riordan could only follow him.

"One of each flavor of cannoli," Wade said, pocketing his phone so he could pull out his wallet instead. The woman working the counter grabbed multiple blue-and-white boxes and set about filling them.

"Are you bringing some back to Ella's?" Riordan asked.

"These are all for me."

"All twenty of them?"

"If you want any, get your own. I don't share my snacks except with my niece."

Riordan shook his head in disbelief, not in the mood for something so sweet. He stood back while Wade got his order and paid for it. He saw the dilemma when Wade turned around carrying three boxes of cannoli and no free hands to eat them with. "Give me the boxes."

Wade narrowed his eyes at him. "I said buy your own."

Riordan sighed in exasperation. "I'm going to hold them so you can eat while we head back to the car."

Wade thought about it for the amount of time it took them to leave the shop before handing the boxes over, already digging a cannoli out of the top one. "Thanks."

"Didn't you eat breakfast?"

"It was a while ago," Wade said, eyeing the pistachio cannoli in his hand. "And these have been on my to-eat list for a few years now."

"I'm pretty sure you can get the same things in Little Italy back in Manhattan."

"Yeah, but those aren't in Boston." Wade bit into it and took a selfie at the same time, nimbly dodging a couple on the sidewalk heading in the opposite direction. "I need to post this."

Riordan shoved down his worry and annoyance. "You need to help us figure out what we're going to do about Niall."

"Yeah, about that. Do you think your clan and Ella's god pack are the only groups Niall is targeting? Have you heard of anyone else having problems?"

"The first I'd heard about Ella's alphas going missing was today. If anyone else's leaders have been taken, I doubt they'd advertise it. My clan certainly didn't."

Wade reached for another cannoli. "Who are the big players in Boston? If I wanted to take over a city, who would I need to take out first?"

The thoughtful question was at odds with the way Wade was

currently stuffing his face. A bit of the creamy filling was smeared at the corner of his mouth, and Riordan had to drag his mind out of the gutter. "My clan isn't the fae he would've gone after if that were the case. He'd have gone after Lady Caith."

"Hm." Wade crunched his way through another cannoli, somehow finishing the top box without Riordan realizing it. He was a little amazed by that. "Is she water-bound like you selkies?"

"No, she's—" Riordan cut himself off, swearing under his breath. "I see what you mean."

"Yeah, it's always about territory with these assholes, and Boston is a seaside town. Niall would have to ensure he owned all his borders, even the wet ones. Are you on good terms with this Lady Caith? Do you think she'd be willing to talk to you about anything going on in her territory?"

Riordan shook his head. "Selkies don't have the clout the *daoine sídhe* have. We're seen as lesser to those fae who can't shed their skin like we do."

"Why?" Wade asked as they crossed the street. He grabbed the empty top box and chucked it in the bin once they reached the other side. "You're all fae."

"We are, but some of us aren't treated as fairly as others."

Wade paused only long enough to somehow cut the string keeping the second box closed and pulling out another cannoli. "Okay, so she's, what? Noble and you're not?"

"My kind are kin," Riordan said, words coming out flat as they walked. "Selkies are insular by nature simply because of our ability to shed our skin and how it affects us."

"The whole being held captive mess, yeah, I can see why you'd want to stick to your own people. So you're saying you and this Lady Caith don't cross paths often. Would she have crossed paths with Niall?"

"If he was smart, no. Lady Caith was cast out of the Seelie Court for reasons I'm not sure of. From what I've been told, Queen Medb tried to entice her to the Unseelie Court, but she declined and stayed in *Éire* before coming here."

"You've only heard it all secondhand?"

"She's older than I am. She was known as the Lady of Wind and Sky past the veil."

"Older and dangerous. Got it." Wade crunched his way through another cannoli, looking at his phone as they walked. "Sage said if we bargain with any fae, she's going to throttle me."

"Maybe you should listen to your dire."

"Eh, I'm pretty sure fae bargains don't work on me."

He said it casually, like the idea of being bound by fae for an eternity wasn't something to worry about. Riordan's eyebrow twitched. It felt like trying to teach some of the younger kin that just because they were fae didn't mean they weren't excluded from the cruelty of their kind. "How sure are you about that?"

"I've never tested it before. Oh, hey, is that a Nutella one?"

Wade swiped the second-to-last cannoli from the second box. Riordan stared down at the mostly empty box in disbelief. "Seriously, what are you? You're putting away more food than most mundane humans outside competitive eating can."

"Do you know I'm forbidden from entering the Nathan's Hot Dog Eating Contest? Jono preemptively banned me for life."

"Probably wise. You'd be the winner every year, and that would be boring."

Wade cackled, the corners of his brown eyes crinkling. He shoved the last bite of cannoli into his mouth and wiped his mouth with the back of his hand. A bit of cream smeared across his cheek, and Riordan had to resist the urge to wipe it off with his fingers.

Maybe his tongue.

He cleared his throat. "You've got some cream on your face still."

Wade wiped it off with his hand again as he laughed. "I can't even blame my niece. Let me grab the last cannoli, and we can toss this box in the next trash can we pass before we get back to my car."

"Are you going to start on the third box? Because if you are, I feel like you won't have any left to play tourist with in Beacon Hill."

"Not if we walk faster."

Wade set off, leaving Riordan to follow, still carrying one box of cannoli. He only hoped no other kin saw him toting around a Mike's Pastry box, or he'd never hear the end of it from his siblings. When they reached the car, Riordan kept the box on his lap while Wade drove with a distracted air while he munched on cannoli.

"Do you even know where you're going?" Riordan asked.

"The map on my phone does."

Riordan sighed heavily, letting his head thunk against the headrest. "There's only street parking in Beacon Hill. If you don't want people to know what kind of car you drive, head for the Center Plaza Garage. It's on the outskirts of everyone's territory there."

"I thought Beacon Hill only belonged to the fae?"

"Mostly. Especially during the day. There's a corner that belongs to the Boston Night Court." The car jerked a little in the lane, and when Riordan glanced over, Wade was scowling out the windshield. "Not a fan of vampires?"

"No," Wade said shortly. "But it'll be fine. We'll leave before sunset."

"You do realize making a mockery of fae territory boundaries isn't much better?"

"I'll take fae over vampires any day." Wade glanced at him, a smirk tugging on his lips. "You're not half-bad, seal-boy."

Riordan let him keep his opinion on that and didn't bother arguing. "Eat another cannoli."

Wade laughed, taking the next turn on a yellow light. "Don't mind if I do."

He reached over to open the box Riordan was holding, somehow undoing the string without needing help. He grabbed another cannoli and took a large bite, driving one-handed. Riordan kept his attention on Wade rather than the road. "What are you hoping to find in Beacon Hill?"

Wade swallowed and licked at a bit of cream, which should honestly be illegal, in Riordan's opinion. "I want to meet with Lady Caith and see where Niall's territory is. He has to be hiding his hostages somewhere."

"Out in the open wouldn't strike me as the way to go."

"I feel like the older some of these immortals are, the dumber they get."

Riordan narrowed his eyes. "I feel like I should be insulted."

"Yeah? How old are you?"

"Almost four hundred."

Wade hummed. "So are you a tween, then, by fae count? Or still a child? Is it like dog years?"

"Am I *what*?" Riordan asked in exasperation. "*No.*"

"Just curious."

Wade somehow finished the third and final box of cannoli by the time they parked in the garage. Riordan had no idea where he'd put it all and knew he probably wouldn't get a straight answer out of Wade if he asked. The other man had a tendency to ignore questions about his background with a cheerfulness that probably put some people at ease and made everyone else walk on eggshells.

"Does your clan have pass-through rights with Lady Caith?" Wade asked as they left the parking garage.

"Yes. Beacon Hill has been her territory since she arrived before World War I. We had to move one of our pubs back then because we weren't in any position to fight to keep the location."

"Lose a lot of business because of her arrival?"

Riordan snorted. "No. We opened up the new pub near Harvard."

"Oh, that's smart. You're never going to lose customers that way." They paused on the sidewalk, and Wade squinted through the sunlight. "All right. Commence with the tour guide duties."

"You know this is a risk, right?"

Wade flashed a smile, and for an instant, Riordan thought Wade's teeth were sharper than they had been. "Don't worry. I'll keep you safe."

It would be laughable, really, if he didn't know what pack Wade belonged to.

Riordan put his hand on Wade's shoulder and turned him around, trying to ignore the firm muscle underneath his fingers and how warm he was, even through the thin fabric of his T-shirt. "This way."

They crossed in the middle of the street, heading for the red cobblestone pathway between two buildings that were only part of a handful built on neutral ground in the neighborhood. This corner of Beacon Hill held the local and state government buildings. On a Thursday, the sidewalks were busy with tourists rather than government workers simply due to the hour. It wasn't noon yet, and everyone's lunch break was still at least a couple of hours away.

Riordan got them past the State House and crossed Joy Street, continuing down Myrtle Street. Redbrick row houses loomed over the one-way, narrow street. It was mostly residential, with a handful of ground floors housing some businesses. The trees were in full greenery, having long since shaken off winter.

"Pretty," Wade commented when they were halfway down the long block. "By the way, we're being followed."

Riordan glanced behind them out of sheer reflex. He got a brief look at two women who appeared mundane human and acting like they were out for a walk. Their expensive athleisure clothes were more for fashion than actual exercise. Both women were exactly a half block away, and if they were wielding glamour to hide their appearance, it was very good. Riordan couldn't sense it at all if that were the case.

Wade elbowed him in the side. "Quit looking."

"What makes you think we're being followed?"

"They have the same pointed ears you do."

Riordan stared at Wade in surprise. "You can see through my glamour?"

"It's not like you're bad at it. Glamour just doesn't work on me."

Another quirk to file away and figure out because Riordan knew glamour *should* work. It was the one kind of magic every fae intrinsically had, no matter their status. It helped them to blend in with a world that would rather they not belong.

"Do you recognize them?" Wade asked.

"No."

"Then let's find out if they're working for Lady Caith or Niall."

With that, Wade abruptly spun on his feet and retreated back the way they'd come with a speed that was *definitely* on the supernatural scale. Riordan didn't react fast enough, belatedly catching up to Wade a few seconds later as the younger man casually dodged a knife one of the women tried to stick in his gut.

"Hey!" Wade squawked. "You tore my shirt! It was a gift from my niece!"

This close now, and Riordan could sense the cold presence of fae, but that took a back seat to Wade's protest because that meant he might have been cut. Riordan really, really did not want to deal with the New York City god pack if he sent Wade back harmed in some way.

"Wade—" Riordan snapped, trying to get between him and the two fae.

The knife in one of the fae's hands was silver, clearly meant to be used against a werecreature. Wade didn't seem concerned, stepping in close so fast he was a blur the other fae couldn't escape. Two seconds later and Wade had the woman slammed up against the side of the building with enough force to crack a couple of bricks. He ripped the knife out of the fae's hand and pointed it at the other one, who froze on the sidewalk.

Something heavy filled the air, pressure like a barometric shift that had Riordan stepping backward out of instinct. The other fae not caught in Wade's grip did the same.

"Are you Niall's or Lady Caith's?" Wade asked, sounding calm even if he looked annoyed. "Don't make me ask twice."

The fae squirmed in Wade's grip, his hand wrapped around her throat and not bothered by the way she kicked at him. She was, Riordan realized, being held at least a foot off the ground, squirming like a pinned bug.

"Lady Caith's," the fae still held at knifepoint got out. "You're trespassing."

"Yeah, that's always fun to do."

Someone walked by Riordan, and he stared in disbelief at the mundane human passing them by without noticing their ongoing altercation. They seemed completely oblivious, and their ignorance wasn't Riordan's doing. He doubted it was the other fae's as well.

Which left Wade.

Wade looked over at Riordan, arching an eyebrow. "Do you think these two are telling the truth?"

"We *are* in Lady Caith's territory. Niall's is in the northwest corner of Beacon Hill," Riordan said. He hesitated, eyeing the fae, who were most likely running some kind of patrol. "She's never usually been so pointed about her borders."

"All right." Wade let the fae go without warning and stepped back, but he kept the silver knife. "Let's go have a talk with your lady."

The fae touched a hand to her throat, eyeing Wade with a healthy dose of wariness that Riordan himself carried. Then her gaze slid past Wade to land on him, a coldness entering her blue eyes. "Our lady has no business with kin."

"He's my tour guide. She'll have business with him because I said so."

Gone was the easygoing attitude Wade had embodied for most of the morning. In its place was a hard-faced young man who stared down the fae with a kind of contemplative focus that made the hair on the back of Riordan's neck stand on end.

The fae on the receiving end of Wade's attention actually flinched. "Fine."

Wade blinked, and that weight to the air disappeared. Riordan found it suddenly easier to breathe. "Awesome. I knew you'd see things my way."

Riordan shook his head in sheer disbelief at how Wade had bullied their way into an audience with Boston's most powerful fae.

CHAPTER EIGHT

WADE SHOOK OUT HIS HANDS, GETTING RID OF THE TINGLING SENSATION AT the tips where his claws wanted to punch through. He resisted the urge to shift mass but let the hint of his aura bleed back into him. He'd learned through trial and error and one grudging telephone call with Reed how to hide his presence so that people didn't register him, which was different from hiding his aura to appear as human. It wasn't quite magic—nothing with spells or command triggers—but something all dragons were capable of so they could stay hidden in the modern world.

He'd used that trick in Seattle when he'd gone searching for Spencer the other year, keeping the locals from seeing him as he dived into a graveyard. Sound was a different problem, but he'd gotten better at buffering a void of silence between his dragon-sized presence and anyone close by not within its boundary.

It meant no one had seen the scuffle—he couldn't even call it a fight—and now the fae were leading them down Joy Street while Riordan seemed tenser than was probably healthy. Wade nudged the other man with his elbow, raising an eyebrow when Riordan turned his head to meet his gaze. His eyes were a deep brown that made him wonder about Riordan's sealskin, what it might look like. But Sage had drilled it into him plenty of times that it was rude to ask questions like that, so he didn't.

"It'll be fine," Wade said.

"You're demanding time with Lady Caith and not going through the proper channels," Riordan said.

"Would those proper channels have gotten us an audience before the end of the week?"

"It's Thursday."

"Exactly. We can call it bad manners if she takes offense. My pack is always yelling at me about those."

"Our lady *will* take offense," one of the fae up ahead called over her shoulder.

Wade made a face. "Then she can take it up with my pack."

"The Boston god pack knows better than to trespass."

"Not my pack," Wade said in a singsong voice.

Riordan winced, but the other man didn't clue the other fae in on what pack Wade came from. Wade would let them wonder about it until Lady Caith asked him a direct question. If she hadn't fought in the Battle of Samhain, he didn't think she would know who he was or even know his pack on sight.

"You are certainly trouble," Riordan muttered under his breath.

"It's a calling."

And right now, it was calling him to a massive redbrick five-story home with a front garden filled with plants that were definitely not a local species. Wade paused just past the wooden gate to poke at something that might have been a rose and which probably looked it with glamour. All the other plants were just as beautiful and strange, the floral scent reminding him of the grove where Gerard and Órlaith had gotten married.

"I think there are laws about invasive species," Wade said.

Riordan hooked a hand around his elbow and dragged him down the walkway to the gleaming mahogany front door. "What the mundane humans don't know won't hurt them."

"That's a lie if I've ever heard one."

He should know. When he was younger and newly orphaned, bouncing from group home to group home, he hadn't known what he was. But those hunters who'd found him had known he was something—something unique enough to tempt a god.

Wade had thought he was a werecreature for most of the years he was a prisoner, mostly because he hadn't known any better. It had taken getting a god-locked collar off his throat and tumbling into Patrick's and Jono's lives to learn his own kind of truth. Sometimes he wondered how things might have been different if his mother had lived long enough to explain what he was. But she hadn't, and he'd never known his father or wanted to find the man. His life was better these days than it ever had been, despite the horror he'd survived.

And if meeting with this Lady Caith to keep others from experiencing it was something he had to do, then he'd deal with her annoyance.

Wade let Riordan drag him to the front door, where a threshold of significant power hummed in his ears. The two fae guards stepped across it easily, but Riordan stayed on the porch, waiting for permission to enter another fae's territory. Wade didn't need any, so he followed the fae inside, earning himself double-takes from each of them.

It also resulted in the pair of them pulling a pair of swords out of thin air to hold them threateningly in his direction. Wade perked up. "Are those magic swords?"

"How did you cross the threshold?" one of the fae demanded.

Wade gave her his most innocent look. "What threshold?"

"I will take hospitality," Riordan said from the porch, still not having entered the home. "Wade will too."

"Sure thing. I hope you're offering chocolate," Wade said. Hospitality was just a way for him to get a couple of bites to eat. Most people offered bread. Most people wouldn't take an offering from the fae if they were smart, but Wade was starting to get hungry again.

The fae didn't put their swords away. Neither did they offer up hospitality. Behind them, another fae walked down the hallway to meet them, dressed like he was on his way to a black-tie event, if fae even had those. Daffodil-yellow hair fell down to his waist, and the fae's eyes were citrine in color, with no warmth to them. He was taller than Wade, broader too, and wore slim-cut dress pants, an actual morning tail suit jacket, a ruffled scarf-type accessory that looked like something Wade had seen in a historical portrait in a museum once, and way too much gold jewelry.

"Who are you?" the new fae asked, staring down his nose at Wade.

"He's here under my protection, Tadgh," Riordan said, hovering in the doorway but still not yet having crossed the threshold. Wade doubted it had anything to do with the kind of power that would keep a vampire out and more about deference to a higher-ranked fae.

"I thought you were under mine?" Wade asked. He waggled his fingers in the face of Riordan's glare. "I need to speak to Lady Caith."

"The Lady of Wind and Sky has a schedule. You are not written in it," Tadgh said.

"So write me in." Wade pointed at the bowl of fruit definitely not from any nearby farms sitting next to a pitcher of what smelled like mead. "The quicker you let me take hospitality, the quicker you'll get rid of me."

"He's dangerous," one of the fae guards said in their language, Wade's head easily translating it. "And he is not human, no matter his appearance."

Tadgh looked at Wade and immediately frowned. "We did not offer you that."

Wade bit into the juicy not-apple-pear-peach fruit he'd taken from the bowl and crunched his way through a bite. "You didn't? It was sitting right there. I thought it was up for grabs."

Tadgh took a step forward, and Wade slowly crunched his way through another bite. The fae's disdain was pretty clear to see, but if he thought his better-than-everyone attitude was going to get Wade to toe the line, then clearly he was dumb as a brick.

Wade took another bite, wondering if Órlaith had any of these fruits she'd be willing to send him. They were really good. "Let me talk to Lady Caith, and then I'll be on my way."

"No," Tadgh said. "Whatever problems the kin have, they aren't ours to fix."

"I'm not asking you to," Riordan said. He seemed to get over being polite and entered the home, coming to stand by Wade. "I promised to show Wade around town."

"Our lady's home is not a tourist attraction."

"I've seen better homes," Wade said. The insulted looks tossed his way by the two fae who'd led them there made him snicker. "Look, the faster we get through hospitality and I meet with your lady, the quicker I'll be out of your way. What aren't you getting about that?"

Tadgh pointed at the door. "You can leave now."

Wade bit at the core of the fruit, the pit there catching his teeth. He bit down on the stone, shattering it, and swallowed the bits that fractured off. Wade blinked, then blinked again, letting his pupils change shape for half a second. "One of yours is taking people and enslaving them, and I don't like that."

Tadgh's finger wavered, dipped, his hand falling back to his side as he stared at Wade. The disdain left his face, replaced with a wariness that proved maybe the stuck-up asshole wasn't as dumb as his silly little outfit made him look. "What are you?"

"You know, my dire keeps telling me that's a rude question to ask."

"Ella has better manners than you."

"Ooh, good try. Still not my dire." Wade ate the last half of the fruit's core, crunching through the stone. "That would be Sage Taylor, of the New York City god pack."

The way the fae went preternaturally still was almost funny to watch. Beside him, Riordan tensed, as if he was going to throw himself between Wade and the others if they attacked, which was awfully sweet of him. Stupid but sweet.

After a moment, Tadgh approached the credenza and poured two glasses of mead, of which he handed one to Wade and one to Riordan. Then he grabbed some berries bunched like grapes but which looked like raspberries if they were bright blue and picked off a few to hand to Riordan. "Both of you be welcome."

Wade tossed back the mead—not as good as Thor's—and stole one of the berries out of Riordan's hand. Riordan sighed at him. "You literally ate your way through almost two dozen cannoli not even half an hour ago."

"Yeah, but the fruit is good."

"Lady Caith will see you," Tadgh said stiffly.

"Lead on," Wade said, snagging another piece of fruit from the bowl before following Tadgh down the hall.

The interior of the house was decorated in a monotonous beige color scheme that seemed out of place for fae. Cold, immaculate—kind of like the Unseelie Court and their fae or an Upper East Side housewife following the latest home décor trend, where nothing was personable. It made him want to let Lillian draw on the walls.

As depressing as the inside was, the back garden was incredible.

Tadgh led them out into a swathe of green and vibrantly colored foliage that looked as if it had been transplanted wholesale from Underhill. The trees lining the back fence were tall, their branches spread wide to block the view of the houses behind them. Flowers and bushes covered the earth on either side of the flagstone path that wound its way through all the greenery in a circular way to the small center grove.

Seated at an ornately carved wooden table beneath a pergola draped in flowering vines with butterflies fluttering about the blossoms was a fae who smelled strongly of magic and just the faintest touch of ozone. Wade would have cut through the grass and the plants, but Tadgh led them properly down the entire circular path. Since Riordan wasn't in any hurry, Wade figured he didn't have to be either. Once they reached the small grove, Wade realized the butter-flies were actually pixies.

He scowled at the bitey little fae, snapping his teeth at one that got too close. "Don't even think about it. Go annoy your friends with the swords."

Riordan coughed and discreetly elbowed him in the side. Wade went where prodded, right up to that wooden table where Lady Caith sat, watching them with fathomless indigo eyes. Her hair was a deep magenta, twisted up in a braided crown atop her head and held in place by silver thread. Jeweled cuffs hid the pointed tips of her ears, and the fire opals that dangled from them made Wade's fingers twitch with the urge to slip them into his pockets. They'd match his new ring nicely.

"Lady Caith," Riordan said, inclining his head in a respectful manner.

Wade just waved at her. "Hey."

Lady Caith set aside the book she was reading, flattening her hand over the leatherbound cover. She wore jeweled rings on every finger, and Wade's attention lingered on the largest, shiniest diamond. Tadgh moved to stand at her back, attentive like a butler.

"You are a long way from New York City," Lady Caith finally said.

"It's not like you're in Los Angeles."

"This isn't your pack's territory."

"Nope," Wade said cheerfully before pulling out one of the wooden chairs to sit, ignoring the soft, slightly strangled sound Riordan let out. "We don't want Boston. Never have, never will. New York City is enough."

"We?" Lady Caith tilted her head, the dappled sunlight making all her jewels shimmer. "You speak for your pack that easily?"

Wade reached for Riordan and tugged on the other man's arm, urging him to sit down. Riordan reluctantly did so, but only after a faint nod from Lady Caith. "I lost the draw this time around, so I was sent out."

Despite the serene gaze she focused on him with, Wade knew fae were rather conniving. "And who are you in your pack?"

"I'm Wade."

Lady Caith raised one finger and then dropped it in a gentle tap that was probably a louder reaction for her than if she'd done a full-body twitch. "I see."

"Do you?" Wade leaned forward. "The Boston god pack reached out to my pack for help because they're magically restricted from getting any within Boston. Riordan here is in sort of the same predicament. One of your people is taking hostages, which isn't nice."

"Niall is not one of my people."

"Oh, good. You know who I'm talking about."

"Niall is not welcome in my territory and holds no claim over mine."

"I heard he stole a corner of it from you."

Lady Caith's dark gaze flicked to Riordan for a split second. "Fae politics are not meant to be shared."

"Niall is indiscriminately targeting the leaders of the preternatural and supernatural communities. Wade offered a point of particular note," Riordan said.

"And what would that be?"

"That you hold dominion over the fae on land in Boston, which makes you a target as well."

"You speak highly of yourself, kin."

Wade scowled and pointed at her. "Lay off. Riordan is with me."

"He is kin. His people's problems are not ours."

"You're all fae. Just because people call you lady doesn't mean you're better than them."

"You forget your place," Tadgh snapped.

Lady Caith's eyes narrowed as she raised her hand in a gesture that had Tadgh staying put. She was pretty, Wade had to admit. Pretty in a cruel way. Definitely not someone he wanted to deal with beyond this not-so-friendly little talk, but he had a feeling that wouldn't happen. Patrick's kind of luck must have rubbed off on him before he left New York. In which case, Patrick could take it back any time now.

"I have it on good authority you got kicked out of the Seelie Court and Brigid hasn't let you back in. Good on you for not throwing yourself in with Medb because wow, would that have been a dumb idea," Wade said. Beside him, Riordan very politely palmed his face. Wade ignored him. "You didn't fight with Brigid in the Battle of Samhain because you're still pissed she won't let you back home until you grovel. Which you won't because you fae are all stubborn. So you took up space in Boston, which, honestly, I would want for the cannoli and clam chowder. Good choice. But now there's some other fae creeping into your territory and making trouble. Niall wants this city, and if you think he won't go through you to get it, then you really are dumber than even Medb was when she tried to throw down with Brigid."

Lady Caith stared at him, never blinking. "You speak rather freely of our goddesses."

"Your crappy hospitality offers aside, you're a better host than Medb was."

Riordan's head snapped around to look at him. "You were taken to the Unseelie Court?"

"Patrick was taken. I tagged along." It wasn't his fault they'd gotten separated from the pack that one time, and he hadn't been about to leave Patrick alone to make dumb decisions without backup. "He's the one the gods favored. Even Brigid. But he's stuck in DC right now; otherwise, he'd be here dealing with this mess, and trust me, you really don't want that. Your city doesn't want that. I'm the much better choice."

Wade leaned back in the chair and crossed his arms over his chest. For a few minutes, no one spoke, the garden quiet. What sounds he could hear came from within the house and the street beyond, but he could see the glitter of wards and glamour running along the property line if he squinted. He bet none of the others could hear the cars driving down the picturesque street they were on.

"You truly believe Niall would dare to strike against me?" Lady Caith finally asked.

Wade tilted his head in Riordan's direction. "I'm betting you won't step foot in the sea, so Niall went after the fae who does. Which means you're the fae he would have to take down next to claim the rest of your people's territory in Boston. He's taken the alphas of the Boston god pack, and I don't think I need to tell you how difficult doing something like that is. Taking them puts all the other packs at risk. I don't know who else is a power player in this city, but if there are any more, then they'd be targets as well."

"The Faneuil Coven would be who he would need to eradicate if he wanted to break up the covens and set them at odds with each other. Their current high priestess is a mage who retired from the Mage Corps."

"Anyone else?"

"Abhartach," Riordan said.

Wade mouthed the name but didn't try to pronounce it. "What's that?"

"Not what. Who. He's the master vampire of the Boston Night Court."

Wade scowled. He absolutely *hated* vampires. It didn't matter that these days, he could eat them and get rid of the problem in one easy bite. Wade would never find any redeeming qualities in them, no matter what Spencer said, because Spencer was always talking with his dick when he did. "Ugh, vampires. Why do they always have to be involved?"

"You have much history with them?" Lady Caith asked.

"You could say that." He didn't elaborate, letting her think whatever she wanted to fill in the gap. "So two fae, a mage, god pack alphas, and a master vampire. Anyone else?"

"None of the other communities who call Boston home have enough clout to be of any threat to our borders."

Never let it be said the fae weren't arrogant. "Do you know if the mage or master vampire are missing?"

"I would assume not."

"Yeah, but you didn't know Harper or Casey were missing or that Riordan's clan had been targeted. You must've been treating Niall as a threat, though, if you were sending out patrols." Wade let out a loud sigh. "I guess that means we have to make sure those other two are still in charge."

The mage would be easy. Most magic users across the board were pretty friendly with his pack because of Patrick. With the Faneuil Coven being led by a mage from the Mage Corps, Wade figured it would be easy to knock on their door, get some answers, and hand out a warning if the high priestess was still around. If she wasn't, it would be just another person he'd have to find.

It was the master vampire he didn't want to deal with.

Lady Caith focused on Riordan. "Which skin did Niall steal?"

"You don't have to answer that," Wade said, doing his best impression of Sage.

Riordan gave him a tight smile. "I know. But Lady Caith already knows one was stolen, so it isn't much of a loss to tell her it's Saoirse's."

"And have you been looking for it?" Lady Caith asked.

"On land and in the ocean."

Lady Caith tipped her head to the side a bit, the motion causing sunlight to splash over her face and head. The fire opals glittered a little brighter, drawing Wade's eye. "There is something dangerous that calls the deep home these days."

"How do you know? You don't live in the sea," Wade said.

"I don't need to swim in the ocean to know there are predators beneath the waves." She folded her hands together over the polished wooden table, thin shoulders straightening. Wade didn't like how she looked at Riordan—like she wanted to hoard him. Which, no, Wade got first dibs.

"Will you give your sister to Niall? Or did he provide you with another offer?"

Wade scowled at her. "What's it to you? We aren't here to bargain."

Lady Caith trained her unfathomable gaze on Wade, which he preferred. "Do you know the history of kin?"

"They're fae, just like you."

"They can shed their skin and be kept, with or without their consent."

"You know, we call that slavery here in this country." Wade leaned forward, digging his fingers into the wooden table, baring his teeth. "I'm gonna take it personally if you try that with Riordan or anyone else in his clan."

"Boston is not your territory."

"Nope. Cannoli aside, I'll take New York City any day of the week." He flattened his hands on the table, reached deep inside for that sense of *self* he could always touch, and shifted mass just enough to break the table into dozens of jagged pieces with what appeared to be a single touch. "But you won't be taking Riordan, or his sister, or anyone else. I know you fae like your games, but this is one you'll lose if you try to play it with me."

Lady Caith staggered to her feet before the shattered bits of wood could fall on her lap, aided by Tadgh's quick hands. She stared at him with eyes gone fractionally wider, a brief scent of fear wafting off her before she could fully shield herself. Riordan had jerked back at the collapse of the table, nearly tipping over, and would have if Wade hadn't grabbed the back of his chair and kept him from falling. Wade casually brushed off some of the wood shards from his lap.

"You accepted our hospitality," Tadgh snapped.

Wade smiled meanly at him. "Did I?"

At his taunt, Tadgh rescinded the offer with "You are not welcome here in our lady's home."

Wade waited. And waited some more. When it was clear that nothing was going to happen—that the home's threshold was not

going to recognize him as a threat and magically kick him out—
Wade tilted Riordan's chair back so all four legs were on the ground,
let it go, and stood. He sketched a mocking bow in Lady Caith's
direction that would probably make Patrick proud. "If you wanted us
gone, all you had to do was ask."

"You are no werecreature," Lady Caith said, the smell of magic
edged with ozone thick like pollen in Wade's nose. It made him want
to sneeze. If she was an immortal of some sort, she clearly wasn't on
the same level as Gerard. Demi-goddess, maybe. Still someone he
didn't want to deal with.

"I'm pack." Whatever she saw when she looked at him would be
human, even after that display of strength Wade had shown. "And
you should remember it was mine that fought and saved this world
against the gods of hell when you didn't heed Brigid's call. Neutral
isn't a good look on you. Maybe you should try rectifying that this
time around when it comes to Niall."

A warm hand wrapped itself carefully around his left upper arm,
tugging a little. Wade glanced at Riordan, who was staring intently
at him and not the other fae. "You don't need to fight for me or my
clan."

"See, that's where you're wrong. This is a what would Patrick do
kind of situation, and Patrick would definitely be pissing people off.
We don't like it when people try to enslave others. We wouldn't want
that to even happen to you, Lady Caith."

That magic scent hadn't faded one bit. Tadgh looked as if he'd
bitten into a lemon. Wade wondered if he was the one trying out
some spells that just weren't hitting. Lady Caith still stood amidst all
the broken wood, having not yet moved, and all her attention was off
Riordan and on Wade, which was what he wanted.

"Your warning about Niall was helpful. I will take it under
advisement," Lady Caith said after a moment.

Tadgh very deliberately looked at her, which would probably be a
spit-take from anyone else. Wade wondered just how unexpected
that careful response was. "You do that. We'll leave you to your

garden party. Oh, and I'm taking the rest of the fruit in your front hall."

He reached up and grabbed Riordan's hand, turning and hauling the other man after him with easy strength. The farther he got Riordan away from the other fae, the better he'd feel. Wade didn't let go of Riordan until they reached the front hall, where he swiped all the fruit in the bowl beneath the glowers from the two fae they'd met on the street. He waved at them on the way out, something like a plum but the size of a large apple clutched in his fingers.

"It's been fun. Next time, offer chocolate," Wade said.

He shoved the fruit in his mouth on the way out, biting through the center stone with ease. By the time they reached the sidewalk, he'd devoured two and was working on the third.

Riordan glanced at him, then did a quick double take. "You really brought the fruit with you?"

"I said I would," Wade mumbled around his latest bite. "It's tasty."

Riordan stared for a moment before shaking his head. "If you're that hungry, I'll get you something to eat."

Wade perked up at that. "Where are we going?"

"I'll give you the address when we're back at your car." They walked for a few minutes in silence before Riordan finally spoke again. "You aren't obligated to get between my clan and Lady Caith, but thank you for trying."

Wade stopped walking, grabbing Riordan's wrist before he thought about what he was doing. Riordan's skin was warm beneath his fingers, and if he dialed up his hearing and focused, Wade could probably hear his heart beating. But he didn't because Patrick was always going on about keeping his nose and ears to himself and respecting people's privacy.

"Just because the way you shift means you lose your skin doesn't mean anyone has the right to take it." Wade let go of Riordan's wrist, plucking at the supple leather jacket he wore. "I meant it when I said my pack doesn't hold with slavery. We all stick our noses into those kinds of problems, even if werecreatures aren't involved."

He still remembered what it was like to fight with a collar around his throat, forced to kill or be killed as entertainment for the rich. The way sometimes someone would pay a ridiculous sum to spend time with him after a fight and do whatever they wanted to him. Wade knew what it meant to be beholden to a master, and he wasn't ever going to let Riordan or his clan experience that if he could help it.

Riordan stared at him with a narrow-eyed intensity that made Wade's breath catch in his throat a little, something warm curling in his chest that he couldn't blame on the fire he could breathe. "If those are the kinds of values your god pack holds, then it's no wonder the gods favored you."

Wade couldn't help the face he made and forced his fingers to stop stroking Riordan's jacket. "Ugh, gods are assholes."

Riordan laughed softly, snagging Wade's hand and pulling him down the sidewalk. "Come on, let's get out of here."

Wade stared at their joined hands all the way back to the car.

CHAPTER NINE

"Got company," Riordan called out as he pushed open the door to the triple-decker home he and his siblings had owned for decades. "Come say hello."

Saoirse poked her head out of the kitchen down the hallway, her hair loose and falling down in waves. She narrowed her eyes at him before her gaze tracked over his shoulder. They widened comically at Wade as the younger man stepped inside, looking around curiously. "Donal said you'd gone off with a lad from the New York City god pack. This him?"

"Hi," Wade said cheerfully, waving at her. "I'm Wade."

Saoirse stepped out of the kitchen and hurried toward them. She met them in the living room, and the polite smile was wiped off her face once she got within sniffing distance of Riordan. She planted her hands on her hips and glared at him. "You smell like you've been traipsing about in Lady Caith's garden."

"I wasn't traipsing," Riordan protested as he nudged the door shut behind him.

She jabbed him in the chest with her finger. "You're not denying you went to her."

"That was my fault. I wanted to check out Niall's territory," Wade said.

Riordan contained a wince, knowing that wouldn't ease his sister's worry. It didn't, judging by the scowl that twisted her lips. She drew in a breath, letting it out on a yell. "Donal! Riordan went to Lady Caith's."

"He did what?" came Donal's muffled shout from upstairs. The heavy sounds of footsteps coalesced seconds later to their older brother entering the living room with his own scowl. "Boyo, I can't believe you—oh. You brought Wade."

"Yeah, Riordan promised me lunch. And don't be mad at him. I was the one who dragged him into Beacon Hill. I wanted to check out Niall's territory, but we got sidetracked with Lady Caith," Wade said.

Saoirse crossed her arms over her chest and tapped her foot rapidly on the floor, glaring at Riordan. "That makes it *worse*."

"We had good reason, and Lady Caith didn't harm me," Riordan said.

"I wouldn't let your brother get hurt," Wade said in a serious voice. "I promise you that."

Some of Saoirse's anger slipped away. She sighed before darting forward to wrap her arms around Riordan beneath his jacket for a hug. He held her tight for a few seconds, kissing the top of her head before she finally pulled away.

"Here." He shrugged out of his jacket and swung it around her shoulders. "Take care of this for me while I make us some lunch."

Saoirse slipped her arms through the sleeves, pulling the edges of the jacket close over her front. It hung long on her, but she didn't care, tucking her nose into the collar to breathe in his scent. He and Donal had been taking turns letting her carry their sealskin around the home to help comfort her. Theirs would never replace hers, but it staved off the skin hunger she felt.

"Thanks," she muttered. "I hope you know what you're doing."

Riordan glanced at Wade. "I think so."

He wasn't just talking about the mess with Niall, but his siblings didn't need to know that. Neither did Wade because Boston wasn't the other man's home. Riordan ignored the sharp stab of want that cut through him, pretending the urge he'd felt earlier to let Wade keep his sealskin was just an illusion.

It would be a lie, but fae were good at those.

Donal gave him an odd look, which he ignored, heading down the hall to the kitchen. Wade followed after him and started poking around the open plan space the second he arrived, opening up cupboards and drawers and peering at all the shelves.

"What are you going to make for breakfast?" Wade asked.

"It's more like brunch at this hour," Riordan said.

"Does that mean we get mimosas?"

Riordan looked over at where Wade had found the pantry and had disappeared into it. "You like mimosas?"

"Hey, guys can like the fruity drinks."

"I'm not saying you can't or that you shouldn't. I can make you a mimosa or something else. We have plenty of alcohol."

Riordan and his siblings couldn't get drunk unless the underlying alcohol was brewed for their people, which meant buying from a fae provider. While they had several bottles of that kind of alcohol in their personal store, he wasn't sure if they'd give Wade any sort of buzz.

"Sure. I can't get drunk, but I like the taste of them. I always have to make sure my niece doesn't try to drink out of mine when I have one." Wade stepped out of the pantry with a bag of tortilla chips, a box of granola bars, and an unopened jar of salsa. "What are you making?"

"I was thinking pancakes or waffles."

"Will you even have room for pancakes if you eat that entire bag of chips?" Donal asked as he came into the kitchen, eyeing where Wade had spread out everything on the other side of the kitchen island.

"He ate two dozen cannoli this morning," Riordan said, then immediately regretted it when Wade spoke up.

"Those were good," Wade said as he ripped open the bag of chips. "I'll need to go back to Mike's Pastry before I leave."

Riordan hastily turned around and made a beeline for the pantry, intent on digging up the box of pancake mix he knew was in there. He could feel Donal's judgmental gaze between his shoulder blades as he searched through the shelves.

"You didn't take him to Modern Pastry?" Donal asked in a deceptively mild voice.

"Wade wanted Mike's Pastry," Riordan said.

"Did you even bother to tell him how Mike's Pastry is inferior to Modern Pastry? Did *you* eat any?"

"No, because Wade wasn't sharing."

"I can't believe you'd betray Modern Pastry in this way."

Riordan exited the pantry and glared at Donal, who was giving him the most disappointed look in his hefty arsenal of expressions. "I just said I didn't eat any."

"You still set foot in enemy territory."

"What's wrong with Mike's Pastry?" Wade asked.

Riordan glanced over at him, unsurprised to see half the bag of chips gone, along with half the salsa. Donal did a double take when he saw how much Wade had already eaten. "Nothing if you like over-priced tourist food."

"Guess we fit right in, then, since we were playing tourist."

"Is that what you were doing when you went to see Lady Caith?" Saoirse asked as she joined them in the kitchen, still wrapped up in Riordan's jacket.

"Some of her fae were following us. I figured we could have a little talk," Wade said.

"And she talked to you? Just like that?"

Riordan dug a frying pan out of one of the cupboards under the island and then pulled a carton of strawberries from the refrigerator. "Wade let them know what pack he was with, and that seemed to be the deciding factor. It was a short conversation."

"She's a target like all of you," Wade said.

Donal leaned against the kitchen island, thankfully out of Riordan's way. "You really think that's true?"

"Niall is going after the leaders of the preternatural and supernatural communities in Boston. You and your clan hold the shoreline and the sea, and she's got everything else. He'd be stupid to try to control you and not her. If he wants Boston, he'd have to go through Lady Caith as well."

"That's suicide," Saoirse said flatly.

"Why?"

"Because the last person who tried to go against her had their body strewn in tiny pieces across the entire path of the Freedom Trail walking tour. The police were bagging evidence for weeks."

Riordan watched Wade bite into a tortilla chip. "Huh. Well, Niall's probably a god of some sort, and Lady Caith smells like a low-grade one as well, so it's probably even odds on which one of them would win in a fight."

"We need to warn the other leaders in Boston," Riordan said.

"All of them?" Donal asked worriedly, clearly thinking about the biggest threat in that group, the same way Riordan had in Lady Caith's garden.

"I dislike the idea of going to the Boston Night Court, but I don't think it's something we can ignore or put off. We lose a chance at future bargaining if we don't at least warn them of a common threat," Riordan said as he started to mix the pancake batter. Saoirse had made herself useful by chopping up the strawberries.

"We don't bargain with vampires to begin with," Donal said flatly.

"We did when Abhartach first came here," Riordan reminded him. Back then, his clan had partnered with several long-since-defunct covens to hold their territory against the nascent Boston Night Court. Those boundaries hadn't changed much, mostly because vampires had no need for the sea.

The problem was they didn't have much contact with any of the covens in Boston these days. The clans kept to themselves, the massive population in Boston making it easier to hide than ever before. If they were to go knocking on the Boston Night Court's door, Riordan would want backup.

"I'll call Ella," Wade said, practically reading Riordan's mind. "She can come with us tonight."

"Tonight?" Donal exclaimed. "That's a little rushed, don't you think?"

Wade crumpled up the now-empty bag of tortilla chips, frowning at Donal. "No? I hate vampires as much as the next person, but you're all operating under a timeline. You don't have time to wait."

Donal winced, and Riordan sighed. "He's right. We can't afford to wait."

"But it's Abhartach," Saoirse said, not bothering to hide her shudder.

"You'll have werecreatures to back you up, and you'll have me," Wade said, almost gently. He looked across the island, catching Riordan's eye, the seriousness in his gaze that of someone far older than he looked. "Do you know where the Night Court's public base is? We'll steer clear of their heart for now."

"For now?" Riordan echoed in disbelief. "Don't tell me you've been in the heart of a Night Court as well?"

"As well as what?" Saoirse asked before Wade could answer.

"He and one of his pack alphas were guests of Medb once."

Saoirse's voice reached near-glass-shattering levels. "And you're still *alive?*"

Wade made a face as he pulled out his phone from his back pocket. "It wasn't my fault we got stuck with her."

Riordan shot Saoirse a warning look, which was enough to get her to shut her mouth and finish chopping the strawberries. "Call Ella and put it on speakerphone."

"Yup," Wade said, already tapping away at his phone.

Riordan carried the mixing bowl over to the stove and the now-warm frying pan. Saoirse passed over the plate of chopped strawberries before getting out of the way. Riordan liked helpers in the kitchen, not other cooks, and set about oiling the pan before putting a ladleful of pancake batter into it.

"Wade?" Ella's voice came from near his elbow. Riordan nearly jumped, surprised to see Wade standing right beside him, having not heard the other man move.

"Hey, Ella. I'm calling about that alliance you agreed to. I didn't want to put anything in writing," Wade said.

The fingers of his other hand were inching closer to the plate of strawberries. Riordan grabbed his wrist without thinking. "Those are for the pancakes."

Wade actually *pouted* at him, and Riordan had to steel himself from giving in.

"Riordan?" Ella asked. "You're still with Wade?"

"Hi, Ella. We have a small update for you and a request."

"It better not be a bargain."

"We promised not to bargain with you under the terms of the alliance. I aim to keep that promise."

"We need to talk with the master vampire of the Boston Night Court, and we need you and those in your god pack you trust to come along as muscle," Wade said.

"You need me to *what*?" Ella exclaimed.

Riordan sighed heavily and scooped up some strawberries to sprinkle them into the pancake batter cooking on the pan, still not letting go of Wade. "We think Niall is targeting all the major leaders of the preternatural and supernatural communities in Boston. We need to see if Abhartach has been targeted yet."

There was silence on Ella's side of the line for a few seconds. "Would it be a terrible thing if that bastard was and had been taken out of the picture already?"

"Agreed," Saoirse muttered.

Riordan ignored his sister. "We won't know one way or another unless we meet with the Boston Night Court."

"Abhartach only allows communication through in-person

meetings. We'd have to meet with one of his human servants today and hope we get a meeting tonight after they speak with him."

"Does he even have a phone?" Wade asked.

"If he does, I don't know anyone who has his phone number."

"Someone needs to tell him that just because he's old doesn't mean he can't get with the modern times. We'll meet you at wherever his daylight proxy human servant is and talk with them."

"The Night Court has an office downtown. Anyone in Boston wanting to set up a meeting has to go through that location. Showing up at his usual haunts without an invitation is a good way to end up dead. We can meet there in two hours."

"How do the vampires even travel across Boston? Don't you all have more churches than most cities?"

"You're thinking of the South."

She rattled off an address on Franklin Street in Downtown Boston, and Riordan nodded even though she couldn't see him. He knew that area well. "We'll see you in two hours."

Ella ended the call first, and Wade shoved his phone back in his pocket. Riordan realized he was still holding on to Wade's wrist and reluctantly let him go. Wade didn't move away though, just leaned over to peer at the pan. "Is this one mine?"

"If you let me flip it, then yes." Wade straightened up and moved away, which Riordan regretted immediately. He focused on the pancakes instead, wondering if the whole box would be enough to make Wade happy. A few moments later, Saoirse draped his jacket over his shoulders, the tingle of his sealskin returned to him making him close his eyes for a second before he slid his arms through the sleeves.

"Thanks," she said, resting her forehead between his shoulder blades. "I feel better."

"I'll make your pancakes next."

"I'm not hungry." She moved away, leaving the kitchen. Riordan watched her go, frowning at her back.

"I'll go check on her," Donal said, leaving the kitchen.

Riordan sighed, using the spatula to flip Wade's pancake.

"Is she okay?" Wade asked from his right behind him, nearly making Riordan lose the pancake. "Sorry, I'll make noise next time."

"It's fine."

"Your sister isn't."

Riordan looked at where Wade had posted himself up against the counter beside Riordan. He wasn't surprised in the least to see at least a quarter of the strawberries were gone, most likely snacked on by Wade when he wasn't looking. "She has skin hunger, and she misses the ocean. It's hard."

Every kin knew what skin hunger was, knew of the need to wrap themselves up in their sealskin and dive beneath the waves, wholly themselves. Parents taught their children when they were old enough the pain of skin hunger by withholding their skin for a few days so they would understand it. They did so as a warning, to caution against losing their skin to people who would only ever keep it to hurt them.

Wade's mouth firmed into a hard line. "I'll go take a walk into Niall's territory tomorrow. See what I can find."

"Don't. It's not safe, and I don't want to have to call up your pack and tell them you got hurt or worse on my watch."

Wade smiled crookedly and shrugged. "He won't be the first god I've handled, and he probably won't be the last."

"I thought the fight was over and we won?"

"Eh, Hermes still comes around from time to time to piss off Patrick. Honestly, I think he's bored now that we don't have to worry about the end of the world."

"Who? Patrick?"

"No, Hermes. I think you're burning my pancake."

Riordan swore because Wade was right. He'd been too distracted by staring into Wade's eyes, and so yeah, one side of the pancake was browned more than it should have been. Wade didn't mind, seeing as he picked it off the pan and took a bite, not even bothering with a plate or butter or syrup.

"Don't let Saoirse see you eat like that. She'll throw a fit," Riordan warned.

"It's good."

"It's burnt."

"Still good." Wade eyed his pancake before tearing off a piece and offering it to Riordan. "Here. I'll prove it to you."

"I thought you didn't share your food?"

Wade rolled his eyes and waggled the piece of pancake at him. "Are you going to try it or not? I even gave you a bit with strawberry in it."

Before Riordan could second-guess himself, he leaned over and bit the piece of pancake out of Wade's fingers, clearly startling him, judging by the surprised sound he let out. Riordan chewed the pancake before shrugging, keeping his gaze on Wade. "It's passable. I'll make you a better one."

Wade stared at Riordan with wide brown eyes, pancake forgotten. The slight flush on his cheeks caught the light strangely before it disappeared in seconds.

"Sure," Wade said in a faintly strangled voice. "I'll eat anything. Mostly."

"Am I interrupting?" Donal asked, a strange weight to his voice.

Riordan desperately wanted to say *yes* because flustered was a good look on Wade. "Wade is eating the test pancake, and then he'll get the next one. I'll make yours after. How's Saoirse?"

"Okay for now. She's cleaning out the trunk."

"I don't think she should come with us into the Boston Night Court's territory."

"I'm coming with you!" Saoirse yelled from upstairs, voice clear as a bell in Riordan's ears due to enhanced hearing.

"Boyo, I could've told you that was a dumb thing to say," Donal sighed.

"Worth a try. It's not like the vampires will be up and walking in daylight." Riordan reached for the strawberries and found the plate empty. He immediately pointed the spatula at Wade. "Quit being a thief."

"Can't be a thief if I pay you back," Wade said quickly.

"Would the strawberries even make it back to me if you tried?"

Wade pursed his lips, looking up at the ceiling as if he were calculating the odds of that happening. "Maybe. Possibly."

Riordan shook his head, amused, despite himself. "Go sit. You can annoy Donal if you like."

"I should probably call my pack and give them an update. Don't eat my pancake."

Wade left the kitchen, Riordan tracking his footsteps to the front door and beyond. He heard Donal, too, as his older brother came around the kitchen island to stand in the same spot Wade had, staring at him.

"Riordan," Donal said carefully.

"It's nothing," Riordan bit out.

"You're fixated."

Riordan scowled, teeth feeling too sharp in his mouth for a brief moment, jacket pulling tight, melding with the lines of his body before he forced it loose again. "I'm not."

"Boyo. Look at me." Riordan sighed, flipping the latest pancake first before obeying his older brother, looking Donal in the eye. Donal's gaze was steady and searching, familiar from all the years where he'd made sure Riordan could stand on his own two feet and swim with the best of them. For all that Donal was the oldest, he was kinder than Riordan, and they both knew it. "You couldn't stop looking at the kid back at the god pack's home."

"He's twenty-three."

Donal snorted softly. "You've lived lifetimes he hasn't."

"He's not human. He's something else, I just don't know what."

"That doesn't mean he will stay. You heard him. His pack is in New York City." Donal reached out and ran his hand up and down Riordan's arm, the way he'd rub at Riordan's back in seal form.

"You've known him not even a day, but you're fixated, and that means he's yours. You know that."

"I won't give him my skin," Riordan got out roughly. He couldn't, even if he wanted to. Not when it was the only thing that might get Saoirse's back.

"Sometimes we don't have a choice when it comes to our mates."

Fixation was different than skin hunger—instinct drove it just the same, but one's heart could be irrational at the best of times. Sometimes kin found a person they wanted, craved, *desired* to give their skin to, and it ached when their love was rejected or they weren't in a position to attempt to be kept.

For Riordan, his clan and his kin had to come first, not his heart.

Not his potential mate.

"Are you burning my pancake?" Wade asked as he wandered back into the kitchen, phone in hand but not pressed to his ear.

Riordan hastily flipped the pancake in the pan. "No. How did your call go?"

Donal moved away, and Wade immediately took his spot. "Patrick is still in DC, and Jono said I wasn't supposed to get into any trouble while out here."

"Did you tell him you're going to meet up with some vampires?"

Wade made a face at him. "Do I look stupid? I'll tell Jono after the fact."

He said it blithely, like he wouldn't be punished for going into danger without notifying his pack. Riordan wondered if he should make overtures to the New York City god pack behind Wade's back just to ensure his clan survived whatever happened. "Go sit down. Your pancake is almost ready."

Wade went readily enough, sitting himself at the nearby dining room table and tapping away at his phone. Donal joined him after getting the syrup from the pantry, the butter already on the table in its covered dish. Riordan made as many pancakes as the batter allowed, saving the last two for himself. When he finally sat down at the table, he was unsurprised to see Wade's plate was empty.

"I don't know where he puts it," Riordan said when Donal just stared at him across the table.

"Bit of a mystery," Donal muttered before finishing what was on his plate.

Saoirse came downstairs when Riordan was eating the last bite of pancake, absently braiding her hair in one long plait. "Trunk is ready."

"We'll be right up," Riordan said.

"Trunk?" Wade asked. "Is it full of weapons?"

Saoirse stared at him. "Why would we have a trunk full of weapons?"

"What else would you have one for?"

"Certainly not that. We keep our guns in the lock boxes."

"We'll be right back," Riordan said as he and Donal left the kitchen. They trudged up the stairs to Donal's room, where their mother's small travel trunk sat at the foot of the bed on a rug that hid enough sigils for spells and wards carved into the wooden floor to take out most threats.

Carved from the wood of a tree found in their homeland past the veil, it was held together by nails made of a metal not found on Earth, one that wouldn't harm them like iron. It used to be easier living in the mortal world before all the cities replaced the forests. Riordan still wouldn't trade the life they'd created for themselves here on these shores for one where they'd be treated as lesser.

Riordan shrugged out of his jacket, shaking it out into the seal-skin it truly was. Donal did the same, and they tucked their skin away inside that trunk with its own spells carved on the inside—ones for protection and keeping safe the most precious things they owned so no one else would own them. Donal locked the trunk, no key needed since the trigger command was spelled to activate by the three of them.

They left the bedroom, Riordan missing his skin already, but he'd rather it be left behind and safe than torn from his body by a vampire. Saoirse and Wade were waiting for them by the front door when they made it downstairs.

"Where are your jackets?" Wade asked.

"Safe," Riordan said, not minding sharing the truth with him. He knew, deep in his bones, that Wade wouldn't use that information for any nefarious reason. Fixation, sure, but Riordan wanted to believe Wade was kind.

Wade nodded slowly. "You could wear them if you wanted. I won't let anything happen to you or your siblings."

"Better to be cautious," Donal said.

"All right. Then let's head out." Riordan locked up behind them, and rather than ride with Donal and Saoirse, he followed Wade to his Audi. Wade glanced over his shoulder at him, raising an eyebrow. "Going to play tour guide again?"

"If you want," Riordan said.

Wade flashed him a smile that lit up his face and nearly made Riordan bite his tongue, fighting the urge to smile stupidly back. "Great. Maybe we can get something to eat along the way."

"Not Mike's Pastry's again."

"You went *where*?" Saoirse shouted from Donal's car. "Traitor!"

Riordan hastily got into the front passenger seat while Wade cackled. "This is your fault."

"It's cannoli. I don't care who makes it, so long as I get to eat it," Wade said cheerfully as he started the engine. "Any other places you can recommend?"

Riordan had lived in Boston for a long, long time, had seen many restaurants come and go. "Plenty, but there won't be enough time to go to all of them before you head back to New York."

"I wouldn't mind taking a trip back here to eat with you."

Riordan stared straight ahead, telling his traitorous heart that Wade was offering to return to Boston for the food scene and not him. "Sure. It's a date."

He only hoped he wouldn't have to stand Wade up if they couldn't win back Saoirse's sealskin.

CHAPTER TEN

THEY MET ELLA ON THE STREET ACROSS FROM THE OFFICE BUILDING WHERE
the Boston Night Court's human servants acted as their proxy during
business hours. The building overlooked the water, and Wade could
smell the saltiness of the sea on the air. It made him want fish and
chips.

He squinted up at the building, shielding his eyes from the sun
with one hand. "What kind of business does a vampire like Abby Boy
run?"

"Who knows? We don't pry. We just try to steer clear of his territory and guard our own," Ella said.

"It's got to be a shell company of some sort."

"You seem awfully interested in how Abhartach makes his
money."

Wade scowled. "I'm just curious if it's through drugs or traf-
ficking or white-collar crime. I'm not above snitching to the
government."

"It doesn't matter. His human servants will never disclose
proprietary information."

"You sound like a lawyer."

Ella shrugged. "I was going to be one before I got mauled and became infected with the werevirus. But the law isn't going to help us with Niall, so let's deal with the human servants and figure out if their master is still running around free."

She gestured at the three god pack werecreatures who had arrived with her for this unexpected visit. Everyone's wolf-bright amber eyes were hidden behind sunglasses, and while they didn't look like they could probably bench-press a car, Wade knew looks could be deceiving.

Ella stalked her way across the street, her pack following her. Wade and the selkies straggled after them. They signed in at the front security desk, though Wade only put down his initials. Then they took the elevator up to the twelfth floor, stepping off it into a hallway that held quite a few suites.

"We want Sanguine Associates," Ella said, already turning left.

Wade shrugged and followed her, content to let her take the lead on this little trip—right up until he got a whiff of a scent that was all too annoyingly familiar.

"Oh, you have *got* to be kidding me," he growled.

Riordan glanced over at him. "What's wrong?"

"A blast from the past."

"Good or bad?" Donal asked.

Wade didn't answer and pushed his way to the front of their little group without using his elbows, but just barely. Ella made a surprised sound, which he ignored, lengthening his stride to reach the office they were heading to first. He gripped the knob and pushed the door open, stepping inside, practically vibrating with indignation.

"What are *you* doing here?" Wade demanded, pointing his finger at the visitor who'd reached the business first and who apparently wasn't alone.

Carmen turned away from the pair of fae she was facing off against in front of a reception desk manned by a pale-faced human servant. She looked at them, and her lips curved in a sultry smile.

Naheed, one of Lucien's favored human servants, stood at her side in bodyguard mode. "I could ask the same of you."

The succubus was gorgeous in a way that always creeped Wade out. Carmen's glamour never worked on him, but he'd been told it was too perfect, every curve of her body meant to play off her sexual nature. Her true self was still beautiful, black horns curving back over her skull and the riot of black curls that fell to her waist. One horn was broken in half, the damage attained during the Battle of Samhain. She'd covered it with a silver cap inlaid with rubies. The dark red pupils in her brown eyes would always mark her as other, the same way as Wade's reptilian pupils would if he showed them. The sexual desire Carmen almost always exuded to some degree to entice men and women and anyone else into her bed always made his nose itch.

"We thought you'd left the country."

"My Night Court's business is no longer yours."

"Yeah? It's gonna be if you're trying to take over the Boston Night Court. Where's your uglier half?"

"Watch your mouth, or I will take offense." Carmen tilted her head, placing one hand on her hip as she eyed him, her gaze tracking to the others who joined him in the reception area like a party none of them were invited to. "These aren't members of your pack."

"Nope, and they're not yours to mess around with. Try, and I will eat you."

"I do so like being eaten," Carmen purred.

Wade rolled his eyes because of course she'd make anything sexual. "Take the threat for what it is."

"My, how you've grown. Your threats are meaningless, and there is nothing tying your pack to my Night Court any longer."

"I didn't come here for you. I came to speak with Abby Boy about a problem."

Carmen reached up and playfully tapped her index finger against her chin. "Is it the same one these oh-so-generous fae have come to discuss and swear they mean no harm about?"

Her smile remained, but her gaze grew cold as she turned to focus on the fae, dismissing Wade and his little group. He wasn't offended, only because he knew Carmen believed everyone was beneath her and Lucien.

Wade crossed his arms over his chest, scowling at her before directing his ire at the two fae who were staring down their noses at everyone. "Are you with Lady Caith?"

"As the Lady Carmen said, it's not your business," the fae with rose-pink hair said.

"*Carmen?*" Riordan exclaimed, echoed by Donal and Saoirse.

Wade glanced at the selkies, wincing at their horrified expressions, which told him they probably knew who Carmen was and who she worked for. "She's no lady."

Carmen placed one hand on her ample chest, smirking at him. "I'm wounded."

"Clearly not enough." Wade jerked his thumb at the fae he didn't like. "They're causing problems in Boston."

"That is no concern of mine."

"It is if you're friendly with Abby Boy. Niall's gunning for his territory." The fae glared at him, and Wade smiled back, showing off his teeth. It was too late now to hide his presence in Boston from Niall or that he was working with Riordan's clan and Ella's god pack now that these two fae had seen him. "Tell me I'm wrong?"

"We are here to discuss a private matter with the master vampire of the Boston Night Court," the second fae said evenly.

Wade caught Carmen's gaze and raised an eyebrow. "Territory fight."

Carmen focused on the fae, the coyness gone from her expression, replaced by a predatory intent Wade remembered all too well from the times he'd had to fight by her side. "Is that so?"

The fae probably thought they could've bullied the human servant into doing what they wanted if they could get past the wards Wade sensed in the walls, but there was definitely no bullying their way past Carmen. The fae sized up the problem in front of them and promptly left without another word, clearly choosing to live another day. Wade watched them go, frowning deeply, before he returned his attention to Carmen. "No, seriously, why are you here? Why aren't you in Mexico or some other country? Tell Lucien South America misses him. He can go visit his cartel."

"*Lucien?*" Ella squeaked out from behind Wade, finally clueing in on who Carmen's boss was.

"Where's the rest of your misbegotten pack?" Carmen asked, bypassing his question.

"Not here for you to annoy," Wade retorted.

"A pity." Carmen's gaze slid from him to everyone standing behind him. "Who are your friends?"

"What's it to you?"

Carmen smiled, nothing about it nice. Nope, Wade hadn't missed dealing with her at all. "You're here for Abhartach."

Wade made a face. "So?"

"We consider him an acquaintance."

Which, for Lucien, was probably as close to an ally as he'd get among vampires. It also meant that Niall would probably regret targeting Abhartach. Wade knew Lucien always considered territory fights and murder a good time.

Wait a minute.

Wade steepled his fingers together beneath his chin, eyeing Carmen contemplatively. "We need an introduction to Abby Boy."

"I'm not the one you should be asking."

"But you and Lucien could vouch for us."

"And why would we do that?"

"Because you both like money."

Wade made a mental note to apologize to Sage and Marek's personal accountant for the money he was about to drop. It would be worth it if it got their little group an audience with the master vampire of Boston's Night Court—even more if they managed to convince the blood-sucking asshole to fight against Niall with them. He was pretty certain if they offered up Niall's territory to Abhartach, then the master vampire would maybe strike up a bargain. It would piss off Lady Caith, but oh well. She'd be the one who would have to deal with the Boston Night Court on her doorstep, not Riordan and his clan.

Carmen hummed thoughtfully. "It's that important to you to see him?"

"Does it matter?"

She tossed back her head and laughed. "No. We'll escort you to Abhartach for a price. His proxy will see to it you're on the list to be seen tomorrow night."

Wade sighed heavily and pulled out his phone. "I was hoping it'd be tonight, but fine. What's your price?"

"Five hundred."

"Please tell me there are no commas involved with that number."

"Oh, fledgling. You know us better than that. Five hundred thousand. I'll give you the wire number when you're ready."

Ella grabbed him by the wrist, leaning in close with a fierce frown. "Wade, no."

"It's fine," Wade promised. He knew how not to make bargains these days, and he definitely knew how to deal with Carmen—pay for her next season's wardrobe and give her someone to kill and she'd be happy.

"Doubly enjoyable for us, as I know it will annoy Patrick," Carmen drawled.

Wade contained his wince. That was so very true, and Patrick was going to yell at him the second he got finished with his trial and whatever new case the SOA wanted his expertise for. "Just give me your wire number."

Like Patrick and Jono, Wade had access to a bank account Sage had set up for the four of them outside the one used for pack tithes. Last he checked, it had a little over two million dollars in it, meant to be used for situations like this. Marek had funded quite a bit of their needs during the nearly two years of lead-up to the Battle of Samhain, and Sage had simply continued that after they got married.

Wade never hurt for money, but he really only used it to buy snacks. The half a million dollars he was wiring to Carmen was going to be flagged and notifications sent off to their accounting people. As soon as he was done with the transfer, he shot off a text in the four-person group chat that was at the top of his list of ongoing text messages.

THAT MONEY TRANSFER WAS FROM ME. DON'T WORRY ABOUT IT.

He shouldn't have been surprised that Jono ended up calling. Wade frowned down at his phone before swiping to end the call and sending another text.

SERIOUSLY. DON'T WORRY. I'M FINE.

ANSWER YOUR DAMN MOBILE.

Jono called again, and Wade knew better than to ignore it this time, so he answered. "Heeey, so—"

"What the bloody hell do you need half a million dollars for?" Jono demanded.

"Not anything illegal!" Wade paused. "Mostly."

"Try again, mate. What is going on in Boston?"

"Nothing I can't handle."

"That's not an answer."

"The wolf sounds annoyed," Carmen mused. "I see some things haven't changed."

Wade made a cutting gesture across his throat with one hand, but it was too late because Jono had clearly heard her. Jono's side of the line went quiet for two seconds before he snarled, "Is that *Carmen?*"

"No?" Wade replied, unable to help the uplift in his voice that turned his answer into a question.

"*Wade.*"

"Okay, okay, look. There's a fae running around taking leaders of the preternatural and supernatural communities up here hostage in exchange for control over territory and more people. We have a lead, and Carmen just happened to be in the same location."

"We? Who is we?"

"Uh, Ella? Dire to the Boston god pack. And Riordan. He's a selkie." Wade glared at Carmen as he kept talking, annoyed by the way she just kept smirking. "We need to talk to an Irish vampire who doesn't even have a phone. Who doesn't have a phone in this day and age? I bet he doesn't even have a computer—"

"Wade."

"Yeah, okay. Anyway, he might be a target, and Carmen says she and Lucien consider him a friend—"

"Acquaintance," Carmen corrected.

"Coming from you and Lucien, that's like best friend material," Wade shot back before refocusing on his conversation with Jono. "Look, Jono. I have it under control. I'll call if I need anything."

"I'm going to send some of the others up to you," Jono said.

"I can handle this. Don't send anyone. Ella won't appreciate that, and I already warned Carmen I'd eat her if she does anything funny."

"You can try," Carmen said. "Tell Patrick we said hello, wolf."

"And we're saying goodbye," Wade said hastily before Jono got any more pissed off. "I'll call you later. Promise. Bye!"

He ended the call and shoved the phone back into his pocket. Carmen smirked at him before half turning to talk to the human servant manning the front desk. "Tell Abhartach we're bringing guests tomorrow night."

"I will inform our master of your request when he wakes," the other woman said.

"It's not a request. He'll understand that." Carmen turned to eye Wade before smirking at him again. "We'll see you at Abhartach's absinthe bar after sunset tomorrow night. Naheed will give you the address. As always, a pleasure doing business with you."

Wade crossed his arms over his chest and scowled at her. "Fine. We'll be there. You better not stand us up."

Carmen sauntered out of the office. Naheed paused only long enough to tell Wade the address of the bar before following after her charge. Riordan came to stand beside him, his arm brushing against Wade's, the touch drawing most of his attention.

"How are you on a first-name basis with Lucien and Carmen?" Riordan asked, staring at the door Carmen had left out of.

"It's a long story and one better told over lunch."

"Then let's get out of here. I think lunch is a good idea," Ella said. She peered around Wade at the human servant. "Apologies for the disruption. We'll be leaving now."

She was polite, all Southern manners, even if she wasn't deferential. Wade hadn't even thought to apologize, but Sage probably would have. Maybe. "Yeah, thanks."

"Never say thank you," Riordan said with a pained expression before snagging Wade by the elbow and hustling him out of the office.

"She's not fae," Wade protested.

"But Niall's people were here, and we don't know for how long or what they were discussing with Carmen before we arrived. So, never say thank you."

"My mama wouldn't stand for that," Ella said from behind them.

They all left the office, and Wade wasn't surprised to see that Carmen and Naheed were nowhere to be found. Neither were the fae. He chewed on his bottom lip, walking with the others back to the elevator. He wasn't sure what Niall would do once he found out Ella and Riordan had found some help, but hopefully, he would make a mistake.

They made it to the street, but rather than head for where they'd parked, Ella walked off in the opposite direction. "We're getting tacos."

Wade immediately perked up. "I *love* tacos!"

"I think you love any kind of food," Saoirse said.

"Yes," Wade agreed heatedly. "So long as it isn't demon-flavored."

Riordan just stared at him in disbelief for several steps before shaking his head. "So you eat things. Carmen called you fledgling. What exactly are you?"

"Hungry."

Wade didn't miss the way Riordan shared a look with Donal and Saoirse, but the other man didn't press the issue, which he thought was nice. Ella snorted delicately but clearly wasn't going to give up whatever information she thought she had on him. She determinedly led the way two blocks over, past a bunch of office workers out on their lunch breaks, to a restaurant that had indoor and outdoor seating and smelled like grilled meat.

They weren't the only ones in line, but their orders were probably going to back up everyone else's behind them. Ella and her pack members each got a dozen tacos, while Riordan and his siblings stuck with half a dozen Baja fish ones. Wade smiled at the person manning the register when he finally reached her and rattled off his order.

Her finger hovered over the screen of her register as she stared at him. "Three dozen tacos?"

"Yup," Wade said. "And a soda."

"Is this a catering order?"

"Nope. All for me."

She didn't look like she believed him, but she dutifully took down his order, and he paid it, taking the little number stand and to-go cup with him over to the soda machine. He poured himself a Coke and then headed through the doors that led to the outside patio and the table the others had claimed. Ella and her pack members still wore their sunglasses, hiding their eyes.

The spot next to Riordan had been left open at the end, and Wade promptly took it, swinging his legs over the bench. The restaurant tables all had benches rather than chairs, lending itself to a more parklike feel than a stuffy place to eat. The colorful paper cut-out flags that looped overhead from a high pergola fluttered in the sluggish breeze.

Saoirse, sitting on the other side of Riordan, craned her head around to eye him. "Are you really going to eat all those tacos you ordered?"

"Yes," Ella and Riordan answered for him in unison, the pair sharing an exasperated look over the table.

Wade laughed. "I'm not sharing if that's what you're asking."

"No," Saoirse said. "I'm just trying to figure out where you put it all."

"That's a question even my pack can't answer."

Truthfully, Wade was just always hungry. He knew it had to do with mass—shifted or not—and his true form. Whatever inherent ability allowed him to shift from dragon to human and back again didn't mean he had a human-sized need when it came to food. He was a growing dragon, as Patrick liked to sigh over every time he had to pay the credit card bill.

Ella leaned forward, peering at Wade over the top of her sunglasses. When she spoke, her voice was barely louder than a whisper to account for the people around them, but Wade heard her clearly anyway. Besides, he'd have warned her if he smelled any kind of threat. Mostly, it was just mundane humans on their lunch breaks. "I won't have my pack owing you. We can't afford half a million dollars for what amounts to an entrance fee to a bar."

"You don't have a debt with us. We hate those," Wade said seriously, thinking about Patrick's soul debt, which had been the catalyst for everything they'd all gone through. "This is a no-strings-attached payment I'm handling to help all of you. We need to know if Abby Boy has been taken or targeted, and if he's still around, I want to try to convince him to go after Niall."

"Ambitious," Donal said from the other side of Saoirse.

"The enemy of my enemy is my friend. My pack and I have played this game before, and it usually works out."

"Usually isn't always," Riordan said, shifting on the bench. His thigh pressed up against Wade's and stayed there, his touch warm through both their jeans. Wade had to squash the urge to lean into the touch, a little panicky way deep down that he'd even thought about wanting it in the first place.

"Uh," Wade said, trying to find his train of thought again. "I mean, we still won?"

Riordan snorted, but there wasn't any judgment in his eyes or his smile. And he had a really nice smile.

Wade wanted to keep him.

Hoarding tendencies were the *worst* sometimes.

"Abhartach can't be trusted," Ella said.

Wade rolled his eyes. "I know *that*. I'm not asking you to trust him. But if we have Niall focusing on the problem of a pissed-off master vampire, that gives us time to search for where your alphas are being kept and where Saoirse's skin might be."

Ella sat back, frowning thoughtfully. "I suppose divide and conquer is as good of a plan as we can hope for."

"*Thank* you. Oh, I think our tacos are coming."

Wade watched hopefully as a few servers weaved through the tables over to theirs, holding plates of tacos set in little stands with three V-shaped dips in them to hold them in place. Wade shoved his soda cup to the side to make room, watching happily as three plates were set down in front of him.

"The rest of your order is coming," the server said.

"Great." Wade piled up the taco stands on one plate. "You can take those back so there's room for the rest."

The smell of street tacos had his mouth watering, and Wade promptly picked up one and ate it in two bites. They were overflowing with meat, onions, and cilantro, but that wasn't a problem for him. Once he had his entire order, he methodically ate his way through the tacos at a pace the others didn't even try to keep up with. Even though he had ordered more than the others, he still finished before them, licking grease off his fingers instead of using a napkin.

He was thinking about maybe getting back in the line to order another couple of tacos when Riordan passed over his last Baja fish taco, dressing dripping out the end from the slaw. "Here. Eat this if you're still hungry."

Wade grinned at him. "Thanks!"

He took the Baja fish taco and promptly devoured it, then started on demolishing the communal chips and salsa bowls everyone else was ignoring in the center of the table.

"Those fae will most likely tell Niall that I've managed to find help despite the spell on me and the others. The same goes for you as well, Riordan. Niall will know by tonight you've got help," Ella said.

"Will you leave your territory to keep him from finding you?" Wade asked.

Ella shook her head. "No. We still need to be available for other packs under our protection."

"I'd send the kin into the sea, but Lady Caith didn't lie about something residing in the deep," Riordan said slowly.

Wade paused in picking up a chip, looking at him. "Oh?"

"There's a danger in the ocean. She's right about that. It feels off." Riordan paused, frowning slightly. "It *sounds* off."

"I can't help you in the sea. But if you don't think it's safe for your people, and you don't want them to stay here, you can always send them out of Boston. Do you have any place they can go to ground at?"

"Bolt holes here in Boston. Salem, maybe, as a last resort, but I still think that's too close to Niall's reach."

"If you're worried about anyone in particular, send them to New York City. My pack can see to their safety until we fix this problem."

"We aren't werecreatures."

"Neither is Patrick. I'd like to see Niall try to go up against my alphas."

It'd be a bloodbath, and none of it would come from Patrick or Jono. Niall would have to be phenomenally stupid to fight the New York City god pack. They had a reputation for a reason these days. It's what had made the five boroughs safer, actually, after the Battle of Samhain. Most of the alliances they'd brokered still held, and the divide between groups within the preternatural and supernatural communities were definitely narrowed these days or gone completely.

"We'll see," Riordan said, promising nothing. Which was fine with Wade. The offer was out there, and that was all that mattered.

"If we're going to that bar tomorrow night, we'll need to figure out a plan beyond one enemy against the other. I don't trust who will be getting us inside," Ella said.

"We can go back to my hotel room. I have plenty of space. I doubt Niall knows where I'm staying," Wade said.

"Yet," Saoirse muttered from down the table.

"He'll probably try to figure out who you are. That puts you in danger," Riordan said.

Wade shrugged. "He can try, and then I'll just eat him."

Ella crumpled up her napkin and drank the rest of her beer in two long swallows. "Will your hotel room even fit all of us?"

"It's the penthouse in the Ritz-Carlton. If we get hungry, I can have the chef make us snacks and send them up."

Ella stared at him for a moment before shaking her head. "All right, let's go."

They left their empty plates on the table and made their way out of the restaurant. Wade thought Riordan would stick with his siblings but was pleased when the other man decided to ride with him again. It eased the twitchiness he got whenever Riordan was out of sight, which had been maybe twice today. He'd known the selkie for less than twenty-four hours, and already Wade didn't want him to be beyond arm's reach.

Maybe it was a dragon thing he didn't yet know about, this desire to keep Riordan close. It was similar to the way he always liked being with his pack and knowing where they were, but different in that none of them had ever made him itch to curl close to Riordan and just hold on.

Just keep him.

Wade got behind the steering wheel and watched Riordan get settled in the front passenger seat. Without his jacket on and in just a T-shirt, it was easy to see how muscular he was. Wade found himself staring at Riordan's shoulders and forearms as he buckled up, noticing there were freckles on his skin there too.

"Something on my shirt?" Riordan asked.

Wade blinked and shook his head, wrenching his gaze away. "Uh, no. Just thinking."

About you. About how I think I want to kiss you.

Ooh, maybe time to call his therapist.

He started the car and backed out of the parking spot, keeping his eyes on the mirrors rather than meeting Riordan's gaze, which he could feel staring at him.

"Thank you, by the way, for helping us. I can't speak for Ella, but my clan appreciates it."

"Sure. I wasn't going to walk away from this once I knew what was going on."

"Other people would."

Wade snorted. "I'm not other people."

"Yeah, I'm starting to see that." Riordan sounded quietly thankful, and his scent, when Wade breathed it in, was salt-tinged relief threaded through with the cologne he wore.

Without thinking about what he was doing, Wade reached over and patted Riordan on the knee. "We'll free Casey and Harper, and we'll get your sister's sealskin back. I promise."

Riordan's fingers wrapped around Wade's wrist before he could pull away, grip gentle, warm fingertips resting right against his now-pounding pulse. "You shouldn't make bargains with fae."

"Bargains don't work on me," Wade managed to get out in a voice that wasn't strangled. Ha. Go him. "And I'll do whatever I want if it'll keep you and the others safe."

Riordan said nothing to that, but neither did he let go of Wade, shifting his grip to fold his fingers around Wade's and hold his hand for the entire drive back to the hotel.

Wade was just glad he didn't crash the car.

CHAPTER ELEVEN

They'd made it down to the Ritz-Carlton lobby after the afternoon meeting in Wade's penthouse suite when Saoirse abruptly stopped walking and spun around to face him. Riordan nearly tripped over his feet to stop himself from crashing into her.

"Go back upstairs," Saoirse said, jabbing her finger into his chest.

"What?" Riordan asked dumbly.

"You're *fixated*." Her gaze softened, even if the next jab of her fingers was just as hard as the first. "Donal is going to drive me home while you spend time with Wade."

Riordan opened his mouth and made a strangled-sounding noise. "I'm not fixated!"

Saoirse rolled her eyes. "Please. You *fed* him, and you couldn't keep your eyes off him during lunch. Go back upstairs."

"How am I supposed to get back home, then? We're not traveling alone."

"Have Wade drop you off. Or don't come home," Donal said, raising one eyebrow.

Riordan palmed his face and groaned. "I'm *fine*."

"You are twitchy as hell, boyo."

"My jacket is at home."

"That's not it, and you know it." Donal thumped him on the shoulder before shoving him around and giving him a push back toward the private elevator they'd come down in. "Give Wade a call. He'll let you come back up."

His terrible, interfering siblings left Riordan alone in the lobby of the hotel, and he couldn't find it in himself to run after them. The idea of staying caught in his thoughts made him turn on his feet and head back to the private elevator accessible only by a key card he didn't have. But he did have Wade's phone number now, and he only hesitated a second before calling.

"Hey," Wade said in that cheerful voice of his. "Did you forget something?"

"No, but can I come up anyway?"

"Sure, I'll come down and get you."

Wade ended the call, and Riordan shoved his phone into his back pocket, ignoring the way he could feel the eyes of the man at the concierge desk staring at him. Riordan's clan had money, and his siblings had more than that with their pub business, but they weren't flashy with it. Riordan knew he didn't look like he was wealthy, but he'd never get to the level that Wade was casually comfortable with.

All thoughts of money and not belonging fled his mind when the elevator doors pinged open and Wade stepped out with a smile and smelling like the cookies he'd devoured at the tail end of the meeting. "Did you still have something you wanted to discuss?"

"Not about Niall. I was wondering if you had any other food spots on your list? I could take you there if you do."

Wade tilted his head, some of his dark brown hair flopping across his forehead. "Are you even hungry?"

"Not really, but I don't mind feeding you."

He didn't tell Wade it was a courting aspect of the kin, that offering food was a way to show he could take care of the other man.

To prove that he could *give* as opposed to *take*. That if Wade were a selkie, then his sealskin would be safe in Riordan's hands.

Wade didn't know that—couldn't know that—not with Niall having cornered Riordan's clan. But Riordan could pretend, for however long they had together here in Boston, that this fixation could turn into something more.

It would be a nice dream if he had to trade his skin for Saoirse's. Something to keep him company in whatever nightmare Niall had planned.

"I eat a lot," Wade warned, the fingers of his right hand tapping against his thigh.

"I'm aware," Riordan said dryly. "I don't mind."

Wade beamed at him, eyes crinkling at the corners. "Is it walkable, or do you need air-conditioning because you'll wilt like a flower?"

Riordan scoffed at him, reaching out to ruffle his fingers through Wade's hair because not touching him right now was impossible. "You're driving."

Wade ducked his head but didn't try to step back. "That means you're playing tour guide."

"Gladly."

"I want lobster rolls this time."

"Okay."

"Lots of them."

"I saw how many tacos you ate." Riordan took Wade's hand and didn't let himself think about the implications of doing so, turning back toward the main lobby and the hotel exit, tugging Wade after him. "I'm taking you to James Hook."

"Like in Peter Pan? Is this a Disney-themed restaurant?"

"What? No. It's a Boston institution."

"My niece would be so disappointed."

"Is she into Disney movies?"

"Yes," Wade said vehemently before proceeding to talk all about her favorite ones and the tea parties they'd have while waiting for the valet to bring the car around. He clearly adored his niece, even if there was no blood relationship involved. But pack, much like clan, wasn't always based on the family one was born into but the one you chose.

The valet pulled up in Wade's rental and handed over the keys. Riordan was forced to let Wade go so they could get in the car and on the road. Inside, even with the air-conditioning running, he could sense the warmth that Wade exuded, a heat that made Riordan want to soak it up.

"You can plug in the address," Wade said.

Riordan reached for the screen on the dashboard. "Head east. It's near where we had lunch."

"You act like I know this city."

Riordan bit down on what he wanted to say—*I wish you did*—and shrugged. "I won't lead you astray."

"That wasn't in doubt."

Wade glanced at him, sunglasses nowhere to be found, gaze open and curious before he returned his attention to the road. "Why'd you come back? It couldn't be just to feed me."

Riordan stared straight ahead and fought the urge to lay his hand over Wade's thigh. He didn't have that right. "I gave an order to my clan that no one travels alone right now. You don't have anyone with you."

Wade chuckled, but it didn't sound as if he was laughing at Riordan. "Trust me. There isn't anything Niall could throw at me that I wouldn't be able to win against."

He didn't smell like magic or werecreature or any of the numerous creatures that made humanity fear the dark. Wade came across as completely human to every single one of Riordan's senses just then—but he remembered that scuffle in Beacon Hill and the weight of a presence that could only be described as predatory.

Wade wasn't human, but he was kind. In Riordan's long-lived experience, that was worth everything.

"You still shouldn't be alone," Riordan said.

"Then I guess it's a good thing you decided to continue playing tour guide."

"I'm always up for showing off Boston."

"So how come you don't want to go back to Ireland?"

"My clan is safer here. And we like Boston."

It had the Boston Harbor and the vast Atlantic Ocean beyond it. Maybe it didn't have the green hills of Ireland, but there was something to be said for the redbrick homes and Fenway Park, the universities and the way the city looked when it snowed.

Boston was home now, and Riordan had made his peace with that years ago.

"I like New York City. I mean, I like cities in general, but Manhattan? That's home with my pack."

Riordan nodded shallowly, thinking of his clan. "Yeah. I get that."

The drive to James Hook & Co. was largely uneventful. Riordan wasn't ashamed of asking all the questions he thought he could get away with if it meant he learned more about Wade. He seemed more than willing to open up, but Riordan was aware of the answers that were glossed over or the questions that were completely ignored, answered with Wade's own questions.

When Riordan asked if Wade had always called New York City home, Wade responded with "So can you change the shape of your jacket?"

"Yes," Riordan said, knowing that was giving nothing away about the magic that tied him to his sealskin.

"So you were wearing your sealskin at Gerard's wedding? It was a fancy coat, but it doesn't look anything like the one you're wearing today."

"Do you like fancy coats?"

"Not particularly. I'm a jeans and T-shirt kind of guy."

"They fit you well."

Wade's fingers—which had been drumming against the steering wheel in time with the radio—paused for a moment before continuing on with the beat. "Uh, thanks?"

Riordan smirked a little. "I don't mind looking."

Wade made a noise that wasn't words in any language before laughing slightly. "Well, that's a first."

"What is?"

"Getting checked out in a nice way."

Riordan glanced over at him. "I find it difficult to believe people don't hit on you."

Wade's jaw firmed at that statement, and Riordan frowned, wondering if he'd overstepped somehow.

"If they do, I don't really notice," Wade said slowly. "I haven't been interested in people like that for years."

Riordan managed not to wince, wondering if he'd been reading the whole situation entirely wrong. "I'm sorry if I've made you uncomfortable."

Wade swiftly shook his head. "You haven't. Really."

He smelled like truth, and that eased the terrible tightness that had wrapped itself around Riordan's chest in the last few moments. "Good. I wouldn't ever want to hurt you."

I want you to keep me.

Riordan didn't give voice to that thought, ruthlessly shoving it down.

"I know you won't."

The conviction in Wade's voice was a balm. Riordan wondered if Wade's instincts were primed the same way his were when it came to each other—that desire to remain close.

Fixation was a terrible, wanting ache. Whether for a lover or the sea, it sang like a siren through him, a song he had to force himself to ignore.

"So why didn't you and your siblings wear your coats to the vampire's office today?" Wade asked.

"It's easy for an enemy to strip us of our skin if they know what we are," Riordan said slowly, feeling as if he was giving up a secret but knowing, too, that Wade would keep it safe. "Better to leave it at home, locked up safe, than be bound by an enemy if we're the ones stepping foot in their territory first."

"But what if Niall goes looking for it? He knows where you all live, right? Once he finds out Ella managed to find a loophole in the spell and she's allied with you, what do you think he'll do?"

"Renege on the week he gave us to decide."

"Maybe it would be better if you wore it tomorrow. I won't let the vampires take anything from any of you. Lucien knows I'll eat him if he tries."

"You never did tell me how you know Lucien."

"It's more that Patrick knew him first, and then the rest of us had the terrible misfortune of knowing him after. Honestly, he's such an asshole."

Wade proceeded to complain all about Lucien and his murderous ways and annoying attitude for the rest of the drive. Riordan didn't mind too much since he got some background on events he only had vague knowledge of from rumors that had run the gamut through the preternatural and supernatural communities some years ago.

"—and then one time he—oh, hey, we're here!" Wade turned suddenly, pulling into the parking lot. It was that weird in-between time between lunch and dinner where the crowds were thinner. Which meant there was a parking spot to be claimed.

Riordan got out, squinting against the sunlight. "How many lobster rolls do you really think you can eat?"

Wade threw back his head and laughed, the line of his throat catching Riordan's eye. "I hope your credit card has no limit."

It did, and Riordan definitely put a dent in it that afternoon as Wade ate his way through at least twenty lobster rolls, half made warm with butter and the other half cold with mayonnaise. Riordan ate a couple of his own, more interested in watching Wade eat his fill while letting the conversation meander wherever it wanted. He just liked listening to Wade talk, hearing him laugh.

"Want another lobster roll, or do you want to go for a walk?" Riordan asked after two hours of lounging at the table in the corner.

Wade licked his fingers free of sauce, and Riordan barely managed not to stare for more than a few seconds. "I thought you didn't walk?"

"I walk."

Wade smirked. "I bet you like to swim as much as I like to fly."

Somehow, Riordan didn't think he was talking about a plane. "Probably."

Wade used the last pile of napkins to clean his hands before standing. "Come on. We'll park the car somewhere else, and then you can take me on a walk."

True to his word, Wade found a parking garage nearby, and they left the car behind, safe from parking tickets. It was late afternoon, and the warm breeze that had blown across Boston all day was starting to cool a little. Riordan wished he had his sealskin with him, but he knew it was safe at home while Wade was safe with him.

Riordan led Wade back toward the street James Hook & Co. was on, taking him down onto the Harborwalk. The shoreline path ringed the majority of Boston, connected by bridges in areas, allowing for pedestrian access to the water and the views that came with it.

Riordan guided them in a more southerly direction. The crowds on the Harborwalk had thinned some from the midday crush, and they weren't nearly as big as during the height of the tourist season in summer. They chatted amiably as he led them across the Congress Street Bridge, passing by the Boston Tea Party Ships and Museum.

"Patrick keeps telling Jono we threw the tea into the harbor for a reason," Wade said with a laugh as he stood there for a few minutes, watching tourists toss anchored packages off the sides of the wooden ships at the behest of a man wearing an old-timey costume. "Jono still can't get him to try any."

"I take it Patrick doesn't like tea?"

"Patrick is in a love affair with coffee so he doesn't murder anyone before noon."

Riordan could relate. They finished crossing the bridge, and

Wade got distracted at the plaza on the other side, courtesy of the ice-cream stand there.

"How much do you even eat in a day?" Riordan asked when Wade came back with two ice-cream cones.

"It's not my fault I'm hungry all the time," Wade said. He thrust out one hand, the cone holding two scoops of chocolate. "You can have this one."

Riordan eyed it, then eyed Wade. "I thought you didn't share your food?"

Wade wouldn't meet his gaze, cheeks faintly flushed. "Yeah, well, you bought me lobster rolls. Consider us even."

Riordan laughed. "I spent close to a thousand dollars on those lobster rolls, but sure, this makes us even."

He took the ice-cream cone because Wade was offering, trying not to read anything more into it. They started walking again, leaving the plaza for the Harborwalk once more. On this side of the Congress Street Bridge, it ran past a small children's park overlooking the water. Not as many people were on the pathway, considering the weekday hour. The smell of the sea was familiar, the salt of it something Riordan could taste in the air. All selkies knew and loved the ocean, and Riordan's home would always be alongside a body of water. For all the peace it gave him, it couldn't completely wash away his unease.

"What if Abhartach doesn't help us?" Riordan asked.

Wade shrugged, licking at his ice cream in a way that made Riordan go a little cross-eyed. "Then I'll pay Lucien more money to convince Abby Boy to cave. Don't worry. I know how to deal with vampires. I'm better at it these days."

"What do you mean?"

Wade was quiet for a long moment, walking beside Riordan but not taking in the view. The grimace tugging at his mouth was something Riordan wanted to smooth away. "I don't like it when others try to keep people as slaves."

The words came out clipped, flat, with a weight to them that spoke of experience that made Riordan want to tear something to pieces with his sharp selkie teeth. Since there wasn't anything around for him to kill, Riordan settled for taking Wade's hand in his and holding on tight. The touch seemed to startle Wade out of whatever memories were haunting him, his head snapping around. Riordan smiled softly at him. "I don't think I've said thank you for all the help you're giving us."

Wade stared down at their hands before raising his head and arching an eyebrow. "Aren't fae not supposed to offer any thanks?"

"I know you won't hurt us." He tugged on Wade's hand, drawing the other man over to the walkway's blue railing so they were out of the way of anyone walking past. His gaze lingered on Wade's expressive mouth and the hint of ice cream at one corner. "Can I kiss you?"

Wade went still, planting his feet. His eyes widened, the sunlight catching bits of gold in the deep brown there. He seemed at a loss for words, but Riordan let him find them, not wanting to push past any boundary that kept Wade comfortable.

"Yes?" he finally said.

"That sounds like a question." Wade bit his bottom lip hard enough the skin there went white from the pressure. Riordan couldn't stop himself from reaching up with his free hand to cup Wade's jaw, using his thumb to gently pry his lip free. "Try again."

Wade drew in a breath that Riordan wanted to chase. "Yes."

This time, the answer was softer, less questioning, but the way that Wade held himself, it was as if he were bracing for a hit. Riordan telegraphed every move he made as he leaned in close, tilting his head only a little since they were nearly of height and pressing his lips to Wade's. He kept the pressure gentle, parting his lips after a moment to flick his tongue over Wade's lips. It was easy to step closer, to lick past Wade's teeth, to kiss him with a careful thoroughness that made Riordan's lungs tighten. The sweetness of their ice cream lingered on his tongue. Wade's response was clumsy, sweet in a way that told Riordan he probably hadn't done this much.

Riordan let go of Wade's hand and settled it on Wade's hip,

which had the unintended effect of causing Wade to jerk back, breaking the kiss, and wrench himself out of Riordan's grip. Riordan immediately froze, staring at where Wade stood just out of arm's reach, breathing a little heavily. It wasn't the reaction Riordan had hoped for; it told him more than he thought Wade realized.

He had to force his voice to stay quiet, to hold back the fury he felt at whoever had hurt Wade in the past to make him react like this. "Are you all right?"

Wade raised his hand to touch his lips, brow furrowed, not looking at Riordan. His breathing had eased some, but Riordan wasn't going to try to crowd him. "Is that what it's supposed to feel like when you kiss someone?"

The words were a mutter, not really directed to Riordan, but they were the catalyst for a fury that sluiced through him like a riptide. "Who hurt you?"

Wade raised his head, blinking at him in surprise, as if he'd forgotten Riordan was there with him. He stared at Riordan, eyes wide, and for a second, Riordan thought his pupils had changed shape.

Wade laughed a little weakly, waving off Riordan's question. "It's nothing. Can we try that again?"

"It's something."

"Just a memory."

Considering the memory had Wade jerking out of his arms, Riordan knew he was going to have to be careful with touch going forward. "Are you sure you want to try kissing me again?"

"Yes." Wade spoke quickly, but there wasn't any scent of fear in the air between them—nothing sour or bitter. He could've been hiding it, putting up a front that Riordan wouldn't be able to see through. Only Wade was looking at him with a curious sort of longing in those brown eyes that Riordan didn't have it in himself to deny.

He stepped closer, easing into Wade's space. Riordan framed Wade's face with one hand, amazed at how warm he felt, like he'd been soaking in sunlight the way a cat might. This time, Riordan kissed Wade with a carefulness that deepened slowly, letting Wade set the pace. Fingers curled around the fabric of his T-shirt, Wade's palm pressing against his chest. He thought, for a moment, Wade was going to pull him closer.

But then Wade shoved him away with a strength that had Riordan nearly falling to the ground in shock, arms windmilling, the remnants of his ice-cream cone going flying. "What—"

Something hot and sharp skimmed across his rib cage. A burning, hideous pain stabbed through his chest, and Riordan curled around the wound iron had made in him with a shocked gasp.

Wade lashed out, hand a blur as he gripped air and *yanked*—and a dagger fell to the ground, clattering over the pathway. He snarled, fingers—no, *claws*—digging into something Riordan couldn't see until he did. Glamour peeled away from Wade's claws, the bright, rainbow lines of magic sloughing off like a weaving coming undone.

The fae held in Wade's grip was dressed in jeans, a Boston Bruins T-shirt, and leather gloves, sharply pointed ears poking out of his shoulder-length honey-colored hair. The fae's other hand was a blur as he reached for the knife on his belt, but it never connected. Wade opened his mouth and belched a literal plume of fire directly in the fae's face, eradicating their head.

Riordan stared in stunned silence at the red scales crawling up Wade's neck and jaw, spreading across his cheeks. More red scales pushed through the skin of his forearms, shining in the sunlight as he shoved the corpse over the side of the railing. A distant splash told Riordan it had made it to the water.

When Wade turned to face him, those brown eyes Riordan had enjoyed staring into were now a vivid gold, bisected by reptilian pupils, and Wade's teeth, when he scowled, were more like fangs. That pressure in the air Riordan remembered from Beacon Hill was back, like he was kneeling before something huge, even if all he could see was Wade.

The fae was dead.

Riordan had an iron wound in his side.

All of that was secondary to the visceral truth Riordan couldn't deny—that Wade was a *dragon*.

No wonder Carmen called him fledgling.

He blinked, and in that scant second, the scales on Wade's body disappeared, and his eyes were back to that particular shade of brown Riordan had found so arresting.

"Riordan!" Wade cried out, rushing over to him. "You're hurt!"

The cut along his ribs ached, and he knew without needing to look that the skin around the wound would be bubbling up like a bad burn. "I'm all right."

Wade made a face. "You know, when my pack says dumb shit like that, I don't believe them, so I'm not going to believe you."

Riordan gently grabbed Wade's wrist, giving it a careful squeeze. "Not the time. You killed a fae in public."

Wade scowled. "Do you think I'd let the asshole hurt you?"

"No. Never. But Wade, someone probably saw that." The Harborwalk wasn't empty, and while it wasn't peak tourist season, someone had to have seen the attack.

Wade shook his head, his other hand already tugging at Riordan's shirt. "No one ever sees me if I don't want them to these days. Let me look at your wound."

"After we get out of here." Riordan let go of Wade and shoved himself to his feet, gritting his teeth against the burning pain that erupted along his ribs with every brush of his T-shirt against the wound. Such a shallow cut would be ignorable if it hadn't come from a blade made of iron.

"Are you like a werecreature where you shift and the wound goes away?" Wade asked as he scrambled to his feet.

Riordan hesitated before nodding. "Similar, yes. But it's harder to heal from iron."

A brief flash of incandescent rage swept over Wade's eyes, turning them gold for half a second. "I should've eaten the bastard."

Riordan really shouldn't have felt so pleased about that reaction.

"It would've been better if you'd left him alive. We could have questioned him."

Wade scoffed. "In my experience, people like that fae don't ever talk when cornered. It's not worth the headache. He was probably working for Niall."

"Making assumptions won't help us."

Wade sidled in close on Riordan's good side, and Riordan took the opportunity to sling his arm over Wade's shoulders. He didn't really need the assistance, but he wasn't going to deny himself the chance to hold Wade close. "It's not an assumption. Lady Caith knows what pack I belong to, and she knows the alliances we brokered before the Battle of Samhain that brought Brigid into the fight. She won't go against me, which means she won't go against you or Ella because she knows doing that will piss me off. That leaves Niall the bastard."

Riordan couldn't fault his reasoning. "He *is* a bastard."

"Yup. Now, let's get you home."

Luckily, the wound wasn't deep or bleeding very much. Riordan didn't leave a blood trail back to the car or stain the leather once Wade deposited him in the seat. The ache of the cut and the iron burn was impossible to ignore. Riordan gritted his teeth during the entire drive back home in South Boston while Wade chatted away at him, worried and nervous in equal measure it seemed like.

They were almost home when Riordan finally gave in to his own desire to calm Wade down by reaching over to settle his hand on Wade's thigh. The younger man cut off midsentence, head snapping around to stare at him with wide eyes.

"Watch the road," Riordan cajoled in a low voice through clenched teeth. "I'm fine."

"I still don't believe you."

He'd be better once he slathered the wound with the salve he and his siblings kept in their first aid kit. A first aid kit that Saoirse met them with at the door once they finally got inside the house, having been warned in advance by a text from Wade.

"Niall's trying to murder you now," Saoirse said, her face pale and eyes haunted.

"I think it was a warning," Riordan grunted as Wade deposited him on the living room couch with easy strength.

"Some warning. Get your shirt off. Donal's bringing down your skin."

Riordan was going to take his shirt off the normal way, but Wade did it for him through sheer expediency by grabbing the collar and tearing the fabric down to the hem. "Hey!"

"It was ruined anyway," Wade said, staring with narrowed eyes at the wound now on display.

Riordan glanced down at his chest, wincing at the slashing burn crawling across his rib cage. The touch of iron was never easy for fae to bear. Those that lived in cities learned to ignore the muffling sense of being surrounded by what amounted to an iron jungle. But touching iron was not something fae did willingly, and the blackened, blistered wound cutting over his ribs was why.

"Hold still," Saoirse warned, already unscrewing the jar that held the magicked healing balm they paid a pretty price for. She slathered the cream over his wound, and the hideous heat of it eased. The pain became something ignorable for the moment, and he let out a thankful sigh.

Donal came into the living room, eyeing Riordan worriedly. "The tub is ready."

"Okay," Riordan said, not yet moving.

"Do you need help?" Wade asked.

"I can make it upstairs on my own."

And he did, with Wade following right behind him rather than his siblings. Riordan was intensely aware of Wade's presence as he joined Riordan in the bathroom he and his siblings had renovated years ago. They'd knocked out a wall and lost half the home office space at the time, but it'd been well worth it for times like this.

Wade whistled softly, taking in the tile stained in shades of blue to make it look like the ocean that covered the floor and walls all the way up to the ceiling. The extra-large, claw-foot bathtub taking up much of the space was presently half-filled with cool water, Riordan's sealskin draped over the curled edge. With a sigh, he started stripping out of the rest of his clothes, prompting him to look over his shoulder at the sound Wade made. Wade was staring up at the ceiling, a flush darkening his cheeks.

"I'll just be leaving," he said.

Riordan kicked his jeans and underwear aside. "Or you could stay."

"Yes, but—" Wade waved his hand in Riordan's direction, still not looking at him. "You're, uh, naked."

Riordan laughed and then instantly regretted it as the wound pulled along his ribs. "You're part of a god pack and surrounded by werecreatures. Aren't they ever naked?"

"No! I mean, yes, but it's not polite to look."

"I don't mind you looking." Wade's face turned an interesting shade of red that was really quite lovely. But Riordan wasn't in the market of making the other man uncomfortable. He reached for his sealskin and wrapped it around his shoulders before stepping into the tub and sinking down into the water. "It's all right. You can look now."

Wade hesitated before dropping his gaze from the ceiling and meeting Riordan's. "Sorry."

"Nothing to be sorry about."

Riordan took a breath and leaned back into the water, his sealskin flowing over his limbs, sliding into his very being. The shift pulled at him, dragging forth the bones and body of a seal out of the human form he lived half his life in. With a twist, he shifted into a seal, the burn of the iron wound disappearing. He slapped his flippers against the side of the tub, sending water splashing over the sides.

"Oh, wow. You're adorable."

Riordan snorted at that, lifting his head and peering up at where Wade now knelt by the tub. He hefted himself up to be at eye level with the younger man, whiskers twitching, and pressed his sensitive nose against Wade's, who laughed and reached out to carefully run his hand over Riordan's head. He twisted his head into the touch and chuffed happily.

"How's your wound?"

In answer, Riordan raised a flipper, showing off the area along his side where the wound had been. While the cut was now healed, there was some discoloration in his fur that spoke of bruising he'd have in human form once he shifted again.

Wade laid his hand gently over the discoloration, and Riordan pressed his nose to Wade's cheek. Wade ducked his head, laughing quietly. "I'm glad you're okay."

Riordan slid down into the tub and twisted, spinning through a shift and rising up as a human, sealskin draped over his lap and a deep bruise pressed over his ribs. He came nose to nose with Wade again, staring into warm brown eyes, wanting nothing more than to kiss him. "I never said thank you for stopping that fae."

"You don't owe me anything."

"And if I want to?"

"Debts are shitty. I won't give you one."

"Then just give me you."

Wade huffed out a breath that Riordan swallowed in a kiss, ignoring the pooling warmth in his gut.

"You're lucky you're cute as a human and as a seal," Wade grumbled when they parted.

Riordan laughed and got to his feet, sealskin still wrapped around his waist like a towel. "Come on. I'm going to lie down for a bit. You can lie down with me."

"Uh, just sleep, right?"

Riordan took Wade's hand and gave it a gentle squeeze. "Just sleep."

He led Wade out of the bathroom and down the hall toward his bedroom, the space mostly clean. He tugged on a pair of boxers and then pulled at his sealskin, letting it wrap around his arms and torso in a soft cardigan sweater.

"Can your sealskin turn into anything?" Wade asked.

"Usually, we keep it as some kind of coat."

"Makes sense."

Wade hadn't made any move toward the bed, still standing in the middle of the bedroom. Riordan tilted his head, studying Wade. "You don't have to stay while I heal if you don't want to."

"I want to," Wade said swiftly, which might have been sheer bravado on his part if Riordan was reading his reactions right. "I just, uh, I might elbow you?"

"Wade. You don't have to stay."

Wade's lips twisted, some of his nervous energy causing him to shift on his feet. "I really do want to."

"It's just sleeping. I promise. I will always ask for what you want."

Wade stared at him, eyes unblinking, before drawing a steeling sort of breath. "Thanks."

Riordan throttled the urge to commit murder on Wade's behalf, knowing that someone, at some point, had violated Wade's boundaries in a way that still reverberated through his reactions. But he wasn't going to ask, and Wade would hopefully tell him if he pushed for too much at any point.

Instead of giving voice to anger that had no place in the bedroom, Riordan coaxed Wade to lie down with him, wrapping the younger man up in his arms and burrowing his nose in dark hair, breathing him in.

"You're better than medicine," Riordan muttered.

Wade let out a slightly choked-out laugh, hands hesitantly plucking at Riordan's sealskin in fabric form. "If you say so."

"I do."

And he meant it. The nap that afternoon was one of the best Riordan had experienced in decades.

CHAPTER TWELVE

"This reminds me of the Upper East Side," Wade said as he got out of the car.

Riordan shoved open his door and got out as well, squinting against the sunlight. "Because it's a rich neighborhood?"

"Yeah. I bet my condo goes for more than these though."

"Maybe one day, I'll see it."

Wade beamed in a way that made him look younger than he was. But then Riordan was reminded of the way he'd backtalked Carmen yesterday. Wade might seem younger, but he'd definitely gone through a lot in his twenty-three years. His confidence was why Riordan found himself standing in front of the home belonging to the Faneuil Coven's high priestess on a Friday morning. Gwen Cattaneo had agreed to a meeting today at Wade's insistence, something Riordan doubted she'd have granted his clan if they'd been the ones asking.

Riordan was tagging along because he wasn't leaving Wade alone. He'd brought his sealskin with him in the form of his usual leather jacket. The weather wasn't so hot yet that he'd get strange looks for his choice of attire. After getting tailed by one of Niall's fae yesterday when running errands in the afternoon, he and Donal had decided not to leave their sealskins behind. They didn't want to risk Niall trying to steal them from their home while they were out.

Riordan and his clan typically steered clear of magic users. Boston was an epicenter for magic, with witches being the predominant type of magic users calling the city and its surrounding towns home. Their numbers had risen and fallen over the decades, with one stretch of history where they'd all gone to ground during the Salem Witch Trials. Territory borders had fluctuated during that time, one of the reasons his clan had been able to claim the shoreline and keep it when they'd arrived in Boston.

The kin kept to themselves and rarely made overtures to the other supernatural and preternatural communities in Boston. He didn't know Gwen personally, only knew the retired major through press releases. She'd taken over the Faneuil Coven two years ago, having been ready to retire when the Battle of Samhain had happened and staying on for the fight and a bit after to see things settled. That was the sort of commitment to duty and people Riordan understood, and he hoped their meeting wouldn't become antagonistic, even with Wade to smooth things over.

Riordan followed Wade up the steps to the porch of the redbrick building that probably went for a cool million dollars easy. Back Bay was an expensive neighborhood to call home, though not as expensive as Beacon Hill. Wade rapped his knuckles on the door, and it opened almost instantly. The young man who answered it seemed to be expecting them.

"Mr. Espinoza," the greeter said politely.

"That makes me sound old. Just Wade is fine," Wade said.

"Wade, then. And is your companion part of your god pack?"

"I'm Bostonian at this point," Riordan said. "Fae if that matters to any of the wards in your home."

He could sense the magic in the walls of the building, a deep well of it that meant the wards were probably laid into the foundation and at least a few decades old. That sort of magic came with a strength he'd rather not be on the wrong side of.

Wariness that hadn't been in the young man's gaze when looking at Wade filled his eyes now. "We weren't informed fae would be joining Wade."

"Riordan is with me. We'll do hospitality if it makes you feel any better," Wade said.

"It would. Come inside, please."

Taking hospitality from a coven wasn't much different than taking it from the fae. Perhaps the bread was a tad stale, but the ice water was refreshing. Wade seemed disappointed at the offering but ate it anyway. "Is Gwen ready to see us?"

"Our high priestess will take the meeting in the ground-floor office. If you'll follow me," the young man said. He still hadn't offered his name, but Riordan opted not to be insulted by the lack of manners. Most people didn't like giving up names to the fae.

Wade leaned in, lowering his voice to just barely above a whisper, but Riordan heard him just fine. "Lady Caith's offering for hospitality was tastier."

It made him stifle a laugh, forcing his expression into bland neutrality when their escort glanced back.

They were led through a neatly furnished home that felt lived in when it came to the small details: a throw blanket tossed haphazardly over a couch in the front room they passed, someone's keys in a glass bowl on a hallway credenza, the books scattered across the dining room table. Riordan could hear voices echoing from the kitchen that he couldn't see as they walked on by the dining area. The ground-floor office was in the back of the building, overlooking a backyard that was full of rosebushes. The window was open to let in the breeze and, with it, the cloying scent of those very same roses.

"High priestess, your guests," the young man said with a formal nod. "Wade arrived with a fae. Hospitality was given."

Gwen looked up from her laptop, blond hair pulled back in a tight bun. Her face was a bit weathered, and even sitting down, she held herself with the straight-backed carriage of one used to parade rest in the military. She wore a neat blouse today rather than a uniform, but she'd worn her uniform just as well, judging by the numerous pictures of her military career hanging on the wall. Two bookcases framed the window behind her, and a side table held an altar, one with a half-melted candle, glossy black feathers, and carved runes.

"Not Persephone, I hope," Wade said with a strange flatness to his voice as he jerked his thumb at the altar in question.

Gwen raised an eyebrow and closed her laptop. "No. My coven worships the Morrígan."

Wade winced. "Uh, not much better."

"I take it you don't believe in our goddess?"

"I believe in too many of them. I just don't *like* any of them."

Gwen stood, coming around the desk to size them both up before offering her hand first to Wade, then to Riordan. "I understand you're here about a territory problem."

"It's your problem as well."

"That remains to be seen. Take a seat. Anywhere you like is fine." Wade opted for the small love seat sofa opposite the altar, and Riordan joined him there, sitting so close their thighs touched. Gwen dragged one of the wing-backed chairs in front of her desk over to them and sat down. "My secretary said you wished to speak to me about a threat."

Wade nodded. "We think a fae is targeting the leaders of the supernatural and preternatural communities in Boston. You're on that list."

"No one in my coven or any others have come to me with reports of being targeted by the fae." Her gaze cut Riordan's way, politely curious in a way he didn't quite trust. "I wasn't aware the kin were in the crosshairs."

Riordan smiled thinly. "It's a recent issue. But we aren't the only ones who have been targeted. The Boston god pack alphas were both taken by Niall, a fae exiled from Underhill. We're trying to find them, as well as something Niall stole from my clan."

Her gaze dropped from his face to his jacket. "Not your skin, but someone else's, I assume?"

Riordan didn't respond to that question. He didn't know Gwen and wasn't about to trust her with the personal details of his clan. She seemed to take his silence as agreement though, which wasn't far off the mark.

"Why reach out to my coven?" she asked.

"Because you're the leader of the most powerful coven in Boston. You hold sway over a lot of magic users, and you're also a mage. I'm guessing Niall wants to control magic users or maybe drive them out and claim your territory as his. I don't know. It's a guessing game at this point, but the consequences have been ugly so far," Wade said.

"And you want my help?"

She sounded skeptical, which Riordan could understand. His clan and the kin didn't mingle with magic users much. He didn't know what sort of relationship the Boston god pack had with the covens. Ella wasn't there to speak for her pack because she'd needed to mediate a territory dispute today between three packs. They'd promised to speak for her though.

"We want the covens to be aware of the threat. Niall won't stop until he's claimed Boston. If it takes years or decades, he'll do it, but we don't think it'll take that long," Riordan said.

"We're pretty sure he's going after the master vampire of the Boston Night Court next. Either that, or he's going to try to negotiate an alliance with them and then probably stab Abby Boy in the heart at some point," Wade said.

Gwen's gaze sharpened, and she leaned forward. "He's targeting Abhartach?"

"He's the next logical choice. We have a meeting with his Night Court tonight."

"And he actually agreed to it?"

"Yes," Wade said with a surprisingly straight face. He didn't mention Lucien, so Riordan held his tongue on that detail as well. "My pack has dealt with vampires before, and I told Ella I'd help keep her pack and Riordan's clan safe when we met up tonight. But Patrick couldn't come to Boston with me, and we're kind of short on magic users. I was wondering if you had any artifacts we could borrow or buy for defensive purposes?"

"Most people would request a magic user themselves when going into vampire territory."

"The fewer people involved, the fewer people there are who can become targets," Riordan said.

"Your magic isn't capable of protecting them?"

Riordan smiled, teeth sharp against his lips, stung by the insult but refusing to show it. "I'm here, aren't I?"

"Hey, that's a little rude. Riordan's doing just fine," Wade said, scowling.

Gwen raised a hand in a calming manner. "I don't mean any disrespect. I'm well aware of how magic differs."

"Then you'll give us an artifact? I just need one that has a shield ward for them."

"Not for yourself?"

"Do you have one?"

Gwen sighed. "An artifact spelled with a shield ward is something we have in our inventory. My coven is not in the habit of selling or loaning them out, but I know Patrick Collins wouldn't have sent you here if there truly wasn't a problem."

"You are in danger, whether you believe us or not," Riordan said.

Wade nodded in agreement. "Yeah, this Niall guy is definitely an asshole. If your coven hasn't been targeted yet, that's great, but that doesn't mean it won't be. We're trying to stop him before he hits anyone else."

"If you're asking for an alliance—" Gwen said.

"I'm not," Riordan cut in. "And I doubt Ella will as well."

He'd speak on Ella's behalf, but he wouldn't speak for her about an alliance without her input. Neither would he place his clan in a quid pro quo position with a coven. Wade initiating the request kept Riordan and his clan from being boxed into a corner, bound by a promise. Fae didn't make promises lightly. Oh, they'd scheme to get a mortal or any other creature to tie themselves to a bargain, but it was rare any fae was the one offering. Fae were taught from a young age that words were a weapon as well as a trap.

"I don't have the authority to ask for any alliance. Boston isn't my territory, and only Patrick and Jono have the authority in my god pack to do something like that," Wade said.

"I understand. But because it is the New York City god pack asking for an artifact of protection, I will let you borrow one of our artifacts spelled with defensive wards," Gwen said.

Wade smiled at her. "Thanks. You should still be on the lookout for threats from the fae."

"I'll warn the members of my coven."

"Niall would be after you since you're their high priestess."

"I'm a combat mage and was in the Mage Corps for twenty years, but I'll take your warning under advisement." Gwen stood and went to open her office door, poking her head out in the hallway. "Grab me the warded box with the crystals from the room upstairs."

Whoever had been standing guard outside the office murmured an affirmative before leaving. Gwen returned to her seat, neatly crossing her ankles.

"We appreciate the help," Wade said.

"It's a temporary loan. I'll expect it returned to me."

"Yup."

A few minutes later, the same young man who had answered the front door stepped into the office, carrying a carved wooden box, the glossy stain on it reflecting the light. Gwen took it and pressed her thumb to the pentagram carved above a metal latch. Soft mauve light cascaded over the box, following the carved lines before disappearing. She opened the box, and Riordan let the hint of magic that escaped it wash past him. "I can offer one artifact. The shield wards aren't military grade and aren't meant to cover more than a handful of people."

"How big is a handful?" Riordan asked.

"Four at the most, but you'd have to be close to each other. The structure of the ward has a limited range."

"That will be fine." It would cover his siblings and himself, along with Wade, though he wondered if it would even work on Wade. Hospitality didn't, and that was old magic in the sense that a home's threshold had been around as long as mortals had.

Gwen lifted a violet quartz crystal hanging from a metal chain out of the warded box. The crystal was carved into a flat disk with a sigil etched into one side. She offered it to Wade, who took it and tossed it from hand to hand before he passed it over to Riordan. "You should wear it."

Wade dropped the crystal onto his palm, the magic lending weight to it he doubted most people could sense. It wasn't magic he was familiar with—his magic dealt with shifting and the sea—but Riordan figured he could handle it easily enough. "What's the command trigger?"

Gwen voiced the phrase, the English words easy enough to remember. Riordan hung the chain with the artifact around his neck, letting the crystal settle against his chest. He'd give it to Saoirse once he made it home.

Warning given, temporary artifact acquired, Riordan felt the meeting was done. He stood, nodding politely at Gwen. "We'll return it tomorrow."

He didn't say thank you, and she didn't seem to expect it of him, judging by the faint quirk of her lips. "I'll look forward to the delivery."

They were escorted out of the coven's home by the same young man as before. The door shut nearly on their heels, which made Riordan snort. Wade seemed just as amused. "I don't think that guy liked us."

"He didn't mind you all that much. It's more that he probably doesn't like fae."

Wade scrunched his nose. "Sage is always on me about manners. He could use some."

Riordan wasn't a stranger to discrimination. It was only one of the many reasons fae used glamour to hide themselves amongst mortals. But he thought it was sweet that Wade was affronted on his behalf.

Riordan tugged on the crystal hanging around his neck, the quiescent magic tickling his palm. "Why don't you travel with something like this?"

"Because I don't need it. But Patrick is still in DC, and I wanted something for you and your siblings. I figured we had to warn Gwen anyway, and what was the harm in asking for some magical help?"

It was a kind gesture, one Riordan hadn't experienced in a long time from someone who wasn't clan. It made him want to wrap Wade up in his jacket, offer up his sealskin, and let the younger man keep him. He swallowed against the visceral *want* of that desire, knowing it was the fixation talking.

It was so tempting to listen to it.

"Thank you."

Wade mock frowned at him. "You don't owe me anything."

"I know." He tugged on Wade's elbow, drawing him close to kiss him on the mouth, just a soft press of lips. "But it's okay if it's you."

"That's just stupidly unfair," Wade mumbled against his lips before kissing back a little harder, a little clumsily. Riordan indulged him there on the sidewalk for a few seconds more, tugging him closer, enjoying the warmth that bled through Wade's clothes. Despite the sun beating down on them, Riordan didn't mind the heat.

"Come on. I'll text Ailín we're heading to the sailing club. He'll meet us out front."

"Okay, but I'm bringing some snacks with us on the boat. It's not like they have a sail-through Dunkin' out there."

Riordan snorted. "Are you going to share them, or do I need to bring my own?"

Wade reached up to pat his cheek. "You're lucky you're cute. My pack knows better than to ask a dumb question like that."

Riordan arched an eyebrow, letting himself be tugged down the sidewalk back to the car, Wade's hand warm in his. "I'm cute, am I?"

"I wouldn't say it if I didn't mean it."

"You can say whatever you like to me, *mo chroí.*"

Wade's flush at the endearment was almost as cute as the way his ass looked in his jeans. His smile was pleased though, and Riordan was proud of the fact that, when he let go of Wade's hand to wrap an arm around his shoulders, Wade didn't pull away.

CHAPTER THIRTEEN

The drive to the Boston Harbor Sailing Club in Downtown Boston was thankfully uneventful. Ailín met them in front of the building, waving at Riordan as they walked up. Ailín was clan, a selkie who also owned a small yacht they used to take the handful of human members of the clan out to sea to join them for a swim. Riordan had requested yesterday for him to take Wade out onto the water while Riordan did his search around the smaller islands in Boston Harbor.

They didn't know where Niall might hide Saoirse's skin, but they were covering all their bases. And Riordan needed to patrol the shoreline anyway, Lady Caith's warning still stark in his thoughts. He didn't know if whatever he'd sensed in the water the other day was aligned with Niall, but if Niall was going after Boston, it stood to reason he'd claim the harbor as well.

"Riordan," Ailín said with a nod. "We're reserved for launch."

"Thanks," Riordan said.

Ailín eyed Wade intently, but there wasn't any malice in his gaze. Riordan didn't know what his siblings had been gossiping about with the clan, but Ailín's focus told him they'd probably mentioned Wade. "You must be the lad our clan chief is spending time with."

"Is that a bad thing?" Wade asked.

"Not unless you mean harm."

Riordan sighed. "I get enough teasing from my siblings. You don't need to start."

"Boyo, the whole clan is going to start" was Ailín's cheerful response before he turned on his heels. "Come on, let's get on the water."

The Boston Harbor Sailing Club was open to the public for lessons and sometimes tours, but being members meant they could head directly for the water. Riordan spotted the launch boat at the small pier, manned by an employee of the club. Directly beyond it, sailboats and small yachts of all kinds bobbed gently in the water, moored away from the shore.

"How many boats do you have?" Wade asked as they approached the small pier.

"We try to keep at least three on hand, moored or anchored in different locations. It was easier to shift on the shoreline when Boston wasn't so built up. These days, if we're swimming as a clan, some of us will shift at the shore, and the rest of us will do so in open water," Riordan said.

The sailing club employee gave them a cheerful hello once they reached the launch boat. They checked Ailín's paperwork for the appropriate mooring location and then set about releasing the boat from the dock to ferry them to the clan's yacht. The *Neptune* was thirty-five feet in length and capable of being handled by only one person if they knew what they were doing.

Everyone in the clan knew what they were doing in the water and on a boat. Ailín didn't need any help getting the *Neptune* unmoored once they were onboard. The launch boat pulled back with a dull roar of engines, heading back to shore. Riordan guided Wade to a bench near the cockpit so they could stay out of the way as Ailín went through the launch prep procedure before he finally untied the yacht from its mooring.

Ailín retreated to the cockpit, and a few seconds later, the engine roared to life, the sound of it vibrating through the deck. Wade looked around curiously as Ailín steered them out of the mooring area and into the open harbor waters, engines propelling them forward through the Boston Main Channel. Riordan had seen it all plenty of times before and was more interested in watching Wade. He manfully ignored Ailín's chuckling at the controls.

"This is pretty cool. I can see why you like Boston," Wade said, twisting around on the bench so he could take in the Boston skyline as they sailed away from it. Riordan couldn't help wrapping his arm around Wade's waist, holding him in place. "How far does your clan territory stretch?"

"We share the water with kin. No one owns the sea," Riordan said.

"Niall wants to."

"Yes."

Wade turned back around to better see him, the lenses of his sunglasses carrying a few stray droplets of water from the breeze. "I won't let him."

Riordan smiled, trying to choke back all the twisted emotion tied to the bitter position he'd been put in. He wanted to believe Wade could help, but Riordan wasn't going to let the younger man risk himself in any way. He couldn't live with himself if he let that happen. So he said nothing in the face of that promise, merely closed the distance to kiss Wade, letting himself catalogue the taste of him, the way he felt pressed so close.

It didn't take very long until they made it out of the Boston Main Channel and were far enough from any nearby boats and barges before Ailín gave him the all-clear signal. "You can shift now."

Riordan reluctantly pulled away from Wade and stood, the movement of the yacht something he easily compensated for. He took a moment to scan the horizon, mentally placing where the yacht was in relation to where he'd be swimming. The Boston Harbor Islands and National State Park was an area his clan and the whole kin in Boston knew well. The clans shared patrol duties, and Riordan knew he wasn't the only one who'd been sensing something off in the waters lately. Lady Caith's warning had been enough for him to sound the alarm with every clan that no one should swim alone.

It was why he had Ailín with him, even though the other man wasn't going to join him below the waves. He'd follow along behind Riordan's underwater trajectory, sticking close and keeping an eye on Wade. "I'll do a circuit around Spectacle Island first and then Long Island. I don't want to go too far out since we have plans tonight."

They were still expected to meet with Abhartach at the master vampire's absinthe bar, and Riordan knew they couldn't miss it. But neither could he shirk his duty as clan chief, not while he still held them.

He shrugged out of his jacket, some deep part of him wanting to turn and hand it to Wade for safekeeping for the handful of minutes it would take him to undress. He swallowed against the urge, doing the expected thing instead and handing his jacket to Ailín.

"I can go with you," Ailín said.

Riordan shook his head. "Stay above with Wade. He doesn't know how to handle a yacht."

Ailín nodded, not arguing his order the way Donal might, but not looking comfortable with it either. Riordan pulled his T-shirt off and stripped out of the rest of his clothes with a perfunctory ease he didn't really think about, not until he clued in to the flush on Wade's face and the way he jerked his gaze away from Riordan. The fact that he'd been looking and hopefully liked what he saw made Riordan want to preen.

Focus.

"Good hunting," Ailín said, handing back his jacket. Riordan slipped his arms through the sleeves, warmth bleeding into his skin.

"Yeah, don't let anything eat you," Wade said.

"Except you?" Riordan couldn't help but ask before diving overboard. Wade's embarrassed squawk became muted by the water that closed over Riordan's head, muffling the world.

The water was cold, the brief shock of it a welcome sensation. Riordan somersaulted forward, sealskin clinging to his body and flowing down his limbs. His legs fused together, fingers too, body expanding into the massive sleek shape of a seal. He used his flippers to propel himself to the surface, head breaking the waves. He unclenched his nose, breathing in a lungful of air, and stared up at the human faces peering over the side of the yacht.

"You fit better in the bay than the bathtub," Wade told him. Riordan barked at him and slapped the surface with one fin. Wade laughed at him. "Go swim. We'll follow."

Riordan dived back underwater, the sounds of ships in the bay distant, muffled vibrations against his body and in his ears. Everything sounded so different in his seal form like this. He could distinguish individual noises and place their location better than with his fae ears on land. While selkies didn't have any echolocation abilities built into their bodies, his magic more than made up for it.

The sea was where selkies thrived; being bound to someone on land against their will meant they would never fully be able to access their magic again. It was tied to their skin, to the vast world they swam through. Their magic would always lead them home, and the cruelest path back would be to follow that ever-present tug and stand on the shore of the place you couldn't visit anymore.

Riordan shook off those thoughts and swam faster, as if he could outswim the problems menacing his clan. The waterways of the harbor were busy today, but he knew best how to steer clear of the various ships traversing the waves. He came up out of a deeper dive and broke the surface, drawing in another lungful of air. Spectacle Island was closer now, the rocky shore fading into greenery that hadn't yet turned brown from summer's heat. Riordan slid back underwater again, swimming through its depths. The push and pull of the tides ebbed against his body as he swam, instinct guiding him around the underwater borders of the island.

Part of this kind of border patrol was to hunt out any water-based threats or encroachment on all the clans' territory. Selkies couldn't scent mark like werecreatures could, but they still marked their territory by embedding bits of their magic in the seabed. The marked points were centuries old at this point, so rich with magic that they shone like lighthouse beacons to his underwater sight. Riordan swam around one particularly large rock protruding from the seabed, nosing around the markings someone had clawed into the stone so long ago. In the murky darkness, the sigils glowed a soft violet in his sight, and he added a bit of his own to what was already there. The pull of it stretched away from the point of contact, disappearing into the depths.

Long gone were the days when the clans could lay active spells to guard their territory. The explosiveness of those spells drew too much attention, and no clan wanted to be responsible for causing the human government to target them. That way lay too many problems. Their kind thrived best when no one knew they walked or swam among mortals. To that end, the border magic was passive, a kind of magical warning system scattered throughout the bay. Selkies could touch that magic and get feedback on any broken area that needed looking into.

Like now.

The dull, discordant vibration that tickled down Riordan's spine made him spin in a tight circle around the sigil stone, the thread of damage tugging his awareness eastward. It wrapped around the southern tip of the small island, passing through other sigils, following the hint of damage to an area closer to the open ocean than the shore—coming from the same direction that unnerving sound had stemmed from the other day.

Riordan swam another circle around the sigil, getting his bearings, before swimming back to the surface and breaking it, getting another breath and to check where the *Neptune* was in the water. He got a flash of it in his peripheral vision, Ailín keeping up with long practice and the familiarity of how they all swam the borders. He dove back under, picking up speed and swimming beneath the waves. Water flowed past him, the murkiness navigable with the help of magic. He swam beneath a handful of sailboats out enjoying the summer day and ignored the distant noise of a cargo ship's engine vibrating through the water.

He followed the ping of broken magic to the southern tip of Spectacle Island, his trajectory through the water curving east. He worried about what could have damaged a sigil stone in the net and when it might have happened. None of the other clans had indicated the warning system had been hit, which meant it must have been recent, possibly even today, and he couldn't ignore the possibility it was Niall's doing.

All of his worry, all of his planning, fled his thoughts as the flow of water changed and something rose up from the seabed floor to slam into him and career them both through the water.

All the air exploded out of his lungs, bubbles fizzing past his eyes as the water twisted into the shape of a nightmare around him. Riordan clamped his nostrils down tight, but there was no air left in his lungs as a fuath wrapped its arms around his body. Claws raked over his skin, clouding the water with his blood. Riordan twisted, jerking his head to the side, trying to bite at its throat. The fuath jerked, its arms loosening a fraction, but it was enough for Riordan to get free with a punch of magic that created a whirlpool at the end of his rear flippers to propel him to the surface. He broke through with a thick gasp, sucking in air, managing a few warning barks that carried through the air with another burst of magic before he hit the water again and went under.

This time, he was prepared.

Nostrils closed tight, air locked in his lungs, Riordan swam after the fuath, following the eddies in its wake as it dived deep. What might have passed as bioluminescence in anything else outlined its body in pale, pale blue, giving breadth to long limbs with spines running down the length and webbed fingers, eyes that took up half its face and a gaping mouth that took up the rest. As it twisted and came hurtling back toward him, Riordan could just make out the stream of kelp that passed as hair beneath the bubbles that sloughed off it.

Riordan met its underwater charge with his own, slamming his body into its scaly one. Fuath were water spirits, a kind of fae that haunted any body of water, be it fresh or salt, large or small, hunting for prey. It clearly seemed to think Riordan was in that category, and he went about disabusing it of that notion by tearing a chunk out of its side with his very sharp teeth.

Bitter blood filled his mouth and the water around them, darkening the area like squid ink. The fuath screamed in a way that was more vibrations than anything else, a dull sound that pressed all along his body. Riordan spat out the chunk of flesh resting on his tongue and kicked all four flippers, swimming out of reach of the claws that sought revenge. He sped for the surface, needing more air in his lungs, and had almost reached it when another fuath hurtled through the water from the north. Riordan somersaulted out of the way in a tight spin, reorienting himself in a matter of seconds. He made it to the surface, broke through the waves, and managed to bark another warning and suck in one lungful of air before something slimy wrapped around one of his rear flippers and *yanked*.

He went under.

The speed at which the fuath dragged him to the bottom of the bay to drown him left Riordan's entire body spinning. He broke the motion by diving down instead of trying to kick free, aiming for the threat with sharp teeth and a blast of water magic that rippled away from him. It hit the fuath like a wave slamming against the rock, forcing the water spirit's tentacle to let go of his flipper. Riordan kicked free, swimming after the fuath with the intent to kill it, but had to pull up with a hard twist as the other fuath attempted to attack from behind.

Claws raked his side as he spun away, lips pulled back over sharp teeth as he bared them in warning at the fuath. The pair of water spirits regrouped, the faintly glowing outlines of their bodies brightening the bottom waters of the bay. With an open-mouthed echoing scream, the fuath attacked, trying to somehow box him in. Riordan reacted with a snarl and twist of his body, biting at anything that came within reach even as he used the smaller claws at the ends of his flippers to keep the fuath at bay.

Another slimy tentacle wrapped around his middle in the melee, squeezing with the intent to force all the air out of his lungs. Riordan kept his throat locked tight, nostrils clenched closed, and furiously bit at the second fuath that was trying to disembowel him.

Then the tide changed, pulling back like a riptide. Riordan braced himself as the tide came back, a wall of water slamming into all three of them, guided by Ailín's sonorous shout. The tentacles holding Riordan in place ripped away, the force of water magic tearing into the fuath. Riordan flapped a flipper at his clanmate as Ailín appeared in the depths, magic caught in his teeth.

Riordan somersaulted to reorient himself, both of them facing the faint glow of where the fuath were regrouping. Ailín rolled close, headbutting Riordan in the side. Riordan nudged at him with a flipper before twisting in a tight roll to indicate what he wanted. There was no speaking deep beneath the surface. Communication happened through body language, and selkies had long since learned how to hold conversations beneath the waves without a word being said.

Ailín dipped a flipper in agreement, breaking to swim to the right, while Riordan swam left. They didn't attack the fuath, not directly, choosing instead to swim in circles around the water spirits at a speed aided by magic. It pushed them faster and faster, spilling from their teeth and away from their flippers to catch the water in a whirlpool that spun tighter and tighter with the fuath at the center.

Riordan spun out the magic, letting it flow from him into the water and the roaring whirlpool they created. The pull of the tightly spinning water forced Riordan and Ailín to alter their swimming trajectory, getting clear of the powerful whirlpool. They kept swimming, kept spinning the whirlpool tighter with their water magic until the glowing fuath were torn apart, bright bits of them getting scattered through the whirlpool.

Riordan somersaulted and let the magic fade. Ailín followed his lead, and they both swam for the surface, leaving the dead to sink to the bottom of the bay. Riordan broke the surface some distance away from the *Neptune*, opening up his nose and throat, hauling in a desperate gasp of air that filled his lungs until it hurt. He bobbed there for half a minute, just breathing, as Ailín swam a nervous circle around him. Eventually, Riordan rolled to his side and smacked a flipper against the small waves and started to swim for the yacht.

Ailín swam alongside him, both of them diving in and out of the water. As they approached, Riordan could see Wade practically hanging over the side of the yacht in an unsafe manner. Riordan barked at him, but Wade didn't know what the warning meant. Diving back underwater, Riordan twisted out of his sealskin, snagging the fur and tying it around his waist before kicking back to the surface. He treaded water near the yacht, aiming a small splash of water at where Wade hung over the railing, hands braced against the hull of the yacht.

"Get back on the boat!" Riordan yelled.

Wade had the temerity to flip him off. "Don't tell me what to do! What was that? I saw you get pulled under, and then there was a whirlpool in the water."

Ailín broke the surface a few feet away in human form, his sealskin draped over his shoulders. "Don't fall out of my boat! You don't have a life jacket on."

Wade scoffed at both of them, clearly not bothered by the risk of falling overboard, before extending one hand. "Come on, I'll help you up."

If Riordan didn't know what Wade was, he'd laugh at the idea that Wade had the strength to haul him up. But he did just that, grasping Riordan by the wrist and lifting him onto the yacht with an ease that left Ailín gaping in the water behind them. Riordan kept his attention on Wade's face, watching the way his dark eyes flicked down Riordan's nearly naked body and back up again, face flushing a little. Riordan preened, ignoring the arched eyebrow Ailín sent his way after Wade hauled his clanmate onto the yacht.

"Clothes," Wade said, tossing outfits at both of them. "Get dressed before someone other than me gets an eyeful."

"Bit prudish coming from someone who is pack," Ailín said teasingly.

"It's more that I don't have any legal clout up here in Boston to talk my way out of a ticket," Wade retorted. Riordan laughed but got dressed quickly to put Wade at ease. His clothes stuck to his wet skin, but it didn't bother him all that much. Ailín got dressed before he checked their positioning in the water. Wade hovered over Riordan, eyeing him critically. "You smell like magic. Was the whirlpool your doing or whatever tried to drown you?"

"Fuath were in the water, and they haven't been for years. We cleared them out at the turn of the century. Ailín helped me tear those two apart with the whirlpool," Riordan said.

"Do you think those things were what Lady Caith warned us about?"

Riordan shook his head. "I think there's something else hiding in the water."

The fuath didn't sound or feel like the presence he'd felt the other day on his patrol. They hadn't filled him with a kind of fear that could drive him to find safety on land. He leaned over to rub at his right ankle, still feeling a lingering ache from being grabbed and hauled about by the fuath. As he lifted his head, a shiny foil Pop-Tart packet was shoved into his face. "Eat this."

Riordan stared past that at Wade. "I know for a fact Ailín doesn't store food on the Neptune."

Wade rolled his eyes and jiggled the packet again. "This is mine, and if you did magic, you need to eat so you don't get hangry."

"Oh."

Considering Wade had seemed willing to bite off Riordan's hand if he stole a cannoli the other day, being offered a treat from Wade's portable snack haul wasn't something he would ever say no to. Pop-Tarts weren't his favorite thing to eat, but it tasted damn good coming from Wade.

Wade crossed his arms over his chest and watched him eat. "So what now?"

"I need to fix the warning sigils they damaged."

Ailín popped his head out of the cockpit. "I can steer us east. Waterway is clear enough for now, but when you go under, I'm coming with you."

"Wade needs—" Riordan protested.

"I know how to swim. Sitting on a boat in the bay while you two do whatever you need to isn't a problem. I'll be fine. I don't know if you will be, and I can't follow you into the water. I'm not built for it," Wade interrupted.

Wade sounded frustrated, brows furrowed in concern. Riordan reached for his arm, pulling it free so he could hold Wade's hand, giving his fingers a squeeze. "Selkies are, and we know how to survive in it."

Wade leaned over to poke him in the chest. "You better, because while I can sit on a boat, I can't steer it. One of you will have to take me back to shore for lunch and dinner because I'm not dealing with vampires tonight on an empty stomach."

Riordan laughed, pulling Wade down to sit beside him on the bench. "I promise I'll feed you."

"Good," Wade said, a smile on his lips that Riordan let himself kiss away.

CHAPTER FOURTEEN

"Man, Patrick is going to kill me," Wade groaned as he got out of the car. They'd ended up parking in the same public parking garage as the other day on the outskirts of Beacon Hill.

"Why?" Riordan said, getting out as well.

"Because he doesn't like it when any of us deal with Lucien alone. I know I have a good reason, but he's still going to be mad."

He didn't mention that Patrick had called him half a dozen times already that evening and Wade hadn't answered any of them, only sending a text to let Patrick know he was fine. It had only caused Patrick to send a bunch of voice texts that outnumbered the voicemails. Wade hadn't listened to any of them yet.

Riordan came around the car, looking far too handsome in his leather jacket. The suppleness of it made sense now that Wade knew it was secretly the other man's sealskin. He itched to touch it but managed to keep his hands to himself.

Riordan wrapped his arm around Wade's shoulders, drawing him close as they headed for the elevator. He wanted to burrow into the warmth but manfully refrained. "But you aren't alone."

Wade wrinkled his nose. "No offense, but Patrick is always gonna think anyone in his pack is alone without him there."

Patrick was overprotective that way, with an attitude of *shoot first, ask questions* later whenever Lucien was in the picture. Not that Wade blamed him. No one in Wade's pack liked Lucien. Given half a chance, Wade *would* eat the blood-sucking bastard.

But Lucien was a known threat; Wade knew what made the master vampire tick. Abhartach was a different problem all together, one Wade didn't have any insight on. Of all the creatures, monsters and legends that existed in the world, his least favorite was an Aztec god, but vampires came in a close second. And vampires weren't to be trusted, no matter what Spencer said.

"I won't leave your side, *mo chroí*."

Wade ducked his head at the endearment, heart beating a little faster. Falling asleep in Riordan's arms yesterday, in his bed, had been something he'd never experienced before outside his pack. But true to his word, they'd only slept while Riordan's body purged the poison from the iron wound. The kisses had been nice, if Wade was honest. They'd been a lot gentler than the ones he'd experienced when imprisoned by Tezcatlipoca, and Riordan had never pushed for what Wade didn't want to give.

It made him want to offer up more, made heat pool in his middle he couldn't blame on fire.

They took the elevator down to the ground floor, and Wade reluctantly pulled away from Riordan. At his questioning glance, Wade shrugged. "Better to not give anything away."

Vampires weren't great at distinguishing scent—the whole not needing to breathe thing working against them there—but they were very skilled at reading body language. Wade didn't doubt for a second that Lucien would figure out there was something going on between himself and Riordan. The longer he could keep Lucien ignorant of that knowledge, though, the better.

Donal, Saoirse, Ella, and two of her pack members showed up a few minutes later, having needed to find parking on a different level from theirs. Wade recognized her pack members as the pair who'd been at her home when Riordan had first arrived the other morning. John Kelly was the older man with the thick Boston accent, while Antonne Wright wouldn't have been out of place in New York City with that Brooklyn accent of his. Wade knew Antonne hadn't been part of the god pack before his took over, but he wondered if the other man had been run out at some point.

"Are you sure Lucien will keep his word?" Ella asked.

Wade would have answered, except he got a whiff of eau de undead and scowled over her shoulder. "Einar."

The blond vampire that blurred to a stop on the sidewalk near the streetlight startled everyone and caused all three werecreatures to shift their fingers into claws. Einar curled his lip at their reaction, staring down his nose at Wade. Since the bitey asshole was tall, it was easy for him to do.

"Lucien half suspected you'd steer clear, even with the payment," Einar said.

Wade crossed his arms over his chest and scowled. "Why would he think I'd waste half a million dollars?"

"You know why, fledgling."

Bad, bitter memories of his time spent locked up in the tunnels of Tremaine's Manhattan Night Court while Tezcatlipoca ran his usual fight rings for the rich flashed through Wade's mind. But he knew better than to let his discomfort show and refused to flinch. "I hope he bet on it and lost. If you're our escort, then start escorting."

Ella shot him a warning look that wasn't as good as Sage's, so Wade opted to ignore it. Einar wouldn't try anything. Wade knew that for a fact because they couldn't entertain Lucien if they weren't in the damn Boston Night Court yet.

Einar curled his hand at them and flashed his jagged, piranha-like fangs in an unfriendly smile. "Follow me."

Einar took off down the street, not so fast that they couldn't keep up, but clearly speeding ahead just to mess with them. Wade sighed and trudged after the vampire, waving for the others to follow him.

"Come on. The sooner we get to the absinthe bar, the sooner we get this meeting over with."

They probably looked like they were a group out to have a good time to anyone passing by. At least they blended in with others in the area that night. Riordan walked beside Wade as they hit Cambridge Street and turned left. The redbrick sidewalk stretched the entire length of that busy street, including past the Green Fairy a few blocks over, which was where Einar deigned to wait for them after rushing on ahead at some point.

Wade squinted at the front of the building, taking in the black paint with gold accents and the neon green halogen lights lining the door. It had no windows, typical of a vampire's establishment, and magic sunk into the wall made his skin prickle. He couldn't tell what sort of spells or wards had been placed around the building. He was glad he'd asked to borrow the artifact from Gwen. Saoirse wore it right now, and he had a feeling she'd drag her brothers close when she needed to use it.

Because it was always *when* with Lucien, not *if*.

The trio of siblings were close with each other and their clan. Riordan was a kind leader, put in a terrible situation that Wade was determined to get him out of. And that meant, right now, dealing with Lucien and Abhartach.

He squared his shoulders and followed Einar inside, wrinkling his nose at the coppery scent of stale blood and the tang of desire filling the air. The others gathered around him just past the door, and Wade took a moment to study the space how Patrick had taught him.

Know your exit points.

The only way in and out was through the door they'd come through. The bar had knocked out the two floors above to create a high ceiling but didn't offer any mezzanine or balcony. Just brick etched with wards that Wade would bet were meant for silence to ensure privacy. Hanging on the walls were numerous paintings depicting historical scenes Wade didn't recognize.

The long bar to his left had two shelves of absinthe bottles and some other alcohol lining the length of the bar. No mirror sat above the bottles, only more paintings. Neither did he see any beer on tap, which was just weird. There were two doors in the back that led to a single restroom and maybe an office of some kind, who knew, but if there was a rear door, Wade couldn't find it.

Find the nearest thing that can be a weapon that isn't you.

All the tables and chairs in the place weren't bolted down, but almost all of them were taken up by vampires. Hidden speakers pumped out what he thought might be classical Irish folk music, but he wasn't sure. Electronics meant there was wiring somewhere that could maybe spark a fire in a pinch. If anything, he knew absinthe burned, so smashing some bottles and setting the liquid on fire was another option.

Call me and I'll come.

Patrick always had, and Wade loved him for that, he did. But he wasn't going to call Patrick or the rest of his pack for this, not when the problem at hand was one he'd been sent to fix. Wade knew what he was now and what he was capable of. He could help himself these days, but it was always nice to know his pack would be there for him, no matter what.

Riordan took half a step forward as if he were going to put himself between Wade and all the vampires who'd turned to look at them. It was a thoughtful gesture, but Wade didn't need to be protected here, either from his memories or the vampire that lazily waved them forward.

"Come meet who you paid to see, fledgling," Lucien said from his sprawled spot on a wooden chair, Carmen perched on his lap in a pair of satin hot pants and a corset top that left little to the imagination. Her stilettos looked like they were sharp enough at the heel to take out an eye. Einar stood behind them both in bodyguard mode, arms crossed over his chest and as still as a statue.

Wade scowled, stalking between the tables of vampires who eyed his group like they were fast food dinner. The human servants keeping their masters company ignored them, while the handful of mundane humans who seemed far too stupid for their own good if they were hanging out at a vampire bar watched them pass curiously. "I can't believe you're in Boston. We all thought you'd fled the country."

"I don't flee."

Wade rolled his eyes, coming to a stop at the round table that sat four, but two of the chairs were empty. He did what Patrick would've done and took a seat without being invited to. Lucien stared at him with those creepy black eyes of his, the left one still marred by a burn scar that stretched over his cheek and forehead and down his neck. It wasn't as bad as Wade remembered it being at the end of the Battle of Samhain when Lucien had done his damnedest to retrieve Macaria.

His efforts had nearly truly killed him. Drinking Patrick's blood—freely offered, which was the only reason Wade hadn't crispifried the master vampire at the time—had been enough to stave off turning to ash. As one of the very few daywalkers in existence, made by the mother of all vampires, Lucien had always been powerful.

And a dick.

Wade put his elbows on the table and focused his attention on the other master vampire they'd come to visit as Riordan claimed the seat beside him. Abhartach was taller than Lucien, even sitting down, with long blond hair so light it appeared white in the dimly lit bar. The features of his face were sharp, almost hollowing out his cheeks, giving him a starved model look. What Wade found most interesting was the master vampire's ears—they were pointed like a fae's. Unlike Lucien's punk attire, Abhartach wore a three-piece business suit Wade was pretty sure was designer. It looked uncomfortable.

"I hear you come with a warning and an offer for my Night Court," Abhartach said in a voice so thick with an Irish accent it reminded Wade of the time he and his pack ended up in a pub on the west coast of Ireland one December. That place had the best fish and chips ever. The Green Fairy was clearly lacking in the food department. "I fear no one in Boston, and I have no need for bargains, especially those given by fae."

"Not even if you're next in line to be targeted? You had fae trying to bully one of your human servants yesterday," Wade said.

"The trespassers would have died for it if my human servant had been harmed."

"Your human servants ended up fine. You have Carmen and me to thank for that."

"I give thanks to no one. Certainly not to someone like you." Abhartach raised a hand, and seconds later, a vampire was at his side, depositing a cut-crystal stemmed glass onto the table. A flat slotted spoon was laid across the top and a sugar cube placed on it. The vampire very slowly poured water from a glass carafe over the sugar cube to dissolve it, turning the drink a cloudy color. It smelled strongly of black licorice to Wade's nose, and he was glad Jono never served the stuff at Tempest.

"Someone like me," Wade echoed. "I feel like that's supposed to be an insult, but honestly, I'm going to rank it a two out of ten."

Carmen laughed throatily, reaching for the martini glass sitting on the table in front of Lucien, who was missing a drink. "You're a little worse at this than Patrick ever was."

"Worse at what? Telling Abby Boy here the truth? That some possibly prayed-into-being wannabe god has the hots for his territory and is collecting people for bargaining chips like a pro poker player? Because that's what I'm saying."

The smile on Carmen's face disappeared and, with it, the glamour she was probably sporting, judging by the surprised little sounds the others around him let out. She always looked like the succubus she was to him, and as pretty as she looked, she was ugly underneath it all, in Wade's opinion.

"A prayed-into-being god?" Carmen asked, sliding off Lucien's lap. "You didn't mention that yesterday."

"You didn't ask."

Carmen shifted on her feet, and a hand settled on Wade's shoulder. He glanced up, finding Ella standing beside his chair, her attention on those seated at the table. "We're not here asking for an alliance. We're here to warn Abhartach that Niall is targeting all our communities in Boston with the intent to take over the city."

Abhartach leaned back in his seat, tapping one long, black-painted nail against the fluted glass. "I see he's keeping to his namesake."

"What do you mean?" Wade asked.

"Niall Noígíallach was a mortal king once who convinced the fae to grant him a long life in Underhill."

"Did you vote to let him in?" At Abhartach's sharp look, Wade pointed at his ears. "You were fae before you were turned, weren't you?"

Riordan grabbed his hand and shoved it down. "That's not a subject we should talk about."

"Why not? He has pointy ears. I didn't even know vampires could turn fae."

Abhartach moved, a blur to Wade's sight, but he still saw the motion. Wade flipped the table faster than Abhartach could reach them, spilling the drinks to the floor as he stood but forcing Abhartach to pull up short, even as the other vampires in the bar rallied to surround the table. The master vampire kept his feet planted where they were, not because of Wade's actions but because of Lucien's words.

"You'd lose," Lucien said casually.

Abhartach's lips peeled back from his fangs, revealing the jagged mess of them to Wade and the others. He towered over all of them except maybe Donal, smelling like blood and that musty undead stench all vampires seemed to carry in their skin. The master vampire's nostrils flared before he looked over his shoulder, clearly dismissing them in favor of Lucien. "You called him fledgling."

"He bites."

Abhartach flicked his gaze back to Wade, who smiled, revealing his own set of fangs for a split second. "Yeah, I bite. Wanna see how hard?"

Riordan pressed up against his back, one hand gripping Wade's T-shirt, as if he were prepared to haul Wade out of the line of fire. Ella stood to his left, her fingernails shifted into claws, while the rest of those with them now faced outward, squaring off with the vampires of the Boston Night Court.

"We're not here to fight," Ella said in a low voice. "We're here to warn you. Consider it a courtesy."

A vampire approached at a slow walk to right the table and kicked the shattered bits of glass aside. The table wobbled a bit, but since Wade wasn't going to be drinking, he didn't care.

Abhartach shot Ella a dismissive look. "You are dire. You have no authority to engage in courtesies or bargains. Where are your alphas?"

Lucien smirked, and Wade really wanted to punch it off his face. "Something tells me Niall has the illustrious pair."

"Don't even think about muscling in on their territory," Wade warned.

"It's not yours to fight over."

"I'd make it mine through an alliance if I have to. Want me to call Patrick? Because I will." Wade pulled out his cell phone and held it up, pressing the button to highlight the screen and show the additional text notifications that had come through since the last time he'd checked, all of them from Patrick. "He's kind of pissed I'm talking to you."

"Do you think I care what he thinks? I'm not bound by my mother's promise any longer. You would do well to watch yourself."

Wade smiled, heat crawling up his throat, flickers of fire tickling his tongue. "I can make the right side of your face match the left if you want. You are *not* taking anyone's territory."

Abhartach smacked his hand down in the center of the table, leaning between Lucien and Wade to break their staring contest. He tilted his head, his long, white-blond hair falling over his shoulders. "I know what you are."

Wade swallowed the fire in his mouth and breathed out a curl of smoke, refusing to acknowledge the faint twinge of old fear at the back of his mind from the close proximity of the master vampire. He tipped his head back and arched an eyebrow in the best condescending look he could manage. Patrick would be proud. Sage and Jono, probably not so much. "Yeah? Then you probably know I could shish kebab everyone in this bar, and none of your bought magic could stop me. I'm not *going* to because you haven't done anything yet to make me need to. Other than invite this asshole in for a drink."

Lucien looked like he was contemplating all the ways he could maybe rend Wade limb from limb, which was just laughable. Abhartach tapped his nails against the wood one at a time in a slow progression. "My Night Court has no quarrel with the Boston god pack nor the selkie clans. I won't make your problems ours."

"No alliance. Got it. But Niall is fae, and so were you once. The only difference now is you're a vampire and he's a maybe-wannabe-god. That's a problem for everyone, or do I need to remind you about the Battle of Samhain?"

Abhartach's lips curled up, revealing his sharp fangs. "I answered my mother's call and fought at the end of the world."

"Great. Then you know how annoying gods are. If you're targeted by one, do you really think you can survive it? Because I know I can, and I'll make sure those with me survive as well. But no alliance means none of us"—Wade gestured at Riordan and the others—"are going to come to your rescue."

Before Abhartach could respond, the door to the bar opened and a person stepped in. Wade couldn't see them, not with his back to the door, but he heard them. What's more, he *sensed* them—so much magic that didn't feel right.

"Casey?" Ella said, sounding far too hopeful.

"Get down!" Wade yelled.

Carmen flipped the table this time, creating a makeshift barrier between her, Lucien, and Abhartach from the threat that just walked into the bar. Saoirse grabbed Donal and Ella since she was closer, shouting out the phrase to activate the shield ward. Bright white magic flared up in a tight dome around the trio, providing a different kind of barrier that Wade shoved Riordan behind and where the other werecreatures joined them.

All of that happened in seconds, not even the length of a breath, but it was still long enough for Wade to get a glimpse of Casey standing in the doorway, expression one of fear and grief, bleeding magic through his skin that Wade could see even if no one else could.

And then whatever spell was wrapped around Casey exploded, the concussive force of pressurized magic ripping away from the god pack alpha's body and through the bar.

CHAPTER FIFTEEN

WADE SANK HIS CLAWS INTO THE FLOOR AS THE CONCUSSIVE BLAST OF THE magical bomb slammed through everyone. He ducked his head, grimacing at Ella's scream of rage, the dire held back from reaching her alpha only by dint of the shield ward. He didn't try to use the ring Gerard and Órlaith had gifted him, not wanting to tip his hand.

A different, high-pitched humming sound hit Wade's ears, nearly popping his eardrums. He glanced up, seeing the wards running from the floor to the high ceiling in the bar were all activated, magical threads tangling through the physical manifestation of the blast radius. He didn't know what the spell was, but it had managed to neutralize some of the harsher aspects of the magical bomb, even if it could do nothing for the concussive force behind the explosion. He did know the silence ward would probably keep anyone outside the bar from knowing what was going on and calling the cops.

"*Casey!*" Ella screamed, clawing at the shield ward Saoirse hadn't deactivated.

The other werecreatures with her appeared just as equally furious and devastated at the cruel way their alpha was being treated. Casey lay unconscious on the floor, magic flickering around his body. Wade could hear that he was still breathing.

One of the werecreatures got halfway to him before skidding to a stop as Niall walked into the bar, radiating power and carrying a faint hint of ozone with his scent. It wasn't anywhere close to how a true god felt, but it was enough of a warning that Niall's magic maybe wasn't just fae magic, and Wade swore softly under his breath.

Maybe he should have called Patrick after all.

Wade could see the fae through the glowing shield ward and wanted to punch that weaselly little smirk off his face. Wade drew his aura down into a tight knot. He wanted to pass as human for this confrontation if at all possible.

"It's never good to try to break a bargain with a fae, my dear dire," Niall tsked as he came to stand beside Casey's unconscious form. He nudged Casey with his foot but thankfully didn't do anything more. Three more fae followed him inside, acting like body-guards, but none of them went further than a foot past the door. They carried swords instead of guns, the edges flickering with magic.

"*You*," Abhartach snarled, stepping forward. "You dare to step foot into my territory like *this*?"

"I told you so," Wade muttered, knowing everyone could hear him.

He shoved himself to his feet, edging around the still-active shield. Abhartach's vampires were all up and prepared to attack, their human servants huddling behind overturned furniture. Every bottle behind the bar had been shattered from the blast, and the handful of mundane humans there for a walk on the wild side were probably regretting their life's choices right about then. So far no one else was dead, but Wade knew how quickly that could change.

Niall's gaze swept the room, lingering on Ella and then Riordan in a way that Wade absolutely hated before the fae smiled lazily at Abhartach. "My mistake. I was under the impression this was a bar owned by magic users."

"Oh, I call bullshit," Wade scoffed. "How long have you lived in Boston?"

"For once, I'm in agreement," Lucien said.

Wade jumped when Lucien appeared on his other side, staring Niall down. Niall's attention slipped to Lucien, and Wade had the absolute pleasure of watching the asshole fae do a double take. Wade knew enough about body language and territory negotiation to know that Niall had just revealed a weakness—he knew who and what Lucien was, and it made the fae wary.

Okay. So *maybe* Wade wouldn't try to eat Lucien tonight.

Niall paused, taking Lucien's measure. "I wasn't aware you would be here tonight."

Carmen and Einar blurred to Lucien's side, and Niall's gaze flicked to them, eyes narrowing fractionally. Wade recognized the smile Carmen gave the fae, the one that promised absolute fucked-up mayhem the moment Lucien gave the word.

In this one instant, Wade hoped Lucien let her have the run of the place.

"Niall Noígíallach, is it? We haven't had the pleasure of a proper introduction," Carmen drawled, her tone arctic. "We should rectify that, seeing as you've interrupted the drink we were having with an old friend."

Niall's attention swung back to Abhartach and the vampires of the Boston Night Court primed to attack, holding back only because their master bade them. Niall seemed to be rethinking his dramatic entrance. "I'm here about a broken bargain. It doesn't concern you."

Abhartach arched an eyebrow and looked down his nose at Niall. "You made it my concern when you attacked my place of business. I've killed for far less."

Niall spread his hands in a faux friendly way. "I'm certain we can come to an accord of some sort."

"The way I see it, Ella didn't break your bargain. You said she couldn't find help with friends, and she didn't. If anyone broke the bargain, it's *you* after you tortured Casey. Which means it's void, and you should give him back," Wade snapped.

The retort earned him Niall's full and undivided attention. Wade met it angrily. "You speak out of turn. I fail to see how a mundane human could aid the dire."

For a wannabe god, he really was dumb. Wade could totally work with that.

"Because clearly, you're an unimaginative dickhead."

Riordan's hand fisted tightly in the back of Wade's shirt, ready to haul him back. "He's right, Niall. You broke the bargain with Ella."

Niall arched an eyebrow. "No, I did not. The dire was meant to keep her mouth shut. Otherwise defiance would be met with death. Her precious alpha is still alive. For now."

To prove his point, Niall drew his foot back and kicked Casey in the gut with enough force to send the alpha rolling. Wade decided right then and there he was going to find Saoirse's skin, get Casey and Harper back as soon as he could, and then eat Niall. The fae would probably give him indigestion, but it would be worth it.

"I guess that's one way to view the situation. You're still wrong, and it doesn't mean you had the right to come blasting into Abhartach's territory like you did," Wade said.

Niall's eyes narrowed, and Riordan's grip tightened to the point Wade thought the selkie might rip his shirt. "You haven't given me your name."

"Nope, and I'm not gonna, so go cry about it."

"Leave," Abhartach ordered Niall. "Now."

The magic in the walls had sucked up the explosion's residue, and now a tangled web of jagged-looking light was forming in the air. Niall looked up, mouth twisting in distaste. "I see you aren't in the mood for conversation."

The magic dropped, but Niall attacked first. He made a cutting gesture with his hand, and light as bright as the sun exploded away from him. Wade closed his eyes against it, but it still burned. The vampires in the bar screamed in fury at the mockery of sunlight that filled the bar from floor to ceiling. It faded after a few seconds, and Wade blinked rapidly, trying to clear his vision of colored spots.

Niall was gone, as were the fae who'd come with him. They'd taken Casey with them, and Wade hoped carting the alpha around would be enough to slow them down as some of Abhartach's vampires gave chase, blurring out of the door. Wade had a feeling they wouldn't catch up with the fae, but if it kept Niall on the run, so much the better.

Abhartach said something in what might have been Irish, and Wade's brain squeezed out a translation. "Send out an edict to the Night Court. Niall and his fae are considered the enemy and have no pass-through rights. I want him found, and I want to be the one to kill him."

"*Finally*," Wade muttered under his breath.

Saoirse spoke the reversal phrase, and the shield ward contained itself in the artifact again. The crystal hanging around her neck glowed for a couple of seconds before all signs of magic disappeared. Saoirse took a couple of steps toward the door before she drew herself up short, shaking her head.

Freed from the protection the shield had offered, Ella staggered toward the space where Casey had been, falling to her knees. Wade figured Casey couldn't have been that bad of an alpha if people were worried about him, but good or bad, he didn't deserve to be treated like that.

Wade twisted around, batting Riordan's hand aside. He stepped around Riordan and jabbed his finger at Abhartach. "You see what I mean about Niall targeting you? You should consider teaming up temporarily with the Boston god pack and the selkie clans."

"That's not how you bargain," Carmen said.

"I'm not bargaining." He just wanted confirmation for everyone else that Abby Boy wasn't going to sit back and take it on the chin. The only silver lining to the night so far was that Niall had gone and overplayed his hand and painted a target on his back with his actions. In attempting to corner Ella and the rest of the Boston god pack by pleading ignorance of territory borders, he'd hopefully ensured the attention of two master vampires, one of whom excelled at murder.

Abhartach took in the destroyed furniture, shattered bottles of absinthe, the scent of all that liquor bitter in the air, and made a gesture with one hand. To an undead asshole, the vampires of his Night Court moved. Some left the bar, while others remained to work with the human servants to start putting things to right. Those mundane humans who'd been caught in the crossfire were escorted from the premises, but Wade didn't have time to worry about them. They couldn't be his priority.

"I need no bargain to secure my borders," Abhartach sneered.

"So you're going after Niall?"

"What do you think?"

"Great. Have fun. Don't kill anyone my pack is allied with." Wade craned his head around and searched out Lucien, catching the other master vampire's eye. "Are you going to help with the murder spree?"

Lucien raised an eyebrow over his scarred left eye. "What do you think?"

"I think I'm going to plead ignorance to all your bloody fun." Wade turned to Riordan and jerked his head at where Ella still knelt on the ground near the door. "Let's get her outside."

"No," Ella rasped. "I'm going after Niall."

"That is a bad idea. Let the vampires hunt him right now."

"He *hurt* my alpha. It's my fault Casey is being tortured. If I hadn't—"

"If you hadn't worked out a way to get outside help, you'd all be worse off than you are. Quit your sniveling and get the fuck out," Lucien cut in, clearly still a heartless bastard.

Wade flipped Lucien off. "Quit being an asshole."

Lucien bared his fangs at Wade, so he returned the sentiment with his own snarl. A warm hand settled on his shoulder, hauling him back until he stood beside Riordan.

"Let's see to Ella," Riordan said quietly.

Wade pointed two fingers at Lucien, then pointed at his own eyes, then pointed again at Lucien in the universal language of *I'm watching you, asshole.* Then he let Riordan pull him away to where Ella was being helped to her feet by one of her pack members. All three of them were ashen-faced, but he was at least glad to see anger in their eyes rather than despair.

Wade made sure everyone else exited the bar first before pausing in the doorway. He looked back at the two master vampires, seeing both of them staring at him. "I know your kind can sniff out blood for miles, but I don't know if the rest of your nose works. So you should know Niall smelled a little like ozone."

Lucien raised his chin, something dark and hungry in his black eyes. "That just means this hunt will be fun."

Wade didn't want to know what sort of powers Lucien had accrued from his mother after the end of the world. Only psychopaths would think hunting a maybe-god was fun.

"You've overstayed your welcome," Abhartach said.

Wade waggled his fingers at the master vampire. "Just admit that I was right."

Hands grabbed him by the waist and hauled him out of the bar. Wade yelped at the manhandling, nearly elbowing Riordan in the face by accident.

"Stop antagonizing the master vampires. My stress levels can't handle it," Riordan said.

"You're handling him well enough," Donal said.

"Hey!" Wade said, trying to tamp down the flush that hit his cheeks. "Uh, we should go."

Riordan snorted. "You don't say."

They hustled back to the parking garage, the streets weirdly calm and normal after the attack they'd just survived in the Green Fairy. Whatever magic Abhartach had bought to line the bar was definitely high-grade, because no one outside seemed to be aware of what had transpired inside. That meant they could leave Beacon Hill without the cops being involved, which Wade always thought was a plus.

They huddled around the pay machine on the ground-floor level of the garage to validate their tickets. Wade tapped Ella on the shoulder, getting her attention. She looked at him, wolf-bright amber eyes still red-rimmed. "Go home. Get behind a threshold. Niall came to target you personally, and you shouldn't make it easy on him."

"He knows where our territory is."

"Do you have a safe house, then? Or maybe someplace outside the city?" The London god pack had owned territory outside that capital. Wade wondered if the Boston god pack had something similar.

Ella's lips firmed into a hard line. "I'm not running away from this fight, not while that bastard has our alphas."

"Niall is going to have his hands full tonight. Abhartach might not have agreed to an alliance, but he's pissed, and he's ordered his entire Night Court to hunt Niall. Lucien's is going to him because he's never said no to murder. Hopefully, that buys us time to find Casey and Harper and get Saoirse's skin back before anything worse happens."

"Vampires are useless during the day."

"Most of them are. But there's one in Boston right now who doesn't mind the occasional sunburn. Niall knows that. He'll probably be cautious so long as Lucien is here in the city."

"I won't have my pack owe that bastard."

"You won't. I promise. Trust me."

Ella nodded. "I do. Despite hating that my alphas are suffering, I don't regret reaching out to your pack."

"Get home safe. We'll talk tomorrow, but if you need me, you have my number."

"Thanks."

Ella and her pack members took the elevator up to whatever level they had parked at. Wade looked over at the selkies. "So what now?"

"I'm hungry. Let's get out of vampire and fae territory and head back to the pub," Saoirse said.

"You're fae."

"Our territory is better."

He couldn't really argue that. They split up like before, with Riordan joining Wade in his car for the drive back to South Boston. Wade was distracted by Riordan's hand resting on his thigh for the entire drive to the pub and how nice it felt.

"Park in our driveway down the easement," Riordan instructed once Wade hit the more residential streets closer to the pub. Most of the street parking was taken, so Wade was glad he wouldn't have to be circling blocks looking for a spot.

Donal and Saoirse were already inside the pub by the time they arrived. The place was packed, almost everyone there smelling like the sea, which probably meant selkies. What caught Wade's nose and attention first, though, was the smell of fried food and lots of it.

"Fish and chips?" Wade asked hopefully as he followed Riordan to the back, where he could see Saoirse sitting.

Riordan laughed. "Sure, I'll go put in an order."

"Do you sell hamburgers?"

"How about I get you a couple of dishes to tide you over while we figure out our next steps?"

"Sounds like a plan."

Riordan headed for the bar counter while Wade went to join Saoirse at the table. Four pints of beer had already been served, and Wade snagged one as he sat down. "Where's Donal?"

"Wrangling the clúrachán in the basement," Saoirse said.

"The what now?"

"A small fae. Merv has been working for us for over a century. He came off a ship and sort of never left." Saoirse wrinkled her nose. "We're short on our Guinness inventory, and Donal is down there castigating him for it."

"So he drank all your Guinness?"

"Yeah."

"And you still employ him?"

"He really is good at inventory, except when he isn't."

Wade took a gulp of his beer. "I don't know how that makes sense."

"Well, we can't exactly fire him. Where would he go? He's practically clan at this rate, even if he can't swim."

Wade silently toasted her for that because from what he'd seen, selkie clans were a lot like werecreature packs. Once you were part of one, it would take *a lot* to get kicked out, and drinking on the clock clearly wasn't going to cut it.

Riordan arrived maybe a minute later, dragging his chair closer to Wade when he pulled it out to sit down. "Orders are in. Saoirse, I put in for a fish pie for you."

"Thanks, boyo."

Wade was about to ask when the food would be ready when his phone rang. He pulled it out of his back pocket and winced at the name on the screen. "I was hoping he'd be too busy to call tonight."

"Who?" Riordan asked.

Wade accepted the call and put the phone up to his ear. "Heeeey, Patrick."

"Don't hey me. I've been stuck in court and late-night meetings with the director for the past two days. What are you doing spending money on Lucien of all fuckers?" Patrick said testily.

Wade tried to think of any excuse to hang up and dodge getting read the riot act. "Uh, I'm in a pub, and there are people around."

"That's not going to get you out of this conversation."

"But they can hear you! Are you sure you want to talk right now?"

"Oh, we're talking since Jono didn't see fit to send someone after you and your bad decisions. We taught you better than this."

"Hey! Since when have I done anything stupid and irresponsible?"

"You want that list in numerical order or alphabetical?"

"Er, okay, but when I'm representing the pack?"

"Exhibit number one would be the wire you sent Lucien."

Wade slumped in his seat, teetering to the side so he could lean against Riordan. "So I guess I shouldn't tell you that Niall was dumb and tried to attack the Boston Night Court tonight and pissed off two master vampires? Lucien is probably going to make a mess of Boston, and I want you to know that's not my fault."

Patrick was quiet for all of five seconds, which was just long enough for Riordan to reach up and scritch his fingers through Wade's hair. He would've melted in bliss if he didn't have Patrick sounding all kinds of pissed off in his ear. Wade knew the anger wasn't directed at him but at the situation Patrick couldn't come and handle himself.

"What were you doing in the Boston Night Court?"

"I paid Lucien for an introduction to Abby Boy."

"Abby Boy," Patrick echoed. "That's not his name, I'm betting."

"He goes by Abhartach, but that's a mouthful, and everyone gets twitchy when I say Abby Boy, which is funny. Anyway, Niall is targeting leaders of the supernatural and preternatural communities here, so I thought the best way to distract him would be to sic vampires on him. Turns out Lucien was in town for a visit and now there are two master vampires gunning for him. Half a million dollars was actually a bargain if you think about it."

Saoirse stared at him as if he'd lost his mind, and Wade could feel the vibrations of Riordan's disbelieving laughter against his body.

"I don't know what's worse. That you convinced Lucien to be your attack dog or that you walked into a Night Court and convinced the *other* master vampire to do the same. Did you even have backup?"

"Yes," Riordan muttered, clearly listening in.

"Ella and some of her pack were with me, and so were the selkies. I know you're stuck in DC, but I *am* handling things here," Wade said.

Patrick let out a snort. "It's vampires. I'm going to worry."

Wade knew why that was the case, and it warmed him a little to know that the care from years ago when they first met was never going to go away. Despite it all, he decided against telling Patrick that Niall was possibly a low-ranked, prayed-into-being god because then he'd definitely leave DC for Boston.

"I can handle them. I handled Takoma's Night Court in Seattle just fine."

"I know, but I feel like you should have backup."

"You can't ditch your job."

"Watch me."

"I'm fine. Really. If anything gets worse, I'll let you know, but I'm not alone out here, and I need to help Ella and Riordan."

"All right," Patrick said after a moment, clearly fighting the urge to get on a plane to Boston. Wade knew that tone in his voice. "I'll tell the others I spoke with you and that I'm staying in DC, but you better pick up your phone when any of us calls next time. And I want you to update Jono twice a day on what is going on. If he doesn't hear from you within twenty-four hours, he'll be coming to Boston."

Ella would definitely not like that, but Wade also knew Jono wouldn't care about niceties if he had to come to Boston. Jono was very protective of his pack. So was Patrick, but between the two of them, Jono was the one who didn't mind ripping people's throats out with his teeth.

"Got it. Have fun annoying the director." Wade ended the call, set his phone on the table, and grabbed his beer. "Good news, which you all probably heard. Patrick isn't coming to Boston."

"I don't know if that's good if we could use the backup. Your pack certainly has a reputation," Saoirse said.

"Niall doesn't know you're New York City god pack," Riordan said.

Wade shrugged, letting Riordan take more of his weight. It earned him a strong arm wrapped around his shoulders, making him want to preen. "He's not going to know until I eat the bastard."

Wade had gone toe-to-toe with plenty of gods before and survived. In a range of godheads, Niall wasn't all that powerful—if he even had one. But he was corrupt and he was a bastard, and Wade was going to enjoy crunching the fae between his teeth.

He wouldn't even complain about the taste this time.

Donal popped up at the table just then, looking harried. "Boyo, it's your turn to talk sense into Merv."

Riordan rubbed his hand over Wade's shoulder, who took the hint and sat up. "What's he done now?"

"Drank the rest of the Guinness we ordered for June and insisted it was part of the May inventory. It's going to take at least a week for our supplier to get us a replacement shipment of kegs. We'll need to buy bottles from the packies to get us through the next few days."

Riordan stood, and Wade immediately missed having him close. "I'll talk to him."

"I'll come with you," Wade said.

"You don't want to wait for your food?"

"It'll be quick, right? Besides, I've never met a clúrachán before."

He knew he had mangled the name, but neither of the three laughed at him for it. Riordan just took him by the hand and led him deeper into the bar to a door with a faded *Employees Only* sign nailed to the wood. They shouldered through it, stepping down a creaky wooden staircase to a cold, brightly lit basement.

"Merv?" Riordan called out.

"Oi, I told your brother the inventory is fine" came the response from deeper in the basement, followed by a loud belch.

"How much inventory do you lose to Merv?" Wade asked.

Riordan sighed. "We can afford it. Mostly."

Wade followed Riordan through rows of shelving filled with boxes of liquor and beer to the back, where kegs were stacked against the wall. Leaning against one and taking a sip of beer from a glass mug with a contemplative expression on a weathered face was a fae who barely came up to Wade's knees. Dark brown hair curled away from Merv's head, and his beard was long and bushy. A bit of foam from his beer coated his mustache, which he licked off after a second.

"Merv," Riordan said, letting Wade's hand go so he could cross his arms over his chest. "What have I said about drinking through the inventory?"

"That leftover amounts are fine for me to imbibe," Merv replied. He belched again, holding the mug up and eyeing it critically. "Ach, but I think this keg's beer is a wee off on the taste profile. I'll have to drink more to be sure."

"No, you won't. Whatever is left of the inventory is fine. Go upstairs and finish the paperwork. Don't make me ask twice."

It was a couple more minutes of grumbling on Merv's part, cajoling on Riordan's, and the stealing of a mug before Merv could be herded back upstairs. He stomped his way up the wooden steps, muttering under his breath about stingy selkies, but he went all the same.

"That seemed easy enough. I don't know why Donal needed help," Wade said.

"He and Merv get along maybe half the time. Merv tends to bite, and Donal always takes offense to that."

Wade laughed. "At least he seems nice?"

"Nice enough. Though I wouldn't want to be bitten by him. It's never fun." Riordan tilted his head, eyeing Wade. "I wouldn't mind it from you though."

Suddenly, the basement felt way too warm. Wade cleared his throat. "Really?"

Riordan quirked a smile at him, warm brown eyes looking nowhere else but at Wade. "I thought I've been obvious about that."

"Admittedly, I'm never looking."

"I find it really hard to believe that no one has ever looked at you before." And just like that, all that warmth fled Wade. Something must have shown on his face, maybe his scent, because Riordan's smile disappeared, replaced by concern and not a little bit of anger. "I really want to find whoever hurt you and kill them."

"You can't," Wade said around the knot in his throat. "He was a god, and the master vampire he was working with in New York City is dead."

A complicated mix of emotions crossed Riordan's face. "If a vampire hurt you, why did you want to meet with Abhartach?"

"Because you needed the help."

"Wade."

He shook his head, frowning hard. "I know what I am now. Dealing with vampires is easier because of it. And my pack made sure the god who enslaved me as a kid paid for it."

"Enslaved," Riordan said slowly, hands curling into fists. "*What?*"

Wade hunched his shoulders, reaching up to scratch at the back of his head as he looked up at the ceiling because it was easier to not look Riordan in the eye. "I never knew my father, and my mother died when I was fourteen or so. I didn't want to stay in a group home, so I ran away, and that was the dumbest thing I could've done. I got picked up by people who sold me to Tezcatlipoca. *He* knew what I was, even if I didn't. Not yet. I was collared and forced to fight to the death for rich people's entertainment, and sometimes after the fight, they...bought me. When I wasn't fighting, I was pickpocketing. I was eighteen when he took us to New York City. That's where I met my pack. That's where Patrick, Jono, and Sage saved me."

He could speak about it now. Years of therapy helped with that, but it still wasn't easy spilling his metaphorical guts to someone who wasn't pack. To wonder if they'd judge him for being a dumb kid or having weird boundaries about personal space and sex and nudity that kept shifting as he grew older.

He shouldn't have worried.

Warm arms wrapped around him, pulling him into a tight embrace that made Wade stiffen for all of a moment. But he took a breath, drew in the scent of the sea and Riordan, and gave in to the urge to tuck his nose against the warm leather jacket collar pressed against Riordan's neck.

"I'll hunt down and murder anyone who ever touched you," Riordan growled.

Wade snorted, burrowing in close, getting his hands beneath the jacket to rest tentatively over the sides of Riordan's rib cage. "That's nice of you, but I'd rather you not get arrested for murder."

"No wonder you hate Niall so much."

"I'd hate him even without knowing what it's like to be someone's prisoner."

Riordan ran his hands up and down Wade's back a couple of times before pulling away. He ducked his head, pressing a chaste kiss to Wade's cheek, which was nice and all, but he was okay with more. So he turned his head, catching Riordan's lips against his own, kissing inexpertly, he knew, but he liked it now. Mostly because it was Riordan, who groaned softly and deepened the kiss, pushing Wade gently up against the shelf full of alcohol and bracketing him in.

They weren't going to *do* anything down in the basement of a crowded pub, but it was really nice to be wanted.

When Riordan broke the kiss, much to Wade's dissatisfaction, the selkie cupped his face with one hand and rested his forehead against Wade's. "I wish I'd known you before Niall."

"I won't let him keep your sister or take you," Wade said.

Riordan didn't say anything to that, but it was fine. Wade meant it.

He didn't like anyone touching what was his.

Riordan reluctantly pulled away. "Come on, let's get back upstairs. I'm sure the food has arrived and is getting cold."

Wade grabbed his hand and hauled him toward the stairs. "Can't have that."

They headed back upstairs, and Wade spent the rest of the evening eating his way through every dish on the menu while holding Riordan's hand.

CHAPTER SIXTEEN

RIORDAN SAW WADE OFF WITH A LINGERING KISS, WISHING HE COULD
follow the younger man back to the hotel, but he needed to be near
his siblings after the night's events. He'd offered to let Wade stay the
night, but Wade had wanted to check on Ella. Riordan didn't like
that Wade would be traveling around Boston alone but knew he'd be
able to take care of himself. A dragon who could pay for help from
Lucien, of all people, wasn't someone most people would mess with.

Only Niall didn't know Wade was a dragon or from the New York
City god pack. Wade cheerfully considered that knowledge his ace in
the hole, and Riordan wasn't going to tell him he was wrong. From
what he'd seen, Wade would be a serious adversary if they were on
opposite sides of a fight.

"You should tell Wade about your fixation," Saoirse said once
Wade's car had disappeared around the corner.

Riordan shook his head, hands tucked into his jacket pockets as
they headed back inside. "I'm not going to put that on him."

He would never make Wade feel obligated for anything, not after
what he'd disclosed in the basement of the pub. It was a wonder
Wade was as cheerful and confident as he was, and Riordan had a

feeling it came down to the core of the New York City god pack. People didn't get to grow and thrive without feeling safe.

Besides, Riordan didn't want to make Wade sad when he inevitably gave leadership of the clan to Donal and traded his skin for Saoirse's. There was no hope of a relationship where he was going. He'd take comfort in a dream of something he'd never had rather than aching over what was lost.

He locked the door behind them, sensing the gentle pulse of the threshold as it settled around the foundation of the home. The threshold was old, having been laid down decades ago, and was strong enough to keep out unwanted visitors, even if it couldn't keep out phone calls.

Riordan's phone rang, piercing the late-night quiet and causing his siblings to pause in their trek upstairs. He pulled it out of his pocket, hoping it was Wade, but his heart sank when he recognized the number Niall had given him the other week when the other fae had first handed down his demands. He didn't want to answer it.

"Who is it?" Donal asked.

Riordan grimaced, finally forcing himself to accept the call and put the phone to his ear. "Niall."

"You must think yourself rather clever for interceding with the Boston Night Court," Niall said in a silky voice full of violence.

"I went to warn Abhartach. You were the one who attacked while Lucien was visiting."

"I was chasing after a broken bargain. It seems I must chase after you as well."

He couldn't stop the way his heart beat a little faster. "We still have time on the bargain."

"Not after tonight, you don't. Tomorrow afternoon, you will give me your skin, or you will hand over your sister. What will it be, hm? Your clan or your family?"

Niall ended the call, and Riordan closed his eyes, the threat ringing in his ears like a sonic boom.

He shook himself back to clarity when Saoirse touched her hand to his chest, pressing her palm over his rapidly beating heart. She looked up at him, face so pale, eyes so big, and he didn't want to ever not see her face in his life. "Don't do it. I'll go to him."

"Like hell you will," Donal growled as he clattered down the steps.

Riordan dragged his little sister into a hug, holding her tight. "Donal is right. You aren't going to him."

"But—" she gasped out against his chest.

Riordan met Donal's gaze over their sister's hunched form, his older brother's expression one of twisting grief. "If it has to be one of us, it'll be me, and I won't let him take the clan."

Saoirse poked him hard in the side. "No. The clan needs you. *We* need you. You're the one we all agreed to lead us."

"This is me leading, *dearthár beag.*"

"Riordan," Donal said softly.

He shook his head, fighting back the surge of fear and grief working its way up his throat. "Let's just—get some sleep. We'll go for a swim in the morning. Do a patrol. Spend the day together."

Figure out how to say goodbye, even if he didn't say it. His siblings heard the unspoken words anyway. Saoirse squeezed him tight enough to nearly crack his ribs for a few seconds more before letting him go. They all went upstairs and disappeared into their bedrooms, getting into sleeping clothes, but ended up sprawled across Riordan's bed in the way they always had when the world got hard. They'd huddled in piles as seal pups when they were young, and that need for closeness and skin contact hadn't ever faded.

If Riordan didn't sleep at all that night, well, he was the only one who knew.

No alarm was set, but they all woke well before dawn. The melancholy quiet of the morning seemed to infiltrate everyone's mood, leaving conversation by the wayside. They got dressed, and Saoirse made coffee, pouring it all into one big tumbler that they all sipped out of on the slow walk to the beach. Saoirse sniffled after every sip she took, causing Riordan to wrap an arm around her and pull her close, matching his stride to hers.

"This is my fault," she said quietly.

Riordan worked his jaw, hating the fact that she even thought to blame herself when she was the victim. "No, it's not. It never will be."

In the shadows between streetlights, he caught Donal looking back at him, his older brother giving a curt nod to Riordan's unspoken question about their sister. He knew Donal would do his damnedest to keep the guilt from eating Saoirse up inside, but he also knew it would be difficult on both of them after he'd gone.

They made it to the beach, all three of them pulling off their shoes and walking barefoot onto cold sand, feet staying dry until they reached the tidal line. In the early morning darkness, Donal and Riordan undressed and shook their jackets out into sealskin, draping the furry warmth over their shoulders. Saoirse bundled up their clothes and settled down cross-legged on the sand, clutching the tumbler of coffee in both hands. "I'll wait for you here."

The only reason Riordan hadn't called on someone else from the clan to keep her company was because she still had Gwen's artifact hanging from her throat. He and Donal left Saoirse on the sand, wading out into the cold waters of the bay, waves lapping against their bodies. Riordan slipped his sealskin off his shoulder as the water reached his chest, plunging it beneath the surface. Before he could sink under as well, Donal caught his arm.

"I don't want to be chief," Donal said in a low, wrecked voice. "The clan was always yours to lead."

"You'll be good at it," Riordan replied, reaching up to grip his brother's hand. "Saoirse will help."

"There has to be another way. Ella could help. There's Wade—"

"Niall cut the time. I don't know when he'll come to collect, but it's today, and I won't let him keep Saoirse," Riordan cut in.

"I don't want that bastard to keep either of you."

Riordan smiled tightly and shook his head. "Let's swim, yeah? One last time."

He needed to feel the ocean against his skin, to swim through the vastness of it and know what home felt like one last time. He was under no illusions that he'd ever step foot in the ocean again. No one whose skin was stolen ever experienced the waves once they were land-bound. Oh, they might see the ocean from a distance, might hear its siren song in their dreams and nightmares, but they'd never swim in it again, not as they were.

So Riordan held his breath and sank beneath the surface, twisting his skin around himself and tumbling into a shift, coming out of the roll in his seal form. Donal was right beside him in the water, just as quick, following where Riordan swam into the deep, dark waters of the sea. He missed having Saoirse with them, but she'd get back in the water soon enough.

They didn't do an official patrol, staying within sight of the shore as they played in the waves. It was bittersweet, knowing what he was losing, but it was worth who he was saving. By the time the sun was up and the water less murky near the surface, Riordan reluctantly called an end to the swim. He got Donal's attention with a nose nudge against his older brother's side, and they swam to the surface. Right before they broke it, a strange, chilling, sonorous echo flowed through the water, coming from the deep waters farther out in the bay, in the open ocean.

It made Riordan want to get back to shore *fast*, and Donal seemed to feel the same. They swam quickly through the water until they reached the beach. Riordan twisted in the shallow waves, riding them in as a human and coming up out of the water with his sealskin wrapped around his waist.

"What was *that*?" Donal asked, swiping a hand over his wet hair.

"A threat Lady Caith warned us about," Riordan said grimly. "You'll need to be careful. Make sure the clans are aware there's something out there in the water that means us harm."

Donal opened his mouth to argue but then paused, eyes narrowing as he looked past Riordan. "Huh. He looks mad."

"Who?" Riordan faced the shore and realized Wade was standing beside Saoirse, arms crossed over his chest and scowling. It was still early enough that no one else was on the beach in their general vicinity. The sun had barely cleared the horizon, sending everyone's shadows stretching out to the west along the sand. "Wade."

"I called him," Saoirse said, a stubborn look on her face. "I told him what you were planning to do."

"Which is *dumb*," Wade said fiercely. "You aren't giving up your skin today. I told you I'd help you stop Niall, but this isn't what I was talking about."

"Wade—"

Wade held up a finger. "Nope. I don't want to hear it. At least, not until I've had a chance to investigate Niall's territory."

"You can't go back there."

"I didn't get to go in the first place. We got waylaid by Lady Caith. And yes, I'm going. I'm good at sniffing out magical hoards, and I still need to find Casey and Harper. Just because Niall gave you an ultimatum doesn't mean you have to give in right away. He wants your skin today? He can come and try to take it one second to midnight, and then I'll fry his ass for the audacity."

Wade was so incensed on Riordan's behalf that the younger man's protectiveness left him feeling warm. And if today was honestly going to be the last day of his freedom, he wasn't going to regret any choices. So he left the surf behind for dry sand, crowding into Wade's space and kissing him deeply. Wade made a sound that he quickly swallowed, licking his way into Wade's mouth with a focus that made his lungs burn.

When they finally parted, Wade just stared at him, a flush to his cheeks that couldn't be blamed on the rising sun. "That's not going to distract me."

"A pity," Riordan murmured.

"Also, you're wet and mostly naked. Get dressed. This isn't a nudist beach. None of us need a ticket."

Donal and Saoirse laughed at that, and Riordan chose to ignore his siblings.

"How's that fixation going, boyo?" Donal asked innocently as he and Riordan started getting dressed.

"What fixation?" Wade asked.

"Nothing," Riordan said hastily. "Come on, let's get back to the house."

"I'll drive you all back."

It was a couple blocks, but Riordan wasn't going to argue, not when Wade had a stubborn set to his jaw. They all piled into his Audi, and he drove for barely a minute back home. They all got out, but Wade didn't. Riordan paused in closing his door, peering at Wade. "Are you coming inside? I'll make you breakfast."

"As much as I really want to, I think I need to get to Beacon Hill," Wade said.

"You're actually saying no to food?"

"I *know*. Don't tell my pack." Wade cracked a smile, and Riordan tried to return it. "Don't stay here today. Go back to my hotel room. I brought you an extra key card. Niall won't know to look for you there."

Wade flipped open the center console and pulled out a little envelope that held an electronic key card. Riordan didn't know how to decline it—what use would he have for it after Niall took him?—but he couldn't say no to Wade. Riordan accepted the key card and pocketed it, unsure how to tell Wade he wasn't sure he'd get to use it.

"What are you going to do in Beacon Hill?"

Wade smiled, his teeth more fangs than anything else, brown eyes flashing gold for a split second. "Hunting."

Riordan wanted to protest, to offer to go along, but he knew that would just put himself within Niall's reach. For all that Wade was a dragon and bargains couldn't work on him, Riordan wasn't so lucky. "Call me when you're done. I'll worry if you don't."

"Sure. Just don't give up your skin to Niall, or I'll have to hunt you next."

Riordan managed a smile before straightening and closing the car door. He waved goodbye to Wade and stepped up onto the sidewalk. Wade drove off, and Riordan watched him go until the car turned the corner.

"Maybe you should've gone with him," Saoirse said.

"I'm not leaving you to Niall," Riordan said.

"Will you go to the hotel?" Riordan didn't answer her as he headed inside their home, making her poke him in the back. "That's what I thought. If you're going to be dumb about all this, then put your skin in the trunk while you handle clan stuff. It'll buy us time if Niall comes back around."

Riordan didn't know if the trunk would be enough to stop Niall from stealing his skin. If Niall was truly a prayer-born god of some sort, he doubted their clan's magic would be capable of keeping them safe. Certainly, he hadn't been.

That fact galled him, and Riordan hated feeling like a failure.

"So what's the plan?" Saoirse asked after Riordan and Donal had locked their skins away in the trunk upstairs. "And don't say giving your skin to Niall in exchange for mine."

"That *is* the plan," Riordan said with a shake of his head. "I won't let him keep your skin."

"Well, we won't let him have the clan."

"He won't if I give leadership over to Donal."

"I don't *want* it," Donal said stubbornly. "I never wanted to be chief, and certainly not like this. You're not giving Wade or Ella enough trust to help us out, and I think you should."

"Wade seems like he could wriggle his way out of anything, and he knows dangerous people that put Niall on the defensive," Saoirse added.

Riordan gave both his siblings a pained look. "I don't think we should rely on the support of two master vampires when they said they didn't want an alliance."

"Then what do you want to do? I'm *not* losing you, boyo."

"I'm with Saoirse," Donal said, meeting Riordan's gaze. "Even if we're on the run until Wade and Ella can get Saoirse's skin back, that keeps you and the clan out of Niall's hands."

"Going on the run means we give up our territory, and *he* wins," Riordan protested. "I won't let that happen."

"Then let Wade do his thing while we go to ground in Boston for a few days."

Riordan wanted to believe their options would work, he did, but he knew what Niall was capable of, and he was terrified of leaving his sister to that fate. "You need to be prepared to take over."

Donal reached out and gripped his shoulders, giving him a shake. "You need to be prepared for us not letting you go."

Saoirse threw her arms around both of them, squeezing in her own hug. "It's all of us or none of us. That's what we promised when we left for these shores."

Riordan closed his eyes and pulled his siblings close into a tight three-way hug. He ducked his head and closed his eyes, breathing in their scents, committing everything to memory. "All right. Let's get the clan safe."

More than fifty selkies were part of Clan Maguire, some of whom traveled west with them centuries ago and all the others finding their way to them over the years. They'd been lucky in that none who'd become clan had ever tried to break the clan up. Riordan was never cruel, and he was willing to work hard to keep the clan and territory safe. He wouldn't ask anything of his clan that he wasn't willing to do himself.

Donal got a pot of coffee brewing while Saoirse went upstairs to pack go-bags for each of them. Riordan settled himself at the kitchen table and pulled out his phone, opening up the group message that had the clan's captains' contacts. Each person in the chat was responsible for notifying upward of ten selkies in their contacts cohort to give out his orders. This way, Riordan wasn't trying to wrangle dozens of people at once. He'd give the orders that needed to be given, and the others would see them done.

He knew none of them would like what he had to say.

Niall has called in the bargain. I want the clan to go to ground in Boston. No arguments. It hopefully won't be for long. If things get bad, Donal will be chief.

"No I won't," Donal said as he set a mug of coffee down beside Riordan. "Because we'll find a way out of this. We always do."

Riordan tapped furiously at his phone as he tried to respond to the anticipated deluge of text messages that was filling up his screen. "Right now, I have to get the clan out of harm's way."

It meant needing to stay at their home for the next few hours because inevitably some of the clan stopped by to try to change his mind and others to figure out how to handle the clan's myriad of businesses. Maguire's Pub could still stay open and be run by the mundane humans on staff. Donal had to revise the schedule, and the pub would be closing early on two of the nights due to staffing short-ages. He'd see if Ella could send some werecreatures around to keep an eye on it.

"Is that it?" Saoirse asked a little impatiently after they'd seen the last clan member out of the home. "Send another text and tell people to stop coming around. We need to leave."

It was close to noon, and so far, Niall hadn't come around, but that wasn't to say he wouldn't. Riordan pocketed his phone and nodded at his sister. "Let's get out of here."

"Our bags are already in the car."

They were taking only one because Donal and Saoirse were insis-tent that Riordan stay with Wade. He didn't like leaving them alone, but they had a condo in Back Bay the two would lie low in for a day or so.

Someone knocked on the front door before they could leave for the garage in the back. Whoever was on the porch felt like fae to his senses.

And they felt familiar.

Donal went to open the door, revealing their guest. "Lady Caith."

Riordan peered over his brother's shoulder at where Lady Caith stood on the porch, dressed in a sleek white business suit with a gold metallic blouse beneath the tailored jacket. Her magenta hair fell down to her waist in styled waves this time, the delicate points of her ears peeking through. She wore minimal jewelry, even if the pair of fae guards with her were practically bristling with weapons most likely glamoured to be hidden. Riordan could pick them out because fae magic was easy enough to sense and adjust for while this close.

"Chief Riordan," Lady Caith said. The use of his title made Riordan blink in surprise, as it was rare to have someone of her stature actually acknowledge his rank. "May I come in?"

"We were just leaving," Riordan said, but he still stepped back, and Donal did as well. Saoirse was practically vibrating beside him with the clear desire to get moving.

Lady Caith stepped inside their home, her guards coming with her. Donal inched closer, subtly putting himself between Riordan and the guards. Lady Caith glanced around, letting nothing show on her face about her opinion of their home. Riordan knew it didn't look like they had money, even if they did, but he was proud of the home he and his siblings had been in for decades.

"My fae tell me that Niall has become the target of the Boston Night Court."

"We didn't broker an alliance with Abhartach. He wasn't receptive."

"Neither was Lucien," Saoirse retorted.

Lady Caith stilled, her attention snapping to Saoirse. "The daywalker is in Boston?"

"Wade seemed friendly with him."

"Not really," Riordan hastened to say. "But they know each other. Neither master vampire was happy about Niall dropping in like he did."

Lady Caith folded her hands together and focused on Riordan. It unnerved him to some degree, but he didn't let it show. "Niall has been testing my territory borders. Several of my guards have been harmed. One has been murdered."

"Nothing's made the news," Riordan said.

Lady Caith's lips curled fractionally. "I know how to keep such disagreements out of sight of mundane humans."

Her words might have been an insult, but Riordan chose not to take them that way. She was here for a reason, and he rather thought he knew why, which meant he wasn't going to muck up their chances of making her an ally, even if only temporarily. "I've told my clan to go to ground for the next few days. We're buying Wade time to scope out Niall's territory right now."

"And do you believe he will be able to find what was stolen?"

"I don't know, but he's trying." Riordan tactfully didn't say it was more than what Lady Caith was doing, but he rather thought the words were heard anyway, judging by how she narrowed her eyes.

"Niall would not hide his hostages out in the open. That was not how he conducted himself when he was mortal."

Some tiny kindle of hope burned in his chest, and Riordan had to try his hardest not to snuff it out. "If you have any ideas on where Niall might be keeping the god pack alphas and my sister's skin, then tell me. I'd bargain with you for that."

Lady Caith tilted her head, eyeing him with an unblinking gaze. "As you would bargain with Niall?"

"I won't leave my sister's skin with him." She had to know the choices that left him; otherwise, he doubted she'd be knocking on his door.

"In that case, I believe we can come to an arrangement."

"We're not jumping from one toxic bargain into another," Donal said sharply.

"I have no desire for your skin. What I want is Niall gone from Boston. Denying him territory is a way to box him in and push him out. Which means I will not let him have yours."

"How kind of you," Riordan said wryly.

"If you were leaving, I assume it was to keep yourselves out of

Niall's reach. In which case, we should discuss terms of an alliance somewhere else."

"Your territory?"

"If you like. It would—"

The window shattered as something crashed through it, magic exploding outward with a concussive *bang* that tore through the air and the threshold, sending them all flying. Riordan slammed into the stairs, all the air leaving his lungs as he landed, knocking his head against one edge hard enough that everything spun in a sickening way.

Then, his entire world went up in flames.

CHAPTER SEVENTEEN

Wade had parked on the street in Beacon Hill rather than the parking garage. He had a general idea of where Niall's territory was located from what Ella and Riordan had told him. Which meant he was fully ready to march over and break into Niall's home and have a look around. He had a nose for magical artifacts and magic in general these days—a skill that helped with the redistribution of wealth, in his opinion—and if Saoirse's skin was anywhere in Niall's home, Wade could find it.

That was the plan.

So of course, Lucien had to be a bastard and derail it.

A motorcycle roared up the cobblestone street and skidded to a stop next to where Wade was walking. Both riders were decked out in Kevlar leather riding pants and jackets. The woman perched behind the driver lifted the helmet's visor, and Carmen's distinctive red-pupiled eyes stared out at him. "If you're looking for Niall, he's not home."

"Is he dead? Tell me he's dead and I can ransack the place," Wade said, crossing his arms.

"What do you think?"

"I think Abby Boy is pissed about the attack, and you're both on daylight duty out of the selfishness of your undead and demonic hearts. Neither of you have ever passed up the opportunity to claim territory that isn't yours."

"The Manhattan Night Court always belonged to me," Lucien said, voice muffled a little through the motorcycle helmet. Unlike Carmen, he didn't raise his visor.

Wade opened his mouth to argue, but considering how that fight played out and ended with his freedom, he'd give Lucien that point. "Fine. I won't argue that, but I will argue everything else."

"You don't know what my Night Court owns."

"I know it's not going to own Boston. Something tells me Abby Boy won't like it if you try."

Carmen rested one elbow on Lucien's shoulder, propping up her helmeted head in one hand. "Niall went to ground last night. Biyu pulled background information on all the properties he owns in Boston, and we went hunting. We're willing to share if you're interested."

Wade was well aware of the skills of Lucien's best hacker. "How much is it going to cost me?"

"How much is your selkie's skin worth?" Lucien asked.

Wade worked his jaw, angry that they'd figured out his current weakness so quickly. "Not enough to bargain for things I don't own, but I'd be willing to pay for it."

It wasn't something he doubted Riordan would be happy about if he tried—him bargaining off territory that wasn't his to save the selkies. Every fight was always about territory when it came down to it. While Wade wouldn't act on behalf of the selkies or the Boston god pack, he'd certainly be willing to tear apart Niall's territory to find those things that didn't belong to the wannabe god.

"We'll never say no to money."

Wade sighed heavily. "Marek is going to be so pissed I'm funding terrorism, but sure, I'll bite. What exactly do I get in return?"

"The location where Niall keeps his hostages."

Wade took a step forward, letting his arms drop down to his sides. "You know where he's keeping Casey and Harper?"

"Yes."

"Do I want to know how you found out so quickly?" Wade narrowed his eyes. "You've been here longer than a few days, haven't you?"

"What I do isn't your business."

"Yeah, yeah, you're only in it for the money. Fine. How much for Casey and Harper's location? And by that, I mean where they're currently located, right now, for me to go rescue. None of this 'you saw them last night, and they've been moved' business."

Carmen laughed. "Oh, you're learning to pick apart the details."

"Sage is a lawyer who works for the fae. Who do you think I learned it from?"

"A pity you learned it at all. The information will cost you one million dollars for each werewolf."

Wade winced but pulled out his phone. "You're that hard up for money?"

"No. We just like annoying your pack."

"Clearly."

Wade sent off another group text about the financial transaction he was about to do and then a separate one to Sage and Marek promising he'd babysit Lillian anytime they wanted to go out on a date as an apology for giving their accountant a headache. "Give me the routing number."

Doing business with Lucien always made Wade want a shower, and he resolved not to tell Ella what he was doing. Still, he got the information he needed once the money was transferred. Carmen's riding glove had a fingertip made with fabric that could track on a touchscreen. When she confirmed the money had been sent, she finally gave him something useful. "Niall owns a hotel downtown. One of those rebranded modern ones that he's putting the finishing touches on. It's slated to open in a few weeks for the height of summer season. Some of our vampires have seen him transporting one of the werecreatures there off and on."

"Casey, I'm guessing? You haven't seen Harper?"

"No, we haven't seen her."

"So you don't know she's there."

"You'll find out when you get there, won't you? But if Niall is keeping hostages, he'd do well to keep one under guard and under threat to keep the other in line. It's what we would do."

"Because hostage taking is such great business."

The corners of Carmen's eyes creased in a way that told Wade she was smirking at him. "It is for us."

Wade tilted his head, phone still in hand and banking app still accessible. "How much to have Biyu hack any security cameras at the hotel to make them go dark when I get there?"

At that, Carmen did laugh. "You have grown if you're thinking like Patrick."

"I'll take that as a compliment."

"It wasn't meant as one. We'll go half a million this time."

"Done."

If it meant he could do some casual breaking and entering without being on camera, so much the better. Wade transferred the additional funds and gave his phone number to Carmen.

"Biyu will call you when the security cameras are down," Carmen said.

Wade didn't question how she'd know when he arrived and just nodded. "Where is the hotel?"

Carmen rattled off the address and flipped down her visor, and then Lucien drove off with a window-rattling roar of his motorcycle. Wade didn't stick around, turning on his feet to run back to his car.

He still needed to find Saoirse's skin, but rescuing Casey and Harper was also something he had to do. And if he could get the pair of them out of Niall's clutches, then that was one less point of pressure for the supernatural and preternatural communities in Boston to worry about. It would also free up the Boston god pack to help the selkie clans fight against Niall.

So Wade made the choice to drive downtown rather than ransack Niall's home, following the GPS directions to the waterfront hotel in question. He parked a couple blocks away in a garage so he wouldn't have to worry about getting towed since he didn't know what was about to go down. All he knew was that if Casey and Harper were inside, he wasn't leaving without them.

He pulled on a baseball cap, stuck a pair of sunglasses on his nose, and started walking like he was a tourist out for a stroll. The hotel in question was easy enough to pick out once he got closer. The pier it sat on wasn't fenced off in any way, which probably meant construction was finished. Wade didn't see any heavy-duty equipment anywhere or construction workers, but the hotel was clearly not open yet. No taxis idled out front, no hotel workers manned the closed door, but the lights were on inside.

Wade clocked the numerous security cameras on the walk up. Before he could start to worry, his phone rang with an incoming call from an unknown number. He answered it, not slowing his stride. "Yeah?"

"The security cameras are down," Carmen said.

"Awesome. Never call me again."

Wade hung up, shoved his phone into his back pocket, and headed for the hotel's front doors. He didn't have a plan, exactly, other than to sniff out where Casey and Harper might be held inside. Magic was easy for him to detect, even if it didn't do anything to him. Hotels were public property though, which meant no threshold would stick, so all he'd have to worry about is whatever spells and wards Niall had set up inside that might make getting Casey and Harper out difficult and anyone on guard duty with guns or other kinds of weapons.

All of which he knew he could handle, even without his pack there with him.

Wade paused in front of the double doors, squinting through the glass at the empty but brightly lit lobby. He gripped one of the long door handles, braced his other hand against the adjacent door, and used his supernatural strength to yank it open, breaking the lock in the process. The glass cracked along the edges from the force of the pull but didn't shatter. Wade slipped inside, not sensing any magic yet in the immediate vicinity.

He breathed in deeply as he headed for the elevator bank, searching for the door that would lead to the stairwell people only ever really used in emergencies. His nostrils flared on his next breath, senses changing as he shifted mass ever so slightly. Everything became *more*—the lights were brighter, the colors more saturated, and the air smelled distinctly of the fae who had passed through, edged with that floral scent that spoke of magic.

And werecreatures.

"Bingo," he muttered.

Wade found the stairwell, and he slipped inside, not needing to break any locks this time. The hotel looked like it was eight stories high, probably restricted from going higher by the pier it was built on and to not interfere with other buildings' views. That still left eight floors that could contain any number of Niall's people and hopefully Casey and Harper.

He'd sniff them out.

Wade expanded his senses, parsing out the ones that didn't matter—bleach and cement and paint, ugh, so sharp—in favor of the almost floral scent that meant fae. It wasn't that they smelled like perfume but that they had an underlying woodsy, floral hint that lingered around them. He didn't know if it was because of their magic or what, but they were easy to pick out of a crowd, even without clocking their pointed ears and strange-colored hair and eyes. Almost as easy as the wet-fur smell of werecreatures.

Living in New York City, with its crush of people in Manhattan in particular, came with a plethora of scents. When Wade had first joined the pack, he'd gone for walks at Jono's behest, senses open, learning to differentiate and pick out particular scents and follow them to their origin. Enhanced senses weren't owned by one particular group, and dragons were very, very good at sniffing out magic and magical artifacts.

Like now.

No threshold would ever exist anywhere in the hotel's foundation, but that didn't mean someone couldn't cast magic in the area. Magic lingered in the air on the third floor, making his nose twitch. He also smelled the scent of werecreatures and blood, which pissed him off. It was never a good situation when people were bleeding.

Wade eyed the door on the third-floor landing for a moment before shrugging to himself. "What would Patrick do?"

Make a scene, which was exactly what Wade did.

He opened the door and waltzed into the hallway like he wasn't on a breaking-and-entering spree. He heard voices down the way and dialed up his hearing, his brain squeezing in the familiar way of translating language.

"—my turn to have some fun with the animal," a fae was saying in their language.

Wade bit back a growl and started to run rather than walk. He was pretty sure he tore through a couple of wards that felt like spiderwebs breaking across his body, but whatever magic they contained never touched him. One of them must have been some kind of alarm to notify its caster because when he reached the hotel room door in question, he didn't even need to knock. It was already opening.

"Oh, hey. Have you seen housekeeping? I need a spray bottle," Wade said.

The fae standing in the door stared at him with ugly orange eyes that widened. "How did you—"

Wade didn't wait for the fae to finish speaking. He aimed an uppercut at the fae with all his strength—which was considerable when one was a dragon.

He tore the fae's head off with that punch, shattering bone and blood spraying through the air and staining his clothes as he shoved the door open and muscled past the falling body. He shook meaty bits off his hand and then had to dodge out of the way of another fae, nearly falling into the bathroom.

"Would you watch where you're going?" Wade shouted.

The fae reappeared in the doorway, magic crackling around their fingers. She was tall and icily beautiful, and Wade ruined everything about her when he roared out a fireball so hot it seared through her upper body in an instant. Wade was a fire dragon, and the fire he could produce even in human form was hotter than lava.

He stepped over the remains of that corpse and swung himself out of the bathroom and into the hotel room proper. Through the smell of charred flesh, the stinging scent of aconite finally hit his nose.

"She's *not* an animal," Wade snapped, glaring at the last remaining fae on guard duty.

They'd certainly treated Harper like one.

Someone had removed the bed, leaving an open space where Harper was chained to the wall by silver chains and cuffs. The carpet beneath her was stained with blood and would have to be replaced before the room was given to a guest. Her arms were covered in burns and whip marks, as was her torso that he could see through the shreds of her clothes, courtesy of the aconite-laced leather whip the fae standing near her held. The fae also held a gun, which was pointed at Wade.

"What *are* you?" the fae demanded, vibrant lime-green eyes wide in his face. His short hair was the same color, and paired with his brown skin, the whole look reminded Wade of a kiwi, just probably not as tasty.

"If I say your worst nightmare, is that too cliché?"

In answer, the fae pulled the trigger.

Wade shifted mass, bringing his scales to the forefront of his human form. The mass behind them he was prepared to shift into place would be enough to deflect the bullets. In full dragon form, regular bullets weren't even noticeable. It was missiles he'd have to watch out for, according to Reed, but Wade was a lot better these days at hiding from radar.

His scales were just in case any of the bullets got through the fire he spat at the fae. Jono always said to have a backup plan whenever he went into a fight. Jono always told Patrick the same thing, to which Patrick always quipped that Jono and the pack were his backup. Wade didn't have his pack with him, but he had all the teachings they'd given him over the last five years or so.

The fae went up in flames, and this time, the heat and smoke were enough to set off the sprinklers overhead. Water poured out in a spray as the fire alarm blared through the hotel in a piercing siren that had Wade immediately dialing down his hearing, because *ow*.

He hurried to Harper's side, kneeling next to her. She stared at him with badly bruised brown eyes, her dark hair matted in places from blood. "I need to touch you."

"Who are you?" she croaked.

"Wade, from the New York City god pack. Your dire found a workaround in the shitty bargain Niall forced on your pack. Can I touch you?"

Despite knowing they were running out of time, he kept his hands hovering over the aconite-laced silver shackles locked around her wrists that impeded her shifting. He didn't know what had been done to her beyond the obvious—being the unwilling punching bag for fae—but he wasn't about to trigger a breakdown with an unwanted touch.

Harper bared her teeth at him. Several were broken, and a couple in the front were gone completely. "Get me free."

Wade shifted a tiny bit more mass, and black talons erupted from his fingertips. Harper flinched, nostrils flaring. He gave her a tight smile, knowing everything about his true form was probably making her uncomfortable. "Sorry."

He carefully slid two talons between Harper's wrist and the cuff, not needing to exert much pressure to slice through the silver. Dragon strength helped with that, and he tossed the broken cuff aside before working to free Harper of the other. The moment she was free of them both, she scrambled away from the wall on shaky limbs, nearly face-planting on the carpet. Wade caught her, mindful of his hands, even if he couldn't be as mindful of her injuries as he'd like because he didn't know the full extent of them.

"We have to go. Can you shift?" he said as he shifted mass again to make his talons disappear. The scales covering his body sank back under his skin, giving no more hint of what he truly was.

"He'll kill Casey if I leave," Harper gasped out.

"I won't let him. Needing to help you both is why I came to Boston. Is Casey here?"

Harper shook her head. "Niall only brought him around to prove to Casey I was still alive. Casey was never held prisoner here."

Well, there went rescuing them both at the same time. "I'll look for him afterward, but you need to come with me. If you stay, you risk your pack."

Wade knew there was a chance he might not be able to keep that promise to her of getting Casey back. She had to know that too, but Harper proved why she was an alpha when she swore before saying, "Okay. Let's go. I can't shift though. Too much aconite poisoning."

That was never good. Wade took a second to pry the fire opal ring off his finger and put it on one of Harper's. "Fae magic, but the good kind. It'll keep you safe while I get us out of here."

She still shuddered, but he couldn't tell if that was her probably newfound aversion to fae magic or the fact he most likely jostled some injuries when he lifted her bridal style in his arms. He could see the magic wrapping around her, the scent of it reminding him of Órlaith. He knew Harper wouldn't find it comforting, but Wade did.

The water pouring down on them was freezing. He stepped over the corpses and out of the hotel room, pitching them both down the hallway at a fast run that he hoped wouldn't hurt Harper too much. He pushed that bit of self through his aura that would make people look away, vision sparkling a little at the edges from a glow only he could see. It was a trick that helped him hide from radar when flying at night and could make people not see him in certain instances, whether in human or dragon form.

It wasn't completely foolproof. He couldn't force millions of people to not see him if he flew during the day, but in moments like this, it worked. They made it to the elevator bank when the doors to the stairwell there slammed open. Wade backpedaled and got him and Harper up against the wall as soundlessly as he could, holding his breath as soaked fae raced by with supernatural speed toward the hotel room, arguing with each other in their language.

Wade glanced down at Harper, seeing she was biting her split lip so hard the skin was white, and it was bleeding again as she tried to hold back an exclamation of pain. She smelled a little like fear and anger to his nose right then, which he couldn't blame her for.

After the last fae passed them, Wade moved to catch the closing door with his foot, shoving it back open so he could swing them around into the stairwell. The fire alarm hadn't stopped, and neither had the sprinklers. He honestly hoped all the water damage ruined the hotel. It would be too much to hope that the first responders would discover the room Harper had been held prisoner in. Wade knew the fae would probably use glamour to hide all the evidence of their wrongdoings, giving an illusion of a regular hotel room.

He wished they'd get caught, but if it took eating Niall to make him pay for what he did, then Wade would gladly take one for the team.

Harper was stiff in his arms by the time he made it to the ground floor, the jostling not helping her wounds any. He wanted to ask if there was anyone with her god pack who handled healing but bit back the question. They weren't in the clear yet.

Which was made abundantly apparent when he hauled open the door to the first-floor elevator bank and came face-to-face with a group of fae heading toward them, probably looking to head up the way they'd just come. The door opening meant they *looked*, and Wade knew it would be a fight to keep them from not seeing him.

So he took a deep breath and let out a roar full of fire that scorched the entire area in front of him—including all the fae. The magic in the ring flared up crystal-white around Harper, protecting her from the heat as Wade burned to ash everything around them. He heard someone shout from farther away, and he scowled, sharp teeth catching on his lips.

"Fuck it. Hold on," Wade warned.

He ran, the world blurring with the speed he put into his stride. The shield held, protecting them from the flying glass of the front doors that he crashed through to get outside. The fire department hadn't arrived yet, but the piercing sounds of sirens in the distance were getting closer. Police and the fire department were on their way, and he wanted to be anywhere else but on the hotel grounds.

Wade didn't stop running until he made it to the rental car a couple of blocks away, skidding to a stop in the garage so hard he ended up falling up against the side of the car from the sudden lack of motion. "Sorry, sorry!"

Harper grunted softly. "It's fine."

"You know, my alpha says the same thing when he's bleeding like you are, and none of us ever believe him." Harper managed a sound that might have been a chuckle, but it turned into a pained huff when Wade finally put her on her feet. She wobbled for a moment, breathing fast and hard as if she'd been the one running. Wade reached past her to grab the car door and open it for her. "Come on. I know a bunch of people who have missed you."

Harper flinched a little, but the relief that flowed across her face was something Wade understood. There was nothing like the feeling of being free.

He helped her into the car, got her buckled up, and then scrambled behind the steering wheel to start the engine. As much as he wanted to career out of the parking garage and speed away, he knew that would only draw attention to them. So he didn't speed out of the parking garage, paid the ticket rather than bust through the gate, and pulled into the street. He was trying to connect his phone to the car's system while watching the road when Harper swiped it out of his hand.

"You don't know where you're going, do you?" she asked.

"If this was Manhattan, I would."

She side-eyed him with her bruised eyes while plugging in his phone. "You pack a lot of fire power. Literally."

"They deserved it. They probably deserved more, but I was in a hurry."

She tapped at the screen on the dash, her home already one of the top choices, considering Wade had been driving between that address, his hotel, and Riordan's home for the past few days. "Is my pack okay? Niall hasn't done anything to them?"

"Niall is a bastard, and he's pissed off a lot of people. He is currently being hunted by two master vampires and their Night Courts."

Harper stilled, fingers resting against the screen. "Two? Boston only has one."

"Yeah," Wade drawled, keeping his eyes on the road. "Lucien was taking a vacation and stopped by to say hi to Abby Boy. Niall thought that would be a good time to drop in for a visit, and guess what? The bastard made things worse for himself, which is a nice change of pace."

"*Lucien* is in Boston? The *daywalker*?"

"Yup. And now you know why Niall's little hostile takeover got derailed." Wade glanced at her and shook his head at the concern he saw on her face. "Don't worry. My pack has dealt with Lucien before. He's not going to stick around, and I paid for all the information, not your pack."

Harper pressed her fingertips carefully to her forehead, as if she had a headache. "You paid Lucien for information?"

"Well, I paid him to get us an introduction to Abby Boy to ask that master vampire to go after Niall. Neither of them was interested until Niall attacked the Green Fairy."

Harper covered her face with both hands and groaned. "Niall is really going after everyone, isn't he? He wants Boston."

"Yeah. Anything I should know about that? Did you maybe overhear where he might be keeping Casey?"

Harper leaned back against the seat, paused to recline it as flat as it would go, and sighed as she stretched out. She was shorter than Wade, built tiny, reminding him of Emma in that way. "The fae think of us as animals. Niall talked around me, not at me, but not about anything I'd consider important. He did say that if I tried to escape, he'd feed Casey to a sea monster."

Wade tilted his head, Riordan's warning about a threat in the sea ringing through his mind. "Out in the bay? Lady Caith warned us there's something in the sea."

"That ice queen finally came out of her redbrick tower to help us mere mortals? I find that difficult to believe."

"We went to warn her about Niall and asked for help. She didn't really seem inclined to join the fight."

"We? You and Ella?"

"No, me and Riordan."

"Ah. Niall did mention he had a selkie's skin in his possession."

Wade immediately perked up at that. "I'm guessing it's too much to hope that he bragged about how he stole it and where he hid it?"

"Sorry. He only mentioned he had it. How's my pack?"

"Uh, good? Ella has kept them safe."

"You said she asked your pack for help?"

"Yeah, Niall forbade her and anyone else in the Boston god pack from asking for help from anyone within the city. He placed a geas on everyone so they can't talk about what he's done, but the loophole meant she could request aid from people outside Boston. So she did, and here I am."

"Thank you," Harper said after a moment, her voice quiet and full of emotion Wade pretended he couldn't smell.

"No thanks needed. It's what pack does."

She nodded before finally removing the ring he'd given her. "Here. This is yours."

Wade took it and put it back on. Conversation lapsed after that, and the silence stayed between them until Wade pulled up in front of Harper's home in the god pack territory. He'd barely put the car into park when the front door to the house slammed open and several blurs streaked outside. One of the blurs resolved itself into Ella, and she yanked open the passenger-side door so hard she shook the car.

"Hey, watch it!" Wade yelped. "This is a rental!"

Ella ignored him in favor of her alpha. "*Harper!*"

At least she unbuckled the seat belt rather than rip it off. Ella carefully gathered Harper into her arms and picked her up out of the car with supernatural strength. Her eyes were shining with tears, and Wade could see other god pack members leaving their homes down the street and hurrying toward them.

"Hey," Harper croaked, beaming at her pack as they crowded in close. "I missed you all."

Wade couldn't see her anymore, not in the crush of werecreatures gathering in the front yard. He leaned over the middle console and cleared his throat. "She needs some potions to reverse aconite poisoning. She won't be able to shift until it's cleared her system. Niall had her chained up in his hotel that hasn't opened yet."

The crowd of werecreatures parted until he could see Ella, who was still holding Harper, her eyes as watery as Harper's had been in the car. "*Thank* you."

"Do you have somewhere safe to go to ground with her until I can find Casey?"

"Yes."

"Good. Don't tell me."

Ella cracked a smile. "I thought you'd be with Riordan today."

"I was. I'm heading back there right now, and then I'll search for Casey. I think I know where he might be or at least where Niall might take him. If I'm right, then I need the selkies to help me."

"Is he being kept on the islands in the bay?"

"It's a possibility I need to check out. Right now, take care of your alpha."

Ella nodded, mouth firming. "We will. Call me when you need backup. You aren't going after Casey alone. Some of the pack has boats."

"You can't swim."

"We're better on land than the selkies, and if he's on any of the islands, we'll find him."

"Got it. I'll keep you updated."

One of the werecreatures closed the passenger door for him, and Wade unlocked the brakes and pulled into the street. He left the Boston god pack to their reunion with one of their alphas and added Riordan's address back into the GPS. Without Harper in the car, he drove a little faster, wanting to get back to Riordan's home to see if the selkies had left yet. He hadn't received a text from them about where they were going, but he hoped Riordan might take him up on the offer of a hotel room.

Wade was optimistic right up until he saw the curl of black smoke twisting through the sky.

"Oh no, no, *no*," Wade said, stomach sinking.

It could be someone else's home on fire, but Wade was of the Patrick Collins school of thought that coincidences never happened.

He pressed down harder on the gas pedal, wanting to go faster but knowing he couldn't go too far above the speed limit and risk getting pulled over or accidentally hitting someone. The smoke grew larger in his field of vision as he drew closer to the residential area where Riordan lived. When he turned onto L Street, he could see farther down that police had blocked off the intersection at the corner where Maguire's Pub was located.

"*Shit.*"

L Street was narrow, and most of the parking was taken. There was one spot at the corner where plastic poles had been set up to discourage parking in the area. Directly behind it was a spot that Wade could fit in, but only if he ran over one of the poles.

He ran over the pole.

Wade pitched himself out of the car, ignoring the police officer who yelled at him to get back as he careened toward the corner.

"I live there!" Wade shouted, lying through his teeth.

He put on a burst of supernatural speed to evade the police officer, dialing his hearing up. Doing so enabled him to hear the Maguire siblings frantically arguing with EMS who were trying to look after them and—yeah, that was definitely Lady Caith. All of them had been corralled some distance from the burning house.

Wade skidded to a halt beside the group. "What the hell happened?"

Heads snapped around to look at him, but Saoirse was the first to speak, voice cracking when she did so. "They're in the trunk!"

No question about what she was talking about.

"Okay," Wade said. "Stay here."

"*Wade*—" Riordan said, reaching for him.

But he was already racing past them, dodging past firefighters who shouted at him to stop, and ran into the burning building.

CHAPTER EIGHTEEN

THE FIRE AND SMOKE DIDN'T REALLY BOTHER HIM, BUT WADE HELD HIS breath anyway as he entered the burning home. Flames licked at him as he skidded to a halt in what had once been the living room. The stairs were on fire and charred all the way through. There was no chance they'd hold his weight if he tried to take them up to the second floor. Neither could he say the second floor would hold his weight, judging by the smoke billowing down the stairwell.

All of the fire smelled like magic. Not hellfire, thankfully—Wade knew that would've been *bad*—but it clearly wasn't set with regular accelerant. Whatever had started it was magical in nature, and no amount of water was likely to put it all out. The fire was going to eat through everything in the house, and Wade knew one of the best ways to disrupt magic was to use fire.

If Riordan and Donal had put their skins in the trunk in Riordan's bedroom for safekeeping and transport and they weren't able to get up there after the attack, then their selkie skins were at risk of being destroyed or stolen.

Wade squinted, shifting mass so that he could see through choking smoke and bright fire. His vision changed, and he could see the crumbling steps better, some of them completely gone. The distance between the first floor and the second was seemingly impassable if one tried to walk it.

He could jump it.

"Hey!" a firefighter barked from behind him. "Are you *stupid?* We need to get you out of here!"

Wade ignored the firefighter, dug his heels in hard to the floor that had lost its carpeting, and used his supernatural strength to fling himself up to the second-floor landing. He ignored the firefighter's shout of surprise, landing with a thump just past the top step. He coughed, blowing smoke out of his lungs, his breathing fine when it wouldn't be for anyone else. Fire licked close but didn't touch him. Even in human form, Wade's body wasn't affected by fire or heat. The clothes he wore might get a little singed the longer he stayed in the house, but they'd last for what he needed to do.

He hurried to Riordan's bedroom, eyes on the burning floor, wincing at the creaking, snapping, and popping coming from smoldering wood all around him. With his enhanced hearing, he could hear firefighters shouting on the street and the cascade of water that sprayed out of a hose into the floor below. The fire had reached the second floor, burning its way to the roof with a speed that was clearly not normal.

Wade shouldered his way into Riordan's bedroom in the back, the space free of flames so far. His gaze went unerringly to the trunk at the foot of the bed, all its wards lit up like neon—and the pack of goddamn bitey pixies trying to pick the lock.

"Oh, don't even think about it," Wade growled. He exhaled a searing burst of dragon flame that skimmed over the top of the trunk, sending some pixies scattering while catching others dead-on. They burned to ash in a flash, and the surviving ones shrieked furiously at him as they dive-bombed his head.

Wade spat out smaller bursts of flame as he approached the trunk, picking off pixies that were worse than mosquitos. One of the last ones flying came directly at his face. Wade went cross-eyed trying to track it, but instead of immediately burning the pixie, he snatched it out of the air with one hand, holding it in a grip that was just a shade up from crushing the tiny fae.

Wade brought it up to eye level as he knelt in front of the trunk. "Did Niall send you?"

The pixie said something in a tiny voice, and Wade's brain squeezed out the meaning after a second. "This isn't mortal business!"

Wade snorted. "Do I look like a mortal to you?"

The pixie's impossibly tiny eyes glared back at him, and Wade let his eyes change color, vision altering a little as his pupils became shaped like a reptile's. The pixie gasped, tiny little feet kicking beneath his fist, shrieking fiercely. Well, he couldn't let them go and report back to Niall. And really, they were the enemy. So he didn't feel too bad about spitting fire at the pixie and shaking the ash off his hand.

With the pixies taken care of, Wade turned his attention to the spelled trunk. All the wards on it and beneath it that kept it anchored to the ground were furiously reacting to the threat of the burning house. While he thought the selkies must have a fireproofing spell on it, he wasn't willing to bet on it.

He gripped the lock in one hand, fingers curled around it, and shifted more mass to bring up his talons. The floor creaked beneath him as a little more mass than he wanted seeped through. He hastily shoved that sense of self back. Magic swirled around the trunk in brilliant colors, the spells on it lashing out. The magic tickled when it hit harmlessly against him, all its power useless in the face of the intrinsic nature of a dragon.

Wade sliced his talons through the lock, wrenching it free of the wood. He winced as the spells went haywire, but there was nothing to be done for it. He yanked the lid open and peered down into the trunk. The wards inside were still activated, a net of magic tangled over a pair of soft brown sealskins. Wade reached for them, hands easily passing through the magic, and he gripped both to pull them out.

"Oh," he said, staring at the sealskin. "They're warm."

He knew immediately which one was Donal's and which one was Riordan's just by smell, even through the smoke. As much as he wanted to bury his nose in Riordan's sealskin, right now wasn't the time. Wade folded them up small and hugged them to his chest with one arm. He looked over his shoulder at the smoke-filled hallway and figured the front of the building was probably not the best way to leave. He stood, eyeing the window that looked out on a small backyard.

Wade hurried over to it, picking up the nightstand by the bed along the way with his free hand. He tossed the nightstand through the window, shattering the glass, and followed after it into open air. He didn't shift mass, just let himself fall to the ground, landing with an "Oof!"

He nearly face-planted, catching himself with his free hand on the grassy ground. Shaking his head, Wade coughed out a plume of smoke before scrambling to his feet. No firefighters had made it to the backyard yet, so he raced for the nearest fence and vaulted over it, clearing it by inches. He did it a couple of more times until he was several houses down the street, hopefully near where the others were waiting.

Cutting down the alley between two homes, he undid the latch on a wooden gate and stepped onto the sidewalk. The street was still cordoned off and full of first responders. He scanned the area, finally getting eyes on Riordan and the others. They'd been moved across the street closer to the corner. He jogged over to meet them, waving his free hand to catch their attention.

"Wade!" Riordan called out, hurrying to meet him halfway.

"I found them!" Wade said.

Riordan didn't reach for his sealskin though. Instead, Wade got pulled in close by his hips and was soundly kissed, right in the middle of the street. He closed his eyes, parting his lips on a soft gasp before Riordan took advantage, and Wade was all for it. He leaned into the kiss, drinking in the taste of the other man. Ever since that moment on the Harborwalk when he'd received what he'd tell his therapist was his first *real* kiss, Wade had been wanting more of them.

Riordan broke the kiss, holding Wade at arm's length, gaze flicking over his face and down his body worriedly. "Are you all right?"

Wade smiled at him. "Fire doesn't bother me."

Riordan snorted out a disbelieving laugh and shook his head. "I can see that."

Donal and Saoirse hurried over, and Wade juggled the sealskins in his arms until he shook out Donal's. He handed it to the other man, who took it with an odd look. "Here you go. I had to break into the trunk to get them, and I think that ruined the spells. Some pixies got there first, though, and were trying to get inside it."

He couldn't help but look past Donal at Lady Caith, who stared back at him unafraid. "The pixies who serve me would never trespass in such a way."

"Somehow, I don't believe that." Wade shook out Riordan's sealskin and passed it over to him. "This is yours."

Riordan opened his mouth, then quickly snapped it shut. He took the sealskin with both hands and held it rather than turn it into a jacket to put it on. "I—thank you."

"I'm sorry about your house."

Riordan managed a tight little smile and finally shook his skin out into the familiar leather jacket he'd been wearing since Wade had met him. He shrugged it on, gaze moving past Wade to the still-burning house, a mournful expression crossing his face. "We're all safe. That's what matters."

"What happened? Was it Niall?"

"Most likely. We didn't see who threw the bomb."

"Were you hurt?" Wade had the sudden urge to strip Riordan so he could make sure the other man was okay, but that would probably result in both of them being arrested for attempted indecent exposure.

"We all got tossed around a bit, but we're fine."

"I came to talk about an alliance with the kin. We were interrupted before we could finish," Lady Caith said as she approached. She looked a little worse for wear, with her fashionable clothes smoke-stained and torn in places, as if she'd been thrown through something that had broken before she did. The guards with her didn't look much better, though they'd managed to keep ahold of their weapons. Wade figured their glamour hid all the sharp blades and the guns that he could see perfectly well. Otherwise, he thought the police would be taking more of an interest in all of them.

"Uh-huh. Funny how you come around, then a bomb goes off," Wade said.

Lady Caith's lips twitched into a slight, condescending smile. "You are not very trusting."

"I have good reason not to be."

"I speak the truth with my intent."

Wade rolled his eyes at her. "Right. You better keep doing that, or I'm complaining to Gerard about you."

"I do not know a Gerard."

"Sure you do. He's Gerard to us mortals. He's Cú Chulainn to you fae."

It was always funny to watch people's faces when they realized Wade was friends with a god. Not like he went around boasting about it, but Sage always said hints were fine in certain circumstances to protect their asses, and an outright statement should only be used like a sucker punch.

Lady Caith went so still she could've doubled as a statue in a museum. She blinked after a moment, letting her arms fall to her sides. Her guards edged a little closer, as if invoking Gerard's formal name could summon him. "If you are an acquaintance of Cú Chulainn—"

"Not if," Donal interrupted with a hard little smile. "Wade was personally invited to Cú Chulainn's wedding, along with his god pack, as special guests."

"Yeah, I met Riordan at the dessert table," Wade said.

Lady Caith pressed her lips together and stared at them all as if she was weighing their worth and getting it right for once. "Very well. An alliance, then, to keep Niall from all our borders. We should not discuss it here. If you are amenable, we can continue our conversation at my home, where your sister will be safe."

"Amenable," Wade muttered under his breath, knowing full well everyone could hear him. "Fae and lawyer speak."

He didn't answer her because it wasn't his right. He looked at Riordan instead, who stared at Lady Caith with narrowed eyes. "You know Niall has her skin. He called last night and gave me until today to either hand Saoirse over or I go in her stead."

Lady Caith nodded. "I can keep your sister from feeling the pull of it in his hands while we think up a plan. But she will need to stay with me."

"If your intent is true for an equal alliance, we'll come to the table. If you mean harm to my sister or any of my clan, I'll hold that against you until I'm satisfied payment has been met for a broken bargain."

"Which would be never," Wade said.

Lady Caith made a delicate gesture with one hand. "My word is true. We will satisfy it between us. There is no need to call down others."

She certainly smelled like truth, at least to Wade's nose. Funny how the threat of a god could get intractable groups to work together.

"Then we'll sit at your table," Riordan said.

"Hopefully not the one I broke," Wade said. At Riordan's glance, Wade smiled at him. "Come on. If you want that talk, let's get out of here before the police claim first dibs."

It took some finagling to leave the scene anyway. The police did want some statements, Wade hid from the battalion chief on the scene, who wanted to read him the riot act for entering a burning building, and the EMS really wanted to send everyone to the hospital for possible smoke inhalation.

Lady Caith proved to have some pull with the people of Boston. The highest-ranked officer on the scene seemed to be aware of her station, and so they managed to leave before the hour was up.

"I parked around the corner. I can drive you all to Beacon Hill," Wade said to the selkies. Lady Caith and her guards veered off from them, presumably heading to their own cars.

"Thanks. The easement is still blocked, so we can't get to our cars, and I have a feeling some of them might be burned," Saoirse said.

Luckily, in all the excitement happening on the street, no one had called in Wade's terrible parking job. They climbed into his rental, and he pulled into the street. Traffic was being rerouted, so it was easy enough to do a U-turn in the intersection and head north. Riordan was already typing Lady Caith's address into his phone's GPS app, which was nice of him.

"Were you able to find anything?" Riordan asked.

Wade drummed his fingers against the steering wheel. "Kind of? I never made it to Niall's house in Beacon Hill. Lucien was scoping the area and said he had information on Harper and Casey. I had to pay him for it, but I found out where they were keeping Harper."

Saoirse leaned forward between the front seats. "Where? Was she alive?"

"His hotel on the waterfront."

"Really? It's supposed to open in a couple of weeks for the summer tourist season."

"Niall is going to have to deal with water damage first. When I left with Harper, all the sprinklers were going off."

Saoirse reached out and ruffled his hair. "Good on you. How was Harper?"

Wade's smugness at property damage faded at her question. "Not that great. Niall was using her and Casey to keep each other in line. Casey wasn't with her, and I'm pretty sure he's being kept on an island in the harbor."

"If he's being kept in the harbor, maybe whatever is in the deep is his jailor," Riordan said slowly.

"We'll get some boats and find out. Ella says her pack is coming with us when we do."

"They can't swim."

"They're better on land than you would be."

Riordan tipped his head. "Fair point. Our alliance with them should still hold, even with Harper back."

"Ella won't go back on her word." She'd gone out of her way to fight a geas in order to save her alphas, but Wade didn't consider that breaking a promise. She'd done it to keep her god pack safe from Niall, and she'd already promised to help them fight to bring Casey home.

"Let's head to Lady Caith's and get Saoirse behind that threshold. If Niall comes looking for her, she'll be safer there than at our condo."

"And if Niall comes looking for you, boyo?" Donal asked.

Wade had to be careful about not breaking the steering wheel with his grip. "He'll have to go through me first."

It was lucky he was braking for a stop sign because Riordan leaned over the console, turned his head to the side, and kissed him so fiercely that Saoirse wolf whistled from the back seat.

"Thanks," Riordan said roughly when he broke the kiss. "For helping us."

Wade cleared his throat, tongue touching the back of his teeth. "You don't owe me anything."

"We'd all be a lot worse off if Ella hadn't brought you here. So thank you all the same."

"Guess I'll keep you, then."

His words put a smile on Riordan's face that didn't fade for the entire drive to Lady Caith's.

This time, when they finally made it to Lady Caith's door, hospitality went quicker. The same fae from before was much more polite, even if he wasn't deferential. That was fine by Wade because the fruit bowl had something that was shaped like an orange but with a deep maroon color to it. The fae was cutting out slices from it, and when Wade shoved his piece into his mouth, he was pleased by the taste. "Reminds me of mango mixed with strawberry. Can I have another?"

The fae sighed but dutifully cut him another piece. Wade munched on it and drank the wine offered to them. With formalities out of the way, they followed the fae to a comfortable room in the rear of the building that overlooked the backyard. Lady Caith waited for them there, drinking out of an intricately designed glass that looked like a stemmed rose. The liquid in its cup was a brilliant honey gold. He assumed it was from some personal store that she wasn't willing to share because no other glasses were waiting for them on the coffee table.

"I am pleased you are willing to meet me at the table," Lady Caith said.

"I do so for my clan," Riordan said.

The cadence of their speech was far too formal, which told him the words probably meant more than just the surface tone. Ritual, maybe, knowing the fae. Wade sat on a chair and got comfortable, ignoring the odd look Donal gave him when he pulled one of the fruits from the fruit bowl out of his pocket. Wade bit into it, the crunch sounding like celery but tasting like apple if it was shaped like a banana. Riordan glanced at him, but Lady Caith was doing her best to ignore him. Wade took another bite, hoping to see her twitch.

He wasn't the best at bargains—though he'd argue he was better than Patrick—but he knew when words were off. Sage was a good teacher, and Wade had spent the last couple of years learning how to help manage the packs under their protection. He'd mediated his fair share of arguments, knocked a few heads together when needed, and in general, figured out what was fair and what wasn't. From what he could tell as Riordan and Lady Caith got into a deep discussion, they weren't asking a whole lot from each other, and the timeframe wasn't open-ended. It was actually kind of hot to watch Riordan get all political with her.

Never thought I'd find border territory politics interesting.

Or really, the man involved in them. Wade chewed his next bite slowly, studying Riordan. He hadn't ever thought he'd find someone he wanted to keep close, not like how Patrick and Jono had each other or how Sage and Marek were together. His therapist had said that was okay, that he'd know when he was comfortable and ready to start a relationship.

But Riordan encompassed everything he found safe in a person—strong-willed, big-hearted, and willing to protect those he cared about—and Wade didn't want to let him go. Which meant he couldn't let Niall take Riordan or keep Saoirse's skin.

"What do you think, Wade?" Lady Caith asked.

Wade blinked, turning to look at her, having only been half listening to their negotiations. He knew better than to completely ignore what was being said. "It's not my place to say. The terms are between your court and Riordan's clan."

"We have a common enemy."

"Yeah, and first chance I get, I'll eat the bastard, but that doesn't mean you need my blessing for this."

Before Lady Caith could respond, Riordan's phone rang. Wade watched him pull it out of his pocket with a frown that flattened into something angry and worried when he looked at the screen. "It's Niall."

Wade couldn't help the way his teeth got sharp. "Put it on speaker."

Riordan answered the call and put the phone on the coffee table. "Niall."

"I don't appreciate your interference," Niall said, voice flat and hard. Wade dialed up his hearing, trying to see who else might be with Niall on his side of the line. Heartbeats thrummed at the edge of his hearing, all of them slow and precise. He doubted any of them were Casey.

"I don't appreciate you *bombing* my *home.*"

"And I don't appreciate you ruining my hotel to get out of our bargain."

"I had nothing to do with your hotel."

"And I never did what you are accusing me of."

"You ordered it," Donal snapped.

"Ah, the siblings are with you. Are you saying your goodbyes?"

Wade had to lift his fingers off the armrest of his chair so he didn't gouge a hole in it. He bit his tongue so he didn't give away his presence. Niall could probably hear the angry beat of his heart, but he wouldn't know it was Wade.

"What do you want?" Riordan asked in a low voice.

"You know exactly what I want. You give me yourself and your clan, or I take your sister."

Riordan closed his eyes, grief twisting across his face. Wade reached between their chairs and took Riordan's hand in his, giving it a tight squeeze. Lady Caith leaned forward, her hair falling over one shoulder. "If you take the selkies in any capacity, I will fight you."

The pause that settled on the line lasted only a few seconds before Niall rallied at her interruption. "Lady Caith."

"Niall Noígíallach."

Names, Wade knew, were important to the fae. He wondered if anyone even knew what Lady Caith's true name was.

"Have you allied yourself with the kin?"

Lady Caith didn't bother responding to that. "You have been playing fast and loose with your words when it comes to bargains."

"You know it's rude to interfere with one that doesn't concern you."

"This concerns me. I know you went after Abhartach and now have two master vampires after you. Congratulations. You have affronted the daywalker."

Wade snorted at that. Lucien never got affronted; he got even. If Niall didn't know that, he'd learn it soon enough.

"The bargain was made, and the selkies must abide by its terms."

"You forced it on them."

"If they weren't meant to be owned, then their skin would never be able to leave their bodies."

"Oh, I'm definitely going to eat you," Wade said, unable to stay silent any longer.

"Ah, the human from the bar. I wondered who sat with you."

"He's not your concern," Riordan said.

"Perhaps I'll find him and take him as well. It would keep you tractable if I did."

"You won't ever touch him." Riordan's words were said fiercely, with a rage that Wade could almost taste. It warmed him, knowing that Riordan was willing to stand between him and Niall's wannabe god ambitions. Wade wouldn't let him, of course. He was more than capable of taking care of himself.

"Perhaps. But I can touch someone else that you love."

Saoirse jerked as if she'd been electrocuted, falling off the couch with an ear-piercing scream. Riordan and Donal both lunged for her, catching her before she hit the coffee table or the floor. Saoirse clawed at her bare arms so badly she drew bright red scratches down her forearms. Her brothers caught her hands, trying to hold her so she wouldn't hurt herself, all while she kept screaming.

Lady Caith picked up Riordan's phone before it could be knocked off the table. Wade threw himself out of the chair and clambered onto the couch the others had vacated. He ripped the gold ring with its fire opal off his finger and stuck his hand into the melee, searching for Saoirse's. "Give me her hand!"

It took both Donal and Riordan to pin Saoirse down and unclench her fingers for Wade to slip the ring Orlaith had given him onto her finger. Magic instantly erupted from the fire opal, wrapping ribbons of ethereal light over her body. It sank into her skin, and Saoirse let out a lung-rattling gasp before going limp in her brothers' arms. Riordan's gaze snapped to Wade, his brown eyes wide. "What the hell?"

"That was the Summer Lady's magic," Lady Caith said, staring at the ring on Saoirse's finger.

Wade saw she'd ended the call with Niall. "Yeah, it was a gift from Órlaith on her wedding day. Doesn't work on me, but it'll work for anyone I give it to. It's spelled to give whoever wears it what they need in the moment."

For Harper, it had shielded her from bullets and magic. He didn't know what it had done for Saoirse.

Lady Caith pursed her lips and tilted her head. "Intent is a powerful thing with our people, and none more strong than those who descend from Brigid. The Summer Lady must find you exceptional to part with such power."

"She likes me."

"So it seems."

Wade leaned back so Riordan and Donal could help Saoirse sit up. She was breathing hard, chest heaving from the need to get air into her lungs, but color was coming back into her face. Donal lifted her up and set her back down on the couch next to Wade, holding her upright until she gave him a tight little nod. "I'm okay."

"No, you're not, *a dheirfiúr*," Donal said.

"Did Niall hurt your skin?" Riordan asked.

Saoirse scrubbed a hand over her face, wiping away her tears. "Yes. It echoed."

"Echoed?" Wade asked.

Riordan grimaced. "When we're forcibly separated from our seal-skin, the holder can do harm to it, and we'll feel it in human form."

"The Summer Lady's magic cut the connection of pain, I assume?" Lady Caith asked.

Saoirse nodded slowly. "I can still feel my sealskin, but not whatever Niall is doing to it."

The haunted look in her eyes made Wade want to murder Niall. "No pain is great, but fuck Niall."

Saoirse stared down at the ring on her finger and made an aborted motion to take it off. "I can give it back?"

Wade reached out to pat her on the head. "Nah. Keep it for now. You need it more than me."

Her shoulders slumped in relief, and she sank down onto the couch.

"What now?" Donal asked.

"I believe it is prudent we figure out a plan of attack. You may stay in my home tonight, and we will hope the vampires cause Niall to be too busy to come skulking around," Lady Caith said.

Wade was all for figuring out a way to get rid of Niall, but he wasn't going to spend the night in territory that wasn't his. "Whatever we decide, we'll need to let the Boston god pack know."

"Then let's call them," Riordan said, reaching for his phone.

Wade sighed and went to claim his seat again. It was going to be a long afternoon of discussions, and he always found those excruciatingly boring. "Do you have any snacks?"

CHAPTER NINETEEN

Wade stepped out of the elevator into the penthouse suite, the lights on and the smell of food saturating the kitchen area. The private chef was nowhere to be found, but when Wade went into the kitchen and opened up the oven, he could see the Dutch oven filled with beef bourguignon on the rack there, and two fresh loaves of bread were covered by a towel on the counter.

"Awesome," Wade said as he reached for the Dutch oven's handles. The metal was warm against his palms, which probably meant it would be too hot for a mundane human or anyone else not immune to fire and high heat to handle. It didn't bother him, and he easily hauled it out of the oven, setting it on the stove. "I asked the chef to make dinner for us because I didn't think I could wait for delivery."

"When did you do that?" Riordan asked as he came up beside Wade. He reached for the lid but then jerked his hand away when he realized it was hot. "Ow."

"It was staying warm in the oven. What made you think it was a good idea to touch it?"

"You touched it."

Wade rolled his eyes and started opening up cupboards to figure out where the bowls were kept. "Heat doesn't bother me."

"You're pretty hot."

"That was the *dumbest* line. Please don't ever say that around my pack."

Riordan laughed and crowded Wade up against the stove for a lingering kiss that definitely burned hotter than the Dutch oven he'd just set down. He tilted his head, parted his lips some, and could have kept on kissing Riordan, except his stomach growled, reminding him he was hungry.

"All right, let's feed you," Riordan said after breaking the kiss.

Wade was torn for a single second between more kisses and food, but food won out. He had a loaf of fresh bread to attack. "There should be some clothes for you in the bedroom. I had the concierge go out and buy some for you since you only have what you're wearing. You can change after dinner or now, whatever you prefer."

Riordan stared at him for a moment before shaking his head. "I haven't even thought about everything we lost. Thank you."

It earned him another kiss, this one close-lipped and brushing soft and gentle against the corner of his mouth. It made his skin tingle, warmth spreading through him. Riordan stepped back and started opening up a few drawers, looking for an oven mitt. He used it to lift the lid off the Dutch oven and take a whiff of dinner. "Smells good."

"I wasn't sure if you'd like it."

"I'd like anything you gave me."

"Well, you also get a loaf of bread you don't have to share with me only because I made sure I got my own."

Riordan laughed and set the lid aside. "Duly noted."

Between the two of them, they found the tableware and utensils, got the beef bourguignon ladled into bowls, and figured out there was a wine fridge in the kitchen island. Wade wasn't a connoisseur of wine in any way, but Riordan seemed impressed by whatever was stored in there. "Do you care what bottle I pick?"

"I'll drink whatever you open," Wade said.

They served the meal on the dining table near the long line of windows that overlooked Boston. The curtains weren't shut, and the sky outside was black due to the late-evening hour. The buildings that stretched out before them glowed with light, making it difficult to see the stars. The view was nice, but Riordan was better looking, even with the stress of the day lending a darkness to his warm brown eyes. Wade wanted to erase the pain he could see there but didn't know how.

The plan they'd come up with at Lady Caith's had essentially been a Trojan horse of sorts. They'd let the vampires have fun hunting Niall tonight. Tomorrow, they would reach out to the asshole—if he was still alive, and Wade could hope he wasn't—and Saoirse would give herself up to Niall. Wade would tag along to help get her skin back and figure out where Casey was being held prisoner in the bay. The Boston god pack would be waiting with the Maguire Clan at the harbor to help search the islands.

Of course, all of that hinged on Niall actually letting Wade join Saoirse as a prisoner. The fae still thought he was human, but Wade had an idea to rile Niall up and allow himself to be taken as an extra prize. Men who had power were never happy when things they considered theirs were damaged or destroyed—like the waterfront hotel—and Wade was certain that arrogance applied to fae as well. Which meant Niall would probably want revenge, and Wade would be the focus of that rage.

Riordan had *not* been happy with the plan, but Saoirse had been stubborn in her determination to place herself in Niall's hands. The ensuing fight between the siblings was what had prompted Wade to leave Lady Caith's with Riordan in tow. If there was anything he knew about pack that could be applied to clan, it was that giving each other space to calm down was the best for everyone.

Donal and Saoirse would be safe with Lady Caith, and Riordan would be safe with Wade.

"Do you travel to help other packs out often?" Riordan asked.

Wade tore off a piece of bread and dunked it in his bowl. "We have alliances with other god packs, way more after the Battle of Samhain than before. But no, generally, we don't. Other cities aren't our territories, and there are some we steer clear of because Sage doesn't want the headache of a lawsuit."

"A lawsuit?"

"Uh, well, Patrick sort of was the catalyst for some property destruction in New York City, Chicago, London, and Paris some years ago."

Riordan stared at him. "The zombies in Paris was your pack?"

"No! I mean, we fought them, but we didn't raise them."

"I can see why you wouldn't want to risk being arrested."

"I miss the macarons and croissants. Sage says I can't go visit even if I fly there myself."

"I don't know about macarons. I like cannoli better."

They debated their favorite desserts, which devolved into arguing over the best snacks. Between Wade's passionate defense of Pop-Tarts and Riordan's love of Boston cream pie, by the time they finished the entire pot of beef bourguignon, Wade was ready for dessert while Riordan was ready for a shower.

"I'll clean up," Wade said.

Riordan disappeared into the bedroom, and Wade heard the shower turn on a minute later. He closed all the curtains first before carrying the dirty dishes to the sink, where he gave them a quick rinse before shoving everything into the dishwasher. He left the empty Dutch oven to soak in the sink and wiped down the table with one hand while he called Jono with the other.

"Hey," he said when Jono picked up. "I'm checking in."

"How are things going in Boston?" Jono asked.

"Fine. I found Harper."

Wade proceeded to update Jono with the day's events, glossing over what he had planned for tomorrow. He knew Jono and the rest of his pack would hate that he was going to hand himself over to

Niall. If they knew, they would probably all fly up to Boston, and no one needed the mess that would cause.

Wade loved them, but his pack could be so overprotective sometimes.

"I'll call again tomorrow," he said, hoping he could keep that promise. Maybe if he called in the morning, his pack wouldn't think anything was wrong.

"Patrick should be home soon. One of us can come out to you once he's free."

"No, it's fine. I got this."

"We know you do, but it's okay to ask for help if you need it."

"I know. Talk to you later." He ended the call, setting his phone on the kitchen island as he tossed the sponge in the sink and washed his hands really quick.

"Hey, I know you said the concierge bought some clothes, but I didn't see them, and I didn't want to go through your things. Are they in the closet?"

Wade looked over his shoulder in the direction of the bedroom and nearly swallowed his tongue. It seemed to be his usual reaction whenever he saw Riordan without clothes. Granted, that was only a couple of times, but still, the selkie was really, *really* hot.

Riordan had a towel wrapped around his waist, showing off all the muscles in his abdomen and chest and arms, and it was a crime he kept all that skin hidden under clothes. Wade's brain short-circuited a little at the sight Riordan presented, fresh from the shower, looking like a literal wet dream and no longer smelling like smoke and magic. All Wade could smell was the hotel soap he'd used to wash up and that intrinsic salt-ocean scent that he'd first noticed in Ella's home.

It still smelled like the best thing ever.

"Uh," Wade managed to get out, tongue a little unwieldy in his mouth.

Riordan left the doorway and crossed the living space, coming to where Wade stood in the open kitchen. He let himself be pushed up against the kitchen island, hands gripping the edge so hard he had to consciously think about his strength so he didn't crack the marble. Riordan stepped in close, the heat from his skin something Wade wanted to burrow into as Riordan's hands settled on his waist, grip surprisingly gentle.

"Or would you rather I didn't get dressed?" Riordan asked in a low voice, the words rumbling in his chest. His pointed ears parted through his damp hair, and Wade had the sudden urge to follow the droplets of water slowly sliding down Riordan's throat with his tongue.

"Yes," Wade said in a voice that was only slightly strangled. "That."

He wanted, in that moment, to have Riordan close. To know what it felt like for someone else's skin to press against his own because he wanted them to. Desire was a foreign sensation, but Wade rather thought this was what it should always feel like—an aching kind of need that buried itself deep in every inch of his body.

His cock twitched, and okay, yeah, he was doing this. With Riordan.

Because it was Riordan, and that's what he wanted.

Riordan's pupils dilated a little at whatever scent he got off Wade, fingers flexing but not in a way that hurt. "I would like you to tell me what you want. I only want to do what you want."

"You. I want you." Wade let go of the countertop and hesitantly reached for the edge of the towel, tugging on it lightly. "Without this."

Riordan smiled slightly, amusement mingling with lust in his gaze, in his scent. "Okay."

He took Wade's hand and, rather than strip right there in the kitchen, led him back to the bedroom. A tiny bit of trepidation slid through Wade's mind, and he squashed it. This wasn't like any of his previous experiences—Riordan wasn't like any of the people who had ever hurt him.

Riordan was *his* choice, and that made all the difference.

For all that Wade wanted this, he had no idea where to start. But Riordan made that easy for him, those warm, strong hands divesting him of his clothes one piece at a time in between kisses that neatly distracted Wade from getting naked with a person of his choosing for the first time in his entire life.

The air in the bedroom was cool from the air-conditioning, but Wade barely noticed, always running hot and feeling hotter in that moment as Riordan finally tossed his towel aside. Wade swallowed thickly and let himself look at Riordan's cock and think about how he wanted to touch it. Then there was no thinking involved, only doing, when Riordan took Wade's hand and guided it to his cock, pressing Wade's fingers around it.

"Anything you want," Riordan said with a soft groan before kissing Wade with a bit more intent. "However you want it. We go at your pace. If you say stop, we stop."

Stroking another guy's cock was *weird*, but in a good way, Wade decided. The way Riordan grew harder beneath his fingers was enticing, and the thought of getting that cock in him hit like an electric shock that held only pleasure and no fear.

Did he want to go that far? He poked at that thought a bit while stroking Riordan's cock before deciding that yeah, he did, because it was Riordan.

"I want you in me," Wade said after a few more kisses that grew increasingly more desperate while his own cock got harder.

Riordan didn't respond in words, which was fine by Wade when he found himself guided backward to the bed. He moved clumsily, distractedly, not wanting to let Riordan go but also wanting to lick the water off his skin. Sinking down on the bed was nice, and having Riordan follow him down should have been nice as well. But the second Riordan caged his body in, Wade went rigid, fingernails one shift of mass away from becoming talons where they pressed against Riordan's ribs.

"Wade," Riordan said quietly, no fear in his voice. "Look at me."

Wade didn't realize his breathing had kicked up fast until he locked eyes with Riordan. "Um."

Riordan eased up a little, revealing more of the ceiling and the room, and Wade found it easier to breathe. "Tell me how you're feeling."

Wade swallowed, steadying himself, refusing to feel ashamed for the reaction he'd just had. "Maybe not like this?"

"Do you still want to? We can stop and just sleep."

Wade shook his head. "No, I want to."

Riordan didn't question his request and immediately pulled back. "Come here."

It took some maneuvering, but eventually, Riordan was leaning against the headboard, propped up by a couple of pillows, and Wade was sitting in his lap with an easy means of escape. Not that he wanted to escape, not with the stupidly hot way that Riordan was stroking their cocks together in one big, warm hand, lube from a bottle that Wade knew he hadn't requested from the hotel easing the friction.

"That wasn't in the bathroom when I first checked in," Wade muttered, head tilted toward where the small bottle was discarded on the bed. The angle let Riordan kiss down his throat in a distracting way.

"Call me hopeful."

"Sure, Hopeful. Just keep touching me like that."

It was honestly difficult to think around the sensation of Riordan's fingers on his cock. The firm but careful drag of fingers over his length sent sparks zinging up his spine, making Wade rock into the touch. He ran his fingers through Riordan's damp hair, over the breadth of his shoulders, memorizing the feel of him. Riordan's seal-skin was draped in jacket form over the back of the chair in the corner, but Wade didn't miss it at all.

He couldn't, not when he had Riordan underneath him, pressed close, the selkie's heartbeat loud in Wade's ears.

It was easy to get distracted by Riordan's fingers and mouth, the flex of muscle beneath his searching hands. But then all his focus snapped to attention, and Wade went still when slick fingers slid over his ass.

Riordan's hands stayed where they were when he turned his head, capturing Wade's mouth in a slow, deep kiss, giving him all the room he wanted to flee if he needed to. "We can stop."

"No, I want to. I just—" Wade broke off, swallowing, staring at Riordan. "I haven't had sex where it didn't hurt and—"

Rage that reminded Wade of a storm's fury flashed across Riordan's eyes, but none of it was in his touch, in his voice. "I promise I will never hurt you."

Wade drew in a shuddering breath that tasted like Riordan, like the sea, filling his lungs with the scent of *them* and not old memories that had no place here. "I know you won't."

That was a belief Wade clung to, realizing it was true on every level as Riordan slowly, carefully slid a finger inside him after Wade nodded his okay to continue, no pain radiating out anywhere. The intrusion wasn't like anything he'd experienced before, and Wade ducked his head, biting at Riordan's collarbone to muffle the sound that wanted to escape his throat.

Riordan took his time, which some part of Wade was grateful for, but by the time he was squirming on three thick fingers, he was desperate for Riordan to *get on with it*. He dug his fingers into Riordan's shoulders, trying to remember that shifting mass right about then would be a bad idea.

"Get in me," he gasped against the curve of Riordan's neck and shoulder, the words vibrating against warm skin.

Riordan made a noise that had to be agreement because he pulled his fingers free, and Wade made a displeased sound that had Riordan laughing. It turned into a sharp moan when Wade bit at his muscle, licking up sweat. "You need to help me out with this. You're taking the lead, *mo chroí.*"

Oh. *Oh.* Well then. He could do that.

Wade's coordination wasn't the best right then, but he somehow managed to rise up on his knees, let Riordan get his hands on him and guide him back down. The press of Riordan's cock against his entrance had him freezing for a split second, but the fingers skating up his thigh to palm his hip and the soft kiss Riordan gave him was distracting enough to push aside everything but the here and now and the growing heat in his gut that had nothing to do with fire.

He sank down onto Riordan's cock, panting against the other man's mouth like he was flying and diving in a dizzying spiral. It didn't hurt, not when he could go at his own pace, not when Riordan had ensured the stretch would be easy and feel good. It still felt weird, but Wade decided he liked it. Then he tilted his hips while chasing after Riordan's mouth for a kiss, and Riordan's cock pressed against a spot inside him that lit up every nerve in his body, and Wade made a noise he didn't know he was capable of in human or dragon form.

"Yeah," Riordan rasped, biting at the edge of his jaw. "Take whatever you want."

"You?" Wade muttered, clumsily circling his hips, wanting to feel that sensation again, trying not to claw open Riordan's skin as he braced himself against the other man's body for leverage.

Riordan laughed, the sound disbelieving and raw as Wade rose up on his knees a little and sank back down on that hard cock. "You gave my skin back today."

Wade groaned as he dug his knees into the bed and figured out how to make his body move to ride Riordan's cock. "Not gonna keep it if you don't give it to me."

He wanted to—desperately wanted to keep Riordan the way he'd never wanted to keep anyone else—but he'd never take someone's heart if it wasn't freely given. A deep instinct had drawn him to the selkie, but it was Riordan's whole personality and kindness that had led Wade into his arms, into his bed, riding his cock with the freedom to stop whenever he wanted.

Only he really didn't because it felt so good when Riordan filled him up, the way Riordan let him set the pace and only ever steadied him, kissed him, made him feel like he was about to burn up in the best way possible. Any lingering remnants of memories of other times he'd done this were washed away by hot waves of pleasure that eddied through his nerves. Everything narrowed down to the undulation of his body as he chased that building pressure of pleasure, to the hands that never left his body, anchoring him to the human shape of the life he preferred to live right now.

Wade's orgasm caught him by surprise, not knowing what the edge felt like until he tumbled right over, desperately grinding down onto Riordan's cock while Riordan stroked Wade's through his release. Riordan kissed away his startled cry, swallowing the noise as he tried to figure out how to breathe.

"Your scales are beautiful," Riordan murmured, lips dragging away from his mouth to kiss his cheek, the edge of his jaw, down his throat, anywhere he could reach.

Wade's chest ached with the need for air, as if he'd done a cross-country flight with no stops, hands gripping Riordan's shoulders tight. He could see the sheen of red scales scattered over the back of one hand out of the corner of his eyes, a trail stretching up his forearm. He didn't remember losing control of his body like that.

Wade hummed, feeling loose-limbed and happy, even as he realized Riordan was still hard inside him. "You didn't come."

"Close," Riordan muttered, tightening his arms around Wade before releasing him. "Lift up."

Wade slid off Riordan's cock and settled on his lap. He watched through half-lidded eyes as Riordan stared at him, breathing hard as he stroked his cock until he came, spilling between them, some of it hitting Wade's stomach. Curious, he wiped up a bit of the cum and put his finger in his mouth. The sound Riordan made was definitely better than the way his cum tasted.

"Might pass on that," Wade admitted.

Riordan laughed, hooking his other hand around the back of Wade's neck and pulling him in for a lazy kiss. "Whatever you want."

You, Wade thought, even if he didn't say it out loud as he leaned against Riordan and let the older man hold him.

It'd be nice if he could make that desire come true.

CHAPTER TWENTY

RIORDAN WOKE UP SUNDAY TO THE DRUMMING SOUND OF RAIN AGAINST THE windows behind the heavy curtains in the hotel bedroom. He was warm even with the air-conditioning on and the sheets tangled around his hips. Most of that reason was lying half on top of him, head resting on his shoulder, one arm slung over his middle and a leg tangled with his, breathing softly against his skin. Wade clung like an octopus in his sleep, and Riordan couldn't say he minded.

He bent his arm, lifting his hand so he could gently run his knuckles up and down Wade's back, following the path of his spine. His skin was fever-warm, a byproduct of being a dragon, Riordan presumed. It made him think of winter and staying in bed curled around each other, a dream he wasn't sure would ever become reality, despite last night.

Letting Wade have his way in bed was the only thing Riordan would ever want in the bedroom. Knowing Wade's past, knowing what he'd overcome, meant Riordan would do everything in his power to never hurt the younger man. It'd been easy to guide him, to show Wade pleasure that made him comfortable, and the best thing about it all had been the laughter. Riordan wanted to remember it all, wanted to be able to hold those moments of joy and heated passion close, because Niall was still a threat.

"You smell like Jono when Patrick has done something stupid and he thinks brooding will solve the problem if tea won't," Wade mumbled, breath tickling Riordan's skin.

Riordan flattened his hand over Wade's hip. "You're awake."

"I'm awake. Kind of want coffee. Kind of want you." Wade's arm curled tighter around Riordan's body, holding him in an embrace he doubted he'd be able to escape without some effort. Not like he'd want to.

"Do you really want coffee over me?"

Wade lifted his head and blearily looked at Riordan. His dark hair was a mess and flopping over his forehead, getting in his eyes. His tanned skin was clear of any dragon scales, though Riordan had been privileged to see them shine through a couple of times last night when they were tangled up together. They'd felt smooth and warm to his touch, just like Wade's skin, patterned in a way that had fascinated Riordan.

"I think I want a shower," Wade decided, being contrary.

To be fair, Riordan did think they both needed a shower after last night. The bedroom was saturated in the smell of sex, but he didn't mind it too much, mostly because beneath it all was the smokey scent he attributed to Wade.

Riordan ran his hand up Wade's spine to drag his fingers through thick hair, making Wade sigh. "Come on. Let's get ready."

Any other day and he would want to stay in bed, exploring Wade's body for hours on end, ordering room service rather than letting the private chef into the penthouse. Any other day and he could let the hours tick away, but not today.

Wade didn't argue, rolling away from Riordan to slide off the bed and get to his feet with a yawn. Riordan immediately missed the warmth of the other man, wanting to drag Wade close again. That itching desire to offer up his sealskin to Wade rushed through Riordan like a riptide, and he had to clench his teeth to keep the words locked away. Wade's confession last night—that he'd never take anything not freely given—was wreaking havoc with Riordan's self-control.

So he channeled that desire into the physical instead, crowding Wade into the walk-in shower big enough for two people once they were in the bathroom. He reached for the knob, turning the water on, not minding that it came out lukewarm first before getting hotter.

"I thought we were cleaning up," Wade mumbled against his lips as Riordan pushed him up against the tiles and kissed him beneath the spray.

"We are," Riordan replied, dragging his mouth and hands down the lean length of Wade's body until he settled on his knees.

"This isn't cleaning up. I'm pretty sure it's—oh *fuck*!"

Wade's head smacked against the tile with a faint crack when Riordan sucked his cock into his mouth, swallowing down to the root. He kept one hand on Wade's hips to steady him rather than pin him. Riordan dragged his mouth back up the length of Wade's cock, licking at the tip as he wrapped his other hand around the base of it, looking up at Wade. "I'm pretty sure I'm going to make you feel good."

Wade's face was flushed, and not just from the steam rising around them. A faint glitter of red scales edged his hairline, and Riordan had the absurd need to see how many more he could bring up through Wade's skin.

"I think you're gonna kill me," Wade moaned. "Do you even know what you look like?"

Riordan smirked but didn't bother answering, preferring instead to swallow Wade's cock again because the sound of Wade's moans against the shower tile was better than music right then. He took his time, working over Wade's cock with a thoroughness that had the younger man swearing and gasping as it hardened in his mouth. Listening to Wade fall apart above him as he swallowed around the cock in his mouth made Riordan feel good, knowing that Wade enjoyed it too. The water was still warm when Wade finally came, cock so far down Riordan's throat he couldn't even taste it.

Riordan looked up, drinking in the sight above him. Wade truly was gorgeous like this, with molten-gold eyes bisected by reptilian pupils and fiery red scales pushing up through his skin in scattered areas of his body, as if he couldn't control himself in the wake of the pleasure Riordan could give him.

He pulled off after a moment, not even breathing hard, and leaned in to nuzzle his face against Wade's stomach. He kissed his way back up warm skin to Wade's mouth for a kiss neither of them shied away from.

"Feel free to do that every morning," Wade said.

Riordan laughed, wanting to believe he could. "Sure."

They didn't spend too much more time in the shower. Wade's stomach rumbled, and Riordan knew they'd need to eat breakfast before they dealt with everything ahead of them that day. He turned off the water, and they left the shower, drying off in the bathroom before Wade finally showed him where all the new clothes were in the closet. Riordan grabbed his sealskin from the chair in the corner and pulled it on as a leather jacket once he was dressed, nerves settling now that it was with him again.

He followed Wade out of the bedroom to the living space beyond. Wade unearthed the remote and turned on the television while Riordan checked out the refrigerator to see what the chef had left that could be used for breakfast. The morning hour meant the channel it was turned to opened up on the local news. Riordan's attention snagged on what was being reported, and he left the carton of eggs he'd pulled from the refrigerator on the counter to join Wade in the living area.

"—fire overnight on a yacht anchored in Cambridge and owned by the same company whose hotel on the wharf had water damage from burst sprinklers yesterday, which has delayed its anticipated summer opening. It's too soon to tell if—"

"That wasn't me," Wade said, looking at his phone and not the television.

"It wasn't anyone from my clan."

"Any other kin who might be out looking for revenge?"

Riordan shook his head. "We don't take on each other's debts that way."

"Ugh. I hate debts." Wade found whatever he was searching for on his phone and pressed it to his ear. Riordan stepped closer, listening in on the call. The ringing stopped, but the line didn't go to voicemail. "Was the yacht your doing?"

"I thought you said you didn't want to speak with us ever again," Carmen drawled. Riordan winced, still amazed at Wade's complete lack of fear when it came to the succubus and the master vampire she followed.

"Extenuating circumstances. Just tell me if Abby Boy is still going after Niall."

"It's been a fun little game, hunting fae."

"Great. Keep enjoying it."

Wade ended the call, apparently happy with that explanation, even if Riordan wasn't. "Are Lucien and his Night Court sticking around Boston?"

"No idea, but I won't be paying for any more of their help."

"I'm betting that yacht belonged to Niall."

"Sucker's bet. I know better than to take them."

"I don't think anyone will be happy if Lucien sticks around after all this."

Wade shrugged, turning to face him. "No one ever is, but he doesn't really settle down. He was in New York City only long enough to keep a promise to the mother of all vampires, and then the second the fight was over, he was gone."

Riordan hoped Lucien only targeted Niall's people and not anyone else. "If Lucien is going after Niall's property, Niall may think what happened at the hotel yesterday was because of the vampires."

"Maybe. But if telling him it was me works to our advantage, I'll shout it from the rooftops."

"I still don't like the plan."

Wade turned to kiss him on the lips, just a quick peck. "Yeah, you yelled about that all day yesterday. I know you don't like it, but I'm not going to let anything happen to Saoirse."

Riordan pressed their foreheads together, hands gripping Wade's hips with tight fingers. He was perfectly willing to give up his skin and his freedom if it meant his sister and his clan would be safe with Donal to lead them. But apparently, Wade and his siblings weren't willing to let that happen. "I'll make us breakfast."

All the eggs in the carton were put to use, as were the two packets of bacon and some shredded cheese. Wade found a loaf of sliced bread in the cupboard and set about toasting the entire thing. When everything was finished, they ate over the pan on the stove, scooping scrambled eggs onto pieces of toast and eating it.

It was enough to tide over his hunger, but it sat heavily in his stomach for the entire rainy drive over to Lady Caith's in Beacon Hill. The home looked intact when they parked out front, no hint of damage in the magic that surrounded it. Niall and his people must have steered clear even after everything, on the run from vampires during the night and the day.

The front door opened before they even reached the porch, Saoirse peeking her head out and smiling in relief at them. "Hey, boyo. Glad to see you in one piece."

"I told you I'd keep him safe," Wade said.

Saoirse wrinkled her nose at Wade when they reached her. "It smells like you did more than that."

"Nope, we are not talking about that."

He didn't sound embarrassed, but Riordan understood why Wade wouldn't want to talk about sex. "Let's get inside. This storm looks to be getting worse."

"Sure thing. Lady Caith has breakfast ready in the dining room."

Wade perked up at that, bustling past her. "Oh, good. I want some fruit."

He disappeared into the home, and Saoirse stepped out of the way so Riordan could enter as well. She shut the door behind him, eyeing him with a faint frown. No other fae were in the hall, their hospitality from before still holding.

"You have your skin," she said.

Riordan reached out to tweak one long lock of her auburn hair. "Of course I do."

"Why haven't you offered it to Wade yet?"

"You know why."

If this plan didn't work, then Riordan needed to be free to offer himself up in lieu of everyone else. He couldn't do that if Wade held his skin, not after the younger man already held his heart, even if Wade didn't know it. Fixation was such a terrible thing when you couldn't give in to it.

"But—"

Riordan shook his head. "Let's find the others."

He wasn't about to discuss anything personal like that in this home that probably had eyes and ears everywhere. The alliance with Lady Caith was built partly on Wade and his god pack's reputation. Riordan would take it, but he wouldn't trust her, not completely.

Saoirse huffed out a sigh and turned on her heels. "All right."

He followed her to the dining room, where he was unsurprised to see Wade clutching a plate piled high with food. It all smelled good, a mix of mundane human food and fae food. There was even a dish of tiny roasted fish piled high that he had to force his older brother to share. Riordan doubted it was typical fare for Lady Caith, who seemed satisfied with her fruit and sweet bread and was probably meant just for the selkies to eat.

"Did you see the news this morning?" Riordan asked after he'd eaten half the food on his plate and was on his second cup of coffee.

"I presume you are referring to the burned yacht," Lady Caith said.

"Yeah. The news thinks it's Niall's."

"They are most likely correct. You told us you would go straight to the hotel last night."

"It wasn't us, if that's what you're asking. It was the vampires' doing."

Lady Caith neatly buttered a piece of fluffy bread. "Ah. Well, good for them."

"Has anyone heard from Ella?" Wade asked before shoving a forkful of food into his mouth.

"No."

"Okay. I'll call them after I eat."

Riordan couldn't shake off the tension that settled in him as they ate. It was barely nine o'clock in the morning, but time felt as if it were dragging. He was a day past Niall's demand, and the only reason Saoirse wasn't writhing around in pain still was because of the ring she still wore. None of them knew the status of her sealskin, and they couldn't go another day without reaching out to Niall. Riordan wouldn't risk his sister's life and sanity any longer.

It was strange, though, that Niall hadn't reached out after his last call. Riordan had thought he would, but perhaps being hunted by vampires and the loss of Harper was making him reassess everything.

Riordan was finishing the last bite of food when thunder rumbled overhead, strong enough to rattle the windows. He glanced up reflexively, listening to the howling wind outside. "I don't think we factored in the rain."

"I did," Lady Caith said. Considering her title, Riordan wasn't going to question the storm any longer.

"We'll still launch the boats, and you have clan leaders to call," Donal said.

Riordan grimaced. "I still think—"

"It was decided," Lady Caith interrupted coolly. "Your protests were noted, but your skin is not the one in Niall's possession. Allow your sister this choice."

Wade knocked his foot against Riordan's beneath the table. "I'll keep her safe. You know that."

"I know," Riordan said, putting his fork down, suddenly no longer hungry. "But it should still be me."

No one seemed inclined to argue with him again, so he didn't press the issue despite how badly he wanted to. Lady Caith didn't seem in the mood to rehash everything they'd fought over yesterday, and the plan in question was already set. All that was left was giving in to Niall's demands.

Riordan kept his phone on him, the weight of it impossible to ignore in his back pocket. The rain meant they all remained inside Lady Caith's home, all of them twitchy. Riordan had wanted to call Niall first, to get it all over with, but Lady Caith had shaken her head.

"Better to let him come crawling to us for what he wants," she had said.

Riordan didn't know if that would make everything better, but he'd agreed to wait, spending time with his siblings in the den, where they huddled together on the couch. Wade stayed close, seated on the floor in front of the couch, resting his head against Riordan's knee.

The storm didn't let up as the hours ticked down. Noon came and went, lunch a tense, quiet affair with little conversation. It was after everyone had eaten, and they were arguing over what to watch when Riordan's phone finally rang, quieting the conversation.

He pulled his phone from his pocket and stared at the screen, Niall's name on the incoming call. Riordan drew in a steadying breath before he answered it. "Niall."

"You must think yourself above me, to play such games with your sister's skin," Niall said in a silky, dangerous voice.

"I take it you didn't get much sleep last night? Vampires keep you up?" Riordan asked, forcing his voice to remain calm.

Niall ignored the question. "We had a bargain, and you broke it. Your sister is forfeit."

"I did no such thing."

"So you say."

"I'm not the one trying to take over Boston."

"A city like this needs guidance."

"Not from you."

"You have a choice, Riordan Maguire. You hand over your sister, or you hand over yourself. Your debt is being called in today."

Riordan made a fist, fingernails biting into the skin of his palm. He looked over at where Saoirse sat, clutching her hands together before her chest, mouth set in a stubborn line. He could smell her fear, but more than that, he could see the determination in her eyes. "Fine. Come make us pay it. We're at Lady Caith's."

He ended the call, in no mood to argue the minutiae of the bargain they'd been forced into. That would happen soon enough. He exhaled sharply, looking over at where Lady Caith stood in the doorway, several of her fae standing behind her. She nodded gravely at him. "He will believe your clan comes first. We know how protective you kin are."

That didn't make any of what they were doing better. Riordan had spent centuries keeping his clan safe, and it felt like the bitterest of failures when the doorbell rang not even an hour later, heralding Niall's arrival, and he would have to choose.

Wade took his hand on the walk through the home to the front door, giving it a hard squeeze. "It'll be all right."

Riordan desperately wanted to believe that, but then one of Lady Caith's fae was opening the front door, revealing Niall standing on the porch, one of his fae servants waiting behind him on the path with an open umbrella. The rain pouring down slanted sideways from the wind, but Niall appeared dry. Riordan could sense the weight of water in the air, his awareness of it tugging at his attention. He thought, briefly, of reaching for it through magic, of using it to lash out at Niall.

But they had a plan, one he'd been outvoted on, and Riordan would do his best to sell it.

"Niall Noígíallach," Lady Caith said, naming him true and not inviting him inside for any sort of hospitality.

"Lady Caith," Niall replied with an insincere smile. It was a mark against his position that he didn't use her title or name her true, either because he didn't know it or he thought using it wouldn't help him. If he was still in the process of becoming a prayed-into-being god of some sort, Riordan wondered if Niall didn't mind the acknowledgment of who he was. "I am not here for you."

"Of course not. You are here for my allies."

Niall's mouth ticked up at one corner, but Riordan couldn't read the reaction. That piercing gaze snapped to him, and Riordan met it without blinking, refusing to show deference in any way. "I am. Kin do so need to be on a leash, don't you think?"

Riordan ground his teeth in the face of that insult. "You play fast and loose with your words."

"I speak the truth." He did, because it was ingrained in the higher fae how they thought of kin. It didn't make Riordan hate him any less.

"Yeah, that still makes you an asshole," Wade said, crossing his arms over his chest.

Niall's attention shifted from Riordan to Wade, and Riordan wanted to step between them. "Ah, the human from the bar."

"Yeah. Little old me who sicced the vampires on you and ruined your hotel. By the way, Harper wants her husband back."

The rage that flashed across Niall's eyes was easy enough to see, like a storm barreling in from the horizon. "You seem not to know your place."

"Oh, I know it." Wade jerked his thumb in Saoirse's direction. "It's with her."

"I'm going with you," Saoirse told Niall, her voice flat and firm, hands fisted at her side. "You can keep me and my skin, and that's all you're getting."

Wade nodded. "And me. You seem the kind of asshole who likes a little revenge. I mean, how much did that yacht of yours cost?"

Riordan could smell the sharp scent of anger for a split second before Niall got himself under control. Wade smiled at him, a hardness to his gaze that would have been foolhardy if Riordan didn't know what Wade was.

"Is this your choice, Riordan?" Niall asked. "You would actually give up your sister to my possession?"

No, Riordan wanted to say. But instead, what came out of his mouth was "You stole her skin, and the cost is too high to get it back."

It took everything in him to choke out those words, not needing to fake how much it pained him to do so. Niall narrowed his eyes but didn't immediately speak, clearly not getting what he truly wanted—which was Riordan's clan and territory to eat away at the rest of the kin.

"The bargain was set, and payment is made," Lady Caith said, her words ringing with a kind of power that made the air feel heavy. "I bear witness."

Something seemed to *snap* around Riordan, that invisible pressure breaking. Riordan stiffened, staring at Saoirse, who swayed on her feet but never lost that determined look in her eyes. She took a deep breath and stepped out of the foyer and onto the porch. Donal had to hold Riordan back from snatching her away from Niall.

They had a plan.

He needed to remember that.

"So where are we going?" Wade asked as he handed his cell phone to Riordan before following Saoirse outside.

"You were not part of the bargain," Niall said.

"It's your lucky day, then, because it's a buy one, get one free sale. Besides, you'll want me. I can tell the vampires to stop messing with your territory."

"That doesn't mean they will stop."

"You won't know unless I try." Wade slung his arm over Saoirse's shoulders, holding her close. He smiled at Niall, showing no fear, and then proceeded to guide Saoirse off the porch and into the rain. "What car are we taking?"

Niall stood there for a moment, his gaze boring into Riordan's. "I don't know what game you think you're playing, but it won't end how you hope. You'll never see your sister again after today."

Riordan bit his tongue until it bled, Donal's grip bruisingly tight on his shoulder. He said nothing to that threat, the bargain paid and witnessed. The Maguire Clan was out of reach of Niall's clutches, but Saoirse wasn't. Riordan dragged his gaze away from Niall and looked past the other fae at Saoirse and Wade, who had paused on the pathway, flanked by two of Niall's fae bodyguards. The rain had soaked through their clothes, plastering their hair to their heads. But they both looked back at him, and Riordan knew the only thing he could do was place his trust in Wade.

He kept his teeth clenched together, words locked away in his chest, his sealskin remaining with him as Niall walked off with his sister and his lover. He didn't call out to them, staying rooted where he stood until the black SUVs double-parked out front finally drove off.

Donal tugged him out of the doorway, letting Lady Caith shut it, closing out the storm. She looked at him, gaze unwavering. "He did not get what he truly wanted. He will come after you again."

"That's what we're hoping for," Donal said in a low voice.

Riordan shook himself free of his brother's grip and pulled out his cell phone, calling Ella. The dire picked up after the first ring. "Did he take the bait?"

"Yes," Riordan said, the words scraping themselves out of his throat. "He took Saoirse and Wade."

"Good. We'll head to the harbor. Have the boats ready."

Ella was all business, which Riordan would appreciate some other day. She ended the call, and the only thing left for them to do was get ready to defend their clan and their territory.

That meant stealing back Saoirse and Wade.

Riordan wanted to believe that Wade would be able to manage that on his own.

CHAPTER TWENTY-ONE

WADE MADE SURE EVERYTHING THAT WOULD HINT AT HIS TRUE FORM WAS locked down tight, all of it hidden how Reed had taught him. That was the easy part. Not hitting back when he got punched in the face by a fae for mocking them took way more effort.

"*Ow*," Wade said, holding a hand over his nose. The pain was a barely there flash that disappeared in a second. The trickle of blood that escaped one nostril was the only bit that would leak out. He wouldn't bruise, but that shouldn't be a problem. He knew bruises and swelling took time to actually come up on a person—he'd seen Patrick suffer through them enough over the years—but they'd hopefully be gone before anyone questioned why Wade looked fine. "If you're trying to break my teeth, you missed."

"Don't," Saoirse said, clutching at his arm where they were crowded in the back seat of the SUV. "Please don't antagonize them."

The fear coming off her was sour in his nose. Wade scowled as he dropped his hand but held his tongue in the face of a smirking fae and the gun trained on them. What he really wanted to do was rip the fae's arm off and then go for Niall's head, but that was a Patrick and Jono kind of plan, and he needed to think like Sage. Which meant he stayed quiet for the rest of the short drive through Beacon Hill to Niall's home in the northwest corner that he'd carved out of Lady Caith's territory however long ago.

Wade's clothes got soaked again when they were dragged out of the SUV and hustled into the fancy-looking redbrick home that reeked of fae magic, and not in a good way. An undercurrent of rotten fish hit the back of his throat when they crossed the threshold, and he had to suppress the gagging noise he wanted to make. A mundane human wouldn't be able to scent like that, but really, how did Niall live in a place that stank like that horribly?

"Take them to the holding room," Niall said once he made it inside.

They were shoved down the hallway, and Wade made sure to keep Saoirse's hand in his. If the fae tried to separate them, Wade would drop the pretense and burn everyone with dragon fire. Sadly, none of the fae gave him that opportunity because both he and Saoirse were shoved into a room that had magic in the walls. None of it touched him, but it drove Saoirse to her knees with a strangled cry.

"What are you doing to her?" Wade demanded, crouching beside her.

"Keeping a disobedient fae in line. Lady Caith's power won't be enough to keep her safe any longer," Niall said, eyeing Wade in a contemplative way he really didn't like.

"Feels like an iron burn," Saoirse gasped out.

Wade moved to block her from Niall's view, settling his hand over the fire opal ring she still wore. His hand blocked the glitter of magic in its depths, the spell somehow knowing what Saoirse needed in that moment—protection and subtlety. The lines of pain pricking the corners of her eyes eased, but she stayed on her knees, pretending to cower.

Niall didn't seem aware of Órlaith's magic, which was odd. For a wannabe god, Wade thought Niall would have sensed the magic. He wondered if Órlaith's magic was just stronger than Niall's, which could work to their advantage.

Wade twisted around on his knees, still keeping himself between Niall and Saoirse. "Where's Casey?"

"The wolf isn't your concern," Niall said coolly.

"That's where you're wrong."

"Such bravado. There is nothing you can do to save them. They broke their bargain with me."

"It's not a bargain if you force them into it."

Niall looked down his nose at them like they were bugs. Wade had to resist the urge to bite him in two. "Well, it doesn't matter now, does it? You confessed to helping Harper flee, which means her husband's life is forfeit."

Wade went still at that, staring at Niall. "Did you kill him?"

"Some sacrifices must be made for those beneath me to learn their place. The sea will take him, and I'll take the land that was his." Niall turned toward the door, speaking to the fae there. "Is she here?"

"She arrived about twenty minutes ago. She waits for you in the study," the fae said.

"You can bring her here. We have business to conduct."

The other fae actually hesitated. "She asked us to bring you to her when you arrived."

Wade wondered who it was they were talking about that made Niall look that displeased. "Fine. Keep an eye on them."

Wade watched him go in confusion. "I thought Niall was in charge. Are you telling me he's someone else's errand boy?"

The fae on babysitting duty didn't bother to answer him. Which was fine—Wade didn't want to have a conversation with him anyway. He turned back around to face Saoirse, catching her eye. She gave him a fraught smile, shoulders tight. "I'm okay."

"Can you tell if your skin is nearby?" Wade didn't bother keeping his voice low, knowing the fae would hear him even if he whispered. The whole reason why they'd let themselves be taken prisoner was to get inside Niall's home.

Saoirse squeezed her eyes shut and shook her head. "No, I can't."

Wade didn't want her to take off the fire opal ring, not if it was the only thing keeping her upright between the room they were in and whatever she'd suffered through yesterday before its magic activated. "Okay."

He closed his eyes and ducked his head, expanding that internal sense he carried within that allowed him to find all manner of magical artifacts and trinkets imbued with bits of magic. It's what had made him a good pickpocket once upon a time, a knack that had saved his life when he was younger. Right now, he used it to save Saoirse's.

Wade kept his aura locked down tight as his awareness drifted through a home saturated with fae magic of various kinds. The tang of ozone was stronger here, probably because it was Niall's home, and it took a moment for Wade to sift through the magic. He concentrated, awareness eventually snagging on the sense of what he could only describe as salt-rusted iron, like the sea was locked away.

Iron hurt fae in the same way silver hurt werecreatures. If Niall had trapped Saoirse's skin inside iron, it might be enough to hurt her the way it had before he'd put the fire opal ring on her finger.

Wade opened his eyes, seeing Saoirse staring back at him hopefully. He mouthed, *I think I found it*, at her, and she was smart enough not to react beyond ducking her head and letting out a shuddering breath.

Footsteps and voices from down the hall caught his ear, and Wade stood. Saoirse tried to get to her feet but fell back to her knees with a grimace. He offered her his hand, which she took, and he hauled her against him, keeping her close. He wished they hadn't had to return the artifact necklace to Gwen because it would've come in handy right about then. The fire opal ring was keeping the pain at bay for her, which was Saoirse's highest need. Wade would have to be her shield.

Niall returned to the holding room, smelling like ozone, but that was because of the fae who followed at his heels. Wade's eyes went wide as he took in the fae who smelled more like a god than Niall and made him think he had the status all wrong.

The newest arrival was a fae shorter than Niall, wearing a glamour over her skin that Wade's vision easily penetrated. To most people, she probably looked like an old woman with green-dyed hair. To Wade, her skin was an almost teal color with shimmery scales over her joints. Her eyes were a murky gray with no sclera showing. Her face was wrinkled, dark green hair clumped wetly together around it in a way that reminded Wade of kelp. Everything about her spoke of the sea, but her scent was all prickly ozone, the marker of a god, demi or otherwise.

Wade stared at her. The fae stared back. A heavy sense of something *big* pressed against his awareness, making his mouth drop open in surprise. "You're a *dragon*?"

Niall wrenched his gaze from Wade back to the fae. "How did he know, Caoránach?"

Caoránach smiled, revealing sharp teeth. "Because he is not as he seems."

Saoirse made a strangled, horrified sound that told Wade whoever this fae was, she was a problem, one they couldn't get tied up in. He tightened his arm around Saoirse's waist and decided it was time for them to get the hell out of there.

He spat dragon fire at the fae, which was met by a blast of seawater that created a swirl of deadly steam Wade didn't stick around to experience. He hauled Saoirse with him to the side wall and punched his way through it with enough strength it damaged the support beam overhead. Pieces of the ceiling rained down behind them as the wall collapsed. He dragged Saoirse out of the holding room, through magic that made the fire opal ring shine like the light in a lighthouse. They ended up in an adjacent dining room, the open-plan kitchen beyond it empty.

Wade opened up his awareness, primed to find treasure, and took Saoirse with him. Shouting echoed through the house, and the walls glowed with magic that chased them up the stairs. A pair of fae stood at the landing up top, actual swords in hand instead of guns.

Wade wasted no time in spitting fire at them hot enough to melt the metal and turn the fae into scorch marks.

"What *are* you?" Saoirse gasped out in shock.

"*Dragon!*" a vicious voice cried out from the first floor.

"She's not wrong," Wade said as he practically carried Saoirse with him down a hallway. "Who was that other dragon?"

"Caoránach? She's an Oilliphéist."

"A what now?"

"Mundane humans would call her a sea serpent." Saoirse shuddered. "She's probably the threat that's been in the harbor and the ocean."

"Oh man, I think I saw one of those on a flight to Ireland once. She must be the god, not Niall. I really don't want to know what they've been doing for him to carry that much of her scent with him." He'd gotten it wrong when it came to what Niall was—still an asshole though—but he'd been right that the problem was a god of some sort. "I don't know what a sea serpent gets out of owning land though."

"Niall's been taking hostages, going after people with magic and power. She has a hunger."

Wade swore. "She can *stay* hungry."

Magic pulsed in the walls around them, and Saoirse let out a pained sound before the fire opal ring sparked with its own magic to counter whatever was being thrown at them. The magic slid right off Wade, useless against him, but he didn't want to put Saoirse at risk any more than she already was.

He paused for half a second to swing her up in his arms, her arms going around his neck as she tucked herself close. Wade spun on his heels and belched out dragon fire in the hallway behind them, setting the space on fire to slow down their pursuers. The scent of the ocean was getting stronger, which meant the sea serpent goddess was probably closing the distance between them. But Wade had one more floor to get to, his awareness of treasure snagging on that salt-iron beacon above.

The staircase at the end of the hallway wasn't guarded at the bottom, but he knew better than to run up it full tilt. He spat more dragon fire ahead of them as a precaution, which was a good thing, because the hail of bullets melted in the heat. Saoirse turned her face away from the fire, holding on tight to Wade as he burned his way up to the third floor.

Fire kindled on the wall, breaking through magic as he ran down the hallway to his right. He didn't see a stairwell leading up, but there was an outline in the ceiling about half the size of a regular door, completely covered in wards that burned bright in defense to their presence.

"Hold on," Wade said as he set Saoirse on her feet again. She leaned against the wall to get out of his way.

Wade jumped, using his strength to launch himself straight up and break through the ceiling entrance with both fists. The door shattered upward from the force of his hit, the spell embedded in it cleaving away in bright lines that hissed and sparked in midair before fading away. He caught the edge of the opening in one hand, hung there for a second, before landing back on the floor with a heavy thump.

Steam exploded from down the hall, and Wade wasted no time in picking up Saoirse and tossing her up through the broken-open entrance above them. Wade followed after her, nearly cracking the floor with the force of his jump. He landed in a tiny space that passed as an attic. He had to duck his head to keep it from hitting the ceiling, but that was fine. He needed to crouch before the iron safe anyway.

Saoirse came up behind him, her heartbeat loud in his ears, quick like a rabbit's. "Is that where he's kept my skin?"

Wade flexed his fingers, talons curving away from the nailbed. "Yeah."

That salt-iron tug was bright in his awareness, treasure waiting to be stolen. Only he'd never keep what was in the safe because it didn't belong to him. It belonged to Saoirse, and he was determined to give it back to her before the sea serpent made it to the attic.

"She's coming," Saoirse breathed in fear. "How are we going to get out?"

"I have a plan," Wade muttered.

First, he needed to break through the safe and all the spells and wards wrapped around it. Iron didn't hurt him, and neither did the magic Niall had set into it. He wondered how any of the fae managed to touch the thing.

Wade placed his talons against the seam of the door and sank them into metal with brute strength, shifting mass a bit to force them through. Saoirse made a surprised sound and scrambled back a few steps. He didn't have time to apologize for making her uncomfortable. Wade used that part of him that could negate magic in breaking through everything laid into the iron safe as he wrenched the door off its hinges and away from the frame itself.

Inside lay some jewelry that reeked of magic, a scepter made out of bone that smelled like a grave, and draped in the back was a soft-looking pile of sealskin that was the whole reason for the mess Riordan and his clan were in. Wade snatched up the sealskin first and tossed it to Saoirse. She caught it lightning quick, flinging it over her shoulders. It shifted as it spun through the air, turning into a cute little cropped leather jacket that she hugged to her body with a ragged sob.

Wade dragged everything else in the safe into that internal pocket where his mass resided as opposed to the ones in his jeans. He didn't know what any of it did, but he knew better than to leave it for Niall to keep. If it was locked up in a magical safe, then Niall thought they were important, and that meant Wade was adding them to his hoard.

"Come on," Wade said as he stood. "We have to go."

"Where?" Saoirse pointed at the broken entrance. "That's the only way out."

"Not the only way. I need you to trust me."

She snorted, letting out a strangled sort of laugh. "You don't need to ask that. I still can't believe you're a dragon."

Wade would always ask, but he didn't tell her that. He reached for her, settled one hand on her shoulder, and gave her a quick little smile. "Whatever happens, I won't let you go."

He could sense the sea serpent getting closer, but he couldn't stick around and fight her, not with Saoirse to worry about. He'd also never fought a dragon before and wasn't sure how he'd get the upper hand with a sea serpent when his element was fire. Wade closed his eyes and opened himself up to the part of him that he locked away from the human form he walked the world in.

Shifting mass was a little like being on the receiving end of an avalanche. It wasn't like how werecreatures shifted, breaking bone and tearing skin and turning it all into something else. Wade's human body was essentially an illusion—solid, yes, but it wasn't his true form.

His true form was what split through the ceiling and floor of Niall's house, breaking free as mass settled back onto earth in the shape of a dragon that destroyed the house better than a wrecking ball. His wings unfurled, arcing upward into the sky, rain and wind lashing at them. His long neck stretched to its full length before he snaked it back down, tilting his head to look at where he carefully held Saoirse in one taloned foreclaw. She stared at him with a slack-jawed expression on her pale face, but she appeared unharmed from having the house come down around them.

The thing about being a dragon in a large urban city was that people would notice you.

Wade could hide himself from radar, and while he could get people to look away, he couldn't make an entire city not see him. At least with the storm, there was cloud coverage, and hopefully, not as many people would be out in the rain. Wade launched himself into the sky, flying straight up toward the low-lying ceiling of storm clouds, both taloned foreclaws curled around Saoirse to shield her from the rain.

Boston disappeared when he made it into the clouds, flapping his wings hard to gain altitude. He was better at navigating direction in this form than on the ground, some other internal sense always knowing which way was up and down and where true north was. He banked on a wingtip in the cloud, sheet lightning cracking above him for a split second, and veered south, heading for the harbor.

He made sure to stay within an altitude that still let Saoirse breathe. The sound of jet engines echoed through the sky, most of them far off at a higher altitude. Wade kept out of the flight paths of the ones heading to the airport, his world gray and cottony-looking, rain pelting his wings and body. He couldn't stay airborne forever though, much as he loved flying. Casey was still missing, and they needed to find him before the sea serpent made it back to the harbor.

Dropping a building on top of a god was probably not enough to kill them.

He could hope it had killed Niall though. It would save Wade from eating the bastard. He probably tasted terrible.

Wade dived lower, the updraft different when he reached the trailing edge of the clouds. He snaked his head down below the clouds, getting eyes on the swath of Boston stretched out before him. The shoreline was closer, and he adjusted his vision to see farther, like a telescope. The water was choppy, all white-capped waves, and none of the boats in the harbor had any sails unfurled.

He rose back into the clouds, hiding himself away from curious eyes, and flapped his wings harder to speed up. He knew vaguely where he needed to go for the meet-up, and the boats waiting for him when he finally dived out of the clouds through howling wind and pouring rain held people that smelled like the sea and others that carried the scents of werecreatures.

He shifted mass as he arrowed toward a familiar yacht. The people on the small rear deck scattered, but they didn't need to. When Wade landed on the deck with a heavy grunt, it wasn't with the mass of a fire dragon but the easy weight of a human. The landing drove both him and Saoirse to their knees, the rocking of the yacht from the storm sending them sliding across the deck.

"Saoirse!" Riordan shouted. "Wade!"

Wade lifted his head, blinking rain out of his eyes. Riordan hurried toward them, keeping his balance against the rocking boat with ease. He crashed to his knees before them, dragging both of them into his arms for a bruising hug.

"He found my skin," Saoirse said, sniffling hard.

"Thank you," Riordan said, pressing a hard, close-mouthed kiss to Wade's lips. "*Thank you.*"

"Not supposed to thank me," Wade muttered.

Riordan laughed shakily before letting them go so he could shrug out of his leather jacket. "Here. You can use this to cover yourself."

Wade was keenly aware of the sharp breath Saoirse drew in. His clothes had been ripped to shreds when he'd shifted mass, and Wade was grateful for the offer, but it was Riordan's *sealskin*. "I can't take that."

"It's only for a little while. We're on our way to the islands."

Wade hesitated but reached for the leather jacket after a moment. It was warm in a way a true piece of clothing wouldn't be. He gripped it with one hand, meeting Riordan's eyes over it as rain poured down around them. "I'll give it back."

Riordan smiled, and the look in his eyes was something Wade wanted to hoard. "I know you will."

Nodding, Wade took the leather jacket and tied it around his waist, gaining a modicum of decency. "I destroyed Niall's house."

"You did what?" Lady Caith asked from where she was braced in the doorway to the cockpit.

"Niall isn't the god, but he was working with one. She was glamoured as some old woman, but she goes by Caoránach."

Wade heard Lady Caith's fingers make dents in the doorframe. "He allied himself with the First Oilliphéist?"

"Looks like it. I'm pretty sure she's not dead and is probably on her way to the water right now."

"Then we need to get to the islands before she makes it beneath the waves."

"I think I saw her that night in the pub," Riordan said, frowning. "She was with Niall and Casey. She didn't act like a god."

"They're good at hiding, but I can always sniff them out," Wade said. Riordan helped Wade and Saoirse to their feet, and Wade swayed on the deck for a few seconds as he tried to find his balance. He didn't mind it when Riordan wrapped an arm around his waist to steady him. "Do we know where Casey is being held?"

Harper popped up behind Lady Caith, peering at him over the fae's shoulder. "No, but my entire god pack is ready to search the islands."

"I will know better where Niall's magic is in the land out there amidst the waves once we are closer. If magic keeps Casey prisoner, my fae and I will do all in our power to free him," Lady Caith said.

"Then let's get out there before we all become fish food," Wade said.

The clock was ticking, and while the sea was the selkies' territory, it was also Caoránach's. He'd fight her if he had to, but the water wasn't his domain, and Wade knew he'd be at a severe disadvantage, especially in the storm. That didn't mean he wouldn't take to the air if he had to.

No way was he letting her or Niall have Boston.

CHAPTER TWENTY-TWO

The small yacht powered through the frothy waves, rocking from the furious seas and the howling wind. The Boston Harbor was empty of all personal boats except for the group belonging to the Maguire clan. Not even the mundane human members of the clan were staying on shore. Most of those captaining the boats weren't selkies, but they knew how to navigate the waves above just as surely as their lovers could the waters below.

Passengers on the boats were fae from Lady Caith's court, the entirety of the Boston god pack, and Wade, who was seated next to Riordan right inside the cockpit on the *Neptune*. He wore Riordan's leather jacket like a kilt, and Riordan had to shove down the smugness he felt at the sight of Wade carrying his sealskin around. He'd take it back when he had to go in the water, but for now, Riordan was satisfied.

Harper staggered into the cabin from a stint out by the railing, soaked through to her skin, hair plastered to her skull. She wasn't sporting any of the wounds Wade had described, but she looked thinner than Riordan remembered from their last meeting about territory borders. She'd been through hell but clearly wasn't letting it stop her from tracking down her husband. Ella hadn't left her alpha's side and followed Harper into the cockpit.

"We're approaching one of the islands. Lady Caith seems to think it's where Casey might be," Harper said.

"Which island?" Riordan asked.

"Great Brewster Island."

That put them about nine miles out from Boston proper, closer to the open ocean than the continent. "There's no docks available on that island, and the water is too choppy to risk getting close to the shore with the boats we're on. We can launch your pack and Lady Caith's people in lifeboats, but the passage will be dicey. My clan will be in the water though. If anyone goes overboard, we'll fish them out and get you to shore."

"We'll take the risk. I'm not leaving without Casey."

Riordan didn't doubt that and wouldn't have even thought to try to persuade her. "We'll get him back."

"I'll get on the radio and notify the other boats," Donal said, shoving himself away from the wall he had braced himself against during the trip through the harbor.

It wasn't even a minute later when one of his clan members flung themselves from the water and somersaulted into human form onto the deck. The rocking of the boat meant they went sliding over the decking and tumbling down the stairs into the cockpit before any of the selkies on the benches outside could grab them.

"Riordan!" Maisie said as Saoirse helped right her, dark brown sealskin draped over her shoulders. "She's in the water!"

He lurched up from the seat, not needing to ask what *she* Maisie was talking about. "Where?"

"Heard her calling in the sea. She sounds angry."

Riordan looked over at where Lady Caith and Harper stood, bracing themselves against the walls. "We need to get you all in the lifeboats."

Easier said than done. Each boat or yacht only had one, maybe two inflatable lifeboats, and the number of passengers far outstripped the number of life vests. Most of the selkies dived overboard, leaving their clothes behind and shifting underwater. Riordan turned to find Wade, locking eyes with him across the deck. "You're going to the island."

Wade set his jaw in a stubborn way that Riordan told himself he couldn't find adorable. "No, I'm not."

"You can't fight underwater, and the yacht can't take your shifted weight."

Wade scowled and crossed his arms over his chest. "I can get up in the air."

"I'd feel better if I knew you were on land." Riordan braced himself against another hard toss of waves, reaching out to keep Wade upright when he stumbled. "Please."

"Fine. But you better not end up in Davey Jones' locker."

"That's a tall tale."

"I know too many of those that turn out to be real." Wade reached for the leather jacket wrapped around his waist. "You're going to need this back."

"Here," Donal said from the cabin, tossing Wade a bright yellow raincoat taken from one of the emergency supply stashes. "Use this to cover up."

Wade swapped Riordan's sealskin for the raincoat that fell to midthigh, offering it back with a freeness that made Riordan swallow hard. Wade patted the leather jacket, a faint smile curving his lips. "Don't let her eat you. Tell the boats to scatter and head to a different island. Have your clan work to get her to the surface, and I'll handle her from there."

"You said she was a god," Riordan said.

"Yeah, I have experience with those fuckers."

Riordan reeled him in for a quick, hard kiss, knowing they didn't have time for lingering goodbyes. "Get on the lifeboat and get to shore."

Wade nodded, sliding over the deck for the railing. Riordan could see the lifeboat bouncing amongst the waves, a selkie attempting to stabilize it from one end by holding the towrope. Wade flung himself over the railing, and Riordan pitched himself to that side of the yacht, looking to make sure Wade made it where he was supposed to go.

He'd ended up in the water, but a selkie was right next to him in the waves, guiding him to the lifeboat. The fae and werecreatures on it helped haul him aboard, and the selkies in charge of getting them to the island grabbed the tow lines and started swimming for shore through the white-capped waves.

"Come on, boyo. We have an Oilliphéist to fight," Donal said.

"We'll need to set up riptides and whirlpools to keep her away from the island. I'll anchor those," Riordan said.

He'd have the entire clan in the water with him this time, blending their water magic together. If they survived this, he'd take them all on a vacation somewhere.

Maybe New York City.

Riordan stripped out of his soaked clothes and dove overboard, Donal close behind him. He cut through the top of frothing waves, going under, cold water closing over him. He rolled into a shift, seal-skin spreading over his body, limbs and body changing into the torpedo-like shape of a seal.

Riordan knew where his clan members were in the vastness of the sea. The magic that tied them to the water let him sense their location with brief bursts of power. The mental map laid out before him grew in pinpricks—a few, then a dozen, then most of the clan stretched out along the length of Greater Brewster Island.

Somewhere far away and coming closer was the echoing, sonorous sound he'd heard before in his patrols—deep and hair-raising. He knew what the threat was now, knew what they'd have to fight against while Harper and the others fought to free Casey on the land. Riordan didn't know if Niall would join Caoránach in the sea, but if that fae did, he'd be fair game.

Riordan twisted in the water, letting his magic flow with the motion. Donal joined him, the pair of them blending their magic together to alter the force of the underwater tides into something different—a riptide of magic that could hopefully act like a barrier against the sea serpent charging their way beneath the waves.

Other clan members joined his efforts, bridging their locations with tightly spun water magic that the selkies further out guided around the ends of the island. Riordan could sense them through the tangle of water magic he was tied to. He wasn't sure if they'd be able to surround the island in time, but his clan would try.

Nose closed against the water, Riordan flicked his flippers and dove down into the dark toward the seabed, hunting for the softly glowing marks he knew were down there. As he swam deeper, one of the marks appeared, shining softly in the dark water. Riordan circled the mark, reaching one flipper out to touch it on one pass. He got immediate feedback, a burst of warning from all the rest in the bay waters. In his mind, he could see the passage of Caoránach through the waters like a dangerous missile, but more than that, he could sense other selkies not of his clan swimming toward them, calling out through the territory marks.

It seemed all the selkie clans in Boston had answered his call. Whether or not they'd get to the island in time to join the fight remained to be seen.

Riordan pushed the information out through the net connecting his clan members, letting his knowledge be shared through their magic. When their magic was all tied together like this, they could share the meaning and intent of their thoughts, even if they couldn't share the actual words.

If Caoránach was truly a god, they couldn't fight her and win, but they could direct her wrath to the surface, where hopefully Wade could handle her. Riordan was putting all of his faith in the younger man's hands—and wings and claws and fire—but he knew it wasn't misplaced. Lady Caith could help Harper and the others track down

Casey. Wade was his clan's backup, and Riordan knew he would fight with them.

Another sonorous cry echoed through the water—deep and malevolent. Riordan swam faster, building the riptides up into the tight spin of a whirlpool. Through the churning water, distant but coming closer, were streaks of bioluminescence in the deep water.

Fuath.

Riordan sent a warning to the clan even as he kicked his flippers and zoomed toward the surface, sucking in another lungful of air. He crested a wave and dove back under, nostrils closing tight. The roar of the storm quieted a little once he was back under. The pull of the underwater tides and the whirlpools his clan was building required more effort to swim through.

Saoirse swam up beside him, smaller and sleeker than him and Donal in her seal form, the brown coloring of her fur something he'd missed seeing. He skimmed a fin over her back for a moment before parting ways, attention on the rapidly approaching fuath.

Again, that sonorous cry echoed through the depths of the harbor's seawater. It made some part of Riordan want to turn and flee, but he shredded that desire like he would fish caught in his seal teeth. Instead, he held fast in the water, determined to fight for his clan and guard their territory shared with the other kin who called Boston home.

It only took a minute more for the fuath to reach their position guarding the approach to the shoreline of Greater Brewster Island. The fuath numbered more than he liked, but his clan was ready for the attack as the first wave of Caoránach's crashed against their defenses like waves against a cliff.

Riordan charged with open-mouthed fury, ramming the closest fuath and ripping its throat out with his teeth in a tight spin. Its bioluminescence flickered before fading out as it sank to the seabed.

Bubbles streamed from Riordan's mouth due to his swift passage through the water as he targeted another fuath, dragging the dangerous riptide with him. It caught the next fuath in its terrible pull, sucking it up into the vicious whirlpool spinning behind them. It ripped the fuath to shreds, bioluminescence fading with its death.

The selkies became bait for the fuath, drawing as many of them into the whirlpools, knowing they were running out of time before Caoránach arrived. Riordan remembered the terror of an Oilliphéist from his childhood spent past the veil centuries ago, the way the beast seemed to encompass the threat of the ocean itself, and he had no doubt that wouldn't be the same today.

It wasn't long until the movement of the underwater tide shifted, heralding the approach of something large. The fuath cried out a welcome that vibrated through the water, making Riordan's heart beat fast as he swam upward in an arc that put him closer to the range of whirlpools his clan had mustered. Amidst the darkness beyond them, a large shadow swam through the depths, bringing with it a sense of terror that Riordan had to shake off. Power crackled through the water, reminding him of an eel's defensive ability, and the hint of magic that bloomed along the back spines of a sinewy monster of the depths revealed a horror that made Riordan freeze in the water for a heart-stopping moment.

Instinct got him moving—away from Caoránach in her Oilliphéist form and into the twisting pull of his clan's magic behind the whirlpools. The dark water churned viciously around the warring sides as fuath and selkies attacked each other. Riordan opened himself up to the water magic he'd been born with, gripping the tightly spinning whirlpool nearest him at the anchoring point and sending it careening through the water. Caoránach dodged it with an underwater roar that echoed through the sea. Riordan swam faster, maneuvering around a fuath and forcing it into the drag of a whirlpool. He aimed for the surface, sensing the threat of Caoránach behind him through the tangle of whirlpools she cut through. How she knew to target him, Riordan couldn't say, but he'd lay the blame at Niall's feet.

Riordan broke the surface, flinging himself as far forward as he could, barking a warning he wasn't sure anyone could hear. He sucked air into his lungs as gravity drew him back toward the waves, rain lashing his body, the wind a roar in his ears. He went under, sliding through the water and directly into a whirlpool manipulated by a clan member that yanked him out of the way of Caoránach's gaping jaw full of ragged teeth.

He kicked his flippers, tumbling down the length of the whirlpool before pitching himself out of it, orienting himself in the water with long practice. Even with the storm raging above and the water darker than it typically was during the day, he could see Caoránach's sinewy form ripping through the water, heading his way. Riordan reached for the nearest whirlpool and dragged its churning core between them, bubbles frothing in the water.

Riordan swam for the surface again, followed by the terrifying bulk of an Oilliphéist that let out a vibrating roar he felt in the bones of his skull. It wrecked his balance for a handful of seconds, disrupting his ability to figure out which way the surface was in the vastness of the sea. The only thing that saved him from being bitten in half was the quick thinking of his siblings.

Donal and Saoirse barreled into him, their teeth sinking into his fur, breaking skin, but he didn't care as they dragged him out of reach of Caoránach's maw. The rush of water that exploded from her jaw snapping shut propelled them away even faster. Donal and Saoirse angled toward the surface, finally letting go of him when he gave a little wriggle.

The whirlpools ripped fuath away from them as they swam through the tangle of water magic. Caoránach tore through each one in her pursuit, the magic fraying and spinning away into the depths of the sea. Riordan and his siblings couldn't possibly hope to outswim the sea serpent, but they didn't need to. They just needed a chance to get her to the surface.

The three of them swam together in a pattern that saw them crossing paths in the water, diving through whirlpools that did their best to slow Caoránach down. Riordan grabbed the frayed edges of magic, trying to spin them back together into something bigger, something stronger.

Something to get an Oilliphéist out of the water.

As clan chief, Riordan's magic was primed to act as an anchor for all the selkies he led. He opened himself up to the sea and the magic found there, spread thin through riptides and whirlpools but still very much present. He somersaulted out of the way of Caoránach's teeth, desperately clawing for magic that could keep her at bay. Donal and Saoirse joined their strength to his, but for all their power, they couldn't go up against a god whose territory was the vast ocean itself.

Caoránach was a master of the sea the way selkies never could be with their smaller stature. No matter how fast they swam, no matter the number of whirlpools they spun, she would outstrip and outlast them.

And she did.

A pulse of magic ripped through the water, shredding the whirlpools spinning beneath the waves. The backlash slammed through Riordan as if he'd been rammed by a ship in the harbor. He faltered, agony lashing through his body as the water undulated all around them, fighting to form a current. When Caoránach wrenched it into a direction he couldn't control, Riordan and the other selkies were drawn with it. He swam against it, trying to flee its clutches. The twisting power of it was something he recognized, and even the strength lent by kin still on their way to fight wasn't enough to free them from the magic tangled around them like a net.

Caoránach roared in triumph, magic erupting in a surge of bubbles and frothy water that spun in an ever-widening circle while rising. The pull of the tide was viciously strong as it punched upward to the surface and the storm raging there. Strong enough to drag Riordan and those selkies nearby within its clutches up with it as someone spun the whirlpool into a waterspout they couldn't escape.

Heart pounding, head aching, magic whittled thin, Riordan fought the current dragging them up toward Caoránach's waiting mouth, the spin giving him vertigo. She roared as sheet lightning illuminated the stormy sky above—a sound that abruptly changed pitch into something agonizing as Wade dived out of the low-hanging clouds and sank his claws into her spiny back, fire exploding from his mouth with a furious roar.

CHAPTER TWENTY-THREE

Wade jumped out of the lifeboat into shallow waters that wouldn't be so bad if the storm hadn't whipped up the waves into a frenzy. He turned to hold the lifeboat steady with the help of the two selkies who'd guided them to shore. The werecreatures and fae who'd weighed down the inflatable boat flung themselves overboard and waded to shore, buffeted by the waves. The werecreatures managed to brace themselves against the sea better than the fae, but everyone made it to shore in one piece.

Wade picked his way around the large rocks filling the shore, heading for the eroding cliff overlooking the sea. He squinted through the driving rain as, around him, the Boston god pack began shifting with bone-cracking ease. Werecreatures—mostly wolves, but Wade saw a grizzly farther down the shore and someone who he thought might be a leopard—raced through the rain and up the sloping ground, scrambling to the top of the cliff.

"There are ruins from the mortals' military on the island. I told Harper that is where I sensed a net of Niall's magic," Lady Caith called out from the base of the cliff, the tide crashing against her feet and ankles as Wade approached.

"Could you tell if Casey was alive?"

Lady Caith shook her head. Her magenta hair had been braided into a crown around her head, but some pieces were escaping the style from the wind. Then she pointed at the sea they'd just escaped from. "Look. Caoránach does not come alone."

Wade spun around, wiping rainwater out of his eyes. He shifted a tiny bit of mass to sharpen his vision, bringing into clarity the distant speedboats cutting through the waves. There were a lot of them.

"Should've paid Lucien to go after more of Niall's property," Wade grumbled.

"It is a bit disconcerting that you are so friendly with that master vampire."

"Oh, we're not friendly. He's just a useful bastard sometimes."

"Clearly." Lady Caith tipped her head back to look up at the cliff they stood beneath. "We need higher ground."

"I can give you a lift." Wade mimed putting his hands together and launching her in the air.

She snorted delicately. "I can make my own way up. Where will you be?"

"Fighting the sea serpent."

"I had wondered what you were. I had my suspicions in my garden. I am not sure I like being right."

"Why not?"

"Your kind makes their own legends. Sometimes they end up like the one in the sea."

Wade frowned at her. "I'm no god."

"You are lucky, then, that I am Tuatha Dé Danann." Lady Caith raised a hand, fingers curling like claws. In her palm, magic spun into being, the color a deep, angry gray, like the storm clouds above. "I left Tír na nÓg for reasons that do not concern you, but I left with the fury of a storm in me. You cannot defeat Caoránach on your own, but we can drive her away. My court will help the Boston god pack retrieve their alpha, as obligated by the alliance we all share. You and I will deal with an Oilliphéist."

"So we're gonna crispifry her?"

Lady Caith shrugged, magic tangling around her wrist and fingers. "I suppose that is one way of describing it."

Wade nodded. "I'll get her out of the ocean and see how much fire she can take. What will you do?"

Lady Caith's smile was small and hard. "Your selkies can call whirlpools. My specialty is with the air and the sea together."

Wade glanced at the sky, frowning at the way the clouds were already starting to spin. "Man, my wings are gonna ache after this."

He stripped off the raincoat and left it piled on the rocky sand, stepping away from Lady Caith. Wade then shifted mass, letting go of his human form, falling into the shape of what he truly was. He stretched, body settling into the clawed legs, long tail and neck, and the heat of a volcano in his belly. He stretched his wings up and out to their fullest, tail lashing against the sand as he sank down on his haunches. With a politeness that would make Sage proud, he offered one foretalon to Lady Caith, allowing her to step into his palm. He lifted her up on top of the cliff, which was honestly safer than if he'd tossed her.

"We need to remove Caoránach from the harbor," she said, pitching her voice a little louder. Wade's hearing in his true form was highly sensitive and enhanced, and he could make out her words perfectly. She stepped up to the edge of the cliff, attention focused on the ocean, hands angled to either side of her body.

The wind picked up, white spray from the waves misting the air over the sea. Despite the daylight hour, the clouds were thick, and there was no sign of the sun. Boston was a distant strip of land, and he hoped the storm had driven everyone inside. If he made the evening news, his pack would be so pissed.

Wade stretched out his wings and looked up at the sky and the clouds that spun there in a way not unlike a hurricane. He really hoped Lady Caith wasn't going to create one of those. He didn't think Boston could handle a storm like that.

He snaked his head around, staring through the rain at the approaching speedboats and the quick-moving shadows he could see in the churning sea. Amidst the waves were spots of faintly glowing lights that darted through the water and the whirlpools that spun offshore. Wade knew what those meant—fuath were harassing the selkies. Ugh, they were as bad as pixies.

Wade spread his wings, digging his hindquarters into the sand, crushing chunks of granite rock as he readied himself to launch. With a snap of his wings, he threw himself into the wind and sky, wings flapping hard to get himself airborne, long tail snaking out behind him. Gravity sloughed away as he rose higher into the storm, the island falling away from him. Lady Caith was soon lost to sight, even if the result of her magic wasn't.

The higher he flew, the stronger the wind became, and Wade had to work to keep himself steady in the air. The Boston Harbor stretched out below him. He adjusted his eyesight, bringing every-thing below him into close relief. As he watched, one of the farthest yachts out suddenly capsized before being tossed into the air by the bulk of a monster swimming below.

Wade adjusted his vision again, bringing Caoránach's shadowy form more into focus. She was fast-moving as a sea serpent, and Wade knew he couldn't get drawn into a battle beneath the waves. He'd lose.

What he needed was to get her into the air and get her away from the island. He could fight her, but he knew he couldn't win against a god. Best he could do was chuck her east and hope she landed hard enough on the water that she'd break some bones. Maybe her neck. Or her spine. Wade wasn't picky; he just wanted her gone as of yesterday.

Some of the whirlpools disappeared below, while others changed size. The wind picked up even more, and Wade had to work his wings harder to stay in the area. The rain came down so horrendously it was almost like a curtain, impossible to see through. Despite the ferocity of the building storm, Wade could easily make out the churning of the water below as it spun in the same direction as the wind and rain above it.

It was rising—*twisting*—into a waterspout created by fae magic.

Oh, he didn't want to fly into that. He really didn't, but it was forming right over Caoránach's position in the sea, the spray circle down there highly distinct, and Wade couldn't leave her down there with the selkies. He wasn't giving her the harbor, and he wasn't giving Niall Boston, and neither of them were getting Riordan.

Wade folded his wings, diving through the sky before snapping them open again. He banked on a wingtip, flying around the open air that wouldn't be open for long once the spinning sea water reached the rainwater in the middle to become a pillar of destruction. He caught a glimpse of Lady Caith on the small cliff, doing her best impression of a lighthouse with how brightly she glowed.

He did another circuit around the rapidly forming waterspout before he finally caught sight of his prey. Caoránach's bioluminescent spines breached the water below at the edge of the waterspout. The selkies' whirlpools around the base of the waterspout had disappeared, and Wade didn't dwell on what that could mean—that the selkies could be hurt, that any of them could be dead. He focused instead on the problem that had led him to Boston, diving down without a roar so she wouldn't hear him coming.

He sank all four taloned claws into Caoránach's body, dragging her out of the sea. Water and blood flowed around his talons where they were embedded in her body, pierced right through scales and skin. Her great head crested a wave, mouth open in an angry roar that reverberated through the air. Wade matched it with his own and a burst of dragon fire as well, burning the nearest glowing spines on her body. They turned black, breaking off at the connecting point to her back.

Her roar this time was something hideous, full of pain, but Wade wouldn't apologize for the agony he inflicted on her. He flapped his wings harder, dragging her bulk out of the waves, belching fire at her when Caoránach's head wrenched around, mouth open for an attack. She spat something black and foul-smelling in his direction, but whatever it was—poison, acid, take your pick—Wade met it with fire. The smell it created when it burned was *so gross*. If he'd been human, he would have gagged.

Something slammed into his left thigh, a sharp edge slicing through the scales there. Wade roared in irritated pain, lashing at the thing—which turned out to be Caoránach's barbed tail—with his own. He kept flapping his wings, using all his strength to drag her fully out of the ocean, clawing at her writhing form.

::Do you think you can cage me, fledgling?::

Caoránach's voice was meant for the water. The way it sounded in his ears, in his mind—bloated and heavy and wanting to echo—gave Wade a headache he didn't appreciate. He didn't bother responding, mostly because he couldn't. His brain's ability to translate languages worked great. His ability to respond to mental conversations was still forming. Reed had told him it would be decades more before that part of his mind fully formed. Until then, he could receive other people's thoughts, just not project his own.

It was weird, sometimes, to think that he'd be a kid in dragon years for centuries to come when it felt like he'd lived a lifetime already.

Wade fought the wind and her writhing body to gain altitude, taking glancing blows from her barbed tail that he forced back with his own, never giving her a chance for what he assumed was a poisoned barb to penetrate his body. He spat more dragon fire at her, aiming for her head. She curled her body down toward the sea to escape the scorching heat, nearly making him lose his position in the air.

He lurched forward, wings beating furiously to keep them stabilized in the air. The churning power of the waterspout was growing, the two sides of the vortex nearly meeting in the middle of the sky.

The wind was gale-force level now, screaming past his ears and buffeting him and Caoránach both.

She twisted in his claws suddenly, and Wade lost hold of her with one of his back talons. Caoránach's sinewy body writhed as her head quickly turned, mouth with its many rows of teeth like a shark opening wide. What he thought were whiskers around her nose turned out to be tentacles, which, also gross, and they stuck to his scales when her teeth sank into the meat of his shoulder with vicious intent.

Wade roared in pain, wings stuttering as agony radiated from the bite. Caoránach had broken through his scales and her teeth were shredding the muscle beneath as she jerked her head from side to side, trying to tear out a bite of him. Worse, a spreading numbness was flowing down that arm, weakening his grip.

Oh, not good.

Wade didn't panic, merely snarled in rage and a little bit of pain while snaking his long neck around to bite down on the closest body part he could get. He sank his own fangs into Caoránach's scaly, slimy body and let loose a punch of dragon fire that blotted out the world. It steamed the rain around his face, and Wade closed his eyes against the heat that would never harm him.

It sure did harm Caoránach though.

She wrenched her mouth free of his shoulder and bellowed furiously. ::*You cannot stop me, fledgling!*::

If Wade was human, he would've rolled his eyes. Gods. Such arrogant assholes.

Wade pulled his teeth out of flesh that tasted like rotten fish, and with a roar, Wade heaved Caoránach into the spinning body of the waterspout. She got tangled up in its force, the sea and sky finally meeting in the middle, solidifying the massive, dangerous column of water and wind powered and controlled by Lady Caith. It spun so tightly that it almost made him dizzy.

Then Wade realized he *was* dizzy and that his left wing wasn't working as well as his right. Which probably meant poison, and that was just the worst. Really. He hated dealing with poison. The best way to clear his system of it was to shift mass, but he'd need to get back to the island for that. Only problem was they'd drifted quite a ways from it during their struggle. Even now, with the waterspout quickly heading out to sea at the behest of Lady Caith's magic, the wind was so strong it was capable of blowing him off course in the rapidly deteriorating condition he was in.

Which left only one option—diving into the sea.

The one place he really didn't want to go.

Wade folded his wings, tucked his legs close to his body, and dived toward the sea below. He pulled up before he hit the surface, stomach buffeted by waves. He snapped his wings out, spreading them as wide as they could go to help catch him before he went under. He was already shifting mass, dizzy and a little nauseous, but forcing through the change. Shoving most of himself *elsewhere* and packing his mind and bits of him into the familiar human body was a little disorienting in the middle of a storm.

With no wings to hold him aloft and only useless arms, Wade fell into the cold water, getting a face full of seawater from a particularly high wave. He inhaled liquid before going under, lungs seizing with the need to get air in them. Even though he ran hot, the water was cold against his skin, the distant numbness at his fingertips from fading poison threatening to creep back through his body with the first hint of hypothermia.

He kicked his legs, trying to orient himself in the churning water, and managed to get closer to the surface. Lungs burning, Wade swam upward, breaking the surface with a ragged gasp. He coughed out water and heaved himself over a wave, trying to drag air into his lungs. He twisted in the water, the waves all around him pulled into different currents from the magic in the water. The last thing Wade wanted to do was get sucked into a whirlpool.

Something cold and slimy wrapped around one ankle, and he got dragged beneath the water anyway.

He managed only a half breath of air, clenching his teeth together as he sank beneath the waves. Vision changing, he got eyes on the fuath below him, staring into an ugly face limned with violet bioluminescence. The soft glow cast the water spirit in eerie shadows, but it was still bright enough for Wade to see the clawed, webbed hands reaching for where he was tangled in its tentacle.

He dived for the fuath rather than trying to kick free of its grip, his own talons flashing in the dim glow. Wade managed to sink his talons into the fuath's closest arm and keep it at bay. The fuath screeched, the sound vibrating through the water between them. Wade tried to twist out of reach of the fuath's other clawed hand, but the sea wasn't the air, and he wasn't quick enough.

Sharp talons dug into his rib cage, scraping against bone, and Wade couldn't help the way his mouth opened on a surprised grunt as he tried to twist away. Bubbles escaped his lips, obscuring the water between them as he twisted in the fuath's grip. The edges of his vision wavered with dark spots as the pressure in his lungs got worse—not from the talons trying to break through bone but from his need to breathe.

Something dark streaked up from the bottom of the sea, slamming into them both. The claws in his skin were wrenched free, the tentacle around his ankle ripping loose. Wade floundered there for a second as the fuath was dragged down into the depths by a selkie, not sure which way was up and losing air.

Then another selkie reached him, the color of his pelt one Wade recognized from when Riordan had swum in the harbor before and lazed about in a bathtub. A cold nose bumped his chest, and Wade wrapped his arms around the large, sleek body, trying to stay out of the way of Riordan's flippers.

They sped toward the churning surface, breaking through the waves. Wade coughed out water and turned his face against Riordan's body, heaving for air. He coughed some more, fire tickling the back of his throat, and he forced it back. Gagging, he spat seawater out of his mouth and clung tighter. A flipper brushed against his side, and Wade finally lifted his head, squinting through the rain and the waves while Riordan kept them steady with ease.

The waterspout was far out at sea now, and he didn't think Caoránach had escaped it yet. If she had, he rather thought Riordan would already be moving. As it was, he bobbed there in the sea until Wade had caught his breath.

"Okay," Wade rasped. "I'm good."

Riordan barked a reply to that before he twisted in the water. Wade floundered a moment before he managed to tighten his arms around Riordan's body. He held on as Riordan swam back to shore, his strength keeping both their heads above the water. Wade was grateful for that because it meant he just had to cling to the other man and get hauled through the water without doing much else.

"You're my very own lifeboat."

Riordan barked in quick succession. It almost sounded as if he was laughing at Wade. Angling his head, Wade focused on not breathing in the water that splashed them as they cut through the waves. Other selkies broke the surface around them on their journey back to the Great Brewster Island, acting as their very own escort.

At some point, Wade's feet dragged against a rocky, sandy bottom, and he dug his heels in, sliding down Riordan's seal body and nearly losing his grip. A few more feet through buffeting waves, and they reached the shallows. He let Riordan go and the selkie dived beneath the water, rising up seconds later in the shape of a man Wade was ridiculously happy to see.

"Thanks for the save," Wade croaked out.

"You saved us first by dragging Caoránach out of the water," Riordan retorted, peeling his selkie skin off his shoulders and passing it over to Wade. "Here, take this."

Wade took the skin, the pelt warm despite having been in the cold water. He wrapped it around his waist, wincing when the motion pulled at the wounds on his rib cage. He lifted his arm to peer at the gouges, about to poke one of them, when Riordan crowded in close and bent to get a closer look.

"I didn't know you'd been hurt," Riordan growled. His fingertips against Wade's side were surprisingly warm, and he couldn't stop himself from leaning into the touch.

"It'll heal." He'd heal faster if he shifted mass again, but he figured twice in one day was pushing it. "Right now, let's find Ella and the others. I'm pretty sure Niall was on his way to the island before Lady Caith conjured up that waterspout."

Riordan straightened but didn't remove his hand. He kissed Wade, the touch of his lips lingering. Wade licked at him, tasting salt and nothing else. He pulled back when he heard a shout from down the shore. Around them, other selkies were coming out of the water, pelts slung over their shoulders or wrapped around their waists, all of them clearly having no issue running around in the nude.

Saoirse approached, and Wade made sure to keep his eyes on her face and nowhere else. "Everyone is accounted for."

"You're sure?" Riordan asked.

Saoirse nodded. "The waterspout was a good distraction, and Wade here kept Caoránach occupied."

"It wasn't all me. We have Lady Caith to thank for most of that effort." Wade looked up at the cliffside and squinted through the pouring rain. He didn't see her at the edge anymore. "We should find her and see where everyone else is in case Niall and his people made it to shore."

"We sank some of those speedboats, but a couple did get through," Donal said.

Wade didn't see any on the shore, but maybe Niall's people tried to swim, and some of them drowned. He could hope. "Let's get up top."

Rather than try to climb the cliff, they headed down the rocky shore for where the land sloped lower, and it was easier to get off the beach. The grassy stretch of land beyond was muddy from the rain. Wade's toes squelched in it as they walked. There wasn't much, if any, plant coverage when they made it up top, so it was easy to see the people scattered near the middle. Wade blinked his vision to something sharper, bringing into focus Lady Caith, Ella, and others. A group of werecreatures was huddled together, most of them looking at whoever was in the middle rather than out. He hoped that meant they had found Casey.

"Let's go join the fun," Wade said.

Even with the saturated ground, everyone moved pretty quickly to reach the others. As they approached, Wade saw that several of Lady Caith's fae guards had their swords drawn and angled around Niall and some of his fae where they knelt in the muck. He didn't look like a rich businessman anymore but rather a beleaguered criminal who was about to get his head chopped off if they all skipped the trial part and went straight to judgment and execution.

Lady Caith didn't turn to look at them as they approached, skin still glowing in a way that had nothing to do with self-care efforts and everything to do with magic. Her magenta hair was a scraggly mess around her head and blowing in the wind, having escaped all its pins. Her clothes were plastered to her body, but she didn't appear cold.

"Caoránach?" Wade asked.

"I am still guiding the waterspout to open ocean," Lady Caith said. For all that she was dragging a serpent god out to sea, her focus never wavered from where Niall knelt before her.

Wade went to stand beside her, looking over his shoulder at the werecreatures behind them. It was easier now to see how they were all crowded around Harper, who was wrapped around a bruised and bleeding but very much alive Casey, with Ella hovering behind both of them. "Is he okay?"

"Niall had him on a sacrificial spell meant to break the territory markers belonging to the kin and feed him to Caoránach, giving her unfettered access to the harbor for her own claim. The spell has been dealt with."

"He's alive," Harper said, not taking her nose away from her husband's throat. "The sooner we get off this island, the better."

"Most of our boats are still seaworthy," Riordan said.

"Oh, good. I'm pretty sure flying everyone to shore would be a bad idea. I don't want to be on the news," Wade said.

"You were never the mundane human you pretended to be," Niall ground out in a low voice.

Wade faced forward again and stared at the fae. "Nope. And the Boston god pack was never mine. I'm from the New York City god pack."

It was funny the way Niall and his people all went absolutely still at that statement. Wade stared Niall down, refusing to blink, and waited the fae out until Niall was the one who dropped his gaze under the pretense of meeting Lady Caith's. "I issued a bargain because we are worth more than the scraps we have been given by mortals."

"There is no *we* in this fight. You would have come after my court as surely as you attempted to go after the Boston Night Court. But Saoirse found her skin, and your hold over the Maguire clan no longer exists. The Boston god pack has found their missing alphas, and your bargain with them is broken. You have no power here," Lady Caith said.

Wade snorted. "You should also know Lucien is a big fan of finders keepers. I don't know about Abby Boy, but between their two Night Courts, you're in for a world of hurt on the financial front."

Lady Caith took a single step forward, looking down at Niall. Her skin still glowed in a luminous way, proof her magic was still working to send that waterspout with Caoránach into the Atlantic Ocean. "What is left of your property and domain after Abhartach is finished with it will revert to the master vampire's control, as he has already claimed it. You have a choice, Niall Noígíallach. You and your court can return under guard to Tír na nÓg and leave Boston behind, or your blood can feed this island. Which will it be?"

Wade thought that was a little too generous of her after the last few days. "Or I could eat him? I'd shift mass for that."

"But not to heal yourself?" Riordan asked incredulously.

Wade shrugged, fighting back a wince as the wound on his rib cage pulled with the motion. "It's healing."

He just needed to focus on it more, but he'd do that once Niall was dealt with once and for all. Riordan sighed and didn't try to argue with him.

"I require an answer," Lady Caith said.

Niall worked his jaw, hate twisting his beautiful face into an ugly expression. "And will you use my subjugation to return your court to Brigid's good graces?"

"Tír na nÓg or a grave. It is your choice."

"It is no choice. Bring me home, Lady of Wind and Sky."

Lady Caith nodded, seemingly satisfied. Wade couldn't stop the shocked cry that escaped his lips when her guards raised their swords and chopped off the heads of every single one of Niall's followers. Niall didn't seem surprised though, nor did he protest the action, face a study in hatred as he glared up at Lady Caith.

"Oh," Wade said as he thought back on the conversation they'd just had. "You only spoke about Niall's life."

Lady Caith tipped her head in his direction. "You know words well."

"Eh, my dire is a lawyer who works for a fae law firm. I kind of have to."

"We should get everyone back to the boats. The storm isn't going to let up anytime soon, and we should return to Boston before the Coast Guard thinks about coming around," Riordan said.

"What about the bodies?"

"We'll take them with us. Some of my clan will carry them out to the sea."

"I'll handle that," Donal said, clamping a hand on Riordan's shoulder. "Let's get out of here."

Wade was all for that. Almost everyone was able-bodied enough to walk out on their own two feet. Niall was led off the island at sword point, while the selkies carried the heads and dragged the bodies of the deceased fae with them back to the shore. Casey wasn't really in any position to walk, much less shift, so one of the god pack members was carrying him.

The selkies in the water were part of other clans, but they fetched the lifeboats scattered across the waves and brought them to the shore for everyone to pile into in groups. The captains of the yachts and other boats steered their vessels as close as they dared in the stormy water. Transporting everyone to the boats took some time, but eventually, Wade found himself clambering up the metal ladder onto the *Neptune*, with Ailín still at the controls.

Some boats had been lost—either capsized or destroyed by Caoránach—but Wade was relieved when he overheard Riordan taking the report over the radio from other boats that everyone in the clan was accounted for.

"Thank you for all you did for us," Riordan said when he returned to Wade's spot in the cabin, squished into the corner on a bench.

"Thanks is a pretty big thing for your kind. Besides, I already told you that you don't need to thank me."

Riordan knelt before him, seemingly unbothered by the seesaw motion of the yacht as Ailín steered them back to Boston. His hand on Wade's thigh was warm, grip gentle. Wade was acutely aware that he still had Riordan's sealskin wrapped around his waist and that Riordan seemed in no hurry to ask for it back. "I mean it."

"Well, I don't want your thanks," Wade muttered, leaning forward to press their foreheads together. "I just want you."

Riordan made a noise that wasn't words in any language Wade's head could translate. But that was fine because Riordan kissed him like they were the only ones on that boat in a storm Wade would fly through all over again for him.

CHAPTER TWENTY-FOUR

RIORDAN WOKE THE DAY AFTER THE FIGHT AND THE STORM IN WADE'S HOTEL
room, spooning the younger man in the hotel bed. His nose was
tucked against the back of Wade's neck, Wade deep asleep like
Riordan wanted to be. He couldn't understand why he'd woken up
until he realized he could hear someone's heartbeat in the kitchen of
the penthouse suite. It was steady and calm, and Wade hadn't
seemed to notice it at all. It made Riordan wonder if Wade was that
deep of a sleeper, something which could be dangerous when their
kind was hunted, or if it was something else.

He was about to wake up Wade, prepared for a fight if one was
going to happen, when Riordan realized a second later why someone
was able to enter the penthouse without Wade noticing or caring.

"Wade," the person in the kitchen said, barely raising their voice
but with an expectant tone of familiarity.

Whoever was out there was able to enter because they were
pack, Riordan realized.

Wade jackknifed up to a sitting position in bed out of a deep
sleep, staring wild-eyed at the open bedroom door. "*Shit*. Crap. Oh
no. He's supposed to be in DC still."

Riordan winced, making the connection immediately. "That's Patrick out there?"

Wade was already scrambling out of bed. "Yes, and I can't tell him you slept on the couch when you're in here with me!"

"Wade," Patrick called again. "Get out here."

"It's not even seven o'clock!" Wade yelled back right before he hastily closed the bedroom door.

"I took an early flight out from DC. General Reed is pissed about yesterday. I'd have flown in last night except he kept me late at the Pentagon discussing your fly-by of Boston. And it was either you got him or me for the lecture, and I know what you prefer."

Wade groaned and rubbed hard at his eyes. "I hate that guy."

"Patrick?" Riordan asked in a low voice, raising an eyebrow in surprise.

"No, his annoying dragon general superior asshole. Ugh." Wade dropped his hands, looking around at their scattered, wet clothes neither of them had bothered to deal with after their arrival last night. "What if you just stay in here? I'll keep the door shut, and you can be quiet."

Riordan's stomach clenched, and not in a good way. "You want to hide me?"

Wade blinked at him before his eyes widened, and he rapidly shook his head. "No! That's not what I meant. I don't want to hide you. Well, I mean. I do, but only from Patrick right now."

"That sounds like you don't want to tell him about me."

Wade groaned, dragging a hand down his face. "I want to tell him? But if he knows you're in here with me, he'll think we slept together, and then he'll want to stab you. He doesn't even have his dagger anymore, but he'd still find a way to stab you. Trust me. I don't want you stabbed."

Some of Riordan's apprehension faded away as he realized Wade wasn't trying to hide their tentative relationship out of regret or shame but because he was trying to spare him a shovel talk. "Patrick is one of your alphas. I should meet him, if that's what you'd want."

Wade gave him a look that was very clearly meant to translate as *your funeral*. It made him laugh, just a little. Wade sighed and returned to the bed. When he got close enough, Riordan grabbed him by the waist and dragged Wade into his lap. Wade tumbled in close without a fight, and Riordan kissed him soundly, ignoring the fact they both needed to brush their teeth and that they were naked, and if Patrick decided to barge in, he was bound to get an eyeful.

Riordan really hoped his first meeting of his lover's family wouldn't be without even his sealskin on.

"Come on," Riordan murmured before they could get too distracted. "Let's get out there."

Wade groaned, and Riordan let him climb back off the bed again. Riordan slid out from beneath the sheets and went to the closet, picking out some clothes from the ones Wade had bought him. Then he grabbed his skin from where it was slung over the chair in the corner, shook it out into a leather jacket, and pulled it on.

They split time in the bathroom for a quick washup at the sink. When Riordan came out after his turn, he found Wade dressed and shifting from foot to foot by the door, chewing on his thumbnail. Riordan couldn't help but hug him, running his hand up and down Wade's back. "It's fine. I mean it."

"Patrick won't be fine," Wade muttered.

That didn't stop him from opening the bedroom door and taking Riordan by the hand to drag him out into the firing range of an over-protective pack member. Riordan peered over Wade's shoulder as they exited the bedroom and had a clear view of the way the redhead leaning against the kitchen island went completely still, gaze sharpening in a way that had Wade's grip tightening around Riordan's hand.

"Hey, Patrick," Wade said, trying for casually cheerful and missing by a mile if Riordan was any judge.

Patrick Collins smelled a little bitter, a little harsh, to Riordan's nose, the other man's scent not typical of any magic user he'd ever met over the centuries. He appeared to be in his early thirties, with messy, dark red hair and green eyes that looked at Riordan the way a hunter might look at caught game, wondering how to skin them.

He was glad, in that moment, to know that this mage was Wade's pack because Wade deserved to be protected. Riordan just had to convince Patrick that Wade didn't need to be protected from *him* because Riordan would rather give up his skin forever than see Wade come to harm.

"There's a Dunkin' two blocks away. Go get us coffee and donuts," Patrick said, never taking his eyes off Riordan.

"You just made coffee! It's percolating right behind you. And the hotel's private chef would totally go get the donuts for us."

"Now, Wade."

Wade bounced on his heels a little. "You just want to get Riordan alone."

"Riordan, is it? The same selkie you mentioned the other day?"

"*Patrick*," Wade groaned.

"There's also a Dunkin' four blocks away. You can go to that one instead."

Wade looked over at Riordan with a faint grimace and an apologetic expression. Riordan smiled encouragingly at him. "It's okay. Go get us breakfast."

Wade reluctantly let him go and headed for the front door. He stabbed his finger in Patrick's direction as he passed the other man. "Be *nice*."

Patrick didn't even look at him. "Bye."

Riordan didn't move, didn't speak, until he heard the elevator descending toward the lobby. "Wade suggested I stay in the bedroom. I told him I wanted to meet you."

Patrick never moved, staring at him with an intensity that Riordan, who'd lived for centuries, found mildly disconcerting. He knew Patrick was a mortal who'd fought against the gods of all the hells, championed by the ones in heaven, and survived the end of the world. But the world's savior wasn't who he stood before.

It was Wade's pack, his family, his older brother.

And Riordan knew a thing or two about older brothers and siblings in general and just what they'd do in defense of their loved ones.

"Give me one good reason why I shouldn't toss you out the nearest window and see if you're as good at flying as you are at swimming," Patrick finally said in a tone of voice that didn't—quite—promise murder, but it was close.

"Because I gave him my skin, and he keeps giving it back to me without hesitation, and he's the only one I've ever trusted to do that. I don't want to stop giving it to him."

It was more than fixation at this point, and Riordan knew the only person who deserved to know that was Wade, but Patrick needed to know he didn't mean Wade any harm. He'd sooner give up his skin forever and suffer all that entailed—the loss of his magic and the sea and his clan—than willingly hurt Wade.

He would never, *ever* do that to his mate.

Patrick finally blinked, and it felt as if Riordan could take a breath. The coffeepot beeped, signaling it was finished brewing, but neither of them moved.

"Wade told me about his past," Riordan said quietly. "About the god that held him prisoner and what was done to him. You need to know I will never hurt him. I just want to keep him safe."

I just want to love him, but Riordan didn't say that out loud.

"I don't know you, so you'll have to deal with the fact that I won't believe a word coming out of your mouth for, oh, let's go with a few years if you stick around." Patrick shoved away from the island and went to the coffeepot, casually putting his back to Riordan in a way that was utterly dismissive in seeing him as a threat, and Riordan decided to not take that personally. "Wade can make his own choices when it comes to relationships. We've always supported that."

"But?" Riordan asked carefully.

Patrick found the mugs on the first try, taking one down to pour himself a cup of coffee but not bothering to pour one for Riordan.

"You're the first one he's had since we took him in as pack. So you can bet your ass no one will find your body if you hurt him."

If it was coming from anyone else, the threat would be melodramatic and laughable, but Riordan had no doubt that Patrick would commit murder for his pack and never feel anything but satisfied. Because that's how Riordan would feel toward a threat pointed at his own siblings and clan. He was relieved that the New York City god pack appeared to operate in the same way. "I wouldn't even fight back."

"You wouldn't get the chance." Patrick turned around and leaned against the counter, sipping his coffee. Riordan wondered if he'd survive getting his own mug and then decided maybe waiting for Wade to return was the better option. "Wade knows better than to fly like he did yesterday, so you're going to tell me what happened and if there's any leftover threat I need to take care of while I'm here."

Riordan knew Wade had been updating Patrick and his pack about what was going on in Boston, but he didn't know all that had been said. So he started at the beginning, with Saoirse's stolen skin and everything that had happened since. He was just finishing up about how they'd all agreed to meet at the Boston god pack's home that morning when Riordan heard the elevator rising. The doors pinged open a moment later, and three people exited it.

"Look who I found in the lobby," Wade said as he made a beeline for them. He held three boxes of donuts in his hand, with a carton containing three to-go cups balanced on top of it. "Witnesses."

"You act like that would stop me," Patrick said.

"Be *nice*. I like them."

Saoirse and Donal trailed after Wade, both of them looking clean and well-rested after what Riordan hoped was a good night's sleep. His siblings had bunked up with some of the clan who had returned to their homes now that the threat from Niall was taken care of. They still didn't have a home to go back to, and that was a headache Riordan wasn't looking forward to.

"Hello," Saoirse said, tone a little questioning as she stared at Patrick.

"Saoirse, Donal, this is Patrick, one of Wade's alphas," Riordan said.

Saoirse's eyes went wide. "Oh! Wade didn't say you were coming."

"*I* didn't know Patrick was coming," Wade grumbled as he set the drinks and donut boxes on the kitchen island.

"I would have flown home to New York if we didn't have to deal with a dragon sighting in Boston." Patrick glanced at Wade before taking an interest in the array of donuts left after Wade had clearly snacked on most of them. "General Reed is suppressing the news stories."

"I'm not telling him thank you."

"I wouldn't ask you to. Hand me the old-fashioned donut."

Wade passed one over, then picked up the chocolate bar that was Riordan's favorite and walked over to hand it to him. "Here. I saved you this one."

"Thanks," Riordan said, taking the donut. "I was filling Patrick in while you were gone."

Wade nodded, taking a bite of a blueberry cake donut and getting flecks of sugared glaze on his lips. Riordan really wanted to kiss him, but Patrick was in the room, and he wanted to live to see another day.

"We're supposed to meet with the Boston god pack today. Lady Caith said she'd take Niall back to Brigid. Boston has a hawthorn path in Back Bay Fens, and they left last night."

"Let's go see how the Boston god pack is doing," Patrick said.

They didn't linger, and when they all made it to the valet outside the hotel, Riordan reluctantly decided to go with his siblings, leaving Patrick to ride with Wade. The sad eyes that Wade turned on him made Riordan almost cave, but he knew Patrick probably wanted to talk to Wade alone.

"We'll meet you there," Riordan said before climbing into the front passenger seat of Saoirse's car. His and Donal's cars had been utterly destroyed in the fire at their home, and Saoirse's had survived by virtue of being parked down the street at the time.

Saoirse got into the back seat, letting Donal drive. They pulled out first, idling for a couple of seconds until Wade pulled out behind them. Riordan watched Wade's car in the rearview mirror, already missing the quiet moment of holding the other man in his arms in the early morning hours.

"Patrick seems a little intense," Donal said off-handedly.

Riordan snorted. "He saw me leaving the bedroom with Wade this morning. I'm surprised I'm not bleeding."

"Is he here to take Wade home?" Saoirse asked.

"Wade was always going to leave."

It ached, knowing they probably only had a few more hours together. With Niall gone and the threat neutralized, Riordan knew there was no further need for Wade to stay in Boston. As much as he wanted Wade to stay with him, Riordan's clan wasn't Wade's pack, and they both had their duties.

"Did you give him your skin?" Donal asked.

"He won't keep it."

Donal snorted. "Boyo, I'm not asking if you let him borrow it like you have been. I'm asking if you *gave him your skin.*"

There was a formality to giving up everything you were to someone you loved when you were a selkie. Riordan desperately wanted to share that with Wade, to give in to the fixation that had hit him in the gut when he'd first met Wade at the dessert table in Underhill. "Someday."

Donal made an aggravated sound before knocking his fist against Riordan's shoulder. "Now would be good."

"Just drive."

His siblings were kind enough to not pester him about his reluctance, but Riordan didn't want to back Wade into a corner. He'd rather they come to an agreement slowly so that Wade had ample time to think about if Riordan was who he truly wanted. Because

Riordan wanted Wade, and he was pretty certain Wade wanted him, but he would never force Wade into anything.

When they finally made it to the Boston god pack territory, they found nearly all of the street parking was taken. Cars were doubled up in driveways, and they had to go further afield to find a spot. Ella must have had someone on the lookout for them because the front door was open when their small group finally walked up. It was interesting to see the way she froze in the doorway at their arrival, attention focused solely on Patrick.

"Oh," she said after a moment. "We didn't know you were coming."

"Just passing through," Patrick said easily. "Wade and I are leaving later today. I came to see how your alphas are doing."

Riordan refused to meet his siblings' eyes at that news even as Wade sidled close, tangling their fingers together.

"Casey is resting. You're more than welcome to come inside."

They all entered the home, and no one asked Patrick for hospitality. Harper came downstairs, going through a formal greeting with Patrick as one god pack alpha to another. The pair got drawn into a conversation that Wade seemed happy enough to escape from.

"This is why Patrick is our alpha," Wade said after he'd dragged Riordan into the god pack's kitchen and started rummaging around in their cupboards. "I'm good in a pinch, but he has authority I don't."

"Authority for what?"

"I'm pretty sure they're hashing out an alliance of some sort. We didn't know Lucien was best friends with Abhartach. If Lucien is going to try to make inroads in Boston for whatever reason, Patrick is letting Harper know we'd be happy to come and deal with him if he becomes too much of a problem."

Riordan almost wished Lucien would stick around, if only to have an excuse for Wade to come visit. "So you'd only come if there was an emergency?"

"Would you only want me to come for an emergency?"

"No."

Wade made a pleased sound and withdrew his arm from a cupboard, coming away with a box of strawberry-flavored Pop-Tarts. He ripped open the top and drew out a packet. "Good. Because I'm planning on asking Marek for a private jet as a present this year so I don't have to keep borrowing his and Sage's."

Riordan stepped close as the younger man tore open the foil packet and shook out two Pop-Tarts. He kept one and offered Riordan the other. Riordan took it, even if Pop-Tarts weren't his favorite snack. Anything Wade gave him, he would eat.

"Why would you need a private jet?"

Wade arched an eyebrow. "To come see you. There's no way I'm driving up here and dealing with both Manhattan drivers *and* Boston drivers in the same day."

Riordan laughed. He settled his free hand on Wade's hip, fingers sliding beneath his T-shirt to press against warm skin. He stroked his thumb over the jut of Wade's hip bone, liking the way it made the other man's breath catch. "But you would if you had to, right?"

"Yeah, I would. But I'd expect to be greeted with all the snacks for having to be stuck in traffic."

"Anything you want, *mo chroí*," Riordan said before kissing Wade in a kitchen that didn't belong to either of them, but it still felt like home with Wade in his arms. "Anything for you."

CHAPTER TWENTY-FIVE

"I have a boyfriend now. There will be no shovel talk," Wade announced as he banged his way into Sage and Marek's home. "Patrick already gave it."

The rest of his pack, sprawled across the couches and chairs watching a game, stared at him in silence for several seconds before they started talking over each other.

"What do you *mean* you have a boyfriend?" Jono demanded.

"Patrick left him alive?" Marek asked.

"I'm getting my laptop to start a background search," Sage said, already standing. "What's his name?"

"Uncle Wade!" Lillian shrieked.

Wade made a face at his pack before striding over to steal his niece off Marek's lap and toss her into the air above him before catching her as she screamed in glee. "This is why you're my favorite."

Jono stood, peering past them at Patrick, who was closing the door to the apartment. "Who is it?"

"I can't believe you're asking Patrick and not me," Wade said.

"One of the selkies who was involved with the whole fae mess up there," Patrick said as he came over to greet Jono with a kiss. "Wade saved his sister, then saved all of them from some sea serpent."

Sage came back into the room, laptop open and cradled in one arm as she tapped away at the keys with her other hand. "I want to know his name."

"Oh, come on. You don't need to do a deep dive on him," Wade protested.

Sage ignored him, looking at Patrick in order to get all the information she wanted, which Patrick happily gave her. "Riordan Maguire. He's a selkie."

"Thank you," Sage said, settling back down in her spot and focusing on her laptop. "I'll tell you what I find."

"Cheers," Jono said. "Wade, come help me in the kitchen."

Wade groaned and handed Lillian back to Marek after blowing a raspberry on her stomach, making her giggle. Then he dragged his feet all the way to the kitchen, slumping against the counter as Jono rummaged through the pantry and came up with a bag of tortilla chips and a jumbo-sized jar of queso.

"I'm allowed to have a boyfriend," Wade said.

Jono nodded. "Yes, and we're allowed to vet him. So what's he like?"

Wade perked up when he realized that Jono wasn't going to try to talk him out of the nascent relationship he was building. To be fair, neither had Patrick, and he knew Sage wouldn't as well. His pack just wanted the best for him, and Wade was pretty damn certain that was Riordan.

So he rambled about his time in Boston, explaining everything that had happened and going off on multiple tangents about Riordan. He went through three bags of chips, two jars of queso, and an entire casserole dish of chili cheese fries that Patrick decided to make and which Lillian loved because she was the best snack niece ever before Wade's story finally wound down.

"He's at least four hundred years older than you," Sage said at the end of his story.

"So?" Wade said.

"So I'm glad he'll be around." Her words came with a gentle smile to take the sting out of them. They all knew Wade would outlive them, and while that fact was one he never liked to dwell on, it wasn't something they fully shied away from.

Wade knew he'd always be there for their pack and the generations that followed. But it was nice to know he'd get to share that with someone.

"Yeah," Wade said. "Me too."

He hadn't ever been in a relationship before, and while he didn't know what to expect, he knew what he wanted—a devotion like what was shared between Patrick and Jono, as well as Sage and Marek. He'd had a front-row seat over the past several years to what love looked like, and Wade thought he'd felt it in the way Riordan had touched him, had held him.

Wade stayed over that night, reinserting himself into the flow of the pack and the bustle of New York City. Lying in the bed in his room that had been his for years, Wade video called Riordan, who answered with an easy smile. "Did you make it home, *mo chroí?*"

"Yeah. I told everyone about you."

"Yeah?"

"Sage did a deep dive on you." Riordan winced, and Wade laughed. "Nah, it'll be fine. She's happy for us."

"I'm glad."

Wade settled down in bed and smiled at Riordan. "How's everyone in Boston?"

They talked until midnight before reluctantly ending the call, and Wade went to sleep missing Riordan breathing beside him. He woke the next morning to a text from Riordan that put a smile on his face.

Morning, mo chroí. Hope you have a great day with your pack. I know you missed them. Call me later whenever you want.

Wade didn't stop thinking of Riordan over the next few days. The texts they exchanged and the video calls weren't a replacement for having the other man by his side like in Boston, but it was good enough for now.

Three days later, Wade left his condo, ready to head to the bar, and rocked to a halt on the sidewalk, eyes going wide at the sight of Riordan getting out of a taxi in Manhattan with a suitcase and a box of what smelled like cannoli. "What are you doing here?"

"What?" Riordan replied teasingly. "You're not happy to see me?"

Wade scoffed and then couldn't help but drag Riordan into a kiss once he made it onto the sidewalk. The carry-on nearly rolled away, and the box of cannoli was held to the side so they weren't crushed as Wade did his absolute best to map out the shape of Riordan's mouth with his tongue.

"Hi," he got out when they finally broke apart. "I missed you. Are those for me?"

"Freshly made today from Modern Pastry, the superior cannoli shop." Riordan kissed the corner of his mouth, his arms tightening around Wade. "And I missed you too, *mo chroí*."

"I was about to head to the bar. I'm meeting the others there. You can meet them too."

Riordan winced slightly but gamely agreed to a date night in pack territory. "Sure. Sounds fun."

Wade laughed. "Don't worry. They like you because I like you." Wade stepped around him to grab the escaped carry-on and then took Riordan by the hand, tugging him toward the front door. "Let's put your stuff away."

He happily led Riordan back inside his home, showing off his condo that no one but the core of his pack had ever been inside. It was his home, the place where he hid his hoard, and Riordan didn't say anything about all the things Wade couldn't bring himself to part with.

"How are Saoirse and Donal doing?" Wade asked.

"Good. They're good. We're working on finding a new place to live in Boston." Riordan dragged his gaze away from Wade's shot glass collection and all the funny sayings on them, a hesitant look in his warm brown eyes as he set down the box of cannoli. "We're also looking for a home in Manhattan. Well, I am."

Wade stared at him, heart beating fast as those words sank in, no translation needed. "You are?"

"Figured if we're going to make this long-distance relationship work, I should have a place to stay. I have an appointment with a real estate agent tomorrow."

They'd talked about it over the past few days, how they each had their responsibilities to their pack and clan that they couldn't and wouldn't give up. But spending time in each other's cities every other week or so was possible so long as there weren't any emergencies to deal with. Marek had already promised Wade he'd buy him a private jet for both of them to use.

Wade knew he and Riordan had the support of their pack and clan, and they could make this work, because he wasn't giving Riordan up, not for anything.

"You don't need to buy a place in Manhattan. You can share with me." The idea of Riordan living in Manhattan but not living here with him made Wade want to lock the door and keep Riordan right where he was.

Riordan smiled, shoulders loosening. "I was hoping you'd say that."

Wade watched as he shrugged out of his leather jacket, the shape of it flowing into the soft pelt of his sealskin. Riordan stared down at it for a moment before he looked at Wade again. "I want you to have this. I never thought I'd ever find my mate, but I'm glad it's you."

He extended his hands, sealskin gripped in his fingers, offering up the whole of him for Wade to keep. Wade made a desperate sound he refused to be embarrassed about as he reached for the sealskin. He took it from Riordan, stroking his fingers over the soft fur, the weight of what it meant a priceless gift Wade had no intention of sharing with anyone.

"I will hoard this like I've hoarded nothing else," Wade promised, finally looking up to meet Riordan's eyes. "But I'll give it back whenever you want it."

Riordan's smile was something Wade knew he'd always want to see for years to come—sweet and warm and full of what he realized just then was love. "I know you'll keep it safe."

"I'll keep *you*."

Riordan groaned, and Wade found himself being yanked close to the other man, sealskin pressed between them, as he was kissed with a thoroughness that left him panting and wanting more.

"I love you," Riordan gasped against his lips, stealing little kisses that Wade happily gave up. "I've wanted you since I first laid eyes on you."

"I love you too." He did, he realized with a dawning awareness. "I love that you make me feel safe. That you give me space. That you don't judge me for everything I've gone through."

Riordan pulled back, swiping his thumb over Wade's lips. "I will never hurt you."

Wade smiled, tasting the truth of those words. "I know you won't."

Riordan kissed him again, and Wade wrapped his arms around Riordan's neck, keeping him there. After a few more kisses, Riordan reluctantly pulled back a little. "We're going to be late if we continue like this."

Wade thought about his pack waiting for him at the bar and how he knew they'd probably interrogate Riordan the second he arrived, but that they'd be happy for him.

"We can be late," he said, pushing Riordan toward the bedroom that used to be Wade's and now was going to be theirs. "So long as we're late together."

Riordan laughed, willing to follow Wade's lead, already yanking off his shirt. "Whatever makes you happy, *mo chroí*."

"You make me happy." Riordan's smile was blinding in response, and Wade couldn't wait to make him smile like that again for the years to come.

They might spend their long lives in opposite elements—Riordan in the sea and Wade in the sky—but Wade knew they'd always meet in the middle at the horizon of a brand-new day.

Do you want more Wade and Riordan?
Visit bit.ly/SS-bonus for a bonus short story.

Want more Soulbound Universe? Check out *A Ferry of Bones & Gold* for the start of an epic adventure with Patrick and Jono.

Don't miss out on sneak peeks, exciting news, and more! Sign up for Hailey Turner's newsletter to stay up-to-date on her upcoming books.

GLOSSARY

Short descriptions of words, acronyms and phrases used in the story that weren't readily explained in text. Included as well are character names.

Abhartach: Master vampire. Is of fae descent. Presides over the Boston Night Court.

Ashanti: Immortal. Goddess and mother of all vampires. Takes the shape of an Asanbosam vampire out of West African myths.

Bailey, Spencer: Mage. Former combat mage with the Mage Corps. Former PIA special agent. Currently an SOA special agent.

Brigid: Immortal. Celtic goddess associated with fertility, spring, healing, smithing, and poetry. Spring Queen of the Seelie Court. Daughter of the Dagda and member of the Tuatha Dé Danann.

Carmen: Succubus. First known recorded appearance was in Venice, Italy.

Caoránach: Sea serpent goddess. First Oilliphéist.

Collins, Patrick: Mage. Former combat mage with the Mage Corps. Former SOA special agent. Currently alpha of the New York City god pack he co-leads with Jono.

Cú Chulainn: (Pronunciation: ku CULL-ann) Immortal. Celtic god and son of the god Lugh. Member of the Tuatha Dé Danann. Irish warrior. Carries the *Gáe Bulg* in fights. Formerly known as Gerard Breckenridge, his mortal identity.

Daoine Sídhe: (Pronunciation: dee-na SHEE) Irish term, plural for People of the Mounds. *See*, Tuatha Dé Danann.

de Vere, Jonothon "Jono": God pack werewolf. Originally from London, England, currently resides in New York City. Alpha of the New York City god pack he co-leads with Patrick.

Dean, Ella: God pack werewolf. Dire of the Boston god pack.

Dire: A rank held only within a god pack. The moniker is taken from the dire wolf but has been shortened to account for different werecreature species. Essentially a rank held by a loyal pack member who helps enforce the alphas' orders.

Duine Sídhe: (Pronunciation: din-na SHEE) Irish term, singular form for fae reference. *See*, Tuatha Dé Danann.

Espinoza, Wade: Fledgling fire dragon. Part of Jono and Patrick's god pack.

Fae: Supernatural beings who reside in Tír na nÓg. There are lesser or higher fae, depending on their status and species. *See also*, Tuatha Dé Danann.

Fatima: Psychopomp. Chose to guide spirits for Spencer Bailey. Takes the form of an ocelot.

Fenrir: Immortal. Wolf in the Norse pantheon. Patron to a god pack.

Fuath: Fae. Water spirits.

Godhead: Primordial power belonging to immortals that gives them life. The strength of their power can be altered by worship or lack thereof.

God pack: A pack of werecreatures infected with the god strain of the werevirus. They act as spokespeople for hidden werecreature packs in their territory. They are supported by monetary tithes from the packs under their protection. Very few retain a connection to their animal-god patrons.

Jenkins, Casey: God pack werewolf. Alpha of the Boston god pack. Married to Harper.

Jenkins, Harper: God pack werewolf. Alpha of the Boston god pack. Married to Casey.

Kohli, Priya: Mage. Director of the Supernatural Operations Agency.

Lady Caith: Fae. Lady of Wind and Sky. Exiled from Tír na nÓg and presides over territory in Boston.

Lucien: Master vampire. Was a soldier in William the Conqueror's army before being turned by Ashanti. Currently a weapons and magic trafficker. Is wanted by many governments.

Mage: Highest rank of magic users and the only practitioners who can tap external power from ley lines and nexuses.

Mage Corps: Military branch under the purview of the US Department of the Preternatural. Accepts only mages.

Magic: Emanating from and powered by a person's soul. Roughly one-quarter of the world's population has magic. Strength varies, with different titles being bestowed depending on a person's magical reach. Casting is divided into defensive wards and offensive spells.

Maguire, Donal: Selkie. Part of the Clan Maguire.

Maguire, Riordan: Selkie. Chief of Clan Maguire.

Maguire, Saoirse: Selkie. Part of the Clan Maguire.

Nexus: Metaphysical lake of power beneath the earth. Usually located in sacred areas or beneath major cities.

Night Court: Vampire group that oversees claimed territory. Headed by a single master vampire. Several Night Courts can exist in the same major city.

Noígíallach, Niall: A former mortal Irish king gifted with immortality. Nearly a prayed-into-being god.

Oilliphéist: Irish sea serpent.

Órlaith: (Pronunciation: OR-lah) Immortal. Daughter of Ruadán. The Summer Lady of the Seelie Court and heir to Brigid.

PCB: Preternatural Crimes Bureau. A PCB is usually found only in the police departments of major metropolitan areas in the United States. The PCB in Seattle is headed up by an assistant chief. It fields detectives specializing in preternatural crimes.

PIA: Preternatural Intelligence Agency. PIA is a national-level foreign intelligence organization overseen by the Secretary of Defense directly through the USDI. The PIA's intelligence operations extend beyond the zones of combat, and approximately half of its employees serve overseas at hundreds of locations and US embassies in many countries. The agency specializes in collection and analysis of preternatural-source intelligence, both overt and clandestine, while also handling American military-diplomatic relations abroad. The agency has no law enforcement authority. (Equivalent to CIA.)

Psychopomp: Creatures, spirits, angels, or deities that appear in many religions and take many forms. Responsible for guiding newly deceased souls from Earth to the afterlife, whether a heaven or hell. Are used most commonly with necromancy and other magic that has an affinity for souls or the dead.

Reed, Noah: Fire dragon. Currently hiding in human form as a three-star Army general who oversees the US Department of the Preternatural.

Seelie Court: Court of the spring and summer fae.

Shields: Ward. Defensive magic used for protection on a large or small scale.

Spells: Offensive magic.

SOA: Supernatural Operations Agency. SOA is the domestic intelligence and security service of the United States that focuses on magical and preternatural crimes and terrorism. Employs human, preternatural and magically affiliated people to field positions for domestic defense. (Equivalent to FBI.)

Takoma: Vampire. Master vampire of the Seattle Night Court.

Taylor, Lillian: Weretiger. Daughter of Sage and Marek.

Taylor, Marek: Seer. CEO of PreterWorld, a social media platform geared toward the preternatural and supernatural community. His patrons are the Norns.

Taylor, Sage: Weretiger. A Diné lawyer who works for the fae law firm Gentry & Thyme. Dire to the New York City god pack.

Tezcatlipoca: Immortal. Aztec god of obsidian, jaguars, war, strife, night sky, and the night winds.

Threshold: Ward. Applied to a hearth and home for protection to keep out negative magic, spirits, and demons.

Tír na nÓg: (Pronunciation: TEER-na-nog) English translation: Land of the Young. A place in the Otherworld past the veil where the Tuatha Dé Danann and lesser fae reside.

Tuatha Dé Danann: (Pronunciation: TOO-ah de-danan) Celtic pantheon of gods. They are considered high-status fae.

Underhill: Another name for the Otherworld.

Unseelie Court: Court of the autumn and winter fae.

US Department of the Preternatural: Employs all manner of magically affiliated and preternatural people for military service. Active-duty combat mages are seconded to the Army, Navy, Air Force, and Marines and are required to go through BTC and joint training.

Veil: The metaphysical barrier between Earth/mundane plane and other worlds/dimensions/planes, such as Faerie and versions of hell and heaven derived from myths.

Wards: Defensive magic.

Werecreatures: Humans who are infected with the werevirus. Can change form into various animalistic shapes. Werecreatures are either infected later on in life or are born with the disease.

Werevirus: An incurable disease that makes those who are infected change into monstrous beasts. Created by an ancient Roman mage, the werevirus was one of the first recorded instances of magically created biological warfare introduced into society. People are born with the werevirus or become infected through intercourse or blood. Two strains exist: a normal strain and a god strain. The god strain has stronger magical properties, which can cause the infected to be susceptible to an immortal patron.

Witch: Most common rank of magic users. On par with warlocks.

AUTHOR'S NOTES

Writing Wade's story was a little daunting because I know how much my readers love him. I hope I did his love story justice. I hope you had lots of snacks while reading. I made myself hungry while writing this book so many times. I won't be discussing the state of my kitchen.

I feel so lucky that you love my characters so much that you clamored for more years after *Soulbound* finished. I wasn't going to rush Wade's story though, so thank you for waiting until I found the right words to create his happily ever after.

My ever and eternal thanks to my usual cohort of friends for supporting me through my bouts of hunger: May Archer, Lily Morton, Aimee Nicole Walker, and Lucy Lennox. A special thank you to Amanda Viecelli, one of my OG ARC readers from way back when, who very kindly agreed to beta read the second draft of this book to Boston-pick it for accuracy and make sure I wouldn't piss any Bostonians off. Any inaccuracies are mine. Another special shout-out to Sandra, my forever editor and friend. The commas would run amok without you.

I would be thrilled and grateful if you would consider reviewing *Secondhand Skin* on Amazon or Goodreads. I appreciate all honest reviews, positive or negative.

CONNECT WITH HAILEY

Keep up with book news by joining Hailey Turner's newsletter and get several free short stories.
readerlinks.com/l/3026697

Join the reader group on Facebook.
facebook.com/groups/haileyshellions

Visit Hailey's website for book news and merch.
www.HaileyTurner.com

OTHER WORKS BY HAILEY TURNER

M/M SCIENCE FICTION MILITARY ROMANCE

Captain Jamie Callahan, son of a wealthy senator and socialite mother, is a survivor.

Staff Sergeant Kyle Brannigan, a Special Forces operative, is a man with secrets.

Alpha Team, the Metahuman Defense Force's top-ranked field team, is where the two collide and their lives will never be the same.

<u>Metahuman Files</u>

In the Wreckage

In the Ruins

In the Shadows

In The Blood

In The Requiem

In the Solace

<u>A Metahuman Files: Classified Novella</u>

Out of the Ashes

New Horizons

Fire In The Heart

M/M URBAN FANTASY

Patrick Collins is a broken mage running from his past.

Jonothon de Vere is a god pack alpha werewolf searching for a home.

In a world where magic is real, myths and legends exist, and gods walk the earth, Patrick and Jono are thrown together by the Fates themselves to fight against an enemy that threatens to consume the world. For if the gods fall and demons from every hell rise up, humanity won't stand a chance.

<u>Soulbound</u>

A Ferry of Bones & Gold

All Souls Near & Nigh

A Crown of Iron & Silver

A Vigil in the Mourning

On the Wings of War

An Echo in the Sorrow

A Veiled & Hallowed Eve

<u>Soulbound Universe Standalones</u>

Resurrection Reprise

Secondhand Skin

LGBTQ+ EPIC STEAMPUNK-INSPIRED FANTASY

Welcome to Maricol, where the land will kill you, kinship turns the gears of war, and burning the dead lest they come back to life is the only way to survive.

Infernal War Saga

The Prince's Poisoned Vow

The Emperor's Bone Palace

The Queen's Starfire Throne

Infernal War Saga Novella

An Emporium of Hearts

CONTEMPORARY GAY ROMANCE

Short stories previously published in the Heart2Heart Charity Anthologies.

From the Heart: A Short Story Collection

AUDIOBOOKS

All of Hailey Turner's audiobooks are available on your favourite listening platform.

Thanks for reading!